Serendipitous Rescue

Lowell Dunn

ESCONDIDO, CALIFORNIA: Word Wizards®

Published by
Word Wizards®
Communications Excellence since 1972
P.O. Box 300721
Escondido, California 92030-0721
United States of America

760/ 781-1227
Internet: http://www.wordwiz72.com

Cover art by Rafael Matigulin

Third printing

ISBN: 978-0-944363-10-2 (Paperback print edition)

CONTENTS

Acknowledgements

Even when only a single name appears on the cover of a book as author, the reality is that many hands and loving hearts contributed to the success of the endeavor.

Thanks to my wife Karen, my brothers Douglas, Dennis and Howard (Jack), and my sisters Gloria, Beverly and Nancy, my daughters Cynthia, Deborah and Marie, and grandkids Lauren, Ryan, Megan and Emily for their help in proofreading and story ideas.

Extra thanks to Doug in handling arrangements for publication and distribution, and Karen for repeated proofreading. Also to Nancy and Mark Ostler, Gloria Wilkinson, and Howard Dunn for their exhaustive work in making story suggestions and fact checking historical names and events.

Further acknowledgements to our wonderful editor, Cassandra Dunn (no relation to the author).

Last but not least are our wonderful illustrators, Pia Bacino, Rafael Matigulin, and Jon Wilkinson.

This book is dedicated to the memory of my mother, Lois Olsen Dunn, who grew up during the Great Depression. She worked in the factories during World War II building B-17 airplanes with her sister Virginia and her brother Lowell. Then she raised a family.

Part 1

1951 - 1971

JJ and Laddie

1

Tutu House

The old woman lay crumpled on the dark kitchen floor, unable to pull herself up. "Is this how I'm going to die?" she thought. A fever had robbed her of her strength. She lived alone. She imagined her nephew coming to check on her, and the horror of what he would find.

The sun was not yet up, but it was beginning to get light outside. A cool breeze gently fell from the open back door. Only the screen door separated her from the outside. Occasionally the aroma of freshly cut grass would enter the kitchen. She had been lying on the floor since the previous evening and was parched with thirst. "I might see one more sunrise," she thought as she drifted in and out of consciousness.

A dog barked. There was a knock on the screen door. A young boy's voice called out.

"Oh," she thought. "It's my boy Jack, come to take me to heaven. But why is there a dog?"

* * * * *

Earlier that evening, after everyone had gone to bed, JJ slipped away from the orphanage. He had been heading northwest, away from Tutu House and out into the country.

It was the middle of June, 1951. JJ was eleven years old. No one knew his exact birthday because of how he came to the orphanage. Tutu House was named by the first orphans who lived there, because of the address: 22 Colonial Drive, Indiana, Pennsylvania. Colonial Drive had a bend in the street, and Tutu House was situated right on the bend, so you could see down the road in both directions. Tutu House was a grand home built in 1920 by a businessman who lost his fortune in the Great Depression. The state claimed the property for back taxes and eventually leased it to the Grace Hope Home for Children. It wasn't exactly a mansion, but to the people who lived there, it was a castle.

Two ladies ran the home for children. Mrs. Barclay was in charge, and Miss Nancy helped. Mrs. Barclay slept in the master bedroom which also served as an office.

At breakfast and dinner, everyone sat at the dining room table. It was twelve feet long and had six chairs on each side, plus one at each end. Mrs. Barclay sat at one end and Miss Nancy at the other. The nine kids who lived at Tutu House populated the other chairs in pretty much the same pattern each meal, leaving three empty places. JJ and the other four boys sat at the end with Miss Nancy, and the girls sat by Mrs. Barclay. The house was a perfect place for an orphanage.

Miss Nancy was JJ's favorite. She was 49 years old and seemed like a grandma to him. She was a thin woman of average height. Her face was kind but showed the signs of a difficult life. Miss Nancy did most of the cooking, and both ladies did the cleaning and laundry. Most people assumed Miss Nancy had never married, but that was another story. She had a room on the second floor, across from the stairs to the attic. There were no pictures on the wall or her desk, but the room had a window overlooking the back yard. Once when JJ was five, he had asked Miss Nancy why she didn't have any pictures like Mrs. Barclay did. Miss Nancy hugged JJ and said the window was her picture. On the table next to her bed was a little music box that everyone loved.

On Saturday nights, everyone would gather in the living room and sit on chairs, couches, or blankets on the floor. Miss Nancy sat in the big chair and read a story, or a chapter from a book, or even made up stories. Sometimes they would listen to radio programs. Miss Nancy would always play the piano as the kids got ready for bed. Everyone looked forward to story night. Miss Nancy liked to say, "Behind everything you see is a story."

Two of the kids who lived at Tutu House, Jon and Shannen, were Mrs. Barclay's children. Mrs. Barclay's husband had been killed in the war. Nearly everyone in town had been affected one way or another by World War II.

JJ often thought it was like they were a big family. They argued and quarreled, but mostly they got along.

In every respect, Tutu House was an ideal place for children, but its days were numbered. The 25-year lease given to the Grace Hope Home for Children would expire in 1959, only eight years away. Then the property would be taken back by the state and sold. It was a worry for Mrs. Barclay and Miss Nancy.

Summertime was the best. Not only was there no school, but they got to go to the movies. Every Wednesday the Mills Movie Theater let the orphans come for free if they arrived at noon.

"I'm glad school's out," JJ said as he came in the front door and walked into the kitchen. He put his school papers and a book on the kitchen table. "I can't wait to go to the movies. I hope it's a Lassie movie."

"It's going to be 'Alice in Wonderland,'" said Miss Nancy, as she placed a dozen potatoes in the oven.

"That's okay," said JJ, watching Miss Nancy. He liked almost any kind of movie, but his favorites were movies about animals, especially Lassie. He had seen all the Lassie movies.

Mrs. Barclay walked in and began chopping carrots. "How was your last day of school?" she asked.

"It was fine," said JJ. "Even Kevin Connor was in a good mood and didn't bother anyone." Kevin was a big kid, three years older than JJ. He had been held back twice. No matter how hard his teachers tried, they failed to teach Kevin how to read. Kevin often taunted JJ about being an orphan and made fun of JJ's clothes. His own clothes weren't much better, and he lived with his grandmother.

"Take your things up to your room," said Miss Nancy. "The ladies from the farm will be here soon."

JJ carried his book, his papers, and a sweater up to his room on the 3rd floor. It was an attic room with a sloped ceiling. There were three other rooms in the large attic that were sometimes used as bedrooms.

As he sat on his bed, looking out his window to the street below, he saw the old truck come down the street and park in front of the house. He ran back down the stairs. "The Friends Ladies are here," he announced as he rounded the stairs at the bottom and ran to the front door.

The two "Friends Ladies," as JJ called them, came every week to deliver eggs, potatoes, butter, milk, and vegetables from their farm. They also brought fresh bread they had baked. They were from the Religious Society of Friends, or Quakers, and their organization ran the orphanage.

"Here you go," said Mrs. Anderson as she handed JJ a basket of eggs. "Be careful." JJ was always careful. Four dozen eggs were heavy and would provide scrambled eggs for Friday, Saturday, and Sunday. Then it would be back to oatmeal.

Shannen, Carol, Jon, Linda, Mrs. Barclay, and Miss Nancy all came outside to help carry the bags of food into the house.

"Your truck doesn't sound too good," said Mrs. Barclay.

"It's been awful," said Mrs. Cooper. "It started running rough about halfway here. We'll need to see a mechanic."

After carefully putting the basket of eggs on the counter next to the kitchen sink, JJ went back out to the truck and opened the engine compartment. It was an old truck, older than JJ. He could see a spark plug wire dangling. He pushed the wire back on to the spark plug and closed the engine cover. He walked back into the house.

"Come and check the truck," he said to Mrs. Anderson. "There was a loose wire."

Miss Nancy and Mrs. Anderson walked back out to the truck with JJ. Mrs. Anderson started the engine, which now ran smoothly.

"Aren't you smart!" she said to JJ.

"Yes he is," said Miss Nancy proudly.

"It was just a loose wire," said JJ modestly.

The two Friends ladies stayed for dinner, made all the more festive by JJ's repair of the truck.

After dinner, the Friends ladies left, and Mark said, "Let's play hide and seek!" The children, already worked up from school being over, tramped up the stairs while Mrs. Barclay and Miss Nancy washed the dishes.

"I guess we don't have any helpers tonight," called out Mrs. Barclay to the kids as they disappeared up the stairs.

By now the kids were in the attic and out of hearing range. Soon, one of them would begin counting while the others scurried down the stairs to various hiding places throughout the house.

Miss Nancy smiled at Mrs. Barclay. "They'll sleep well tonight." Both ladies were used to the sounds of kids running up and down the stairs. Playing hide and seek was a common occurrence on rainy days.

That evening, when JJ went to bed, he was happy. He was an average-looking eleven-year-old boy with blond-brown hair and brown eyes. He loved living at Tutu House, and he loved his room on the 3rd

floor. "This is going to be the best summer," he said to himself as he lay in bed.

The next few days were consumed with bike riding, going to the library, playing tag, and other outside games with friends and each other. The boys had their toy soldiers, toy cars, toy trucks, and marbles. The girls had their dolls, doll clothes, a toy farmhouse, jacks, and a dollhouse that had been donated.

Wednesday was finally the first movie day of summer. Everyone was looking forward to a trip to the movie theater. Not every Wednesday was a movie day. It depended on the movie. "Alice in Wonderland" would be a good one for the kids, figured Miss Nancy. It would also be a chance for Mrs. Barclay and Miss Nancy to relax and take a break.

Walking together in a group to and from the Mills Movie theater was part of the fun. After the show, they stopped at the store for penny candy. It was an old tradition. On the way back, JJ and Jon bolted as they turned the corner to Colonial Drive.

"Race you to the house!" said Jon as he started running.

JJ and Jon ran toward the house. Jon reached the front door and stopped to wait. JJ ran to the back door. "Back door's the winner!" said JJ as he dashed around the house. Jon started chasing JJ.

"Hey!" said JJ as he spied a small dog sitting on the back porch. He stopped running and walked over to the dog and picked it up. The little dog licked JJ's face. Jon came from behind. The back door opened. Linda and Carol came out.

"Look!" said ten-year-old Carol.

"Oh, he's cute," said twelve-year-old Linda.

Miss Nancy came out as well. "My goodness," she said, as she looked at JJ and the children playing with the dog. "Where did he come from?"

"He was on the porch," said JJ.

"Can we keep it?" asked Carol, looking up at Miss Nancy.

"It's my dog," said JJ. "I found him."

"Nobody's going to have a dog," said Miss Nancy. "Poor little thing."

"He's hungry," said JJ.

"He's also young," said Miss Nancy. "He's either lost or abandoned." She looked in the direction of the nearby park but couldn't see anyone.

"I'm going to call him Lassie," said JJ.

"I don't know about that," said Miss Nancy. "I don't think we can keep a dog here. Besides, it's a boy dog."

"Okay," said JJ. "He must be Laddie then, like in the movie. Can we at least feed him?"

Miss Nancy knew it wasn't a good idea but did it anyway. She always had a special place in her heart for JJ, who had latched on to her immediately after arriving at Tutu House as a baby. For quite some time, Miss Nancy was the only one who could console him.

She made a meal for the hungry pup by putting some meat and broken bread crust in a bowl with some milk. Laddie stood on his hind legs and followed the dish as it was lowered to the porch.

"Aw," said the girls.

The kids surrounded Laddie and watched as he quickly ate the meat and bread. He kept licking until the milk was gone. Then he looked up at Miss Nancy.

"He sure was hungry," said JJ.

Laddie was brown, with a little white patch on his head. He was no bigger than ten pounds. He bounced over to JJ like he wanted to play. "He seems like a puppy all right," said Miss Nancy. "I don't know what we're going to do with him."

"I'll take care of him," said JJ.

"But what about nighttime?" asked Miss Nancy.

"Well," thought JJ. "We could put him in the garage."

All the kids played with Laddie in the back yard. Sometimes they ran around with Laddie chasing them. Sometimes they rested in a circle on the grass and took turns petting Laddie. Laddie was full of energy, and the children were cheerfully noisy.

Mrs. Barclay was not enthused. "We can't keep a dog here," she said to Miss Nancy.

"I know," said Miss Nancy. "We'll make a poster and put it out front. We'll keep the dog here for a few days, and if no one comes to claim him, we'll call the dog pound."

Miss Nancy was deliberately vague, attempting to delay the inevitable. Even though Mrs. Barclay was in charge, Miss Nancy was a little older, and Mrs. Barclay would often go along with Miss Nancy's ideas.

While the children ate dinner, Laddie whined at the back door. Mrs. Barclay was irritated. After dinner, all the kids ran back outside to play with JJ and Laddie. Even sixteen-year-old Jon was having fun.

As it got dark, Miss Nancy said, "It's time to put the dog in the garage."

"We need to make a bed for him," said JJ.

"I'll get some rags," said Miss Nancy.

She rummaged through the laundry room and returned with some worn out pajamas. People who struggled through the Great Depression rarely threw things away. She also had an old cereal bowl.

"Here's a dish you can use for water," she said.

Carol, Linda, and Shannen helped JJ take Laddie to the garage and made a bed with the old clothes. JJ filled the dish with water from the hose and put it by Laddie's bed. He closed the garage door, and everyone returned to the house. "Good night Laddie," he called from the back porch. It pained him to hear Laddie barking and scratching at the garage door.

JJ gave Miss Nancy his usual goodnight hug and climbed the stairs to his room. Laddie whined and barked. Mrs. Barclay gave a sigh.

"He'll probably calm down after a while," said Miss Nancy hopefully.

Up in his room, JJ could faintly hear Laddie barking in the garage. As he lay in his bed, he couldn't sleep. Every time he heard Laddie bark he got more anxious. After a while, JJ got out of bed and tiptoed down the stairs. He peeked around the corner to see where Miss Nancy and Mrs. Barclay were sitting. They were out of view, sitting in the living room, listening to the radio.

Laddie was soon quiet. Mrs. Barclay was relieved but waited anxiously for the barking to resume. The whole situation with the dog was unnerving, in ways she couldn't explain. They didn't see or hear JJ unlock the back door and step outside. He was now in the garage, sitting in the dark with Laddie.

"I'm sorry," said JJ, as he held Laddie in his arms and stroked and patted him. He was waiting for the two ladies to go to bed. Then he realized they might check the back door and lock it again.

JJ carried Laddie back through the unlocked back door, locked it, and climbed the stairs carefully and quietly to the third floor. There were two bathrooms downstairs and two bathrooms upstairs, but no bathrooms in the attic, so it wasn't unusual for someone to be walking up and down the upper stairs during the night.

JJ could still hear the radio as he closed the door to his room. Fortunately, Laddie remained quiet.

JJ placed Laddie on his bed and slipped under the sheet. Laddie curled up next to JJ and looked at him. As they gazed at each other in the semi-darkened room, JJ thought about the Lassie movies. "You're my dog now," said JJ. "We have to stay together."

The next morning JJ was up before anyone else. He carefully looked down the stairs to see if anyone was up. Miss Nancy and Mrs. Barclay always left their doors open a little, but the coast was clear. He went quickly down the rest of the stairs and carried Laddie outside. As other kids woke up and came out to play, they were delighted to see that

Laddie was still there. Once again, Miss Nancy gave Laddie some food. Mrs. Barclay was disappointed that Laddie hadn't run off.

Laddie stayed close by and wanted to play with anyone who came outside, especially JJ. When everyone went inside for lunch or dinner, Laddie sat by the back door and waited and whined. JJ gobbled his food quickly and spent all day outside. Miss Nancy scraped the small remnants of leftover food from the other dinner plates to make a meal for Laddie.

"What are we going to do with Laddie when we go to the movie next Wednesday?" asked Miss Nancy.

JJ hadn't thought about that problem. "Well," he said, thinking. "We could tie him up to the tree, and he could rest in the shade."

Miss Nancy looked at her favorite tree. "Yes," she said. "That would be fine."

Miss Nancy watched as JJ and others ran around the yard with Laddie. She thought to herself, *I don't know how this is going to work out.*

For the next few days, JJ picked up Laddie at night and carried him up to his room. One time he fell asleep in the garage with Laddie and ended up spending the night there. He knew he couldn't keep doing this. Mrs. Barclay seemed irritated. JJ heard her asking Miss Nancy when they planned to take the dog to the pound. JJ decided the only solution was to run away. After all, that's what Tom Sawyer had done. JJ was smart, but he was only eleven.

That evening, after the children were in bed, JJ sneaked out to the garage. The two ladies sat together in the living room resting and listening to the radio. Mrs. Barclay sipped a cup of tea. They heard Laddie settle down like he did each evening. JJ picked up Laddie and sadly walked quietly toward the street. As he headed away from Tutu house, Miss Nancy talked to Mrs. Barclay.

"I'm worried about JJ," said Miss Nancy.

"Being attached to the dog?" asked Mrs. Barclay.

"Yes," said Miss Nancy. "He loves it so. Would it be so bad to let him keep it?"

"I'm not used to having a dog around," said Mrs. Barclay. "How would we afford it?"

"It's just a small dog," said Miss Nancy. "He could eat table scraps."

Both ladies thought about how seldom they wasted any food. "He wouldn't eat much," said Miss Nancy.

Mrs. Barclay didn't say anything. In her heart, she knew it was too late to get rid of Laddie.

"There are worse things a boy can get into," said Miss Nancy.

"I suppose you're right," said Mrs. Barclay. "There's no fence here."

"It doesn't seem likely that Laddie will run off," said Miss Nancy.

"No, I guess not," said Mrs. Barclay. She thought about how Miss Nancy had been her dearest friend for twelve years and rarely asked for anything.

Mrs. Barclay sighed. "I wouldn't be surprised if that dog was up in his room right now."

"He's a good boy," said Miss Nancy.

"I know," said Mrs. Barclay. "But what happens when he has to leave?"

"I don't know," said Miss Nancy. "Hopefully that's a ways off."

Mrs. Barclay agreed to let the dog stay. JJ never heard that conversation, and now his adventure was underway. And that brings us back to where we began.

He and Laddie had walked five miles by the time it started to get light. Up ahead was a small farmhouse with a barn. It was set back a distance from the main road. The house and the barn were both old. JJ decided to rest. He was getting hungry and thought maybe he could ask for some food. Perhaps he could sleep in the barn.

The barn was off to the right at the end of a dirt driveway. JJ figured he could sneak into the barn if no one was up or paying attention. As he got closer, he picked up Laddie and carried him. He had to open a gate across the driveway. As he walked toward the barn, Laddie started barking and looking back toward the house. Laddie squirmed so violently that he broke loose from JJ's arms and ran to the back door, pacing back and forth. JJ had no choice but to get closer, and when he did, he heard someone quietly moaning inside. It sounded like someone was sick. He knocked on the old wooden screen door. He could barely see inside.

"Hello!" called JJ. "Are you all right?" He carefully opened the door and looked inside. Lying on the floor was an old woman.

"Water," she was barely able to say.

2

The Farm

JJ quickly found a cup and got water from the kitchen sink. It was an old-fashioned manual pump, but he knew how to use it. He took the cup of water to the woman and tried to lift her head so she could drink. Laddie stayed close by.

He could tell that the woman had a fever and was ill. The woman was able to drink a little and then closed her eyes. JJ felt bad that she was lying on the hard floor and grabbed a pillow from the couch in the living room. He placed it under her head. She woke again. This time, she looked at JJ with half closed eyes and asked him to help her to the couch. He helped her sit up and then used all his strength to help her to the couch. The house was small, and the living room was right next to the kitchen.

The woman lay down on the couch. JJ found a dishrag, rinsed it in the sink, and placed it on the woman's forehead. He'd helped Miss Nancy with sick kids before at Tutu House and had been asked many times over the years to get a wet rag to help cool a fever.

JJ had acted almost without thinking, but now the seriousness of the situation made him nervous. He sat in a chair, not knowing what to do next. Perhaps the cool dishrag helped, because the lady started moving and managed to sit up slowly. It was obvious she was sick.

"What's your name, boy?" she asked.

"JJ, ma'am."

The lady looked at JJ, then at Laddie, through half-shut eyes, and asked for another drink of water. JJ brought her the glass of water, and she slowly sipped. Then she closed her eyes and asked if he could get another cold rag. He quickly rinsed the dishrag and brought it back. She lay back down on the couch and closed her eyes.

JJ was starving and tired. It was now 6:30 am. He was too worked up to try to rest so he went to the kitchen and looked around. He found a loaf of bread in the breadbox. He was so hungry he could have eaten the entire loaf by himself, but at Tutu House he'd learned you should always try to figure out how much there was to go around. He cut off a piece of bread and shared some with Laddie. There was a small refrigerator humming quietly and what looked like a gas stove. He looked out the back kitchen window and saw a cow. He opened the refrigerator door and saw a jar of milk inside. "That must be a milk cow," thought JJ. He poured himself some of the cold milk and let Laddie finish drinking from his cup. As he drank the milk, it occurred to him that if it were a milk cow, it probably hadn't been milked recently.

The old woman was still asleep on the couch, so he went back outside. The back porch was covered and ran the entire length of the house. There were some shelves, an old washing machine, a broom, a mop, and a chair.

In the back, off to the side, was the barn. It seemed like a beautiful place to JJ, but there were signs of wear. Quite a few weeds were growing around. Inside the barn, he saw an old lawnmower, an old car, and some boxes and old tools. Everything was old and covered in dust.

JJ grabbed a bucket from the shelf and washed it with the garden hose. He had milked cows before when he visited the Friends Ladies' farm. They had explained how important it was for cows to be milked regularly. JJ patted and stroked the cow's head for a minute and then sat beside the cow. He milked the cow for a while and filled the bucket to overflowing. He kept milking until it seemed the milking was done. He brought the bucket back into the house and poured some of the milk into two clean jars he found in the cupboard and put them in the refrigerator. Then he poured some milk over some bread in a dish for Laddie just like Miss Nancy had done, and drank another big glass himself.

JJ sat down on a chair in the kitchen and heard the woman say something. He got up and walked back to the living room where the couch was. "What did you say your name was?" the lady asked again.

"JJ, ma'am. And this here is Laddie."

"Do I know you?" she asked.

"No, ma'am. I'm from the orphanage."

"Can you get me another drink of water please?"

JJ filled the glass with fresh water and rinsed the wet rag.

"Thank you, JJ. How old are you?"

"I'm eleven."

After a short pause, the lady said, "Can you help me up, please?"

JJ helped her to her feet, and she slowly walked to the bathroom. Then she went into her bedroom and lay down on her bed. It wasn't eight o' clock in the morning yet. JJ was so tired he lay down on the bed in the other bedroom, crosswise. The bed had a slightly dusty smell, but before JJ could even think about it, he was asleep, with Laddie resting next to him.

JJ woke up a few hours later when he heard the sound of the lady walking to the bathroom. He jumped up, not knowing where he was for a moment. By the time the lady was back in her bed JJ was awake. She asked for the wet rag again. JJ got the rag, rinsed it, and brought it to her. She put the cloth on her forehead, closed her eyes, and said, "What are you doing here, JJ?"

"I ran away, 'cause they were going to get rid of my dog."

"I see," she said. To JJ, she looked like she was 100 years old, but she was only 72. "My name is Beverly."

"Pleased to meet you, ma'am."

"Pleased to meet you, JJ. I'm pretty sure you saved my life."

"I hope you don't mind, I milked the cow," said JJ.

"Oh my land, the cow! Thank you so much!"

"You're welcome."

"I've got to rest. Can you take care of yourself for a while?"

"Yes, ma'am. Do you want me to call anyone for help?"

"There's no phone dear. I have some soup in the cupboard if you're hungry. I wouldn't mind just a taste myself."

Beverly closed her eyes and appeared to be sleeping again. She was about the same height as JJ, but heavier.

JJ walked around the house. On the mantel over the fireplace were a few pictures. One was an older man, and another was an old picture of Beverly holding hands with the same man, but younger. Another was a picture of a young man in a military uniform. Next to it was a Gold Star service banner, folded neatly.

JJ walked out the front door and stood on the porch. It had a roof and ran along the full length of the small house, like the back porch.

Laddie followed close by wherever JJ walked. JJ returned to the kitchen and found a can of Campbell's soup. He mixed it with milk in a pan on the stove. As he stirred the warming soup, he wondered what Miss Nancy would be fixing for lunch.

He sliced a piece of bread and ate a bowl of soup. He put some more soup in the bowl and gave it to Laddie. Then he got another bowl and put in a small amount of soup and took it to Beverly. She was grateful for the food and ate a few spoonfuls of soup. She wanted to rest again, so JJ took the bowl and let her go back to sleep.

It was now a little past noon. Outside, clouds were moving in, and it looked like rain.

* * * * *

At Tutu House, Sheriff Doug was talking to Miss Nancy and Mrs. Barclay. All the kids were outside with their noses pressed against the window trying to hear what was going on inside. After a time, Sheriff Doug walked outside and to the police car. He talked on his police radio and returned to the house. Miss Nancy's eyes were red from crying. Soon, two more police cars arrived. The sheriff deputies talked together and then began looking around the yard. There weren't any clues to follow because JJ had simply walked down the street. Sheriff Doug sent cars out in all directions while he headed South. They drove around for a while, but found nothing. It started raining. Sheriff Doug returned to Tutu House and spoke with Miss Nancy and Mrs. Barclay. "I'm guessing the rain will bring him home. I don't expect a young boy will want to stay out in this. Most kids who run away come back within a few hours."

* * * * *

JJ walked out to the barn. It wasn't raining hard, and he was interested in the lawn mower. Even though he was tired, nervous energy made him restless. He needed something to do.

The weeds and tall grass made walking in the yard difficult for Laddie. JJ dusted off a gas can that was sitting in a corner and poured a little gasoline into the lawnmower. He tried to start the lawnmower but had no luck. After some difficulty he finally got the dry carburetor primed and pulled the rope several times. The engine sputtered to life. Laddie didn't like the smoke and the smell and stayed by the open door, almost getting wet from the rain. JJ fiddled with the levers, figuring out which was the choke and which was the throttle. He let it run for a few minutes, then turned it off. It was after three o' clock now, and the rain was letting up.

He went back to the house to check on Beverly. She was still sleeping, so he came back outside and started the lawnmower. The backyard past the back gate on the left was a mess, making Laddie disappear into the tall grass and weeds.

Everything was slightly wet from the rain, but JJ started mowing anyway. The back area was large, nearly an acre. JJ mowed an area from the barn to the back fence about twenty feet wide. It was only a small part of the yard, but it provided a nice area where he could walk around with Laddie.

Inside the house, Beverly woke to the muffled sound of the lawnmower outside. It brought back pleasant memories. She could easily imagine her husband out working in the yard and her little boy playing with his toys.

JJ turned off the lawnmower and put it in the barn. He took his jacket and dried Laddie, and walked back into the house. Beverly was sitting on the couch in the small living room. Laddie jumped on her lap, and she started petting the dog. JJ smiled and said he was glad she liked dogs.

"I've never liked dogs before," she said. "I don't know why this one likes me."

Beverly paused for a moment and got a sad look on her face. "My boy Jack wanted a dog, but we never got one."

Then she said, "Well, JJ. Tell me more about why you ran away."

JJ told all about Tutu House, and how Laddie had become his friend. They talked for a long time. Beverly told him about her husband, how he had died almost four years ago, and about their son Jack, who had been killed in the war. She didn't seem at all ashamed to let tears roll down her face as she talked. "I remember quite clearly when Jack was your age. What I wouldn't give to have that time again."

"Is that a picture of Jack?" asked JJ as he pointed to the photograph above the fireplace.

"Yes," said Beverly. "He was a wonderful son. He never married. He and Tom, that's my nephew, were always together until the war."

"I'm sorry you have to live here by yourself," said JJ. After a moment he said, "Maybe you should get a telephone."

"Yes, I should," said Beverly. "Everything costs so much. I'm glad you came by, but if it wasn't getting late, I'd send you home. I'm feeling much better."

"I'm worried about being gone from home," said JJ. "But I'm afraid I'll have to get rid of Laddie."

"You need to get back home," said Beverly. "I'm sure they're worried about you."

"It makes me sad to think about them," said JJ. "Especially Miss Nancy."

"First thing tomorrow morning we'll have breakfast and you can be on your way. I'm doing better now thanks to you and Laddie. You can take a message for me to have them call my nephew."

After a moment, she added "You can let Laddie live here. I'll take care of him for you. You can come and visit." That made JJ feel a little better.

It was starting to get late, but not completely dark yet. "We've got plenty of hamburger meat," said Beverly. "We could make spaghetti for dinner if you could do the work."

"It seems like you've got plenty of food," said JJ. He thought about the dusty old car in the barn. "How do you get to the store?"

"My nephew comes by now and then to check on me and take me shopping. He was here just the day before yesterday. I also have the milk cow and the chickens. If I can just sit in the kitchen, I'll show you how to make dinner."

JJ helped Beverly to the kitchen where she could sit at the table. He had helped Miss Nancy make spaghetti many times before and just needed to know where everything was kept. Beverly told him where to find a pot, the strainer, the sauce, and everything else. The only tricky part was pouring the water out of the cooked spaghetti without spilling the food.

By the time dinner was ready, it was starting to get dark. JJ tried to switch on a light, but it didn't work. Beverly said, "The lights don't work. I think I blew a fuse yesterday. My nephew usually fixes those things for me."

"Where's the fuse box?" asked JJ.

"It's out on the back porch."

"Do you have a flashlight?"

"Oh dear," said Beverly. "Where would that be? There's one around here somewhere. Might be out by the fuse box."

JJ looked around the back porch. Over by the washing machine, close to the corner, was the fuse box and there was a stool nearby. On a shelf right under the fuse box was a flashlight. JJ turned it on, but it was almost dead. The sun had set, and it was getting dark quickly. JJ opened the fuse box and could see there were only four fuses. He knew about fuses from watching Mrs. Barclay replace a burned out fuse at Tutu House. It had a fuse box with eight fuses.

He unscrewed one fuse and looked at it, but it seemed ok, so he screwed it back in. It made a little spark, so he knew it was ok. He unscrewed another fuse and looked through the small glass window. It looked like it was blown, but it was hard to see. There were three spare fuses on the shelf where the flashlight had been. He grabbed one and screwed it in. Instantly there was light inside the house.

He put the flashlight back and climbed down off the stool and walked back into the house. The kitchen and bedroom lights were on.

"My, isn't that wonderful," said Beverly. "Aren't you smart!"

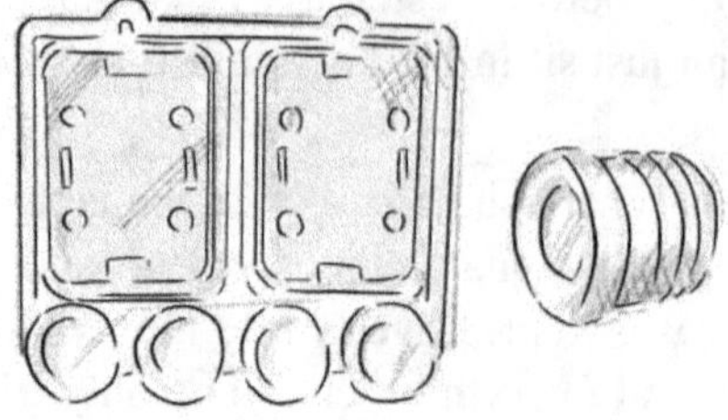

An old-fashioned fuse box with screw-in fuses

"It was just a fuse," said JJ. He finished setting the table and sliced some bread. He was hungry and glad for the food, but Beverly didn't eat much.

After dinner, JJ washed the dishes and Beverly said, "Turn out the lights and let's look at the fireflies."

Here and there, throughout the fields behind the farm area, a few flickering lights bobbed around. JJ helped Beverly outside and onto the chair on the porch. JJ sat on the edge of the porch.

"So how did you learn about things like lawnmowers and fuses?" asked Beverly.

"Mr. Johnson comes by now and then to fix things," said JJ. "We call him Uncle Larry. He and I fix things. He shows me how they work. He takes care of other places too."

"You seem pretty smart," said Beverly. "You must like school."

"It's ok," said JJ. "I do pretty well, actually."

"I'll bet you do," said Beverly. "I bet you're the smartest one in the class."

"Well, on some things. I'm good with arithmetic and reading. I learned to read when I was still in kindergarten."

"My goodness," said Beverly. "That's wonderful. What's your favorite book?"

"Lassie Come-Home. I have my own book in my room."

"You have your own room at the orphanage?"

"Yes, at the top in the attic. It's a very big house."

"It sounds like a nice place," said Beverly.

"Miss Nancy and Mrs. Barclay help me with schoolwork. They're nice. I've been there since I was two. I don't remember anywhere else."

"So where did you learn to milk a cow?" asked Beverly.

"The people who are in charge of the orphanage have a big farm. We go there every summer to learn about things."

"My farm used to be a lot bigger," said Beverly. "When I was first married we saved our money so we could buy this place. We were married in 1900, right at the beginning of the century. It took us nine years, but we did it. Jack was born in 1915, right here in this house. My brother lived in town and had a boy, Tom. He was a few years younger than my Jack. Those were good days."

Beverly sighed and then continued. "Jack worked this place with my husband and me. Tom worked as an electrician. The war changed everything. None of us were the same after that. After my husband died, I sold off most of the farm. Now, Tom wants me to sell the rest and live with him. He's the one who checks on me and helps me with groceries. I admit it would be easier to be living with him, but I don't know how I can leave this place and all my memories. Everything seems so unfinished."

JJ didn't say anything and just thought about things. Finally, he said, "It seems life is a big mixture of good and bad things."

It was quiet for a while. Finally, Beverly got up and gave JJ a hug. "I need to get back inside and rest. I'm feeling much better."

JJ helped Beverly back inside to the couch in the living room. He asked, "Can we listen to the radio?" He had seen a radio in the living room corner. It was the big, old-fashioned kind.

"Why yes! That would be good." JJ walked over and turned on the radio. The light on the radio dial came on, and after about half a minute, it started to make a sound. It was already on a station, but the tuning wasn't quite right, so he adjusted the dial until the sound was pretty clear. A man was talking, so he changed the dial around until he found some music. It was old "Big Band" music. Beverly smiled, and JJ sat on the couch. Off in the distance was some rain, and the occasional lightning would make a popping sound on the radio. With the fireflies outside, the lightning in the distance, and the crackling sound on the radio, it felt magical.

JJ was getting sleepy. They heard a news item on the radio about a lost eleven-year-old boy, asking for anyone with information to call the police.

"I'm sure they're worried about you," said Beverly.

"I know," said JJ. "I shouldn't have run away."

"Get some rest tonight and you can be on your way first thing in the morning."

Beverly found some pajamas for JJ. "These used to be Jack's. I've kept so many of his things." JJ gave her a hug. Then he took Laddie to the other bedroom and lay on the bed. Laddie jumped up next to him and licked his face.

"I sure do miss home," he said to Laddie. "I could go back now, but what if Beverly gets sick again? I better wait till morning. But what will happen to you? I don't want you to have to live so far away."

JJ slept fitfully, dreaming of Tutu House, and stories of Lassie.

The next morning Beverly and JJ were both up early and made breakfast with sausage and eggs. While JJ cleaned up, she went to her room to write a message for JJ to take home.

* * * * *

At Tutu House, JJ still had not returned. Miss Nancy and Mrs. Barclay hadn't slept all night. Sheriff Doug was disappointed that JJ was still missing. He decided to do more searching and sent more officers to ask around.

"I've put out another bulletin," he told Mrs. Barclay. "The boy will get hungry eventually. Someone will find him, or he'll show up back here. Meanwhile, we'll keep looking." No one wanted to think about the alternative.

Officer Lowell drove around, looking for a likely place where an eleven-year-old might want to hide. He checked out parks and some wooded areas but found nothing. No one saw or knew anything. It wasn't known exactly what time JJ had left, so it was hard to figure how far he might have gone. Officer Lowell kept driving around. The houses thinned out. He decided to go ten more miles on each of the main roads before giving up. He came to a small farmhouse and decided to stop and check it out.

3

A New Life

Officer Lowell parked in the driveway of the little house, and walked to the front door. JJ was washing the dishes when he heard a knock on the door. Laddie started barking. JJ opened the front door. Officer Lowell and JJ stood there and looked at each other. "Hi, I'm JJ."

"What the heck are you doing here?" asked Officer Lowell. "Everyone's looking for you."

"I'm sorry," said JJ. "I was going to come back, but I found Beverly. She's sick. There's no phone here, and she needs help."

Beverly walked slowly into the room with her message. "Oh dear," she said. She almost collapsed. Officer Lowell and JJ helped her to the couch. Laddie was still barking. "If you could call my nephew he could come and get me," she said.

Officer Lowell walked to his car and got on the police radio. Within minutes, Tutu House was notified that JJ was safe, and Beverly's nephew, Tom Robinson, was on his way. Officer Lowell waited for Tom and listened to Beverly and JJ tell their story. Soon, another police car arrived. It was Sheriff Doug. "Boy, are we glad to see you," he said. While Officer Lowell was explaining to Sheriff Doug, another car pulled up. It was Tom Robinson and his wife, Laura. Two police cars, a lost boy, a dog barking, and sick Aunt Beverly made for quite a scene.

Officer Lowell explained the whole situation to Tom and Laura. JJ gave Beverly a hug and each said goodbye. Beverly called out, "Don't forget – I can take care of Laddie if you need. Thank you, JJ."

Sheriff Doug helped JJ and Laddie into the police car and said, "Let's get you back home." As he pulled up and parked in front of Tutu House, Miss Nancy and Mrs. Barclay were standing on the front porch and came running. There was much hugging and crying.

"JJ, we were so worried," said Miss Nancy.

"JJ is a hero," said Sheriff Doug. He relayed the story to the ladies as the other kids gathered around.

"I'm sorry I ran away," said JJ. "I was worried about Laddie, then we found a sick lady."

"Don't worry," said Mrs. Barclay. "We're just glad you're home and safe!"

JJ looked up at Mrs. Barclay, then at Miss Nancy. He looked at Laddie, and his heart was heavy. Mrs. Barclay knelt down and looked directly at JJ and smiled. "JJ dear, Miss Nancy and I already decided Laddie can stay."

JJ's face lit up. The children were ecstatic. Tutu House was filled with merriment. JJ was glad to be home. Miss Nancy and Mrs. Barclay were relieved beyond measure and Sheriff Doug was glad for the happy outcome.

The children played with Laddie and visited with JJ while Miss Nancy made an early lunch. JJ wasn't hungry, but the others were ready to walk into town to see "Treasure Island" at the Mills Movie Theater. Mrs. Barclay took the older children and left JJ with Miss Nancy.

"I'm really tired," said JJ. "I didn't sleep well last night or the night before."

He and Miss Nancy climbed the stairs to his room. Miss Nancy sat on the edge of his bed and talked. It was different seeing Laddie on the bed with JJ.

"I really like Beverly," said JJ. He already sounded sleepy. "She lives all alone, and her husband died a few years ago, and her son was killed in the war."

"I'm glad you were able to help her," said Miss Nancy as she stood up to leave. Hearing about a widow living alone made her feel melancholy. She walked back down the stairs and let JJ sleep. She was tired, too, and sat down in the big chair to rest, keeping an eye on the two youngest. She was exhausted and felt bad that Mrs. Barclay had to take the kids into town alone. I'll give her a break when she gets back, she thought.

After a short while, Miss Nancy woke. "Oh dear. I must have dozed off," she thought. The house was still quiet, but everyone would be coming home soon. Lying next to her in the big chair was Laddie. JJ was still asleep in his room, and the kids were still playing with their toys. Laddie sat up and wagged his tail. Miss Nancy couldn't help patting him on the head. "Well, Laddie, I don't know what to think of all this." Then he rested his head on her lap. "I can see why JJ loves you."

When Mrs. Barclay and the children returned from the movie, Laddie started barking. JJ woke up and came downstairs. Miss Nancy and Mrs. Barclay fixed dinner. Things were getting back to normal, except for Laddie being in the house. After dinner, JJ told his story to all the children again. He thought of the little farm house and said, "There really is a story behind everything, just like Miss Nancy says!"

Dinner was a challenge for Mrs. Barclay. She didn't like having a dog in the house during dinner but kept her feelings to herself. The other children all wanted to feed something to Laddie, and it was chaotic. Mrs. Barclay could only hope that things would eventually settle down. Getting ready for bed took forever. Everyone kept going to JJ's room to see Laddie on the bed.

The next day started early with children running up to JJ's room. Kids and dog ran around the house until they were told to go outside. After lunch a lady from the newspaper came over. She wanted to hear all about JJ running away and saving an old lady. Once again, he told his story.

After dinner Laura Robinson called on the phone to ask if they could bring Beverly by tomorrow to visit JJ. Mrs. Barclay said it would be fine and gave Laura the address.

JJ was excited about seeing Beverly. Miss Nancy and Mrs. Barclay were curious.

The following day all the children wanted pets. Mrs. Barclay was afraid this might happen but said, "Let's just take care of one thing at a time."

After dinner, as the children ran around the yard with Laddie, an older car pulled up in front of Tutu House. A man, a woman, and an older lady got out. Shannen ran inside yelling, "Somebody's here!"

As Tom, Laura and their Aunt Beverly walked toward the front door, JJ ran out and gave Beverly a hug. She appeared to be doing better. Tom had a newspaper in his hand. Miss Nancy and Mrs. Barclay greeted them at the door.

"My, what a nice house!" said Beverly.

They all walked inside, shaking hands and greeting each other. Tom smiled and asked if they had read the newspaper. "I brought you a copy," he said and gave it to Miss Nancy. There, on the lower right-hand corner of the first page, was a story about an orphan boy who rescued an elderly woman.

Everyone smiled as they walked into the living room. Tom and Laura looked all around the house. Miss Nancy and Mrs. Barclay examined the newspaper.

"This is certainly a day to remember," said Miss Nancy.

"So, JJ," said Tom. "We didn't get a chance to meet you the other day."

"Aunt Beverly wanted to come by and see you," said Laura. "We wanted to meet you, too. It's amazing how you came along and saved her."

"Aunt Beverly says you fixed the lawnmower and mowed the yard," said Tom.

"Well, part of it," said JJ.

"Where did you learn to work on things like that?" asked Tom.

Miss Nancy said, "JJ is quite a clever boy. He's been keeping our lawnmower running since he was eight. He even fixed a problem our friends were having with their car."

"What do you do, Mr. Robinson?" asked Mrs. Barclay.

"I'm an electrician," said Tom.

"We're trying to rebuild the business," said Laura. "The depression and the war have been hard on us."

"It's been hard on everyone," said Miss Nancy.

"Were you in the war?" asked Mrs. Barclay.

"Yes," said Tom. "I was in Europe."

"My son died in France," said Aunt Beverly.

"My husband died in the Pacific," said Mrs. Barclay.

For a moment, no one said anything. Then Miss Nancy got up, smiled, and said, "How about some cookies and milk."

Without waiting for an answer, she walked into the kitchen. Mrs. Barclay followed her. They returned with a plate of cookies, a pitcher of milk, and glasses.

"I just wanted to make sure JJ wouldn't have a problem with the dog," said Aunt Beverly. "He's welcome to leave Laddie with me."

"We're hoping to have Aunt Beverly come and live with us," said Tom. "We've got a little house in the back she can stay in."

Aunt Beverly started to say something but stopped and just smiled.

They enjoyed their snack and visited politely. Soon the other kids wanted cookies and milk.

"It's very nice here," said Laura.

"We love it here," said Mrs. Barclay.

"Do you want to come up to the top and see my room?" asked JJ.

"Well, not this time," said Beverly. "I'm still a little tired."

"When you get better, you can come back."

"Ok, I will. You can call me Aunt Beverly if you want."

They talked more about JJ's adventure, and how fortunate it was that he came along when he did. As they got ready to leave, Aunt Beverly gave JJ a hug. JJ waved as the car drove away.

"Well, that was interesting," said Mrs. Barclay.

JJ and Laddie ran outside to play with the other kids.

"Yes," said Miss Nancy. "You look like you're thinking of something."

"I was just thinking what a nice family they would be for JJ."

Miss Nancy's face gave away an inner feeling of panic.

"Well, think about it," said Mrs. Barclay. "They live locally, and if JJ were placed with them, he would never be far away. Tom has a trade he could teach JJ. It's just a thought."

It was quite a thought, indeed.

* * * * *

For now, having a dog in the house wasn't so terrible, but it was different. Neither Miss Nancy nor Mrs. Barclay had ever had pets. Fortunately, JJ didn't have any trouble getting Laddie to go outside when necessary.

On Saturday, story night was extra fun. Laddie was worn out from playing with the children all day, and was quiet, resting next to JJ. It was a good time to be reading "The Story of Dr. Doolittle."

Sunday afternoon produced another phone call from Laura Robinson. Again, Mrs. Barclay answered the phone. "I really hate to bother you," said Laura, "but Aunt Beverly wants to see JJ again. She's agreed to come and live with us. We're hoping maybe we could occasionally bring her by to see JJ and Laddie."

"That would be fine!" said Mrs. Barclay. "We would love to see you again! Why don't you come for dinner tomorrow? The children aren't in school, and we can eat anytime you like. What time does Tom get home from work?"

"Tom is usually home by late afternoon, but I was just thinking of bringing Aunt Beverly over by myself."

"Why don't you bring Tom, too," said Mrs. Barclay. "We don't eat fancy."

"Neither do we," said Laura.

The next evening was Monday. Tom, Laura, and Aunt Beverly arrived at 5 pm. While Miss Nancy finished getting the meatloaf and mashed potatoes ready, JJ took Aunt Beverly upstairs all the way to the attic rooms.

"My, what a nice room," said Aunt Beverly, nearly out of breath. "And look at that window."

JJ showed Aunt Beverly his Lassie books and other things he had in his room. Laddie jumped onto the bed while Aunt Beverly held one of the Lassie books.

"Laddie doesn't look like Lassie," said Aunt Beverly with a smile.

"No, he doesn't," laughed JJ.

When JJ and Aunt Beverly came down from the attic, everyone was ready to sit at the big table. For the first time in recent memory, all fourteen chairs at the large dining room table were filled.

Five-year-old Mary, sitting next to Laura, said, "I'm glad you're here."

"Why is that?" asked Laura with a smile.

"'Cause we get soda pop at dinner."

"Soda pop at dinner?" repeated Laura with a smile.

"Mrs. Barclay said if we promise to be extra good we can have soda pop at dinner."

Laura laughed, and Mrs. Barclay smiled.

After dinner, JJ took Aunt Beverly outside, and the other children followed.

Mrs. Barclay spoke to Tom. "You're very fond of your aunt, aren't you?"

"Her boy was my cousin. He was like an older brother. It was devastating when Jack didn't come back from the war. Before that, when my mom died, Aunt Beverly was like a mother to me. She took care of me and now we take care of her. I just wish she was happier about coming to live with us."

"She sure seems taken with JJ," said Mrs. Barclay.

"Yes, she does," said Tom. "I guess it's not too surprising."

There was silence for a moment. Mrs. Barclay walked to the window where she could see the children playing outside in the back. Tom and Laura followed. Outside, JJ was holding Aunt Beverly's hand and was walking back toward the house.

Once inside, Aunt Beverly said, "Tom, one of their bicycles is broken. See if you can fix it."

"What's the problem?" asked Tom.

"It's Carol's bike," said JJ. "The frame broke. Uncle Larry tried to fix it, but he said it needs to be welded."

"Tom knows how to weld," said Aunt Beverly. "He could fix it."

"I could try," said Tom. "I don't have my welder with me."

"Why don't the three of you join us for story night on Saturday?" said Mrs. Barclay.

"What's story night?" asked Laura.

"Well," said Mrs. Barclay, "after dinner, we turn on the radio and listen to Annie Oakley while we have dessert. Usually, it's just cookies. Then Miss Nancy plays the piano, and the children sing songs, or we just listen to some music. Then Miss Nancy tells or reads a story. We're reading Dr. Doolittle right now. After that, the children start getting ready for bed."

"That sounds lovely," said Laura.

"Oh, I hope you can come for story night," said JJ.

"We'll be back, and Tom can bring the welder," said Aunt Beverly.

Tom and Laura just smiled.

When it was time to leave, Tom, Laura, and Aunt Beverly said goodbye. As they walked out the door, Mrs. Barclay called out to them, "I meant for you to come for dinner too."

"Okay," said Aunt Beverly.

Late Saturday afternoon, Tom, Laura, and Aunt Beverly were greeted by enthusiastic children. Miss Nancy prepared a nice stew. At the table, JJ sat between Miss Nancy and Aunt Beverly. The children were once again curious about Tom, Laura, and Aunt Beverly. Dinner was especially good.

Afterward, the kids went outside to play while Miss Nancy washed the dishes. JJ was happy to show how he could ride a bicycle. Thanks to the generosity of others, the children who lived at Tutu House all had a few nice toys, clothes, bicycles, tricycles, and wagons. Sometimes Miss Nancy and Mrs. Barclay even used their own savings to get something a child needed.

JJ brought out the broken bicycle, and then helped Tom carry the welder from the car. JJ watched with interest while Tom clamped wires onto the frame of the bicycle and cleaned the broken area with a brush. He put on a welder's mask and told JJ and the others to stand back. He began welding and in a matter of seconds, sparks were flying, and the cracked frame was repaired. JJ was amazed. He had never seen anything like it before.

"Wow," said all the children who had come to watch.

"Can you teach me how to do that?" asked JJ eagerly.

"We'll see," said Tom.

"Can you fix my light switch?" asked Carol, timidly.

Tom had to smile. "What's the matter with it?" he asked.

"It doesn't make the light go on," she said.

"Well, let's see," said Tom. "Let's get this stuff back to the car and we'll take a look."

JJ, Jon, and Carol helped carry the welding equipment back to the car. Tom enjoyed his attentive helpers. He put the welding equipment away and picked up a few tools, a small box with two wires dangling from it, and one of the spare switches he always carried. He gave each child something to carry. They showed him which room was Carol's.

"Let's see what the problem is," said Tom.

He unscrewed the switch cover and did something to the switch. The light flickered for a moment.

"Did you fix it?" asked Carol.

"No, but I can see what the trouble is."

JJ and Carol watched while Tom replaced the light switch. In two minutes it was fixed. Carol smiled and said, "Thank you Mister Robinson."

Tom was pleased. JJ was amazed that Tom carried a spare light switch in his car.

At Tutu House, they only had dessert on story night or special occasions. Sometimes they had Oreo cookies but this morning Miss Nancy had baked oatmeal cookies.

Not everyone sat still to listen to the Annie Oakley radio program, but most did. Aunt Beverly sat with JJ and Laddie while Tom and Laura visited with Miss Nancy and Mrs. Barclay in the kitchen.

"That was a very nice meal," said Laura.

"Thank you," said Miss Nancy.

"Thank you for fixing Carol's bicycle, and the light switch," said Mrs. Barclay.

"You have a wonderful home here," said Tom. "What happens when the kids grow up?"

"The older ones usually graduate to facilities in Pittsburgh," said Mrs. Barclay. "They try to get them trained for jobs and apprenticeships. There's a girl's home and a boy's home. We feel our home here is an ideal place for young children."

"There's hardly a year that goes by when we aren't saying goodbye to a child we've learned to love," said Miss Nancy.

"We do keep in touch with most of them," said Mrs. Barclay.

Mrs. Barclay and Miss Nancy both smiled.

When the radio program was over, Mrs. Barclay told the children to make a place on one of the couches for the guests. The younger kids brought blankets from their rooms and sat on the floor, even though there were plenty of chairs and two other couches.

Miss Nancy sat at the piano and played different songs which the children named. The younger kids sang along with some. "Für Elise!" said JJ. Miss Nancy played the song that for some reason JJ had always liked. Then she closed the piano and walked to the bookshelf, filled with many well-worn books. "Let's see," said Miss Nancy. "Where did we leave off?"

When the evening was done, Tom, Laura, and Aunt Beverly got ready to leave. Laura and Aunt Beverly thought everything had been very nice. Miss Nancy thanked Tom again for fixing the bicycle and the light switch. Tom enjoyed how the kids liked him for fixing things. Aunt Beverly was still talking with JJ, and the other kids were heading to bed. Mrs. Barclay looked directly at Tom and Laura. "I'd like you both to think about an idea I have. What if JJ came to live with you? He can't stay here forever, and living with you would make your Aunt Beverly happy. You could teach JJ about your work, and he would learn a trade. He's already interested in what you do."

Tom and Laura were both shocked and didn't say anything.

"Just think about it," said Mrs. Barclay. "Nothing would make us happier than to find a good home for JJ close by. He's clever, polite, and loves to help. He's one of the nicest boys we've ever had."

Tom tried to say something, but he was truly in shock. Laura just said, "Oh my." It was silent, except for the sounds of children getting ready for bed. Emotions swirled inside him. He and Laura had not talked about children since the death of their little girl so many years ago.

"I'm sorry if I made you uncomfortable," said Mrs. Barclay. "Just think about it."

Aunt Beverly walked over. "Think about what?" she asked.

"We'll talk in the car," said Tom.

"It was a very nice evening," said Laura.

"No matter what," said Mrs. Barclay, "Please come back for story night again."

Tom, Laura, and Aunt Beverly walked to the car, and JJ called out "Goodbye! We'll see you next week!"

"My goodness," said Miss Nancy as the door closed. She was nearly in a panic. In her mind, JJ would be with them until he was thirteen or more. But Mrs. Barclay was right. Who knows what would happen to him then? What could be better than a home right here in town? It was all so sudden.

"I'm going to do my best to make this happen," said Mrs. Barclay. "For your sake and mine."

"I know you're right," said Miss Nancy, "but, oh dear."

At the Robinson home, there were some serious discussions. Aunt Beverly was surprised and delighted at the prospect of having JJ come and live with them. Neither Tom nor Laura was sure what to think.

"Didn't you enjoy being with the children today?" asked Aunt Beverly. "I sure did. I felt young again."

Tom and Laura had to admit that it had been the nicest evening they had experienced in more than ten years, and Tom would do almost anything for his aunt.

"I kind of like the idea," said Laura.

"I don't know," said Tom. "I enjoyed being there too, but it seems impractical to think about having a child here now."

That made Laura sad. "If Baby Karen hadn't died we would have a child now. Would that be impractical?" She went into the bedroom.

That thought made Tom depressed. It was a horrible memory.

"That's not what I meant," said Tom to his aunt. "It's not like JJ is our own child."

"But he could be," said Aunt Beverly. "I like him. He saved my life."

"I know," said Tom. "But I wasn't prepared to think about taking in a kid."

"He's not just any kid," said Beverly. "How many boys his age would have milked my cow for me?"

"He is an unusual kid," said Tom. "There's no doubt about that."

"Thomas," said Aunt Beverly in one of her more serious moments. "JJ can't replace Baby Karen. But I want you to think about this for me, for JJ, and for Laura. I know you two haven't been as happy as you could be. Life has been hard. But I have a good feeling about this."

Tom apologized to Laura. He said he would try to make things work. He wanted his wife and aunt to be happy, but this was so sudden. Besides, he was busy and behind schedule. It wasn't easy finding work, and he was currently on a big job that needed to be completed soon.

The next few days were touched with anxiety, waiting to hear what the Robinsons would decide.

JJ could tell something was up. He worried that it might have something to do with Laddie.

On Wednesday, there was no trip to the movie theater because it wasn't a good movie for kids. Miss Nancy was glad to have all the children around. That evening the telephone rang. Miss Nancy was cleaning up from dinner. Mrs. Barclay answered the phone. "Hello, Mrs. Barclay. This is Tom Robinson. We've agreed to your suggestion about JJ."

4

A New Home

Thursday and Friday had been strange days. The mood at Tutu house was unsettled. It pained both ladies to prepare JJ for this next step. Miss Nancy reminded herself that this was an ideal situation. Over the years she had said goodbye to many children. It was always hard, but she had taken care of JJ from the time he was a baby, and this would be her most painful farewell. Mrs. Barclay and Miss Nancy talked to JJ about going to live with Tom and Laura.

"We don't want to see you go," said Mrs. Barclay, "but if you went to live with the Robinsons you would always be close by, and your future would be settled. Mr. Robinson could teach you about his work."

JJ was smart enough to understand the situation. He already had worries about having to go to the home in Pittsburgh. This would be a big change, but at least he would still be in town. "Can I take my things with me?"

"Of course you can," said Miss Nancy.

"What about the bicycle?"

"You can take it if you want but it would be nice if you left it for Greg," said Mrs. Barclay.

"I guess I could leave my Lassie books here for someone else to read. I'm probably too old for them anyway."

"Nonsense," said Mrs. Barclay with a smile. "You can certainly take your Lassie books. You're never too old for a good book."

"If it doesn't work out you can always come back," said Miss Nancy hopefully.

"Someday I'll have to leave here anyway."

"Yes," said Mrs. Barclay, "but this would be much better than going to Pittsburgh."

For JJ, a lifetime of security was evaporating.

"Life doesn't always give us what we want," said Miss Nancy. "Sometimes we just have to deal with what life gives us and do the best we can."

Saturday morning, JJ made his bed for the last time. It was an odd feeling for him. He gathered his favorite toys and books and put them in two paper bags. His clothes were placed in an old suitcase purchased from the thrift store. Every orphan who had ever left Tutu house had been given a suitcase that had been donated or purchased for a good price.

"Now remember," said Miss Nancy, "the first few days are the hardest, but it gets better over time. Just be a helper. It's going to be strange for Mr. and Mrs. Robinson, too."

"Miss Nancy knows what she's talking about," said Mrs. Barclay reassuringly.

"You'll be fine," said Miss Nancy. "Before you know it you'll be all settled."

"At least I won't be far away," said JJ.

"That's right," said Mrs. Barclay. "And we'll be seeing you often."

Tom and Laura had agreed to come back for story night every Saturday for the rest of summer. They would consider this a trial period.

That evening, Tom, Laura, and Aunt Beverly came for dinner and story night. It wasn't as jolly as before. Everyone felt some tension, but made an effort to be cheerful. When the evening was done, it was time for the children to get ready for bed. JJ said goodbye to everyone and said he would see them next week. Miss Nancy gave JJ a hug and whispered, "We'll see you soon."

The other kids were happy for JJ, and Miss Nancy and Mrs. Barclay tried to be happy too. They believed it was the best thing, but it was still terribly hard to say goodbye. With school out for the summer, it was a good time to make a change.

* * * * *

The Robinsons lived in a three bedroom house. It was old but had lots of character.

In back of the house was a small one bedroom residence. It had a small living room, a tiny kitchen, and a bathroom. It was perfect for Aunt Beverly.

A young couple had been renting the small house from Tom and Laura and had agreed to move to Beverly's farm. Everyone was satisfied with the arrangement. The young couple was glad to have a bigger place and liked having the cow and chickens. Aunt Beverly was finally living with Tom and Laura, but had her own place. It was different for her, but now she didn't need to worry about doing chores or getting sick. A telephone was finally installed at Beverly's farm house.

JJ's first night away from Tutu House was strange, and even difficult. For one thing, Tom and Laura weren't used to dogs and hadn't considered that JJ would want Laddie to sleep in the house. They couldn't understand the attachment JJ and Laddie had for each other. Tom proposed that Laddie could sleep in the garage until they could build a dog house. JJ was sharply disappointed. Aunt Beverly said, "It's ok. Laddie can sleep in my house." Tom wasn't going to argue with his aunt.

Living with Tom and Laura was quite different than being with Aunt Beverly on the farm. They brought the bed that JJ had slept in at the farm, but now it smelled fresh and clean. For the first time in many days, he was going to bed without Laddie. Laura tried to be pleasant and talked to him for a while. Finally, she said, "It's nice to have you and Aunt Beverly here." Then she turned out the light. As JJ lay there in the dark, he couldn't help but wish he was saying "good night" to Miss Nancy, and climbing the stairs to his room. He didn't sleep for a long time. He could hear the muffled voices of Tom and Laura talking in the other room. Tears filled his eyes. At least Laddie was close by. He thought about what Miss Nancy had said about the first few days being the hardest. He thought about the other orphans he knew who had grown up and left. "If they can do it, so can I."

Tom and Laura talked about the day. It was stressful for them as well. "I just hope this works out," said Tom.

"I know," said Laura. "But JJ is such a nice boy, and now we have Aunt Beverly here with us. She is much happier with JJ being here."

"It's going to be a lot to get used to."

"I know," said Laura. "But it's not so bad, is it? You've wanted Aunt Beverly here for a long time."

Laura was hopeful that this new family arrangement would bring cheer into their sad home.

At Tutu House, Miss Nancy and Mrs. Barclay stood in JJ's room and looked around. It was hard to see the room empty and silent. "JJ still has his winter coat and gloves here," said Mrs. Barclay. "We can have them drop by to pick them up. We'll see how JJ is doing."

"Yes," said Miss Nancy quietly, holding back a tear.

"As much as I hate to see JJ leave," said Mrs. Barclay, "I believe this is the right thing. I have a good feeling about Tom and Laura, and at this point in JJ's life, I believe they can do things for him we just can't."

"Yes, I know," said Miss Nancy. "But it just breaks my heart. I hope things work out."

"I'm sure they will," said Mrs. Barclay as she gave Miss Nancy a hug. "We'll be seeing them on story night, so it's not like he's gone for good. Let's go down and check on everyone."

At the little house in the back of Tom and Laura's, Aunt Beverly got ready for bed. Laddie jumped up on the bed next to her. "I'm sorry you can't be with JJ," she said to Laddie, petting him softly. "I'm sure things will work out."

Sunday wasn't much better. JJ was up early and went out to Aunt Beverly's house. He, Aunt Beverly, and Laddie all came back into the main house for breakfast. Eating at the small kitchen table with just the four of them was different from the large dining room table at Tutu House. Tom was not happy with Laddie being in the house but didn't say anything. It surprised him how Aunt Beverly's attitude toward dogs had changed. Fortunately, she did enough talking for everyone.

Laura and Aunt Beverly spent some time fixing up JJ's room. JJ played with Laddie outside, but was bored and lonely. Tom went to work for a while, even though it was Sunday. He was behind schedule.

After lunch, Mrs. Barclay called to let them know there were a few more clothing items, and asked if they could come by and pick them up.

When Tom got home, they all drove over to Tutu House. It was good to have something to do. JJ was happy to see the kids and give Miss Nancy a hug. Miss Nancy took JJ and Aunt Beverly into the kitchen for a cookie and then outside where the kids were playing. Mrs. Barclay took Tom and Laura up to JJ's room. "Is everything going ok?" she asked as they climbed the stairs to JJ's room.

"Well, it's an adjustment," said Tom.

"Of course it is," said Mrs. Barclay, as they reached JJ's room. JJ's coat and gloves were lying on the bed. "I'll keep JJ's room for him for a while, just in case. He is always welcome back, but if you can make things work, he will change your life."

Tom and Laura looked at each other, and Tom said they would make an effort.

"Please remember we've had JJ here since he was in diapers. We've raised him like our own. He's like a son to Miss Nancy. It's our job to place children in good families like yours, but that doesn't mean it's easy for us."

"I understand," said Laura.

After a short visit, the Robinsons said goodbye. As they walked out the door, Mrs. Barclay said, "Why don't you come over on Wednesday for the Fourth of July? We'll have fireworks here, and it will be fun."

"We'll be here," said Aunt Beverly.

Tom was surprised that Mrs. Barclay and Miss Nancy would have their own fireworks at Tutu House.

On the way home, Laura had Tom stop at the store to buy some ice cream. When they got home, she let JJ open a new can of Hershey's chocolate syrup and with the ice cream it helped lighten the mood. At least everyone was smiling as they got ready for bed. Once again, JJ took Aunt Beverly and Laddie to the little house in back and JJ said good night to Laddie. He stayed a long time and talked with Aunt Beverly. He was unhappy about leaving Laddie. Aunt Beverly said, "Give them a chance. They just need to get used to Laddie. I'll do what I can." She was sitting on the couch holding Laddie when JJ left.

Laura said good night to JJ. She could tell he was sad about not having Laddie with him. As she got in her bed, she wondered if they were doing the right thing. But if they returned JJ to the orphanage, what would happen with Aunt Beverly? Were they doing this for the right reasons? Wasn't this Mrs. Barclay's idea?

"I think we all just need a little time to adjust," said Laura. "It's a big change for everyone."

"I know," said Tom. It was obvious Tom was also thinking about everything. "I just don't know if we're making a better life for him than if he stayed at the orphanage with his friends." Tom was glad to have his aunt with them. He just wished it was simpler than having to include JJ. He wished JJ didn't have a dog. He wished his little girl hadn't died. He wished life wasn't so hard. He wished so many things.

Tom couldn't sleep. He got out of bed and walked quietly around the darkened house. He looked at the door to the room where JJ was sleeping. He liked JJ just fine, but it was different knowing he was in that room. The other bedroom still had Baby Karen's things. Looking at that door made him sad. He sat down in the dark living room on the couch to think. Sometimes he wondered why he even bothered being alive. He hardly enjoyed work anymore. There was once a time when the future seemed bright. Thinking about things wasn't helping. After a while, he got up and went back to the bedroom and got in bed.

Laura wasn't sure what to think anymore. She was also having a hard time sleeping. She was worried, and wondered if it would take a miracle for things to work out. But fate, or God, or serendipity itself had decided it was time for Tom and Laura to have a better life. JJ *was* their miracle. Tom just couldn't see it yet. This miracle needed a little nudge.

The next morning, everyone was polite at breakfast, but even Aunt Beverly could feel the strain. Tom felt pressured to try and make things work and worried what people would think if he failed.

When he got home from work, the sun was setting. Laura sent Tom to the store with Aunt Beverly to pick up some groceries. After a while, Laura and JJ heard the car return and then some shouting.

Laura ran outside, and JJ followed. Tom was holding his right hand in great pain, yelling and cussing. Aunt Beverly had slammed the car door on Tom's hand.

"I didn't mean to," cried Aunt Beverly. "I didn't see his hand there."

"Oh no," thought Laura to herself. "This isn't going to help at all."

She called out, "JJ, help Aunt Beverly with the groceries. Tom – hold still and let me take a look at your hand."

Tom moaned, "I think it's broken!"

"Laddie, get down!" said Laura. "Aunt Beverly, call the doctor and let them know we're coming. The number's on the side of the refrigerator."

Laura put Tom in the car. As they drove off, Aunt Beverly said, "Come on, JJ. I'll call the doctor and you can help me get supper started."

JJ set the table and helped Aunt Beverly cook potatoes, vegetables and pork chops. "Don't worry," she said nervously. "Everything will be fine."

Dinner was on the table when Tom and Laura returned with Tom's hand in a bandage. "It's only a broken thumb," said Laura.

The meal was uncomfortably quiet. Laddie could be heard faintly barking from Aunt Beverly's little house. Tom was grumpy. "This is a heck of a thing. I've got lines to pull tomorrow on the Davis project. I'm never going to get caught up now."

JJ thought about what Miss Nancy had said about being a helper. "I can help," he said.

"That's a good idea," said Aunt Beverly. "Tom, you should put that boy to work. Let him help you. You know how smart he is."

Tom was doubtful, but had no other option. He decided to wait until after the 4th of July before making up his mind about what to do with JJ.

Tom was in a sour mood as he got ready for bed, and Laura was depressed. In the dark that night, she cried silent tears. It seemed everything was falling apart. As far as she could tell, things were worse than ever. Sometimes it's hard to tell you are in the middle of a miracle.

The next morning was Tuesday. It had been another strained, uncomfortable night for JJ. He was up early to go out back and see Laddie at Aunt Beverly's place. Laura fixed a nice big breakfast, but there wasn't a lot of conversation. Aunt Beverly was optimistic like usual. Laura made a lunch sack for Tom and JJ. They drove off, a nervous JJ and a grumpy Tom. Laura was beginning to feel that the right thing to do was to return JJ to the orphanage. Perhaps they could bring Aunt Beverly over for visits. She tried to think of different ways to make this work. The day dragged on slowly. Aunt Beverly and Laura sat outside for a while in the shade of a tree. Aunt Beverly tried to get Laura to pet Laddie. Laura made a half-hearted attempt but was clearly worried about everything, and very sad.

On the way to the worksite, Tom thought to himself "I'll probably be the laughingstock of everyone." He had wanted to complete this part of his work before the Fourth of July, and now that seemed impossible.

When Tom and JJ arrived at the site where an office building was being constructed, he and JJ got out of the car, and he handed JJ a tool that looked like a spool of wire. Then he grabbed a large box of wire from the trunk and carried it toward the unfinished building, with JJ following. He felt embarrassed about the whole situation. A plumber called out "Hey Tom, who's the kid?"

Without thinking, Tom held up is bandaged hand and said, "It's my nephew. He's going to help me out today."

Tom and JJ walked around to the back of the building and over to what looked like a fuse box but had switches instead. "Is that a fuse box?" asked JJ.

"It's a circuit breaker panel," said Tom. "We don't use fuses anymore." Inside the panel were what looked like the ends of many pipes. Tom put the box of wire on the ground and said, "We need to pull wires through each of these conduits."

JJ tried to imagine pushing wires through long pipes. "Gosh, how do we do that?"

Tom said, "I'll show you. Bring the fish tape over this way. You're going to have to help me with this." They walked into one of the unfinished rooms and over to where an outlet was going to be installed. The room smelled of new wood, wet concrete and plaster, and JJ liked it.

"We're going to push this fish tape down the line from here, and it will go back to the circuit breaker panel," said Tom. He explained how to start unspooling the fish tape, which was like a stiff, flexible thin and flat wire, and push it through the conduit pipe, which was next to where the outlet was being installed.

"Oh, I get it," said JJ as he started pushing the fish tape through the open end of the conduit pipe. It took two hands and sometimes it was hard, but he kept pushing. A painter named Scott walked in from the other room and said, "Hi, Tom. Is that your boy?"

Tom showed his bandaged thumb again and said, "My nephew is helping out. I broke my thumb."

Scott watched JJ for a moment and said, "Hey – pretty good." He joked, "when you're done with that you can come over and help me paint!"

Tom had to admit to himself that JJ was doing a good job. "I'll go back to the service panel and tell you when the fish tape wire comes through," said Tom.

JJ kept pushing the fish tape wire down the conduit until Tom yelled out, "Ok! Got it!"

JJ came over to see Tom fastening the actual wire to the end of the fish tape. It was hard with only one hand. "Oh – I get it," said JJ. "Now we just pull the wire back down the conduit."

"Right," said Tom. "You go back and start pulling, and I'll try to feed the wire to get it started."

JJ began pulling on the fish tape he had previously pushed into the conduit, and Tom said, "Ok – it's going good. Keep pulling."

"Wow, this is hard," said JJ as he struggled to pull on the wire. He used both hands and pulled and yanked and soon the wire appeared. JJ could see how Tom had attached the wire and unhooked it from the fish tape without Tom having to say anything. "Very good," thought Tom. The plumber walked by, saw JJ working, and said, "Hey Tom – you should bring him every day!"

JJ was breathing hard from pulling the wire but was pleased with himself. "Ok," he said. "Let's do the next one."

"Ok," said Tom. "We just did the longest one. The others will be easier."

Pulling wires was faster and easier when Tom could be on one end and JJ on the other. The work moved along more quickly than when Tom worked alone without a broken thumb. The other men working in the area liked JJ and his cheerful attitude. "So how do you like working with your uncle?" asked the plumber.

"It's great!" said JJ. He liked having something to do rather than sit around the house.

By lunchtime, all the lines had been pulled. The guys working there ate lunch around the same time, and they sat around talking. "You're really moving along there," said Scott, the painter. "Good thing you brought your nephew along."

They were right, thought Tom. "Next," he said to JJ, "we'll be connecting the wires to the breakers."

"So how do the circuit breakers work?" asked JJ.

Tom explained, and JJ could see it was a big improvement over fuses. As they ate their lunch, they talked. Tom found himself having a good time explaining what they were doing. It gave him the same good feeling he had had fixing Carol's bike and the light switch. They talked about the wiring at Aunt Beverly's farm and why the fuses kept blowing there. Tom was amazed at how much he enjoyed talking with JJ, and how quickly JJ caught on to things. During the afternoon, JJ got to see how Tom used a meter to test the lines to make sure each had been connected properly. Tom even let JJ use the meter while he switched different breakers on and off to test each circuit. For JJ, each task they did was fun, and Tom had tools JJ had never seen before. As they worked together, Tom explained some of the basics of house wiring.

Everyone working there liked JJ. At the end of the day, Tom was ahead of schedule. It was clear. JJ was an asset, broken thumb or not. As Tom and JJ packed up their tools and got ready to leave, the other guys all said goodbye and said they hoped to see JJ again on Thursday. Everyone wished each other a happy Fourth of July.

The ride back to the house was quite different from the ride to work. Now they were talking to each other. Tom enjoyed answering JJ's questions and explaining how things worked. It was obvious JJ was soaking up everything he said.

"You were pretty helpful today," said Tom. "How would you like to keep working with me for a few days?"

"That would be neat!" said JJ with a big smile.

Laura and Aunt Beverly were waiting with anticipation, dread, and worry. They had started working on Tom's favorite dinner and were each taking turns watching out the front room window. It was the middle of summer so it would be light outside for some time. A fan was humming in the living room, creating a nice breeze. Around 4:30 they saw the car turn and pull into the driveway. "Oh dear," thought Laura. "They're early."

Laura stepped outside while Aunt Beverly waited inside. Tom opened his door, got out, and he was smiling, finishing a conversation with JJ. JJ opened his door, and he was smiling too. "Well, how did it go?" asked Laura.

"It was fine," said Tom. "That boy's a good worker, and he catches on fast."

Laura's relief was indescribable.

"It was fun," said JJ. "I got to do all kinds of stuff, and Uncle Tom has really neat tools."

Laura was astonished and mouthed the question, "Uncle Tom?"

Tom just shrugged his shoulders and smiled. Laura hadn't seen him smile that way in a long time.

The atmosphere at the dinner table couldn't have been brighter. Conversation was non-stop. JJ described each step of the job as though it were an adventure. Tom just said it was normal stuff and dropped food crumbs to Laddie under the table. Aunt Beverly had been right about JJ. For Tom, it was the beginning of a new life.

After dinner, JJ caught a glimpse of Tom and Laura kissing and hugging in the kitchen. Aunt Beverly saw it too and pulled JJ into the living room. They sat and played with Laddie until Tom and Laura came in and turned on the radio. Laura was radiantly happy, and Tom was in the best mood anyone had seen in years.

That day, Tom gained a partner and a friend. JJ got a career. Laura got her husband back. Aunt Beverly got peace, and Laddie got to sleep in the house.

The next day was a holiday, and the Robinson family was finally in a holiday mood. In the morning Tom let JJ see more of his tools and explained what they did. He even brought out the welder and gave JJ his first lesson. The sparks from the welder reminded JJ of fireworks. Going back to Tutu House in the evening for fireworks now seemed like fun to Tom.

After dinner, Tom, Laura, Aunt Beverly, JJ, and Laddie all drove to Tutu House. It would be an hour before it would be dark enough for fireworks. Tom's hand was in a bandage, but he appeared to be happier than ever. Mrs. Barclay and Miss Nancy were pleased to see JJ so happy, describing the adventures of working with Tom during the previous day. Carol brought her bicycle over to show that it was working fine and thanked Tom for fixing it.

"Seems like things are working out," said Mrs. Barclay.

"They certainly are," said Laura with a smile.

5

Settling In

JJ loved working with Tom, and they became the best of friends. JJ learned how to use a welder and even got to do some painting. The few days turned into every workday for the summer, and JJ was paid a small allowance for helping. Tom's hand healed perfectly. They almost always finished early. Tom enjoyed JJ's company, and JJ liked having something useful to do. They continued enjoying story night at Tutu House.

Things had indeed worked out. The Robinson household was now a happy home. Tutu House felt empty without JJ, but Mrs. Barclay and Miss Nancy were at peace. They looked forward to story night more than ever. JJ often had his own story to tell. The four ladies were becoming friends.

Tom found himself enjoying story night more than he would have thought. He was a favorite of the other kids, who looked forward to the visits. There was often some little thing that needed fixing and Tom was happy to help. JJ assisted, and Tom explained what he was doing.

Meals were now a happy time, and there was no shortage of conversation. They listened to the radio at night, played Monopoly and other games, and were a happy family. When the day was done, JJ walked Aunt Beverly to the little house in the back while Laddie walked around to pee. Sometimes it seemed to JJ that Aunt Beverly was not as steady, but he thought it could be his imagination. Or perhaps the heat was bothering her. By now it was hot and humid, and everyone had a fan running at night.

One evening in late August, after dinner, they were all sitting at the kitchen table drinking cold sodas. Moisture was dripping from their cold glasses. Laura had just finished cleaning up the dishes and was sitting by the fan. "I don't know how people ever lived without electric fans," she said.

"You can say that again," said Aunt Beverly.

"I could just stick my head in the refrigerator and take a nap," said Laura jokingly.

"Hey," said JJ. "Why can't we just open the refrigerator door and let it cool down the kitchen?"

"I've thought of that," said Aunt Beverly, "except the food would probably spoil."

"That's a good question," said Tom. "And there's a reason why it wouldn't work."

Tom could see by JJ's face that he was interested, and continued.

"Go feel the back of the refrigerator," said Tom.

JJ got up and reached around the back and said, "Hey, it's hot back here." It was almost hot enough to burn his hand.

"A refrigerator doesn't just cool things down," said Tom. "It trades heat for cold. It moves the heat out of the inside of the refrigerator and moves it to the outside. If you left the fridge door open, it would be cooling and heating the room at the same time. You'd get nowhere."

JJ thought for a minute. "What if you could stick the back side of the fridge outside but keep the door inside?"

"JJ," said Tom, "you are indeed a clever lad. That's exactly how air conditioning works. How would you like to help me do just that?"

Everyone looked at Tom with astonishment.

"Cut a hole in the wall?" asked JJ.

"No," laughed Tom. "I've had this idea ever since the war where I learned about air conditioning. I'm thinking of taking an old refrigerator apart and cutting out the cooling mechanism and putting the hot part outside and the cold part inside. Maybe we could make our own air conditioner."

Tom and JJ spent the next few days planning their attack on the next refrigerator they could find. "I'll tell you," said Laura to Aunt Beverly,

"Tom seems more like a kid than ever." Aunt Beverly couldn't be happier.

Tom came across an old refrigerator and took it to the shop. He and JJ pulled it apart. They separated the condenser and evaporator units, and then re-attached them with a length of copper tubing they purchased from Stewart's hardware store. They hung the evaporator unit inside the office part of their shop and the condenser unit outside. They charged the line with Freon using some tools Tom had brought home with him from the Army Air Corps and turned it on. It worked. The evaporator unit looked a bit odd, but it got cold. They used a fan to blow air across and cool the room. Outside they used a fan to blow air across the condenser coils. It wasn't pretty, but it made cool air. At least it was at the shop and not at home. Tom and JJ were pleased.

* * * * *

After a wonderful and productive summer, it was time to register for middle school. Tom was not looking forward to the start of school, and neither was JJ. Tom would miss having JJ with him. Henderson Electric, named after a family relative no longer involved, had been struggling to recover since the war ended. There wasn't a lot of money yet, but the economy was picking up, and the future looked good. Tom was the owner and sole employee, and any contribution from JJ made a huge difference. "Now I just need to find more work," thought Tom.

Laura walked with JJ to the new school. His name from the orphanage was listed as Jark Jackson. He was two years old when he was found walking by himself at the grocery store. At first, people looked around for his parents. Then the police were called. He could barely talk, and when asked his name, he said something unintelligible that sounded like "Jark." He had been examined by a doctor who said his best guess was that Jark had been born somewhere around the beginning of March. His official birthday was set as March 1, 1940. Before he was three, he had become known simply as "JJ."

JJ liked middle school better than grammar school. There was the occasional run-in with Kevin Connor, but JJ liked most of his teachers. It was nice going to different classes instead of staying in the same room for the whole day. At lunch, he met with his friends and told them about his new life. Steven and Michael were impressed by JJ having a job, sort of.

After school and on weekends, JJ was able to work with Tom. It was more fun working with Tom than doing homework.

Unfortunately, Kevin Connor lived only five blocks away from Tom and Laura's house. JJ worked out a route to school which ensured he wouldn't run into Kevin on the way. The school was bigger, which made it easier to avoid him in the morning.

All in all, things were going well. They settled into a wonderful routine. Every morning JJ and Laddie would get Aunt Beverly for breakfast. Laddie would jump all over her, and she would reach down and pet him. Sometimes, when they slept in, Aunt Beverly would come in the back door yelling "Yoo Hoo!" and Laddie would jump off the bed and run barking to see her. Life was different now for Tom and Laura. They had a dog living in the house, Aunt Beverly was always happy, Laura was always smiling, and Tom liked dogs and kids. "How life can change," thought Laura.

One time JJ remarked to Aunt Beverly, "Uncle Tom and Aunt Laura sure do hug and kiss a lot."

"That's the way it should be," she said. "They've been sad for so long it's good to see this. They got married a few years before the war, you know, and had a little girl named Karen who got scarlet fever and died when she was just three years old. While Tom was in the war, Laura worked at the restaurant. When the war was over, and Tom got back, nothing was the same. It seemed their happiness was gone."

It was a lot to think about. JJ was glad they were happy now.

In the Fall, everyone looked forward to the holiday season, starting with Halloween. "Why don't you all come over for Halloween?" Mrs. Barclay said to Laura. "The kids all have fun. We'll have a little party."

JJ was happy to go trick or treating in familiar territory with his friends. Tom, Laura, and Aunt Beverly were happy to be doing something jolly.

By Thanksgiving, it was getting cold. The Robinson home was warm and filled with the aroma of cooking and baking. For Tom and Laura, it was the best Thanksgiving in years, and there was much to be thankful for. Laura and Aunt Beverly enjoyed preparing food. Tom gave a nice blessing. JJ said he was thankful for Laddie, his new family, and his friends at Tutu House. Aunt Beverly said she was thankful JJ had come into their lives. Tom said he was thankful that business was picking up and that he had JJ to help him. Laura said she was thankful everyone was healthy and happy. Tom was amazed when he thought about how only nine months ago, JJ was a complete stranger. Now, he truly loved JJ. As they were going to bed, Tom and Laura discussed the need to go ahead and get the adoption completed.

The next day they visited Tutu House and brought pies they had baked. As usual, Mrs. Barclay and Miss Nancy were glad to see them. "I can't believe I was ever doubtful about JJ," said Tom. "We can't imagine life without him. In fact, it's hard to imagine life without you folks, too."

Mrs. Barclay smiled. "Families come in all shapes and sizes. You're a fine man, Mr. Robinson. I hope we always see you and Laura and JJ around here."

Mrs. Barclay was pleased with the whole affair. She could tell by the way Tom and Laura looked at each other that they had a happy family.

"I'm glad to see JJ so happy," she continued. "We really do miss him around here."

After Thanksgiving, Aunt Beverly's excitement for Christmas was spreading to everyone. For the first time in many years, Tom was looking forward to finding a Christmas tree. They all went together on a Saturday. It was mid-afternoon, the sky was overcast, and the air was chilly while they walked around the Christmas tree lot. The ground was covered with sawdust, and the air was filled with the smell of a thousand Christmas trees. Indiana, Pennsylvania was the Christmas tree capital of America. JJ was amused by Aunt Beverly as she examined all the different trees. They settled on a six-foot tree that everyone liked. Tom and JJ fastened it to the top of the car. It was beginning to feel like Christmas.

When they got home, Laura found the old box of ornaments and Christmas lights, and they spent the evening decorating the tree. Aunt Beverly and Laura were both having so much fun. There had not been a Christmas tree in either of their homes for many years.

After decorating the tree, Laura fixed dinner and Tom helped. The lights in the living room were turned out except for the Christmas tree. JJ sat on the couch with Aunt Beverly and Laddie and admired the tree. When dinner was ready, Aunt Beverly stood up and reached up to the angel on top of the tree and adjusted it just a little. JJ noticed that she gazed at the angel in a thoughtful way. The last person who had placed that ornament on a Christmas tree was her son Jack, and it hadn't been used since.

The next few days were cheerful. School was out for Christmas vacation, and JJ was able to work with Tom. There still wasn't a lot of business yet, but it was always more fun working with each other. It also provided a chance for Tom to take JJ shopping for Laura and Aunt Beverly.

Christmas morning was merry. JJ was overjoyed when he saw a new red bicycle that he knew was for him. He missed the one he had left at Tutu House, but it would be used by other orphans, just as it had been passed down to him.

Aunt Beverly had come over extra early yelling "Yoo hoo," but everyone was getting up anyway. It was fun to see that Tom was almost as excited as a kid. Laura was pleased by some earrings JJ had picked out himself and bought with his own money. Tom was happy with a new flashlight JJ had picked out. Aunt Beverly was thrilled by a necklace.

They had hot chocolate and toast for breakfast. Outside was chilly and cold, but JJ was anxious to try out his new bike. Tom, Laura, and Aunt Beverly held cups of hot chocolate and watched as JJ rode up and down the street with Laddie running along. All in all, it was the picture of a perfect family.

That night they all sat quietly on the couch in the darkened room, looking at the lights on the Christmas tree and thinking about the day. Laura was wearing her new earrings, Aunt Beverly was wearing her necklace, Tom was fiddling with his new flashlight, and Laddie was sound asleep on the floor next to the tree. It had truly been a merry Christmas. JJ spoke quietly, "It's been such a wonderful day with the four of us all together."

"It has been nice," said Laura with a smile, as she put her arm around JJ. "But in a few months, there will be five of us."

6

New Business

On January 9, 1952, JJ became the legal son of Tom and Laura Robinson. Aunt Beverly, Miss Nancy, Mrs. Barclay, and all the children from Tutu House accompanied Tom, Laura, and JJ to the courtroom. Even Sheriff Doug and Officer Lowell showed up.

Judge Hansen was pleased to see the small crowd. It was the first order of business that morning. He called Tom, Laura, and JJ into his chamber. A few minutes later the door opened, and he asked for Aunt Beverly and Miss Nancy.

"You have quite a family," said Judge Hansen. "And quite a story."

Miss Nancy and Aunt Beverly cried during the short procedure. Judge Hansen congratulated everyone and wished them all a good life. "This is the best part of my job."

* * * * *

On March 1, they celebrated JJ's 12th birthday, his first birthday away from Tutu House. Tom and Laura got him a set of tools. Also included was a trip to Tutu House for birthday cake. It had been almost a month since their last visit. Aunt Beverly said she felt tired and wanted to stay home and rest.

The whole day ended up being grand. JJ showed his new tools to everyone, and Miss Nancy examined each one. Miss Nancy and Mrs. Barclay were happy to hear about Laura expecting a baby.

* * * * *

May 26 was Memorial Day, and JJ got to see where Baby Karen was buried. It was the first time in years that Tom and Laura had visited the grave together. Tom held Laura's hand as they stood by the grave. Tom wiped his eyes several times. It was the first time JJ had seen him cry.

JJ tried to imagine Baby Karen as a little girl, smiling, walking, talking, happy to see her daddy come home from work, and Laura dressing her in little clothes. Then, getting sick, and how sad it must have been to finally kiss their little girl goodbye. It made him sad just to think about it. Instinctively he gave both of them a hug.

Aunt Beverly remembered that awful time in 1942. The war was starting, and her son Jack left for Europe. Those were dark days. Then Tom left, too. In the summer of 1944, Beverly was notified that Jack had been killed. He had been buried in France. She would never see that place.

From then on, Laura became close to Beverly. Two years after Tom returned from the war, his uncle died. It seemed that sadness was all that kept this family together, until now.

Nobody spoke on their way back home. It was a day of mixed feelings. The past was sad, but Laura was expecting, and JJ had changed their life.

* * * * *

In June, a whole year had passed since JJ ran away and met Aunt Beverly. Sometimes there are little events that end up changing your life forever, like finding a lost dog, or smashing your thumb in a car door. Today would be another one of those days.

It started with a bicycle ride to the big store. JJ had been saving to buy a headlight set for his bike. It was a nice, sunny day, and JJ had no trouble riding his bicycle to the large store on the other side of town.

When he arrived at the parking lot, he noticed a couple of men standing around a white Cadillac. One well-dressed man standing next to the driver's door didn't look happy. The engine hood was open, and JJ could see inside. The man was talking to another man about the car not starting. Both men headed inside the store. When one of the men returned a few minutes later, JJ had his hands in the engine and was doing something.

"Hey kid, what do you think you're doing?" said the man. He was a big guy, a head taller than average.

"Hey, mister. I think I found the problem. Try it now," said JJ, with a serious look on his face.

The man looked quizzically at JJ but got inside the car and turned the key. The engine roared to life, and the sound made JJ jump backward. Then the engine died. The man got out of the car. "Look, here's the problem," said JJ pointing to the engine.

"You don't say," said the man.

"Look," said JJ. "Your distributor is clamped down by these two little things right here, see? Well, one of the screws underneath is stripped and keeps coming lose."

By now the man was laughing. "You're quite a kid. How old are you?"

"I'm 12, sir."

"What's your name, kid?"

"JJ."

"Pleased to meet you, JJ, my name is Howard Mills. You seem to know something about engines."

JJ had a big smile. "Yeah. I like to fix things. We could take your car over to my dad's shop, and he could fix it, but we need some tape."

"Your dad's a mechanic?"

"No, he's an electrician, but he's pretty good with things, like me."

Mr. Mills laughed out loud. He was 47 years old, tall, and a bit heavy. He immediately liked JJ.

By now the store manager had come out. Mr. Mills walked over to him and said, "Hi Sam. Thanks for helping out. Can you watch JJ's bike for me until we come back to get it?"

"Sure thing," said Sam. "What do you want me to do about the Triple A?"

"Tell them to hold that service call. Let's see what happens here. And I need some tape."

"No problem, Mr. Mills. What kind of tape do you need?"

"I need some duct tape," said JJ.

"We need duct tape, Sam," said Mr. Mills with a laugh.

"Ok. I'll be right back."

"So what are you here for?" Mr. Mills asked JJ.

"I'm getting a headlight for my bike."

Mr. Mills looked down at the bicycle lying on the ground. "Not a bad looking bike. Reminds me of when I was a kid. We used to tie flashlights to the handlebars to ride at night. Didn't hardly work at all."

JJ looked at Mr. Mills and tried to imagine him on a bicycle. Mr. Mills must have guessed what JJ was thinking. He laughed out loud again. "I was smaller then!"

Sam came back out with the duct tape. JJ started wrapping the tape carefully around the distributor cap and the supporting bracket. "This probably won't last long, but hopefully it will last long enough to get us to the shop."

They got into the car, and Mr. Mills turned the key. The engine started right up. Mr. Mills looked at JJ and JJ looked right back with a smile. "Ok, kid. Show me how to get to your dad's shop."

After a short drive, they pulled into the driveway. Tom came out to see who this was. Mr. Mills and JJ got out of the car, and Mr. Mills walked over to Tom and introduced himself. "I'm Howard Mills. JJ here did a temporary fix on my car. He says you can fix it."

"Gosh, I don't know," said Tom. He looked at JJ, who had that look that said he knew his dad could fix anything. Then Tom asked, "Any relation to the Mills Theaters?"

"Yeah, they're mine. You like movies?"

"You own the Mills Movie Theater?" exclaimed JJ. "Oh my gosh! I love to go there!"

"Well, I'm glad you're fans," said Mr. Mills.

"A pleasure to meet you," said Tom. "Let's see what we can do with this."

Tom opened the hood of the car and saw the duct tape. "What's the problem, here, JJ?"

"It's a broken screw on the distributor cap," said JJ. "You can fix it easy, Dad."

Tom unwrapped the tape and took a look at the broken screw. By now it was getting quite warm outside. "Why don't you take Mr. Mills into the office to wait while I take a look at this," said Tom.

"Do you mind if I use your phone, Tom?"

"Oh, sure, go right ahead. Right there in the office."

JJ took Mr. Mills into the office. JJ couldn't help staring at Mr. Mills, even though he knew it wasn't polite. When they got inside, Mr. Mills said, "I see you folks have air conditioning." Tom and JJ had set up their homemade cooling system again. It wasn't a proper air conditioner, but the office was small, and it worked well enough.

"Yeah," said JJ. "My dad made it and I helped. He's pretty smart and taught me how it works."

"You don't say," said Mr. Mills. He dialed up his office. "Hello, Gloria? This is Howard. Yes, it did. Hey – I'm over at Henderson Electrical on Magnolia. Yeah, I'm running late. Great. Thanks."

Laura was working in the office and asked Mr. Mills if he would like a drink of water.

"Sure, thanks!" he said.

Laura brought him a glass and said, "So you run the Mills Theaters."

"Yes I do. I see JJ here likes movies."

"He certainly does. He still talks about going on Wednesdays when he was at the orphanage."

Tom walked in, and Mr. Mills asked how it was going.

"Well," said Tom, "I think I've got something that will work a little better than the duct tape, but you'll need to go to the dealer and have them replace the mounting bracket. This should last for a while, though. Sure is a nice car, Mr. Mills."

"How much do I owe you?"

"Oh gosh," said Tom. "I didn't really do much. How about some movie tickets?"

"You got it!" said Mr. Mills. "I'll have someone drop them by. I've got to get going. Ok if I drop JJ off back at the store?"

"That would be great," said Tom.

"Ok, JJ. How about we go back and get your bike." They got into the Cadillac and drove off.

"Well, that was strange," said Laura, after they left.

"You can say that again," said Tom.

On the way back, JJ and Howard Mills talked.

"So your dad's an electrician but he made his own air conditioner?"

"He's very clever and wants to get into air conditioning. He thinks it's going to be big business."

"Your dad's right about that. What's he doing to get started?"

"I don't know. I think we're saving up to buy a real air conditioner so we can sell it to someone."

"So you work with your dad?"

"Yup. After school and on weekends. In the summertime I get to work almost every day."

"And you used to live at the orphanage?"

"Yup. Up until last year."

When they arrived back at the store, JJ and Mr. Mills walked inside to the manager's office. "Hi, Sam. You got the bike ok?"

"No problem. Right here in the office."

"Great," said Mr. Mills. "Good luck with the light set, kid. We'll see you soon. Oh hey, Sam, JJ here wants a light set for his bike. Can you help him out? Get your best one and put it on my account."

"Sure thing, Mr. Mills. See you later."

When Howard Mills got back to his office, he sat behind his desk, thinking.

His receptionist and office manager, Gloria, came in and asked what happened with the car.

"Gloria," he said. "I may have stumbled onto the opportunity of a lifetime. I want you to do something for me." He gave her some instructions and then made a phone call.

"Hello, Mrs. Robinson. This is Howard Mills again. Is Tom there?"

Mr. Mills waited until Tom came on the line.

"Tom, how are you doing? Thanks again for fixing my car. Yeah, no problem. JJ tells me you're interested in the air conditioning business. Yes, he's quite the kid. Look, I need to set up air conditioning in my theater, and I'd like to know if you're interested. Yes, that's right. Well, that wouldn't be a problem because I can order the supplies directly. Why don't you come here tomorrow morning and let's discuss it? 9 am would be perfect. Great. Ok, see you then."

When Tom hung up the phone, the blood was gone from his face.

"Tom! What's wrong?" asked Laura.

"You aren't going to believe this. Mr. Mills wants me to come to his office tomorrow morning to discuss setting up his theater with air conditioning."

"What? How?"

"Apparently something JJ said in the car on their way back."

"Oh, honey. Are we ready for this?"

"No money out of pocket. He'll buy all the materials and pay us per hour. It's a dream job."

There was nothing else to say. They hugged each other.

For the next few hours, Tom poured over the industrial catalogs he'd been collecting. At the dinner table, there was nothing but talk of movie theaters, Cadillacs, free bike headlamps, and air conditioning.

And, of course, the occasional "What did I tell you?" from Aunt Beverly. After dinner, JJ hooked up the headlight and generator – the kind that rubbed against the wheel and turned on the headlight when the bike moved. JJ took his bike out for a ride in the dark, but his excitement over the headlight was overshadowed by the events of the day. Later, while JJ lay in bed, Tom stayed up, going over his plans. No one went to sleep quickly that night.

The next morning, at 8:55, Tom was at Mr. Mills' office above the theater. "You must be Tom Robinson," said Gloria. "Come right in."

"Good morning Tom!" said Howard Mills. "I see you met Gloria, my office manager."

"Yes," said Tom, as he shook Gloria's hand. "Pleased to meet you."

"Ok," said Howard. "Come in and let's get right to it. I want to hear your thoughts on this."

"My first question," said Tom, "is whether you want to cool the theater only or do you want to do the offices too?"

"Not sure, Tom. Let's see what kind of costs we're talking about."

"We want to cool the whole office," said Gloria from the other room.

Tom smiled and put his papers on Mr. Mills' desk. "The way I figure, it will cost about this much to do the theater, and this much to do the rest of the offices. My normal rate is $2.75 per hour and I figure it will take about fifteen hours to rework the heater and install the evaporator coils, about eight hours to set up the compressor and condenser coils, four hours to run the electric, and maybe another eight hours or so to run the copper lines. It's going to be different for the office because it's a boiler-radiator heating system."

"Very interesting, Tom. I like your numbers. I like them a lot. Let's get going on this right away. Get those items ordered and have them shipped here. Have anyone call my office if they need confirmation. A lot of those other chains are already air-conditioned, and I'll be out of business if I don't move fast. Oh, and let's do this office for sure."

"I'll get on it right away," said Tom. "There's a backlog on some items because of the copper and aluminum shortages, and now everyone's worried about Korea, but we'll get it figured out."

"That's why I want to do business with you. What's the name of your company again?"

"Henderson Electrical."

"Who's Henderson?"

"He was my dad's brother in law."

"He's not involved now?"

"No, he died a long time ago."

"You need a new name. Maybe something like 'Robinson Electric and Air Conditioning'."

"Ok, I'll think about it." Tom could see that Mr. Mills was a man of action.

"All right, Tom. Give me a call every day and keep me posted. And here, this is for you and your family." It was a special laminated theater pass. "Come in as often as you like and bring whoever you want."

"Holy smoke!" said Tom. "JJ is going to flip! Ok – see you later!"

Tom grabbed his papers and walked out of the office and into a brand new world.

Gloria walked into Howard Mills's office and looked at Howard. "Are you really going to have these guys do the air conditioning? And why the generous mood? I've known you a long time, and I think you're up to something."

"Let's see how they do," said Howard. "I'm a pretty good judge of people, and I'm betting that in a few months we're going to be partners. I believe there's some real talent here, and I don't think Tom knows how to run a business. Besides, there's something about that kid."

7
New Friends

Within an hour of meeting with Howard Mills, Tom had picked up JJ and returned to the theater to start measuring things. JJ was ecstatic about the free pass.

Installing the air conditioning units would require electrical wiring, copper tubing, and some sheet metal work. They were experts at electrical, ok with the copper, but had limited experience with sheet metal. That didn't faze them, though.

"I see you boys are already at work," said Howard Mills as he came out of the office to check on them.

"Gee, thanks for the neat pass, Mr. Mills," said JJ with a big grin.

"I'm going to try to get this ordered today," said Tom.

"Why don't you go ahead and order enough for two more theaters, while you're at it," said Mr. Mills.

"Holy cow!" said Tom, "I need to see them first and see what we need. Are you talking about the ones in Pittsburgh?"

"I've got five in Pittsburgh, but there's two I'm most interested in right now," said Mr. Mills. "I'll have Gloria give you the addresses so you can check them out. Can we get this done by July first?"

"Wow, that's tight," said Tom. "Kind of depends on how fast we can get everything."

"Well, give it your best shot," said Mr. Mills.

"Will do," said Tom.

"We sure will," said JJ.

They had less than two weeks. It would have been easy for an established company, but they had no experience with commercial air conditioning. As things turned out, it was easier to have Gloria do the ordering. Tom showed her what he needed, and Gloria did the buying. It's doubtful Tom would have gotten anything on time without Gloria's help. She was able to find the right people and was good at following up.

While they waited for the equipment to arrive, Tom and JJ began wiring the 480V circuits they would need to run the large compressors. It was fun working outside the theater and hearing the muffled sound of the movie playing inside. They made numerous trips to Stewart's hardware and got to be on a first name basis with Alex Stewart, the owner.

On one of their trips to the hardware store, they walked to the back, expecting to talk to Alex and saw a tall, lanky man sitting behind the counter.

"Holy cow!" said JJ.

Tom and JJ stopped short of the counter and stared in amazement. At the same moment, Alex appeared from around the corner.

"Hello boys," said Alex. "Ever met my son before?"

"Are these guys friends of yours?" asked Jimmy Stewart with a smile.

"Yeah," said Alex with a chuckle. "They're good guys."

"Well now," said Jimmy with his acting voice. "This is quite a situation we have here." He reached over the counter to shake Tom and JJ's hand.

"Gosh!" said JJ.

"It's an honor to meet you," said Tom.

"Well now, any friend of pop's is a friend of mine," said Jimmy.

"Jimmy's a pilot," said Alex, as he put his hand on his son's shoulder. "He flies his plane home once in a while for a visit."

By now, others were coming to the counter to see the visiting celebrity. It was a fun shopping trip and gave Tom and JJ something to talk about at dinner time.

As things would have it, nothing arrived on time. The first unit arrived at Theater 1 in Pittsburgh, which was about 60 miles away. By now they had the wiring ready and hoped they had calculated everything properly. These were big commercial AC units, not quite what Tom imagined they would be doing for their first job. They worked all day and into the night. When they worked on the theater close by, they could go home for dinner and then go back to work. In Pittsburgh, they ate at a diner, and JJ thought it was great fun. One advantage of working late was that it wasn't so hot outside.

They would often get home well after dark, and Laddie would be glad to see JJ. Laura was grateful that Aunt Beverly and Laddie were around while Tom and JJ were gone. Laura and Laddie were becoming good friends.

By July 1 they had two of the theaters finished, and Howard had done a grand re-opening of each. They finished the third one by the end of the day on July 3. Howard Mills was a good sport and paid them weekly for their work. That money came in handy for eating at the diner. Everyone was pleased, and Howard Mills did more grand openings, announcing the new air-conditioned theaters.

As Howard counted out their weekly pay, Tom asked if the new air conditioning was helping.

"It's working great," said Howard. "Attendance is already up. I'd like to get the rest of the theaters done now."

"That's great!" said Tom.

"Let's have Gloria start ordering for the other theaters," said Howard.

"Will do," said Tom.

"You boys have sure done a good job," said Howard, as he gave Tom a handful of cash. "What are you going to do with the extra money?"

"I've been thinking," said Tom. "I'd like to buy this window AC for my house." He showed Howard a page from the wholesale catalog and pointed to a model. "I was hoping that since we're already doing business with them, we might be able to get a discount."

"I'll bet Laura's not happy with the heat we're having," said Howard.

"You can say that again," said Tom. "Her condition makes it all the worse. I thought about setting up my home made unit at home for her, but it's not enough to cool a house. I'd like to install a good one."

"Hmm," said Howard. "I'll have Gloria check into it."

The next afternoon Tom stopped by Howard's office to check on the material Gloria was ordering for the remaining theaters.

"That air conditioner you wanted," said Howard, "Gloria said they're from a different department. The only way to get a commercial discount is to buy three or more."

"Dang," said Tom.

"So I ordered three," said Howard.

"You what?" said Tom.

"I expect we're going to need experience with these as well as the commercial units," said Howard. "And it's going to be a company expense. You and I need to talk about where this is all going, but for now, I want you to set one up at your place, and one at Gloria's house. We'll sell the third one. Oh, and one more thing. I had Gloria order the 240V version so it will have plenty of cooling power. You better start setting up your electrical for that. And I'll need you to help out at Gloria's house as well."

"Holy smoke!" said Tom. It was hard to keep up with Howard.

Tom and JJ drove right over to Stewart's Hardware to pick up circuit breakers and wire. After dinner, they spent the evening running a line to where they would put the AC unit. Laura was excited.

Two days later the units arrived and were immediately installed. Laura was quickly spoiled. Gloria loved hers.

"How about you?" Tom asked Howard.

"I've had a couple of smaller units for some time, so I'm ok," said Howard. "Eventually, I want to set up a whole house system."

For now, it was back to work. Tom and JJ worked long hours to get two more theaters set up plus a store belonging to a friend of Howard's.

* * * * *

On July 15, JJ got a baby sister. She was named Lois, after Laura's grandmother. JJ had never seen such a tiny baby before, and Laddie seemed just as interested. Aunt Beverly was ecstatic. Having a newborn baby in the house was a huge change, and Laura was glad for Aunt Beverly's help. When JJ sat on the couch and held Baby Lois, he couldn't believe how small and light she was.

Two weeks later, Howard announced that he had a surprise for them. He asked Tom to bring Laura and JJ into his office above the theater. Aunt Beverly stayed home with Laddie and the baby. Helping with the new baby wore her out, but she relished her job.

When Tom, Laura, and JJ arrived at the office, Howard removed a cloth covering a large object, revealing a brand new television. It was a nice one, with a 16-inch screen. They all stared at it, not knowing what it meant.

"It's yours," said Howard. "A bonus for all your hard work, and the work remaining."

"Holy smoke!" said JJ.

And that's how the Robinsons became the first family on their block to have a television. JJ helped Tom install an antenna on top of the roof while Laddie barked at them from below. The only television stations were in Pittsburgh, so the antenna had to be tall. Having an antenna on the roof was a mark of distinction. Television changed the way they lived, and so did Baby Lois. A new routine of watching TV after dinner began.

It was almost time to start school again. JJ wanted to visit Tutu House and see Miss Nancy and everyone and tell them what he had been doing. "Why don't we all go," said Laura, who was doing well. Aunt Beverly was tired again, so she stayed home to rest and watch TV. The four of them drove to Tutu House with Laddie and had a nice visit. Even though JJ loved Tom and Laura, he still thought of Miss Nancy as a sort of grandma and always would. He was happy to see her, and she was keenly interested in Baby Lois and everything going on in his life. He told her all about the work they were doing and the new television. They didn't stay too long on account of Laura and Baby Lois. Miss Nancy and Mrs. Barclay thoroughly enjoyed holding the baby.

"Placing JJ with the Robinsons has worked out even better than I hoped," said Mrs. Barclay.

"Once again, you were so right," said Miss Nancy. "I never imagined things would work out so well."

* * * * *

As JJ started his second year of middle school, Howard Mills started introducing Tom to other businesses. It was the middle of September, and Howard wanted to talk. "Tom," said Howard, "I think we've got a chance to do some real business here."

Tom wasn't sure what the "we" meant, but he was interested.

"You probably never changed the name of your company, did you?" asked Howard. He already knew the answer.

"No," said Tom. "Been way too busy."

"I've got a proposition for you to think about," said Howard. "I think we should go into business together. Mills and Robinson Air Conditioning and Electric. My name is well-known, and I've got contacts and connections. Gloria can handle the office work and do the purchasing. Laura can stay home with the baby. I believe I can make a lot of money, Tom, for both of us."

It was not something Tom had been expecting. "Gosh, I don't know what to say."

"You think about it. Discuss it with Laura. I think we could be great partners."

"I sure will, Mr. Mills."

"And stop calling me Mr. Mills. From now on it's Howard." He reached out and shook Tom's hand. "Let's not take too long to think about this. I've got lots of interest, including the big store where I met JJ."

* * * * *

At school, the kids wanted to know about the new television. When you're one of the few houses with an antenna on your roof, word gets around. Toward the end of September, as JJ was leaving school, his old nemesis, Kevin Connor, came out of nowhere and punched him in the stomach. Then he just walked off.

When JJ got home, Laura could tell something was wrong. After some prodding, JJ told her what had happened.

"Oh dear," said Aunt Beverly.

"Why do you think he did that?" asked Laura.

"Who knows?" said JJ. "Kevin hates everyone. No one likes him. He's mean to everybody. I just wish he would die."

"Oh now let's not talk that way," said Laura.

When Tom got home, Laura told him about Kevin. Tom decided they should to go over to Kevin's house and talk to him. JJ didn't like that idea. Laura wasn't sure about it either. Tom was aware of Kevin Connor being an old problem and wanted to do something.

After dinner, Tom drove JJ over to Kevin Connor's house. It was a Thursday evening and almost dark.

There was an old car in the driveway where Kevin lived. The hood was up, and an engine was sitting on the ground next to it. Further down the driveway was more junk. What looked like a washing machine was lying on its side and had been partly taken apart. Tom knocked on the door. An older lady opened it. Tom explained who he was and why he was there.

"Well, I'm not surprised at all. The way my grandson is going he'll end up in jail just like his father. Kevin! Get out here and tell me what this is all about!"

JJ felt horribly uncomfortable. When Kevin came into the room, he looked bigger than ever. Kevin gave JJ a "wait till I get you alone" look.

"I understand you hit JJ today," said Tom.

"What of it?" said Kevin.

"Why are you always causing trouble?" said his grandma.

"I was hoping we could figure out what the problem was," said Tom.

Kevin crossed his arms, looked at Tom, and said, "I don't know. What do *you* think the problem is?"

Tom tried to think of what to say. Kevin was only fifteen years old, but he was the same height as Tom, and heavier. It was an intimidating situation. JJ looked down at his shoes. Tom was beginning to feel like he had made a mistake. He felt flushed and uncomfortably warm. At that moment the phone rang. Everyone watched awkwardly as Kevin's grandma walked over to answer the phone.

"It's for you," she said to Kevin.

Kevin walked angrily toward the phone, picked it up, and gruffly said, "Yeah?" After listening for only a few seconds, he almost shouted into the phone: "The car will be ready when it's ready!" He slammed the phone and stood there with an angry look on his face. As Tom looked at Kevin, he thought he saw a trace of desperation in Kevin's eyes.

In a split second, Tom had an idea. "I see you're working on that old car," he said.

"What of it?" said Kevin.

"I was wondering how you got the engine out."

Kevin's expression changed from anger to annoyance. "Duh – I unbolted it and pulled it out."

Tom almost interrupted by asking: "I mean, I don't see a crane or anything."

Kevin's expression mellowed, ever so slightly. "It's not a big engine. I just lifted it out."

"Wow," said Tom.

"He does like to work on things," said his grandma.

"You mean he can fix things?" asked Tom.

"He takes things apart but doesn't always get them back together."

"What about that washing machine outside?" asked Tom.

"I could fix it if I had any decent tools," said Kevin, scowling.

"What do you think the problem is?"

"The dang pump is clogged. If I had a proper Allen wrench, I could get at it."

"I've got a set in the car."

Kevin's expression changed once again, revealing bewilderment and confusion.

"I like to fix things too," said Tom. "I'm curious about the washing machine." He turned and spoke to JJ. "Go get the wrench set and a flashlight out of the car."

JJ was only too happy to get out of there. As he returned with the tools, Tom and Kevin were out in the driveway. Tom took the flashlight and shined it on the washing machine. Then he handed the wrench set to Kevin. Kevin gave Tom a curious look, glanced at the wrench set, and picked the correct size wrench without hesitation. In a few seconds, he had the pump apart and found the clog. Then he put the pump back together as Tom watched with careful interest.

Tom asked Kevin more questions about the car. Kevin's attitude was gradually transforming. He was soon having a normal conversation. His grandma was now outside as well. What Tom said next shocked everyone. "Kevin, would you be interested in a job?"

"A job!" said his grandma. "He can hardly read and write."

Kevin looked hurt, but Tom continued. "I believe Kevin's got a talent, ma'am. I could use a guy like this. He could work after school and on weekends, like JJ here."

JJ didn't like the sound of that at all.

"Let's see," said Tom, thinking. "Tomorrow's Friday. Can you come over to the shop Saturday morning?"

Kevin was speechless but managed to say, "Sure, I guess."

"Look," said Tom. "We've got to get going. No hard feelings?"

Tom shook Kevin's hand. Kevin seemed almost bewildered, a completely different person. Then Kevin reached out to shake JJ's hand. "Hey, I'm sorry. I don't know why I did that. Oh, here," said Kevin as he bent down to pick up the wrench set.

"You know what," said Tom. "Keep it. I've got another set at the shop. We'll see you Saturday?"

"Ok. Sure," said Kevin. "Thanks, Mr. Robinson."

JJ and Tom got back into the car and drove home. "That was sure weird," said JJ.

Back at the house, JJ told the story of what happened to Laura and Aunt Beverly.

"Well, I sure hope it works out," said Laura.

"You always were a smart one, Tom," said Aunt Beverly.

At school the next day, JJ was extra nervous. Kevin was waiting for him. "Hey, how's it going?" asked Kevin.

During lunchtime, others were surprised to see Kevin and JJ eating lunch together. Kevin was curious about the business and all the projects JJ had worked on.

It was a turning point for everyone. Tom got his first employee, Kevin got an occupation, and JJ lost an enemy. The future had been altered in a way no one could have imagined.

8

Expansion

Kevin showed up first thing Saturday morning. It was the day they were finishing the installation at the big store across town where JJ had met Howard Mills.

Tom's original plan was to start on Friday, but he had decided to wait until Kevin and JJ were both present. Tom let JJ explain how they had run the 480V wire from the circuit breakers to where they had installed the compressor. "You want to be real careful with that voltage," said Tom.

"Our job today is to run the copper lines from the compressors to and from the evaporator units," said Tom. "Then we'll charge the lines with Freon."

There were three separate AC units to handle this building, each with its own thermostat, compressor, evaporator, and blower motor. Kevin caught on quickly.

Tom told JJ to get the copper tubing and start running the first unit. Tom explained how you have to be careful bending the tubing. "So it won't kink," finished Kevin.

"Well, that's a good start," thought Tom.

"So we're going to solder the pieces together?" asked Kevin.

"That's right," said Tom. "But here's the thing. Everything in this business depends on getting a good solder joint, or the Freon leaks out. Any loose connection, bad solder joint, or pinhole ruins the whole job. Even worse, everything seems fine and then a year or two later it doesn't work so well 'cause the Freon has started leaking out. Have you ever soldered copper tubing before?"

"Not really," said Kevin.

Tom explained the basics and cut a few pieces for practicing. He showed Kevin how to do it and let him try. Kevin took the small blowtorch, heated the copper and applied the solder like a seasoned professional. Then he did a little trick with the torch and applied a second touch of solder.

"Hmm," said Tom. "What was that?"

"You said it was important to get a good seal and in my mind I could see the solder flow and when I saw it do that little thing I changed the heat."

"What little thing?" asked Tom.

"It's hard to describe," said Kevin.

Tom examined the test joint Kevin had made. It was as perfect as anything he had ever seen. "Look at that, JJ," he said.

Kevin really did have a knack for mechanical things. It was like he saw how things worked in his mind. Tom let Kevin make the connections on the actual system using his special technique. The pressure test was perfect. The joints all looked good and were completely sealed. "Gosh, this is great," said Tom. "Ok, you two start running the lines for the next unit, and I'll get this one charged with Freon."

What had been expected to be a weekend job was done by 7pm that night. Tom called Laura on the phone to say they were staying late to finish up, and they would have Sunday off. He called Kevin's grandmother and explained that things were going well, and he would be late bringing Kevin home.

When they finally pulled up in front of Kevin's house, Tom said, "That went really well today. How about we start at one dollar per hour and see how things go?"

"Gosh, Mr. Robinson. That would be swell."

"I'll line up more work for next weekend. Here's ten bucks for today's work. JJ, you can keep Kevin informed of our schedule for the weekend, ok?"

"Sure," said JJ.

As they drove off and headed for home, JJ said, "Kevin sure is a strange person."

"I wonder what Miss Nancy would say about him," said Tom.

"Probably that there was a story there," said JJ.

They got home and had a late dinner. Laura was happy they would be staying home tomorrow instead of working. Their first job with a new employee worked out well. As they were eating, Tom started smiling.

"What?" said Laura.

"Well," said Tom, "I was just thinking. I've got JJ here who's only twelve, and a kid who can't read, and everything is working great."

Tom roughed up JJ's hair, and they all smiled.

At school, the teachers noticed Kevin hanging around with JJ, and even Michael and Steven. In a few days, Kevin was part of a regular lunch group.

Two weeks later, Tom decided to go to the school and talk to the principal about Kevin. He was curious why Kevin struggled so hard in school.

"Hello, Mr. Robinson, I'm Dennis Miller. I understand you're interested in Kevin Connor."

"Pleased to meet you, Mr. Miller. Yes, Kevin started working for me recently. I'm curious about the trouble he's having in school."

"We don't normally discuss a student with someone who isn't a parent or guardian, but Kevin's change in attitude these past couple of weeks is nothing short of miraculous. We all appreciate what you've done for him."

"I'm sure glad to hear it. How is he doing so far this year?" asked Tom.

"Well, I've got to be honest with you. Kevin has serious learning problems. He's been held back several times."

"That's so odd," said Tom. "When he uses tools or works with mechanical things, it's as if he's studied them for hours. He seems to have an uncanny ability to figure things out."

"I didn't know that," said the principal. "But it's not unheard of. Sometimes people with a deficiency in one area make up for it with a special skill. In addition to everything else, Kevin's home life hasn't been ideal, as I'm sure you're aware."

"So what does it mean for Kevin's education?" asked Tom.

Dennis Miller looked at the floor and scratched his head. "I shouldn't say this but frankly, what we're doing here is pretty much a waste of time."

"I'd like to talk to his grandmother about pulling him out of school. What would you think about that?"

"If this were high school or he was eighteen it wouldn't be a problem," said Dennis. Kevin is what, about fifteen?"

"He's almost sixteen," said Tom.

"I don't know," said Principal Dennis. "The law is the law, even if it isn't working well here."

"There must be something we can do," said Tom.

Tom left without a solution. He talked it over with Howard Mills. Howard was intrigued by Kevin's ability. "He showed me a technique I'd never seen before," said Tom. "We could increase our reliability and reduce service calls if we all used Kevin's method for making copper joints. Personally, I believe the poor kid is suffering in school while we're suffering for lack of a good employee. I'll bet I could double our workload if I could hire him full time."

That was enough to get Howard Mills involved. He called the school superintendent and arranged a meeting with the principal, Tom, himself, and Kevin's grandma. The meeting lasted a little over a half hour. Everyone was in agreement that school as they knew it was not working for Kevin. They just had to figure a way to make something work. Principal Dennis suggested classifying Kevin's new job as a work related training program and the superintendent agreed.

"Dennis and I could probably get in trouble over this," said the superintendent. "So let's keep this to ourselves. I hate to see anyone suffer, and that includes our frustrated teachers. Tom, I would appreciate it if you'd keep us up to date on how this works out with Kevin."

When Kevin got home after school, he was as glum as ever but surprised to see Tom at his house. His grandma spoke first. "Mr. Robinson has some interesting news, Kevin."

"I understand you don't enjoy school," said Tom. Kevin just gave a sigh.

"Would you be interested if today was your last day?"

"Of school?" asked Kevin.

"You're all done, if you want," said Tom.

Kevin was speechless.

"I don't have a full load of work yet," said Tom. "But I want to hire you part time and eventually full time. I've got permission from the authorities to take you out of school. We've got a chance to pick up some large projects. What do you think?"

Kevin's grandma had tears in her eyes as Kevin shook Tom's hand vigorously. "Sure thing, Mr. Robinson. That would be the best thing ever."

And so began the first real employee of Howard and Tom's new air conditioning and electric company. Tom told Howard they could now double their workload and Howard went right to work on it. "This is exactly the right direction," said Howard.

JJ was a little jealous of the idea that Kevin Connor would be out of school and spending more time with Tom than he was. At dinner, Laura could tell something was wrong. She had just finished feeding Baby Lois, and the four of them were sitting down to eat. "Is something bothering you?" she asked.

"Well, it bugs me that Kevin gets to stop school and go to work," said JJ.

JJ was reassured that this was a good thing and wouldn't subtract from his life. "Somebody in this family needs to get an education," said Tom. "Howard has big plans, and this company is going to grow."

That night the TV stayed off.

After dinner, Laura said, "Let's go sit in the living room. JJ, can you hold Baby Lois while I take care of this diaper?"

"Here," said Aunt Beverly. "I'll take care of it."

"Thank you," said Laura.

JJ sat on the couch holding Baby Lois and Laddie jumped up next to him. Tom sat down next to Laddie and Laura sat down next to JJ.

"Let's think about it this way," said Tom. "Are things better or worse now that Kevin is working with us instead of being a bully?"

"Well, better, of course," said JJ.

"And not just for you. Things are better for me, for Howard Mills, and everyone. Our company is going to grow, thanks to Howard Mills, and eventually you're going to play an important role. School isn't hard for you and you need to take advantage of it. For now, the best thing is for you to stay in school and learn the things our company will need."

JJ sat with Baby Lois, Laddie, his mom and dad, and felt better. Aunt Beverly came back into the room. He wondered what Kevin was doing right now, all alone with his grandma, and felt sorry for him.

*****

The following Saturday was another dinner and story night at Tutu House. There always seemed to be so much to talk about. Aunt Beverly came with them this time. Tom and Laura enjoyed their visits with Miss Nancy and Mrs. Barclay. The kids always loved to see Laddie. Miss Nancy and Mrs. Barclay enjoyed holding Baby Lois and hearing the Robinson news.

When they got home later that night, Aunt Beverly said she was tired and wanted to go bed. JJ walked her back to her little house while Laddie walked around. "Good night, Aunt Beverly."

"Good night, JJ." Aunt Beverly kissed him on his forehead and gave him a hug. "You're a wonderful boy. Thank you for everything."

The next morning, JJ walked over to the little house to get her for breakfast while Laddie walked around to pee. He knocked on the door, but there was no answer. It was the first time Aunt Beverly hadn't answered right away. JJ knocked again. It was cloudy and cold outside, and a light breeze was blowing. JJ opened the door, which was never locked, and called out to Aunt Beverly. He walked in and saw her sitting on the couch. It reminded him of seeing her resting on the couch that day when he first met her and she was sick. In her lap was the photograph of her son Jack.

He could tell something was wrong, and thought perhaps she was sick again. He reached out to feel her head, thinking she might have a fever. The coldness of her forehead was a shock he would never forget. Although he knew she must have died, he felt confused. He ran back to the main house and by the time he got back inside he was crying. Tom and Laura were just getting up when they heard JJ. As they came out of their room, they could tell something was wrong. JJ hugged his mom and cried. "It's Aunt Beverly." There was little doubt what that meant.

A stroke had given Aunt Beverly a quick and peaceful end to her life. The next few days were spent making arrangements for the funeral. Everything that had to be done just made JJ sad. The weather matched everyone's mood – it got dark early and was cold and cloudy.

Tom gave the eulogy at the funeral and talked about how Aunt Beverly had changed their lives forever, and how she had loved spending time with their new family, how she liked having breakfast with them each morning and how she had learned to love a little dog. "Aunt Beverly was a happy person, always optimistic. She brought sunshine and joy into our lives."

JJ said a few words about how he loved Aunt Beverly, and how he was glad they could make Aunt Beverly happy. Laura talked about their good times and how Aunt Beverly was now with Baby Karen, her son Jack, and her husband. She was glad Aunt Beverly got to see Baby Lois and help out. Aunt Beverly had had a good life, especially this past year.

As per Aunt Beverly's wishes, she was cremated, and her ashes were mixed with the ashes from her husband's urn. At the farm, they all walked out to the furthest corner out back, on the left side of the property in the area where JJ had mowed the weeds. It was cold, and the wind was blowing. It would be snowing soon. Tom brought a shovel and dug a small hole and JJ poured the ashes in. Then he covered the ashes with dirt.

They were a different family now. Breakfast and dinner were much quieter. Soon Baby Lois would be eating with them in a high chair and filling the house with baby sounds, but it would never be the same without Aunt Beverly.

* * * * *

As the weeks passed, Tom and Howard had more business discussions. Howard Mills wanted to form a new company. It was clearly the off season for air conditioning, yet they had plenty of orders for work. Between his electrical jobs and the air conditioning work, Tom and Kevin were constantly busy. Howard had managed to sell a number of multiple unit systems to some large office buildings locally and in Pittsburgh. Tom had mastered Kevin's method of soldering and JJ was practicing. Their new angle was to give a four year warranty.

Tom and Laura invited Howard for Thanksgiving, along with Kevin and his grandmother. It was going to be a big feast this year. Kevin's grandma was only too happy to help in the kitchen. Gloria was invited, but already had plans with her big family.

As they sat down at the dinner table, Kevin's grandma made a sort of toast: "I would just like to say 'thank you' for inviting us into your lives, and for making such a difference ours."

Then Tom said, "I'm thankful for Howard Mills and our new business."

Howard said, "Well, I'm thankful for that day I had car trouble and met JJ. Otherwise we wouldn't be together today."

Laura said, "I'm thankful for Aunt Beverly, and the good times we had. If it weren't for her, we would have never met JJ."

"I'm thankful for Laddie," said JJ. "Otherwise, I would've never met Aunt Beverly in the first place."

"I guess it's true," said Tom. "Everything affects everything else, just like in the 'It's a Wonderful Life' movie."

"Remarkably true," thought Howard Mills to himself.

Howard looked at JJ and Laddie, Kevin, and his grandma, and this prosperous new family with their new baby. He thought about how everyone's actions had affected each other and how everyone was so much better off. He spoke again. "I have an important announcement to make. Tom and I have agreed to reformulate the company into a corporation. The new name is going to be "Mills and Robinson Air Conditioning and Electric. Tom and I are going to be 50-50 partners."

"And I want you boys to call me Uncle Howard," he said to JJ and Kevin.

This was the first time Kevin had been to a real Thanksgiving dinner where it felt like Thanksgiving. He was thankful for a lot, more than he would feel comfortable saying out loud.

After dinner, they gathered into the living room and played charades. It was fun because Kevin had never done it before, Howard wasn't good at it, and Laura and Grandma Connor were the experts. They snacked, visited, and played other games. It was after 11 pm when Howard said it was probably time to leave. He got up, and so did Kevin and his grandma. As Howard stepped out the door, JJ said, "Good night, Uncle Howard. It sure was fun."

Then Kevin did the same. "Good night Uncle Howard."

As Tom, JJ, and Laura cleaned up and put dishes in the sink, they talked about how things were changing. "I wonder," said Laura, "if we could afford a clothes dryer."

"I don't see why not," said Tom with a smile. "What do you think, JJ? Do you think we could hook one up?"

The next day Tom and JJ picked up an electric clothes dryer at the big store and brought it home. Then they took a trip to Stewart's Hardware for wire and connection hardware. Setting up an electric dryer was easy for them. It was a nice early Christmas present for Laura. And it gave them all an idea for another Christmas present.

* * * * *

As Christmas approached, Tom purchased lights to go around the outside of the house. JJ and Tom had a lot of fun putting them up, and made jokes about how hard it was, them being electricians and all. It would be their first Christmas without Aunt Beverly, but they were determined to make it a good one. They also helped get a big Christmas tree for Tutu House.

JJ, Tom, and Laura were invited to Tutu House for a Christmas Eve dinner. Tom had a Santa Claus hat and a bag of toys. Actually, three bags. They also had a special surprise for Miss Nancy and Mrs. Barclay.

When Tom, Laura, JJ, Baby Lois and Laddie arrived at Tutu House in their new company truck, it was already getting dark. They could see the candle that Miss Nancy put in the window every Christmas

Eve. Children came running out the front door to meet them. Carrying in three bags of toys with children cheerfully yelling and a dog barking made for quite a commotion.

JJ thought of Uncle Howard and Kevin. They would be on their way over to Gloria's house to share a Christmas Eve dinner with her and her three daughters.

Inside Tutu House, it was nice and warm, and not just because the oven was on. There were decorations everywhere, mostly homemade, just like every Christmas. Miss Nancy and Mrs. Barclay had always managed to have a Christmas tree with lights and ornaments.

The roast cooking in the kitchen smelled heavenly. Howard had purchased food for Gloria and the orphanage. He wasn't good at picking out gifts and Laura had suggested that buying Christmas dinner would be a perfect gift.

"Dinner will be ready in about a half hour," said Miss Nancy. "While we're waiting, the kids have practiced a few songs they want to sing."

The kids formed a tiny choir, and Miss Nancy played the piano. They sang "Silent Night," "Up on the Housetop," and "Rudolph the Red-Nosed Reindeer." Everyone clapped and the children were quite pleased.

Miss Nancy said, "Now JJ, how about you read us 'The Night Before Christmas?'"

When JJ finished, everyone clapped again. Then they made their way to the dining room. As usual, Laddie was allowed to find whatever dinner scraps happened to land his way. Laura had long since learned to live with a dog in the house and would say to herself, "Floors can easily be mopped, but lost memories can never be recovered." That philosophy would come in handy in a few years when Baby Lois would write on the living room wall.

After dinner, the kids opened their presents and began playing with their toys. Then Tom motioned to JJ, who said, "We have one more present. It's out in the truck."

JJ and Tom walked out to their truck and returned carrying a large present on a hand truck. It was obviously quite heavy. They lifted it up the front porch stairs and wheeled it into the house. The wrapping paper was already starting to tear. "Go ahead and open it," said JJ as he looked at Mrs. Barclay and Miss Nancy. Miss Nancy tore off the wrapping paper, and underneath was a cardboard box with markings indicating that it contained a large air conditioner.

"Oh my," said Mrs. Barclay.

"Oh my goodness," said Miss Nancy with a curious smile. Both ladies took turns touching the box.

"It's going to take some work setting this up," said Tom, "But it should be ready in time for summer."

With a light snow on the ground and a chill outside, it seemed an odd gift, but the two ladies knew full well what summer would bring. One never quite gets used to 90% humidity.

By the time the Robinsons left, it was the best Christmas JJ had ever had, and it wasn't even Christmas day.

* * * * *

The large air conditioner presented two problems, though. One was the old wiring in the house, and the other was the old wiring along the street. The old fuse box at Tutu House would have to be replaced with a new circuit breaker panel. Tom and JJ could easily handle that. But the utility company would have to take care of putting in a new transformer out on the street.

By February, Tom was getting nowhere with the power company. Colonial drive wasn't scheduled for upgrades for at least another year. Maybe longer.

That's when Howard Mills stepped in. He had Gloria do some checking around and managed to get a meeting with the local director. Their conversation went something like this:

Mills: "Thanks for seeing me on this important matter. I understand your schedule for the Colonial Drive upgrade is out another year or two."

Director: "Yes, it's a complicated matter getting all these upgrades handled. Colonial Drive is quite a distance from the substation."

Mills: "You realize there's an orphanage on that street, and we want to set up air conditioning."

Director: "Yes, I know. But we have certain priorities on the schedule."

Mills: "Can't you just install a new transformer?" Howard had been clued in by Tom.

Director: "We could, but it wouldn't be the right kind for the new upgrades."

Mills: "Can't you just replace the transformer when the upgrade is completed?"

Director: "In theory, yes. But it's extra work for our crews. I'd have to special order the transformer."

Mills: "Look. I'm trying to help you out, here."

Director: "How so?"

Mills: "You should know that we've donated a large air conditioning system to the orphanage. The big store is donating a new fence for the yard. We plan to get some publicity out of this for our own benefit. We'll be having newspaper and TV coverage. It would be silly for the power company to get a black eye over something so simple."

Director: "I see."

Mills: "We sure would like to have good publicity all the way around."

Director: "Let me see what I can do."

Mills: "I'll keep you posted. Why don't you come and be part of the event? We can mention how the power company helped us out of a pickle."

Director: "I can feel my arm being twisted, but I admit it's not a bad idea."

* * * * *

March 1 was JJ's 13th birthday. This year Tom and Laura decided to celebrate JJ's birthday at Tutu House. It wasn't so much that JJ was still adapting, it was more a case of Tom and Laura thinking of the orphanage as part of their family. His birthday was on a Sunday this year, and they had a nice birthday celebration and dinner. The kids loved singing "Happy Birthday" to JJ, and Laddie was once again happy to be looking for crumbs under the table. Baby Lois was walking. The kids thought it was great fun to watch her and have her come this way and that. For his birthday, JJ got a magic set. He'd seen it on TV and was planning on saving up for it. It was a great surprise, and he was able to do some simple tricks right away. The kids all enjoyed JJ's magic, and everyone had a lot of fun.

"It's hard to imagine we have a teenager," said Laura. They could barely remember life without JJ now.

By the beginning of May, there was a new transformer on the telephone pole outside Tutu House. It was connected to the new circuit breaker panel Tom and JJ had installed.

When Tom and JJ purchased the electrical supplies at Stewart's hardware store, Alex asked about their project.

"It's for the orphanage," Tom Explained.

"Oh really?" asked Alex. "How are they doing these days?"

"They're doing great!" said JJ.

"JJ grew up there," said Tom.

"How about that," said Alex, looking at JJ.

"We're installing an air conditioner for them," explained JJ.

"No kidding," said Alex. "In that case you have this stuff at cost."

"Thanks," said Tom.

Tutu House still had old wiring inside, but at least it had a modern electric service panel. It also had a new 240-volt line running to the living room for the air conditioner.

By the end of the first week in June, it had been almost two years since Laddie showed up and JJ ran away. During the past few weeks, a new fence was installed, and Tutu House had been repainted. Howard Mills had worked out a deal with a local paint company in exchange for a good discount on an air conditioning system. The big store where JJ met Howard Mills had donated fence materials. Tom and JJ had cut a hole in the living room wall and installed the air conditioner.

On the day of the event, Miss Nancy and Mrs. Barclay finally got to meet Howard Mills.

"It's a real pleasure to meet you," said Miss Nancy.

"It's nice to finally meet you, too," said Howard. "I hear about you all the time from JJ."

"It's a nice thing you do for the kids here to let them come to the movies during summer. They really look forward to it. I know JJ sure did."

"Well, I'm glad," said Howard. In reality, he had started the free orphan day for publicity, but he was genuinely glad it was appreciated, and he did have a place in his heart for orphans.

The lady from the newspaper, as well as a TV reporter from Pittsburgh, were there, along with a power company representative, the owner of the paint store, and Sam from the big store. The police were even there. Sheriff Doug came by and was happy to see how things had worked out with JJ and the Robinsons. They had Miss Nancy turn on the air conditioner and within minutes ice cold air was blowing out.

"Oh my land," said Mrs. Barclay with a laugh. "It's getting cold in here!"

All in all, it was a festive day, and the six o'clock news had a thirty-second story about Tutu House toward the end of its broadcast.

9

Strike One

Summer was the time JJ loved best. He was out of school and working full time with his dad and Kevin. Working outside in the heat was often uncomfortable, but he enjoyed it. Business was booming, and this was their busy season. One of the next jobs they got after the publicity at Tutu House was the sheriff station.

JJ and Kevin were now good friends and enjoyed working with each other. JJ had finally mastered Kevin's soldering technique. Kevin was pleased that he could teach something to someone else. He also liked being needed. His strength came in handy almost daily. He could single-handedly carry a large AC unit from the truck to the point of installation.

It was fun to visit Tutu House during the summer. Tom, Laura, JJ, and Laddie often came for story night. Miss Nancy and Mrs. Barclay never got tired of telling them how nice it was to have air conditioning. When it was extra hot and humid, they would let the children camp out in the living room at night where it was cool and dry. They no longer used the sleeping porch.

On July 4th, everyone gathered at Tutu House for fireworks. It was a Saturday, and JJ invited Kevin, Uncle Howard, and Gloria. Kevin brought his grandma and Gloria brought her daughters. It was the first time Kevin had been to Tutu House. "Wow. So this is where you lived," he said to JJ.

Miss Nancy and Mrs. Barclay were happy to meet Kevin and his grandma, and Kevin was happy to meet more of JJ's "family." Miss Nancy was thankful for JJ remaining in her life. She was also grateful for Tom and what had happened with Kevin. It was hard to believe Kevin and JJ were now friends.

Tom and Laura brought hot dogs, hamburgers, sodas, lemonade, and fireworks. They also brought an idea. Laura had mentioned a few weeks earlier about how she enjoyed the clothes dryer and felt badly for the two ladies at Tutu House not having one. In the humid summers, it could take a long time for clothes to dry outside. Financially, Tom and Laura were better off now than they could have imagined even a year ago. They decided to check out the possibility of installing one at Tutu house.

Outside it was hot and humid, but inside was nice and pleasant. Laura got some snacks out, and Tom started setting up the barbecue he brought. Everyone knew that Miss Nancy loved hamburgers. While Tom was cooking, JJ and Kevin walked around the house. JJ showed Kevin where the gas line ran, and Kevin measured things in his mind.

Everyone ate inside and had a pleasant time visiting with each other. To Miss Nancy and Mrs. Barclay, Howard Mills was a celebrity. Miss Nancy seemed concerned about something and Tom asked if everything was okay. Mrs. Barclay explained to Tom and Howard that in six years they would have to leave Tutu House because of the expiring lease.

As it started getting dark, the kids had fun with sparklers. Then JJ and Kevin took charge of lighting fireworks. While everyone was enjoying the fireworks, Howard thought about the expiring lease, and a promise he had made to himself decades ago.

* * * * *

A week after their Fourth of July party, Tom, JJ, and Kevin came back to Tutu House in the company truck with a large cardboard box. It wasn't Christmas, but would soon feel like it. Miss Nancy and Mrs. Barclay were curious. JJ and Kevin ripped the cardboard apart to reveal a brand new clothes dryer. It was a gas model, much more difficult to install than an electric model, but cheaper to operate. Kevin brought a bunch of pipe and plumbing material from the truck and began connecting a gas line from where it came into the house to the laundry area where the washing machine was. It didn't take long for Kevin to run the gas line. JJ was always amazed at Kevin's ability to figure out and handle plumbing. Tom visited inside while JJ and Kevin worked. He wished the age for driver's licenses was 16 like in California. It would be nice if Kevin could have driven JJ over today. Then Tom wondered how Kevin would ever be able to get a license if he couldn't read.

It was hot working outside, but afterward, they had sandwiches and lemonade and a short visit. JJ showed the two ladies how to operate the dryer, and he and Kevin cleaned things up and put their tools away. As they got ready to leave, Miss Nancy and Mrs. Barclay gave them hugs and thanked them for everything. JJ always liked giving Miss Nancy a hug, but this was new for Kevin. From Kevin's perspective, JJ had been a lucky guy growing up here.

* * * * *

Summer was over, and JJ had earned enough money to last all year. Baby Lois was more than two years old. These were semi-sweet times for Laura. Lois was nearly the same age as when Baby Karen got scarlet fever and died. It was hard not to worry. Fortunately, everything was fine, and Lois was healthy and strong.

* * * * *

This year they decided on Howard's house for Thanksgiving. It was a good sized home and was filled with a nice crowd. Everyone came, including Gloria and her kids. After dinner, Howard had a TV on in one room, some of the kids were playing Monopoly in another room, and the adults sat around visiting. This was becoming a tradition everyone enjoyed and looked forward to. It was sometimes hard for Kevin's grandma to believe how nice things had turned out. Everyone had something to be thankful for.

* * * * *

On Christmas Eve, Tom invited Howard, Kevin, and his grandma to Christmas dinner at Tutu House, and to help bring in presents for the kids. Gloria had long-standing plans with her family.

Once again there was a little Christmas program. JJ read "The Night Before Christmas" and the children sang.

Howard enjoyed the evening as well. He admired Tom and Laura, and couldn't help thinking what would have happened to Kevin if Tom hadn't intervened. He also had an idea for Tom to consider, and spoke to him after dinner.

"Tom, I've been thinking about the lease problem for this place. What would you say to the idea of having our company buy this property?"

"Gosh, I don't know," said Tom, quite surprised. "It would be great if we could somehow save this place. What do you have in mind?"

"Well," said Howard, "I've had Gloria do some investigating. We might be able to purchase this place cheap, and we could keep it available for the orphanage."

"Sounds like we wouldn't be making any money," said Tom, with a smile. "What makes you so interested?"

"I have my reasons," said Howard. "Are you ok with it?"

"Sure," said Tom. "If you think we can afford it."

"Well, here's my plan. We put in a bid for the house, a low bid, with the state. They'll tell us we can't bid for another five or six years. We counter by claiming we believe we can get the current tenants to terminate the lease. If we can make a deal, we'll donate it back to the orphanage, or something, I'm not sure yet, and take a tax write-off. It'll still cost us money, but maybe not so much."

"I'm all for it if you think we can swing it."

"I still need to work out some things with the accountant," said Howard. "But I'm sure we can do something. Let's talk to the ladies. I'd hate to see that air conditioner you installed here go to waste," he said with a smile.

Howard asked Mrs. Barclay if they could talk. She motioned to Miss Nancy, and they all went into the den, just off the living room.

"Howard's got an idea he wants to discuss with you," said Tom.

"I've been thinking about this place," said Howard. "I can't guarantee anything right now, but I think there might be a way I can make an offer to buy this place from the state so you won't have to leave in 1959."

"Oh my!" said Mrs. Barclay and Miss Nancy together.

"I'm going to talk to the state revenue people about it. In order for us to be able to proceed, they will likely contact you and ask if you're willing to give up the remaining years on your current lease. It could be risky because as soon as you agree to terminate your lease, anyone could bid on the property. There's a good chance no one will notice, and we'll be able to get this property into our company. I'm not sure of the details yet, but I need to know if you are willing to take a risk on this idea."

"My land!" said Mrs. Barclay. "It's an incredible idea. What do you think, Miss Nancy?"

"I don't know what to think," said Miss Nancy. "If there is any chance at all that you could make this work I'm all for it."

"What do you need us to do?" asked Mrs. Barclay.

"Nothing at the moment," said Howard. "These things take time. I wanted to check with you first before doing anything else."

"I can't tell you how wonderful that would be," said Mrs. Barclay.

"I'll let you know how things go," said Howard.

That night, neither Mrs. Barclay nor Miss Nancy fell asleep early.

* * * * *

Another birthday and another summer came and went. Business was thriving. JJ was fourteen years old and starting to pay more attention to girls.

Thanksgiving once again brought everyone together at Uncle Howard's house. After dinner, Tom and Howard were discussing business and Tom asked about one of Howard's appointments.

"No good," said Howard.

"One of those?" asked Tom.

"Yup," said Howard.

JJ was curious. "What happened?" he asked.

"Well," said Uncle Howard. "Some businesses can be trouble, and you'll never make them happy. The object isn't to sell to everyone; the object is to make money. You want to avoid people who are going to be trouble."

"Gosh," said JJ. "How can you tell?"

"You can't always tell," said Howard. "But often you can. I'm pretty good at reading people. One of the things I look for is how they react to Gloria. If they have trouble with her being a member of the team, then we don't want to do business with them."

"You mean because she's a Negro lady?" asked JJ.

"Yup. It seems to bother some people."

"Wow," said JJ. "I'm glad you're the one figuring out that stuff."

* * * * *

After another fun Christmas at Tutu house, another new year, and another birthday, JJ, was fifteen. Baby Lois was talking. It was a lot of fun. There was hardly a time when the Robinson home was quiet. It had been another good year for the company, even better than the previous year. JJ enjoyed working with Kevin, and Howard was glad they could grow the company. With Kevin, they could do more than twice the work of Tom alone, and during the summer with JJ working, they were able to keep up with every project Uncle Howard could sell.

1955 was a big year for school kids and their parents. The previous year had been a successful test of the new polio vaccine developed by Jonas Salk at the University of Pittsburgh. This year school kids all across the country were getting the vaccine at schools, fire stations, and other public places. For some, it was too late. There were those, like Howard Mills' wife, who suffocated as a result of being paralyzed. Others recovered, but were left crippled or with deformed limbs. Even a former President was not immune. Nearly every school in the country had a few polio survivors. Laura, like most mothers, hoped the new vaccine would put an end to polio.

* * * * *

JJ had a crush on Deborah. He had known her since grammar school. He was fairly popular at school now. He had nice clothes and made good money. He even had one of the new transistor radios, made by a small Japanese company that would eventually go by the name of Sony. Nearly everyone knew he could go to the movies for free. He often brought friends with him to see a show.

JJ and Deborah had one class together – math. It was beginning algebra, and Deborah wasn't getting it at all. JJ enjoyed helping her.

One afternoon when he was helping with homework, he asked if she liked movies.

"Oh, yes," said Deborah.

"Me too," said JJ. "I've seen all the Lassie movies."

"Hmm," said Deborah. "I saw one but didn't like it."

JJ was shocked.

"What about the Lassie TV show?" asked JJ.

"It's not my kind of thing," she said. "I love 'Gone With the Wind.' I've seen it three times."

JJ had heard of it. He heard adults talk about it.

"How about 'Tom Sawyer?'" he asked.

"It was ok," said Deborah. "Kind of long and boring."

"Boring!" thought JJ to himself. He had seen that movie twice and looked forward to seeing it again.

"How about Casa Blanca?" asked Deborah. "It's such a great movie. Have you seen it?"

"Gosh," said JJ. "I never did. I was wondering if you wanted to go and see 'War of the Worlds.'"

"Not really," said Deborah. "Sounds dumb to me."

And that was that. They went back to their homework, and the romance was over without them ever going on a date.

10

Strike Two

Summer was another good season. They made quite a few trips to Pittsburgh to install large commercial AC systems. JJ and Kevin were now being paid $2 per hour, and Tom was making twice that. Howard Mills was wheeling and dealing and kept everyone busy. He continued to be the company salesperson and was doing a great job. Gloria was being paid more than she could have imagined. She was instrumental in the smooth operation of the company.

She was also instrumental in another project. Gloria had been talking with people in the state department of revenue and had come up with an idea. If they could get Tutu House designated as a state historical landmark, it would become much more difficult to sell, which would make it easier for Mills and Robinson to purchase the property for a low price. The paperwork had been processed, and they were waiting for a public hearing.

*****

Tom and Howard wanted to expand the business. The next logical step was to get a truck for Kevin. He was now eighteen – three years older than JJ. Kevin knew the rules of the road and had been practicing with JJ who read the instructions to him. It didn't seem likely that Kevin would be able to pass a written test, though. Tom called Sheriff Doug and explained the problem. He asked Sheriff Doug if he knew anyone at the DMV office.

Howard, Tom, and Sheriff Doug took Kevin to the DMV and spoke to the director, Mr. Ryan. They explained the problem and asked if Kevin could take the written test orally.

"Everyone knows you shouldn't park within 15 feet of a fire hydrant," said Howard. "But how many people actually know how far 15 feet is? Kevin does."

The fact that these people, including Sheriff Doug, were all with Kevin convinced Mr. Ryan to let Kevin take the test. He called to Marie, one of the workers, and told her what they were doing. "Take Kevin into my office and ask him the questions," said Mr. Ryan.

After a few minutes, Marie and Kevin came back out. Marie said, "He only missed one."

"Ok," said Mr. Ryan. "Let's go ahead with the driving test."

The driving test was a snap for Kevin.

Howard thanked Sheriff Doug and asked how his air conditioning was working. "Just great. Thanks a lot. I'm glad to see you are all doing well." Sheriff Doug shook everyone's hand and left. He thought to himself, "If we had more folks like Tom, we'd need fewer folks like me."

Tom and Kevin could now go to job sites independently. Howard worked out a deal with the local Ford dealer who needed an air conditioned showroom.

Each day after work, Kevin parked the new truck in the driveway of his grandma's house. On each side of the truck were written the words "Mills and Robinson Air Conditioning and Electric." Grandma Connor was proud.

* * * * *

As the fall school season started, JJ had over a thousand dollars saved. He had stopped being shy with girls in general. Sometime after his failed attempt with Deborah, he developed a crush on Cynthia, a girl in his English class who used to have a crush on him. He asked if she would like to go see a movie.

"Sure," she said. "How about Friday night?"

"Sounds good," said JJ.

On Friday evening, Tom was still out on a job, so Laura drove JJ to pick up Cynthia. It would have been more impressive if he didn't have to get a ride with his mom and little sister.

They had a good time after Laura dropped them off at the theater. JJ liked Cynthia but couldn't tell if she liked him.

A school dance was coming up so he asked Cynthia if she would like to go.

"I'd love to!" she said. Cynthia and her friends had been to every school dance whether or not they had dates.

"This would be good," JJ thought to himself. She lived two blocks from the school, and he wouldn't need his parents to give him a ride.

"Cool," he said. "How about I come by your place around 8 pm?"

"Sounds good," said Cynthia. "See you then."

He still couldn't tell if she really liked him. On the night of the dance, he walked over to Cynthia's house. She looked nice, and they talked on the way to the school. It was chilly but not cold. As they walked, a dog barked from one of the houses.

"Do you have any pets?" asked JJ.

"No, do you?

"Yeah, a little dog named Laddie. He always barks when I have to leave."

"I'll bet the neighbors don't like it."

"Well, he's in the house, so it's not that bad. He calms down pretty quickly."

"Your dog's in the house?"

"Yeah."

"He's not in his doghouse?"

"He doesn't have a doghouse."

"Where does he sleep at night?"

"He sleeps in my room."

"Wow. That's weird."

"Yeah, I guess it is," said JJ, feeling slightly awkward.

They got to the school and walked into the gym that had been decorated for the dance. Cynthia immediately ran to her friends.

"You all know JJ, right?" she announced to her friends.

Cynthia was a good dancer. It seemed Cynthia spent as much time dancing as JJ spent working.

Other boys, mostly seniors, came over and danced with Cynthia. She loved dancing with all of them.

JJ had a good time, but realized Cynthia didn't have any feelings for him. She was just a nice girl.

Later, as he walked her home, she said, "That was fun. Let's do it again."

Lots of sixteen-year-old boys and some fifteen-year-olds had "steady" girlfriends. JJ wished he had a girlfriend, but it wouldn't be Cynthia.

11

Romance

The rest of the school year passed pleasantly enough. Another holiday season came and went, and JJ turned 16 in March. The school season ended, and JJ spent another summer working with Kevin and his dad. He was now a junior in high school. He was almost six feet tall and shaving every day. His life was about to take another big turn.

One fall afternoon, after school, JJ took Laddie out for his walk to the downtown area. On his way back home, he had one more corner to turn when he came upon a house with a chain link fence in front. It was a house he had walked past many times, but to which he had paid little attention.

In the yard was a cat. Laddie saw the cat and barked. The cat walked back and forth and then walked away. The following day the same thing happened. Within a week, Laddie was anticipating the house and looking for the cat. Gradually, the cat got closer and closer to the fence. In time, the cat was waiting by the fence for JJ and Laddie.

Then, a funny thing happened. Laddie and the cat began going nose to nose through the fence. This happened day after day. JJ could swear the two had become friends.

One day, while Laddie and the cat were greeting each other, the front door opened. It startled JJ, and he said, "Oh – hi. It looks like my dog likes your cat."

"I know," said the young woman who came out the door. JJ could see she had braces on her legs and was also using some crutches, the kind that grasped around the arms. JJ recognized her as one of the kids at school who had polio. She was nearly as tall as JJ, had brown hair, brown eyes, and a big, cheerful smile.

"Oh," said JJ. "I didn't know you lived here."

"Hi! My name's Anna. I've seen you at school. Do you live around here?"

"Yeah, just around the corner and down a ways. I'm JJ. This here is Laddie."

"I think he's cute!"

"Thanks," said JJ. "What's your cat's name?"

"This is Princess."

After a few moments, he said, "Well, nice to meet you." He waved and smiled and off he walked.

The next day when JJ came by the house with the chain link fence, Anna was already outside, and the cat was by the fence.

"Hi again," said Anna. "It's funny how my cat waits for you to come by."

Anna was sitting on a chair on the porch. "Why don't you open the gate and see what they would do together?" said Anna.

For some reason, that made JJ nervous, and he felt strangely shy. Anna seemed to radiate cheerfulness, and JJ thought her smiling face was absolutely beautiful. "Ok," he said, and picked up Laddie. He opened the gate slowly and stepped inside. He knelt down, carefully holding Laddie. Princess backed away at first, then came slowly up to Laddie, who was wagging his tail right in JJ's face. Laddie and Princess were now nose to nose again, so JJ slowly let go of Laddie. Laddie tried to sniff the cat and then jumped back, wagging his tail high, like he wanted to play. Laddie stood two feet from Princess and waited. Princess walked slowly to Laddie.

"It looks like they want to be friends," said Anna with a smile.

"Wow," laughed JJ. "Wait till my mom hears Laddie is friends with a cat."

Anna said, "So what grade are you in?"

"I'm a junior," said JJ.

"Oh. I'm a senior."

They talked for a while and then JJ said he had to leave. "Well, I've got to get going," said JJ

"See you later," said Anna, smiling.

The next day when JJ came by, Anna was just coming out the door to sit down. Princess was already by the gate. "Hi, JJ," she said. "Come on in."

This time, JJ opened the gate and walked in with Laddie. He couldn't understand why Anna made him so nervous. Laddie and Princess immediately went nose to nose and started playing.

"That is so cute!" said Anna. She sat down on the top step of the porch, her braces clinking quietly.

JJ leaned against the gate.

"So what does your dad do?" asked Anna.

"He does electrical and air conditioning work. I work with him on weekends and in the summer."

"We'd love to have air conditioning here," said Anna. "Do you set up air conditioners for houses?"

"Sometimes," said JJ. "Mostly we do large buildings and offices. That kind of thing. We did the Mills Theaters."

"Really?" said Anna. "How neat! I remember when they got air conditioning. We love to go there, especially in the summer."

"You like movies?" JJ asked.

"Sure," said Anna. "We just saw Davy Crockett."

"I liked that one," said JJ. "How about Creature from the Black Lagoon?"

"Oh yeah," said Anna. "How about Gone with the Wind?"

"I haven't seen that one," said JJ. "How about Lassie?"

"Who wouldn't love Lassie!" said Anna. "I've seen all the Lassie movies. Did you name Laddie after 'Son of Lassie'?"

"Pretty much," said JJ.

They talked about Tom Sawyer, 20,000 Leagues Under the Sea, Peter Pan, War of the Worlds, and even Casablanca. JJ blurted out how he could go to the movies any time he liked.

"Then you'll have to take me to see a movie," said Anna with a big smile.

It actually seemed like a good idea to JJ.

"Tarantula is playing now," said JJ.

"I know," said Anna. "I want to see it."

"Maybe I should get your phone number so I can call you, and we could figure out a time," said JJ.

"That would be fun!" said Anna. She got herself up and said, "Wait here and I'll get a paper and pencil." She came back out, and JJ stepped up onto the porch. She handed JJ a slip of paper with a phone number. JJ took it from her and said goodbye. As he looked at her face close up, something about the way she looked back at him made him feel nervous, or odd, or something he didn't quite recognize. It was like she was gazing into his soul.

When he got home, he told his mom about wanting to take Anna to the movies. Laura was a little surprised, and curious about how JJ met Anna. JJ told the story about Laddie wanting to play with Princess, and how he had started talking to Anna. "She's real nice, and she likes movies, too. Anna wants to go and see Tarantula. I was hoping you or dad could take us."

"Why don't you just walk like you normally do?"

"She can't walk long distances because she has braces on her legs."

Laura realized who JJ was talking about and said, "Your dad or I will be happy to take you."

When Tom got home, JJ told him about Anna, and how they met, and how he wanted to take Anna to the movies. "I don't think she can walk all the way to the theater," said JJ. "So I wonder if you or mom could take us."

"I don't see why not," said Tom. "Which day do you want?"

"I have to call her, but I wanted to check first."

"You have any problem with that?" Tom asked Laura.

"No, that's fine," she said.

JJ called Anna on the phone. They decided to see the 7:30 showing the next night, Friday. While JJ was talking with Anna, Tom noticed that Laura seemed concerned. Laura explained she was worried about JJ getting involved with Anna.

"Well," said Tom, "maybe nothing will happen. Let's wait and see. Didn't JJ already have trouble with some girlfriends?"

"Yes, but..."

"Are you worried because Anna is handicapped?"

Laura didn't say anything. That night she had a hard time sleeping. She hated herself for having these worries about JJ's new friend. "What if little Lois had polio," she thought. She would still want Lois to have a good life and meet someone like JJ. Baby Karen could have had polio just as well as scarlet fever.

The next morning, before he left for work, Tom made a suggestion to JJ.

"Why don't you bring Anna here after school tomorrow. We can meet her and have dinner. Then I'll drive you to the theater."

The next day, Laura called Anna's mother on the phone.

"Hello, this is JJ Robinson's mother. How are you doing?"

"Oh, hello, Mrs. Robinson. I'm doing fine."

"I suppose you know JJ and Anna want to go and see a movie tonight," said Laura.

"Yes, that's very nice. JJ seems like a nice boy."

"I'm taking my little girl out for a walk in a while," said Laura. "I wonder if I might drop by."

"I think that would be lovely," said Mrs. Kurzmann.

Laura finished cleaning up the kitchen, looked for a few more things to take care of, put a sweater on little Lois, and started out for a walk around the corner. "I don't know why I'm even doing this," she said to herself, now starting to feel silly.

It didn't take long to walk around the corner. It wasn't hard to find the house with the chain link fence around the front yard and a cat on the porch. Laura opened the gate. Little Lois was interested in the cat. Laura held Lois's hand and walked up the steps and knocked.

Mrs. Kurzmann opened the door. "It's very nice to meet you," she said. "Do come in. My, what a cute little girl. How old are you dear?"

"I'm five," said Lois."

"Anna was four when she got polio," said Mrs. Kurzmann, looking at Lois. "Would you like some water? I don't have any tea or lemonade made up."

Laura realized with a sudden shock that if Baby Karen hadn't died, she would be Anna's age. It was hard not to wonder what Baby Karen would have looked like all grown up.

"Oh no, that's fine," said Laura. "I just wanted to meet you and see if it would be ok to have JJ bring Anna by our place before they go out tonight so we can meet her, and if it wouldn't be a problem for Anna to walk back to our house just around the corner."

"That shouldn't be a problem. She's learned to manage quite well. I understand your husband is in the air conditioning business."

The two mothers chatted for a while. Laura said she was happy to get to know her better and said goodbye. As she walked back home, she felt much better.

When JJ got home from school, he took Laddie out for a short walk and stopped at Anna's house. He opened the gate and walked to the front door and knocked.

Mrs. Kurzmann opened the door and said, "Hello, JJ. Anna just got dropped off from school. She'll be ready in a minute."

Laddie and Princess played with each other while JJ waited for Anna. Anna came out shortly and said with a smile "Hi, JJ. Nice to see you again so soon." They had seen each other at school. "Hi, Laddie."

"You kids have fun," said Mrs. Kurzmann.

"We will," said Anna.

JJ and Anna walked with Laddie to his house around the corner and down the street.

"How would you kids like some spaghetti?" asked Laura.

"Great," said JJ.

"Sure," said Anna. "What a cute little girl."

"That's my sister Lois," said JJ.

"I'm five," said Lois.

"Hi, Lois," said Anna.

Lois walked over to Anna and touched the leg brace with her finger. "What's that?" she asked.

"It's my leg brace. I got sick a long time ago, and my legs never got better, so now these help me walk."

"Oh," said Lois. She looked up at Anna's face and back at the braces. "I got a tricycle."

Anna laughed congenially. Laura got to visit with Anna while getting dinner ready. When Tom came home, he was happy to meet Anna.

"What time would you like to leave for the movie?" asked Tom.

"Maybe 7:15," said JJ.

While eating dinner, they talked. Laura and Tom learned that Anna was an accomplished seamstress, played the piano, and liked to paint. She was cheerful and obviously quite smart. Anna thanked Laura for the dinner, and they got ready to leave. JJ helped Anna into the car.

Tom drove them to the Mills Movie Theater and dropped them off in front. Tom waved goodbye and drove home. JJ walked Anna past the short line at the ticket office. The lady waved at JJ and said the usual: "Enjoy the movie JJ." They walked inside, and the ticket taker said, "Hi there JJ. Got a date tonight?"

JJ's face flushed, but he was enjoying his status.

"Wow," said Anna. "You're really a somebody."

JJ just grinned and said, "Yeah, it's pretty cool. The guy who owns this place is like an uncle to me."

Meanwhile, back at the house, Tom and Laura talked.

Tom said, "Well, she seems like a nice girl."

"Yes she does," said Laura. "Her mother is nice as well. I walked over and talked to her this morning."

They sat down with little Lois to watch a rerun of "I Love Lucy."

At the theater, JJ and Anna sat down to watch a scary movie about a huge tarantula in the Arizona desert. When the monster appeared on the screen, Anna instinctively grabbed JJ's arm. "Oh – sorry," she said and laughed. "That one got me."

"I know," said JJ. "Me, too."

JJ put his hand on hers, and she gently grabbed back. Her hand was soft and almost moist. JJ couldn't know how nervous Anna was. For the rest of the movie, they held hands. Fortunately, the monster tarantula was destroyed, and humankind was saved.

"That was great!" said JJ.

"It was really fun!" said Anna.

Anna made her way to the ladies room while JJ called on the pay phone for Tom to come and pick them up. As they walked out of the theater, JJ kind of wished Anna didn't have to use crutches. He would like to hold her hand again.

Tom dropped them off in front of Anna's house and drove home. JJ helped Anna up the three steps and to her door. "Thank you, JJ. I had so much fun."

"Me too," said JJ.

"See you soon!" said Anna, as JJ left.

Back home, Laura asked how the movie was. "It was neat," said JJ. "We liked it."

At the Kurzmann house later that night, Anna's mother heard her singing an old lullaby she hadn't heard for many years.

The next day was Saturday, and JJ went to work with Tom. "We're going to meet Kevin over at the Mickelson office building," said Tom.

Kevin had picked up some AC units the day before and brought them to the job site.

When they arrived, Kevin was already there and smiling. "You look all happy," Tom said to Kevin.

"I went on a date last night with a nice girl I met," said Kevin.

"Well, do tell," said Tom to Kevin.

It turns out that last month when they installed an AC at one of the office buildings, a lady who worked there asked Kevin if he knew of a reliable plumber. A friend of hers was having trouble getting a new washing machine installed.

"Well heck," said Kevin. "I do that kind of stuff."

He had gone over to this lady's house to see what the problem was. Her name was Patty. She was from Greensburg. Her mom and dad had bought her a washing machine for her birthday, but the hoses didn't match the existing plumbing. He looked at the washing machine, checked out the laundry area, and said he needed to go to the hardware store and get some fittings. He came back with several small pieces of plumbing hardware.

"Did you find an adapter?" asked Patty.

"There's no adapter for something like this," said Kevin, "They didn't put the right kind of pipes in here, so I had to figure something out."

"I'm surprised you didn't have to write anything down or measure anything," said Patty.

"Well, I'm kinda odd that way," said Kevin. "I have a thing that makes it hard for me to read and write but when I look at mechanical things I can see the problem exactly in my head."

"That's very interesting," said Patty.

Kevin worked for about ten minutes.

"I'm almost finished. The old pipe is completely wrong, but this should take care of it."

When he was finished, he hooked up the washing machine and moved it into place.

"You're an interesting fellow," said Patty. "You do electrical and air conditioning work too?"

"That's my main job, actually," said Kevin.

"How did you get a job if you couldn't read?"

"It's a long story."

"I'd love to hear it," said Patty, and sat down on her couch.

Kevin told her about his life, his problems with school, how he met Tom and got hired, and how he had dropped out of school. They visited for a while, and Patty wanted to get to know him better.

"I'm pretty lucky," said Kevin. "I had so much trouble with school and didn't get along with my teachers. Now I have a great job and work with great people. I drive a company truck and make good money."

Patty smiled and said it was fortunate. "How much do I owe you for this?" she asked.

"Heck, that's ok. I've enjoyed my visit."

"At least let me pay you for the parts you bought."

"That didn't amount to much. I get a good discount."

"It was nice to meet you, Kevin. I hate to see you go."

"Do you like to go to the movies?" asked Kevin.

"Sure," said Patty. "Do you ever go hiking?"

"No but it sounds fun," said Kevin.

They agreed to go on a date and exchanged phone numbers.

"By the way, what do you do?" asked Kevin.

"I teach third grade," she said.

"Well I'll be darned," said Kevin.

That Saturday evening when JJ got home from working with Tom and Kevin, he got Laddie and headed off for his walk. It was almost getting dark outside, so he decided to cut his walk short. He really just wanted to go by Anna's house, so he walked around the block to come to Anna's house the same way he normally did. When he arrived at the fence, there was no cat in front, and the lights were out. The front porch light was on, and it was obvious no one was home. JJ was surprised at how disappointed he felt.

He got home and Laura said, "That was a quick walk. Did you see Anna?"

"No, they weren't home."

JJ didn't say much, but he thought about Anna and her smiling face all evening.

On Sunday afternoon, JJ took Laddie for a walk. Once again impatience got the best of him, and he took the short route. When he came to Anna's house, no one was outside. He looked around for a minute, and Laddie looked for the cat. Suddenly the door opened, and Anna came out. "Hi," she said. "What are you doing here?"

Princess came out of the house and ran over to the gate. JJ didn't quite know what to say but felt relieved. Anna said, "Nice to see you. Come on in. Thanks again for Friday night. I had so much fun."

JJ opened the gate and came over to the porch steps. "Me, too," he said. It was breezy out and slightly chilly.

"Would you like to come inside?" said Anna.

"Sure," said JJ and he walked up the steps. "Is it ok for Laddie to come in?"

"Of course," said Anna, smiling.

JJ sat on the living room couch, and Laddie jumped onto his lap. Princess walked around in circles by his feet. Anna's mom walked in and said, "Hello, JJ, nice to see you."

"Nice to see you, too, Mrs. Kurzmann."

"Anna said you watched a fun movie about a giant spider."

"Yeah, it was pretty cool," said JJ. For some reason, it was hard for him to think of things to say.

"Your dad and mom sure seem nice," said Anna.

"They sure are," said JJ. "I'm lucky to have them."

"We were visiting my aunt and uncle in Pittsburgh yesterday," said Anna.

"How's school going?" asked Mrs. Kurzmann.

"It's ok," said JJ. "Everything but history."

"My problem is math," said Anna. "But I love history. Maybe we could help each other."

"Sure," said JJ.

"We could do homework together," said Anna.

"Sure," said JJ again.

They agreed to have JJ come over after school. After visiting for a while, they said goodbye and he left. When he got home, he told his parents about their plan to do homework together. To Laura, it seemed to be rushing things. She suggested that maybe they could alternate and have Anna come over to JJ's house sometimes.

On Monday after school, JJ walked to Anna's house with his homework. "Where's Laddie?" asked Anna.

"I wasn't sure if I should bring him," said JJ.

"You can bring him. He can play with Princess."

"Ok," said JJ. "I'll bring him next time. But my mom said you can come over to my house and do homework too. Maybe we can trade off."

"That would be fun," said Anna.

On Tuesday, it was Anna's turn to come to JJ's house. He walked over to Anna's house with Laddie to bring her back to his house. As they were getting ready to leave, Anna explained how one leg was stronger than the other. "If I could hang on to you, I'd only need one crutch," she said. They walked back to JJ's house, with Anna holding JJ's hand for stability. He didn't mind at all.

While they were working on their homework, JJ said, "'Invasion of the Body Snatchers' will be playing this weekend. Want to go?"

"Sounds scary," said Anna. "I'd love to!"

After homework and dinner, JJ walked Anna home.

On Friday, they went to the movies again. They were in the habit now of only using a single crutch for Anna so JJ could hold her hand. When they watched the movie, they didn't need a scary part to hold hands.

It made JJ happy to see Anna at school, and he looked forward to homework sessions. During one of their sessions, Anna asked JJ if he would be interested in going to the dance at school that was coming up after Halloween.

"Well," said JJ, thinking about his earlier experience. "I'm not a very good dancer."

"Do I look like I'm going to be doing a lot of dancing?" laughed Anna.

JJ had to laugh too. "I haven't been to many dances," said JJ.

"I've hardly ever been," said Anna softly.

"I would love to," said JJ.

By now, Tom and Laura realized JJ and Anna were not likely going to tire of each other. It was obvious that Anna was a wonderful person who liked JJ very much.

On the night of the dance, Tom drove JJ to Anna's house and waited outside in the car. JJ knocked on the door, and Anna's mother answered and invited him inside. Anna came into the living room looking happy and pretty.

"Wow, you look beautiful!" said JJ.

"I made this dress myself."

"Holy cow. I can't believe it."

"You look quite handsome yourself," said Anna, smiling.

Anna's father and mother came in, looking proud and happy. "You both look so nice," said her mom.

"You guys have fun," said her dad.

JJ helped Anna out to the car. They were both used to Anna only using one crutch now, and hanging on to JJ or holding his hand for support. It didn't take long to get to school. Tom wished them a fun time and drove off. JJ and Anna walked to the gym that had been decorated for the dance. They stood around, sometimes just holding hands, and sometimes saying "hi" to various friends. Anna's best friend, Lauren, was there with her date, Eric, and was happy to see Anna. JJ, Anna, Lauren, and Eric walked over to a table and sat down to visit.

After visiting for a few minutes, Anna and Lauren decided to use the restroom. Eric left to meet some friends and JJ helped Anna over to the women's rest room area. While he was waiting, a couple of boys he didn't like came over to ask how he liked dancing with the crippled girl. JJ was used to being teased and ignored them. At the same time, Kevin walked in with his girlfriend and recognized the boys who were bothering JJ. He walked up behind the two boys, put his arms around the shoulders of each one and said, "Hi guys! You aren't bothering JJ are you?"

"Oh hey – we were just saying hi to JJ. See you later."

Kevin didn't let go immediately. As he held on, he said, "You boys aren't forgetting that JJ is my best friend, are you?"

As the two boys quickly walked away, Kevin greeted JJ. "Hey JJ, how's it going!"

"Good. What are you doing here?"

"Oh, I just thought I'd drop by and check things out," said Kevin with a smile.

Right then Anna and Lauren came out, and JJ said, "Hey Anna. Have you met my friend Kevin?"

Anna was surprised, along with Lauren. They only knew of Kevin's reputation as a bully who had dropped out of school.

"Oh, hi, Kevin," she said, not knowing what to think.

"Kevin works with me and my dad," said JJ.

"You look gorgeous," said Kevin. "This is my friend Patty."

"Thank you," said Anna. "Pleased to meet you, Patty."

"Yes, nice to meet you," said JJ.

"It's nice to meet you, too," said Patty. "I've heard a lot about you."

Lauren also said it was nice to meet him and walked over to the dance area to find Eric.

JJ, Anna, Kevin, and Patty walked over to the little table and sat down and talked. Kevin and Patty didn't stay long.

"Well, look," said Kevin. "We're going to be heading out. I just wanted to drop by and say hi." Kevin admired the way JJ helped Anna get around.

"Thanks, Kevin. See you later. Nice to meet you, Patty."

After Kevin and Patty had left, Anna smiled and said, "You'll have to tell me all about that."

"It's a long story," said JJ with a smile.

Lauren came over with Eric and sat down. Lauren was happy that Anna was here at the dance with a date.

A slow dance started. Anna pulled on JJ and said, "Let's dance." JJ was not sure what to do. Anna put down her only crutch and grabbed JJ. "We can just dance right here."

They held each other and rocked back and forth to the song "On the Street Where You Live." Lauren smiled at Anna, and Anna looked back with her own smile. After a moment, Anna pulled JJ close and held him tightly, partly out of necessity, and partly because she was deeply in love. She hoped he would learn to love her.

It was the first time JJ had his arms around Anna, and he liked the feeling. When the song ended, they stopped dancing, but JJ was slow to let go. Then "Que Sera, Sera" began playing, and they kept dancing. As Anna held JJ, she wondered what the future would be.

They danced and visited until 11:30pm. JJ called his folks, and Tom came to pick them up. He dropped them off in front of Anna's house and drove home. It was getting cold outside. Anna asked JJ if he wanted to come in for some hot chocolate. JJ was only too happy to say yes. While Anna was making hot chocolate, her parents came in and asked how the dance went.

"It was super nice, and we had a great time," said JJ.

"It really was," said Anna. She had such a nice smile on her face.

"We're going to bed," said her mom. "Don't stay up too late."

JJ was in uncharted territory now. He had never been this serious with a girl before. They spent another hour visiting and drinking hot chocolate. As they sat together on the couch, he told the story of how he became friends with Kevin Connor, his life at the orphanage, how he came to live with Tom and Laura, and all about Howard Mills. "Wow," said Anna. "You've had an interesting life."

When it was time to leave, Anna said, "Thanks for taking me to the dance. I had so much fun."

She started to stand up, and JJ held her arm to help. She grabbed JJ's arm and gave him a big hug. And then she kissed him. He held her tight and kissed back. They stayed that way for a few minutes. Finally, Anna said, "Good night, JJ."

He said, "Good night," and smiled. Anna smiled back as he walked out the door. He walked around the corner and back to his house, thinking about the dance and kissing Anna.

Laura was still up, and asked how everything turned out. JJ told her about the evening, how nice it was, and how beautiful Anna looked. "She made her own dress, and it was like something you'd buy at a fancy store."

"I wish I could have seen her," said Laura. "Would you like me to make you some hot chocolate?"

"That's ok," said JJ. "I had some at Anna's house."

Laura had to smile. She could see faint traces of lipstick on JJ's face.

"So you really like Anna?" said Laura.

"Yeah, mom. I really do."

"She does seem like a nice girl," said Laura. "Probably one of the nicest girls I've ever met."

The day before Thanksgiving, the Robinsons brought a turkey to Tutu House and had dinner with them. Miss Nancy was as curious as ever about JJ's new girlfriend. Little Lois was old enough to play with some of the younger kids. "You'll have to bring Anna by here so we can meet her," said Miss Nancy.

The next day, at Howard's house, Thanksgiving felt a little off for JJ. It was a nice party as usual. Kevin brought his grandma and his girlfriend, Patty. JJ was with all the people he loved, but he missed being with Anna.

Gloria said, "Hey JJ. I understand you have a girlfriend."

JJ blushed and said, "Yeah."

"Your mom says she's very nice."

"Yeah, she is."

"Well, maybe next time you can bring her."

JJ wondered what his life would be next time. Would he and Anna still be friends? What would they be doing a year from now if they were?

* * * * *

Howard told Tom they were ready to make their move on the Tutu House property. To the state of Pennsylvania, Tutu House was not considered anything important and had raised no public concern. "We're going to offer $25,000 to buy the property," said Howard.

"Wow, that's a lot of money," said Tom.

"Not for a house like that," said Howard. "That place is worth a bundle. Gloria believes anything less would jeopardize our bid."

* * * * *

The annual Christmas dinner at Tutu House had become a tradition. This time, JJ brought Anna. Tom and Laura had done their shopping for the kids and had lots of presents. Their arrival was met with the usual excitement. The children were curious about Anna and her braces. Miss Nancy gave Anna a hug and said how nice it was to finally meet her. Anna was equally curious about JJ's former home. Each had heard so much about the other.

Tom warned Mrs. Barclay that they would soon be notified by the state about a party being interested in buying the property, and they should agree to a request to end the lease. They only had three years left anyway. "Howard Mills told me to tell you that he would personally help find another situation if the deal fell through," said Tom.

"I wonder why he is doing this for us?" asked Mrs. Barclay.

"He hasn't told me why," said Tom. "But he's as serious about this as anything."

The children sang, Miss Nancy played the piano, and JJ read "The Night Before Christmas" as had become the custom. Anna thought it was positively darling.

They had a wonderfully warm and happy dinner. Tom and Laura were glad to have Anna with them. Dinner was never quiet at Tutu House, but Anna loved everything. Miss Nancy was happy to hear that Anna could play the piano, and that she made her own dresses. Anna had a wonderful time visiting with Miss Nancy and Mrs. Barclay. Miss Nancy told JJ how pleased she was that he had chosen such a nice girl. "You could say it was Laddie's doing," said JJ.

When it was time to leave, Miss Nancy gave Anna another big hug. "I hope we'll be seeing you again soon."

Tom and Laura dropped JJ and Anna off at her house and drove home. JJ walked Anna into her house. They hugged and kissed. As Anna held JJ tight, she whispered in his ear, "I love you JJ."

"I love you too, Anna," he whispered back.

* * * * *

They continued to do homework together and go to the movies. They saw "Around the World in 80 Days," "The Great Locomotive Chase," "The Ten Commandments," "The King And I," and many others. JJ was an expert at being Anna's extra crutch. He had learned how to help her take her braces off when she wanted to relax and watch TV. Anna truly loved JJ. She loved his family, his dog, his friends, and everything about him.

The more Tom and Laura got to know Anna, the more they liked her. Anna could look at a dress in a store, or even a picture of a dress, and be able to reproduce it. She was talented and smart. Most important of all, she was sweet and kind. She loved JJ dearly, and JJ loved her. Tom and Laura wanted the best for JJ, and Anna seemed to be that person.

A few weeks before his 17th birthday, JJ walked to Anna's house to do homework. He found her wiping tears from her eyes. He had never seen her cry before. "My father is being transferred to Pittsburgh."

12

The Move

The news about Mr. Kurzmann being transferred was upsetting to JJ as well as Anna. But JJ had made many trips to Pittsburgh with his dad and Kevin. Since they did business there nearly every week, JJ vowed there wouldn't be a week without a visit.

Anna's father was struggling with a dilemma. He needed to take the job at the steel mill, but he hated to move the family. "What if I just commute each day?" he asked at dinner that night.

"I don't know," said Mrs. Kurzmann. "It's awfully far."

"I could do it for a while," he said, "and see how long I can manage."

"Oh, Daddy!" said Anna. She hugged her father and was sad and happy at the same time. She loved her parents dearly but didn't want to be away from JJ. On the other hand, she didn't want her father suffering such a long drive every day.

As they got ready for bed, the Kurzmanns talked. "It's a heck of a thing for this to come up right now," said Mr. Kurzmann. "I haven't seen Anna this happy since I can't remember."

"I know," said Mrs. Kurzmann. "But how can you manage such a drive?"

Pittsburgh was about 60 miles away. It wouldn't be easy. It was one thing for Tom or Kevin to make the trip when it was convenient for business, but driving there every day? This was Anna's last year in high school, and JJ was the most important thing in her life. He had to try.

A week after Mr. Kurzmann started work at his new job, it was time to celebrate JJ's 17th birthday. The crowd of friends and family was growing. Besides JJ's family, Uncle Howard, Gloria and her daughters, Kevin and his grandma, there was Kevin's girlfriend Patty and of course, Anna and her parents. It made for a warm Saturday afternoon in more ways than one.

JJ blew out his birthday candles and said, "My best birthday present is Anna being here with us."

Everyone clapped, but it was a reminder that Mr. Kurzmann was now working in Pittsburgh. Tom asked, "How's your new job going, Mr. Kurzmann?"

"Well, so far so good," said Mr. Kurzmann. "I have to leave by 6:30 in the morning to make sure I'll get there in time. I'm back on the road again by about 5:30 and back home by 6:45 or 7 pm. Mrs. Kurzmann and Anna have dinner ready when I get home, so it's not so bad. I'm making more money so I can afford the gas, but I'm worried about driving the car to death."

Everyone loved how JJ and Anna were sweethearts, and felt bad for Mr. Kurzmann. They knew he was making this sacrifice so Anna could stay in school and be with JJ. The birthday party turned into a problem-solving session.

"Kevin and I can help with the car," said JJ.

"Absolutely," said Kevin as Patty gave him a hug.

"I can get tires cheap," said Uncle Howard.

"I'll help any way I can," said Tom.

"I don't know what to say," said Mr. Kurzmann.

"There is one thing you could do for us," said Patty. "Or I should say Anna could do for us."

"What's that?" asked Anna.

"There's a dress Patty wants, but it's expensive," said Kevin. "We thought maybe you could make it for her."

"If you can show me at a store or get a picture, I'll take a look," said Anna.

"I think Patty has a picture in her purse," said Kevin. He turned to Patty and asked, "Do you have it here?"

Patty opened her purse as everyone watched. She unfolded a page from a magazine and handed it to Anna. Everyone gasped at the picture of a wedding dress.

"Why Kevin!" said Tom.

"Patty!" said Anna and Laura together.

"Oh my," said Grandma Connor.

Patty hugged Grandma Connor and then everyone was hugging everyone.

Finally, Kevin asked, "Do you think you can make it?"

Everyone looked at Anna. "This is one thing I've never made," she said. "How much time do I have?"

Now everyone was looking at Kevin and Patty.

"We're thinking August or September," said Patty.

Laura gave Patty another hug and Anna said, "That should be plenty of time."

Everyone's attention was now focused on Kevin and Patty. Mr. and Mrs. Kurzmann held each other's hand, and each was thinking how nice the family was. Hopefully one day they would see their Anna in a wedding dress. The Kurzmanns couldn't imagine a nicer group of people to be involved with. Mr. Kurzmann couldn't help but think to himself what they would have missed if he had moved his family to Latrobe a few years ago.

It turned out to be a memorable birthday. The best one so far, JJ thought. As things were winding down, Kevin spoke to Mr. Kurzmann. "Why don't you bring your car over to my place tomorrow afternoon and I'll check it out?"

Patty gave Anna the picture of the wedding dress. Uncle Howard told Gloria to take Anna to a fabric store and charge it to the company.

It had been a long day, and it was after 9 pm by the time everyone left. The Kurzmanns thanked everyone and said how glad they were to meet everyone. Little Lois had already gone to bed. JJ and Anna decided to walk back to her house and watch TV. Being a Saturday, the TV stations wouldn't sign off until after midnight. It didn't matter what was on because they wouldn't be paying much attention.

The next day, Sunday afternoon, Mr. Kurzmann took his car to Kevin's house. Kevin began the first of many checkups and tuned up the engine.

Tom, Laura, JJ, Anna, Little Lois, and Laddie drove over to Tutu House to visit and share the news about Kevin Connor. Little Lois loved to play with the kids there. Miss Nancy and Mrs. Barclay loved to see JJ and his family and hear how everyone was doing. JJ was bigger and more mature than when he left almost six years ago. Now here he was, with a sweetheart. Anna and JJ looked so natural together.

* * * * *

April 12 was Anna's birthday. She was now eighteen. For the past five weeks, JJ and Anna had been the "same" age. On Friday evening, they had a birthday party at Anna's house with a few friends, which included Tom, Laura, Lois, Kevin, and Patty. Anna had a birthday cake and made a wish when she blew out the candles. "What did you wish for?" asked JJ.

"I can't tell you!" laughed Anna. "It might not come true!"

Everyone had a good time. It would only be a matter of months before her wish would come true.

* * * * *

By June, plans were well underway for Kevin and Patty's wedding. They were going to be married at her parent's farm in Greensburg. Anna had finished the wedding dress, and Patty was pleased that it had turned out so well. It had taken Anna many days of work, but she enjoyed making the dress. She started working on three bridesmaid's dresses. Mr. Kurzmann brought his car to Kevin's house several times for a tune-up. The car was running great after new brakes and a clutch. He said his car had never run so well.

* * * * *

The end of school for summer brought another big event – Anna's graduation from high school. Once again everyone was together. Uncle Howard loved all these family events, and Anna was considered family now. Everyone was proud of Anna's determination. At the graduation ceremony Anna was surrounded by friends and family, including

Lauren and others who had graduated with her. The Kurzmanns were once again accompanied by their new friends, proud that Anna had graduated with honors. Kevin felt a little bad about how he would never be standing up there with a diploma, but he was happy and content. Next year would be JJ's turn.

After graduation, there was a reception in the Kurzmann's backyard. Laura had helped Mrs. Kurzmann prepare sandwiches, cookies, and punch.

* * * * *

Grandma Connor had been to Patty's apartment several times with Kevin and liked where Patty was living. One evening when Patty was at the Connor home having dinner with them, Grandma Connor joked about how they should switch places. It wasn't a bad idea, but Kevin thought of another idea. "Why don't we add on to this house, or build a small house out in the back?" he said.

When Kevin mentioned this at work, Uncle Howard frowned and thought for a moment. "I don't like the idea of your grandma living all alone," he said, "But you and Patty should have a place of your own." Then he said, "Kevin, see if you can find a house for sale that you and Patty like that is near your grandma's house. I'll buy it, and you can rent from me. Down the road, if you like it, we'll work something out."

Kevin and Patty scouted the neighborhood and talked to a realtor. They found a nice little two bedroom house just two blocks from Grandma Connor's place. It had a long driveway and a garage in the back. The backyard was quite large and off in the corner of the yard was a workshop. The house had a good sized living room and kitchen. Patty loved it, and Kevin thought the workshop was the best feature. Gloria worked out the details with the realtor, and soon Howard became the owner of another piece of property.

They decided to move Patty's furniture into the house and have Patty move in before the wedding and live there. Grandma Connor was delighted with the whole arrangement and happy that Kevin wouldn't be far away.

"Gosh," said Grandma Connor, "It's going to be so quiet around here."

"What you need," said Kevin, "is a dog."

"Or maybe a cat," said Patty.

"We'll see about that," laughed Grandma.

* * * * *

The wedding was set for Saturday, September 14, 1957. The week before, Patty's folks came up for dinner and to see the new place. Kevin and JJ had spent the day running wiring for two new air conditioners, a large one for the house and a small one for the bedroom. Patty's folks were impressed.

At first, they hadn't understood what Patty saw in Kevin, but they had to admit he was a decent, hard-working fellow. Patty had initially been attracted to Kevin because he was good-looking, big and strong, had a career, and was an unusual person. Kevin's life had changed for the better. He had a big heart, and she loved him dearly.

The wedding itself was fun. Most of Patty's friends and family lived in the Greensburg area. Patty had always wanted a wedding at their farm. Greensburg was about an hour's drive from Indiana, not quite as far as Pittsburgh. Tom, Laura, JJ, Little Lois, Anna, and Laddie rode in one car. Gloria rode with Howard in his car. Kevin, his grandma, and Patty had driven down the night before and stayed at the farmhouse.

Patty was a beautiful bride in her wedding dress, and Anna was proud of her work. Chairs had been set up outside, and everyone hoped the weather would cooperate. Tom was the best man, and JJ and Howard were ushers. For Grandma Connor, watching Patty walk down the aisle to her grandson was one of the highlights of her life. Once again, Howard enjoyed being part of a celebration.

Food and refreshments had been set up by Patty's family. It was a little breezy, but all went well. Kevin had never looked so handsome. Patty was beautiful. As she walked with her father to Kevin, Anna squeezed JJ's hand, and they both smiled. Kevin and Patty were pronounced "man and wife." and after they had kissed, Kevin gave Tom a hug.

In the evening after the party, everyone headed home. Kevin and Patty dropped Grandma at her house and began their new life together. Howard dropped Gloria off at her house. Tom, Laura, Little Lois, Anna, JJ, and Laddie were glad to get home. It was about 9 pm, but

Lois was still up. Everyone was sitting around the living room and talking about the day. Tom was slumped back on the couch with Laura next to him resting her head on his shoulder. Anna was sitting next to JJ on the couch with JJ's arm around her. Little Lois was sitting on the floor next to Anna's feet playing with a doll. Laddie was also on the floor, lying on his side, asleep.

"Wow," said JJ. "What a day. It was fun, but I'm glad to be back where it's just the five of us."

"It's been a wonderful day," said Laura, with a smile. She put her arm around Tom. "Soon there will be six of us."

13

Anna's Day

I t was now the fall of 1957. Anna was out of school, and JJ had one more year. Little Lois was five. Laura was expecting in January. It had been a busy year and was far from over. It would also be a significant year for Mills & Robinson AC and Electric.

* * * * *

Kevin and Patty were happy in their new home. Each workday Patty drove her car to the elementary school, and Kevin drove his truck to work at Mills & Robinson. They didn't have a lot of furniture yet, but they were making good money and had decided to buy a new item for their home each month.

Uncle Howard had purchased quite a few plumbing and automotive tools for Kevin to keep in his workshop. Howard found it helpful to be able to call on Kevin for nearly any kind of problem. Kevin loved how people needed him, and he liked being useful.

* * * * *

At breakfast one morning in September, JJ made an announcement. "Anna and I are going shopping for an engagement ring."

Laura was caught off guard. She couldn't think of what to say. She thought to herself, *they're so young.*

Tom Looked at Laura and saw the expression on her face. "Well," he said. "I guess we shouldn't be too surprised."

"Yeah," said JJ. "I kind of get butterflies thinking about it."

"It's sure a big step," said Laura, concern still showing on her face.

"Yes, I know," said JJ.

"When are you thinking about getting married?" asked Laura.

"Is JJ and Anna getting married?" asked little Lois.

"Yes, sweetie," said Laura to little Lois. "Someday they will get married."

"I don't know exactly," said JJ. "But her dad can't keep driving to Pittsburgh every day."

It was true, and Tom and Laura knew it. Mr. Kurzmann had already had one close call when he almost fell asleep driving home last month.

"Getting married young can be a problem down the road," said Tom.

"Well, I know," said JJ. "But I can't bear the thought of not being around Anna either."

"I like Anna," said little Lois. "When they get married will Anna come and live with us?"

"No sweetie, they will go live in their own house," said Laura.

"Oh," said Lois.

Everyone but Lois knew events were conspiring to push JJ and Anna into an early marriage.

"We've talked a little about it," said JJ, "and we're thinking maybe September or October after I graduate, sometime after the busy season."

The thought of an actual date gave Laura the chills.

"You would just be eighteen," said Laura. *You've only been with us for a few years*, she thought.

"We were thinking maybe we could start off living out back in Aunt Beverly's house."

That made Laura feel a little better. But married at eighteen?

"Well," said Tom. "It sure is something to think about." He gave Laura a hug and said, "Remember we married at 19."

She smiled. They both remembered how their marriage almost didn't survive.

At work, Tom and JJ mentioned the developing plans to Kevin, Gloria, and Howard.

"That's no surprise," said Howard with a smile. Then he changed the subject. "JJ, as you know, we've been busier than ever. Gloria could really use some help. Why don't you ask Anna if she'd like to work in the office here and help Gloria out?"

"Sure, Uncle Howard. I'll ask her."

It surprised Tom and Kevin but made perfect sense. After work, when Tom and JJ returned home, JJ asked if Anna could come over for dinner.

"Of course," said Laura. "What's up?"

"Uncle Howard wants Anna to work in the office," said Tom.

"Oh my," said Laura.

"I'll go get her," said JJ. He ran out the door, down the street, around the corner, and over to Anna's house. He knocked, and Mrs. Kurzmann opened the door.

"Hi, Mrs. Kurzmann. How're you doing? I need to see Anna." Anna came out from her room. "Uncle Howard wants to know if you want a job working in the office."

"Wow," said Anna. "I was thinking about sewing, but it sure would be interesting working in the office."

"Gloria is getting swamped," said JJ. "She needs help with the phone and other stuff. It would be cool if you worked with us."

JJ turned to Mrs. Kurzmann and asked, "Can Anna come over for dinner?"

"I don't see why not," said Mrs. Kurzmann. "Let me know what you decide about the job," she said to Anna.

JJ walked Anna back to his house and got ready for dinner.

"It will be so cool to have Anna working in the office with us," said JJ.

"Now remember," said Tom. "You and I are gone from the office most of the time."

"I know," said JJ. "But it would be neat if Anna was there."

"When would I start?" asked Anna.

"Well," said Tom, "knowing Uncle Howard, I'd say tomorrow morning. What do you think?"

"I'd like to try, that's for sure," said Anna.

"We can pick you up in the morning and take you with us to the office," said Tom.

"Should I take a lunch or something?" asked Anna.

"You won't need one," said Tom. "Howard buys lunch. How about we come by around 8:30 tomorrow?"

And so began Anna's new career working in the office. Every morning JJ and Tom picked up Anna after breakfast and brought her home after work. Sometimes when Tom and JJ were stuck on a job, Gloria would take Anna home. Anna started by answering phones but soon learned their file system and became a competent office worker. It was also the beginning of a new friendship between Anna and Gloria. Not only was the help a welcome relief, but Gloria also enjoyed having another lady in the office. There was an elevator on one side of the building which was used mostly for bringing supplies up to the second floor, and it came in handy for Anna. Over the next few weeks, Gloria and Anna tidied up the elevator and organized more office space.

Eventually, the subject of marriage came up again. From his work during the summer, JJ had more than enough money for a ring. In the middle of October 1957, JJ and Anna became officially engaged. They planned to get married sometime after next summer.

This, of course, was an occasion for a visit to Tutu House. They picked up Anna and drove over for story night. Miss Nancy and Mrs. Barclay were interested in seeing Anna's engagement ring. JJ explained the situation with Anna's father and how her parents would eventually need to move to Pittsburgh.

"Everyone's worried about us getting married too young," said JJ to Miss Nancy.

"Of course they are," said Miss Nancy. "It's hard for a marriage to survive when people are married so young. No one wants you or Anna to ever be hurt. People change and can fall out of love."

"It's hard to imagine not ever being in love with her," said JJ.

"Not everyone who gets married young has trouble," said Miss Nancy. She had such a nice smile on face and almost seemed like she was far away. JJ could tell she was thinking about something. "If you always admire each other you'll be fine."

Miss Nancy gave JJ a hug and said she was proud of him. "I just hope you come and visit often," she added. "I've learned to love Anna."

* * * * *

Tom was making more money than ever before. Kevin and Patty were doing well, Gloria was doing better than ever, and Howard was buying more property. Howard wanted to grow the company to a new level, which meant hiring more employees. Tom convinced Howard to wait until after JJ had graduated from high school, but that was about to change.

Christmas was a turning point for the company.

Thanksgiving was once again at Howard Mills' house. After dinner, they sat and talked. Tom mentioned that it was time to start shopping for toys for the kids at Tutu House. "You really like doing that, don't you?" said Howard.

"Yeah," said Tom. "We look forward to being Santa Claus. Every year is just as good, maybe even better. One nice thing about having extra money is being able to do this kind of thing."

"Oh, it's a lot of fun," said Laura. "You should see those kids when we bring in the toys and then when they open their presents."

Howard thought about how he had enjoyed the last Christmas at Tutu House. He also thought about the past. He spoke to Gloria. "I want to do this Santa Claus thing like Tom and Laura. Can you find another orphanage and see if they would be interested?"

"No problem," said Gloria with a smile. "I'll have Anna get on it right away."

Anna and Gloria found a home in Pittsburgh with seventeen kids. Howard tasked Gloria and Anna to buy presents for all seventeen plus arrange for a big Christmas dinner. He asked Kevin and Patty to help deliver everything. Arrangements were made to visit the home the day before Christmas, early in the afternoon.

Howard drove over to Kevin and Patty's house, and they all drove to Pittsburgh in a company truck, loaded with seven bags of toys. It was 29 degrees outside when they arrived. The kids were already excited. It took several trips to bring the bags of toys inside. There was much merriment as the toys were handed out. Howard had purchased three presents for each child, and each package had a name. Howard, Kevin, and Patty were each pulling out a toy and reading a child's name, so it was a happy mix of glee and chaos. When they were finished, Patty noticed it was cold.

"Seems a little chilly in here," she remarked.

"Yes," said Mrs. Adams, the lady in charge. "The old furnace is out again. The repairman won't be here for several days. It's only warm in the kitchen. We keep the oven on."

"Oh, no!" said Patty.

"Kevin," said Howard. "See if you can take a look."

It was an old house with an ancient furnace and no thermostat. There was a dial on the wall with a cable running down to the furnace in the basement. Kevin looked it over and went down the stairs into the basement. He came up, went out to the truck, got a flashlight, and went back down to the basement. He looked at the furnace and within a half minute he could see how it worked. He came back up and fiddled with the dial on the wall.

"How does it look?" asked Howard.

"Never seen anything like it," said Kevin, "But I'm not an expert on furnaces. Looks like the cable from this here dial is broken. I'm going to see if I've got something in the truck. For now, I've manually forced the furnace on."

Kevin walked back out to the truck and brought in some tools and some wire and headed back downstairs. Meanwhile, it was getting warmer.

"Oh, that feels good," said Mrs. Adams.

After about 10 minutes Kevin came back up and fiddled with the dial on the wall again.

"I've got it working temporarily, but I think I can fix this. I just need a little help making an adjustment."

He told Patty to stand by the dial and went back down into the basement. After a minute, he yelled to Patty to turn the dial to the "off" position. Then back to the "maximum" position. After a few more minutes he came back up. "Ok," he said. "Should be working."

"Oh my word," said Mrs. Adams. "Thank you so much. The only thing is I can't pay you anything at the moment."

Uncle Howard laughed out loud. He could have been imitating Saint Nick. "No charge for that, Mrs. Adams."

The next three hours passed quickly. The kids were noisy as they played with their toys, the house was warm, and they had a nice dinner. Howard admitted to himself that Tom was 100% right. Kevin gave Mrs. Adams his phone number in case there was any further trouble. They hated to leave but wanted to get back to their homes before it got dark. Uncle Howard thought about how Tom and JJ had installed an AC unit at Tutu House. "It's a great idea," he thought to himself. "Maybe another publicity story…"

A few days after Christmas Kevin got a phone call.

"Hello, this is Mr. Christianson, with Christianson Heating and Plumbing. Am I speaking to Mills and Robinson AC and Electrical?"

"Yes," said Kevin. "This is my home number."

"I understand you fixed the heater at the children's home."

"Yeah, we were there for Christmas, and the furnace wasn't working," said Kevin.

"That's mighty impressive young fellow," said the man, obviously much older than Kevin. "I've only got one technician who knows how to work on those old heaters. Are you the owner?"

"No, that would be Howard Mills," said Kevin.

"I'd like to talk to him," said the man. "Can I give you my number and have him call me?"

Mr. Christianson gave Kevin his phone number, and Kevin passed it on to Howard, who called immediately. Mr. Christianson explained how he wanted to retire. He was hoping to find someone who might be interested in buying out his business. Howard was definitely interested in expanding into the heating business.

The following Monday, Howard, Tom, Kevin, and Gloria drove to Pittsburgh for a meeting with Mr. Christianson and his employees. Howard could tell immediately that this was the kind of company he could work with.

During the meeting, Mr. Christianson told a little about each employee. When he came to Mark Johnson, he explained how Mark had flown P-51's during the war. "You were a Red Tail?" interrupted Gloria.

"Sure was," said Mark.

"My husband was a Red Tail," said Gloria. "He didn't make it back."

"I'm sorry to hear about that," said Mark. "What was his name?"

"Louis Walker."

"I knew him," said Mark. "He was a super nice guy and a real leader. I would often see him pumping up the troops with his little speeches."

"That would be Louis, all right," said Gloria. Mark could see that Gloria was starting to get emotional, so he continued.

"You should know that Louis was a real hero. He died in a fierce battle over Germany. There was a big bombing run with B-17s, and he was ahead of us, leading the way. It was an awful fight, and many of us didn't make it back. Our job was to protect the bombers. We saved a lot of B-17s that day and struck a serious blow to Hitler."

"I sometimes wish he had just saved his life for me," said Gloria. "It's been hard without him."

"Louis believed that if Hitler won, there would be no life for people like us. He believed that whatever the cost, he wanted his family and loved ones to have freedom. He said that many times and we all believed it. I still believe it."

Gloria wiped her eyes and thanked Mark for giving her this information.

"It's a pleasure to meet you," said Mark to Gloria. "You'll have to meet my wife sometime. There are a number of us here in Pittsburgh."

Howard and Tom shook hands with Mr. Christianson. Everyone believed this would be a good business move. To the Christianson employees, it seemed the folks at Mills and Robinson were a good bunch. Howard worked out a deal for Mills & Robinson to gradually take over Christianson Heating and Plumbing. It wasn't the biggest merger in history, but Mills & Robinson expanded by nine employees and was on its way to becoming a full-service company. They taught the Christianson employees about air conditioning and in turn learned more about heating systems. There was a lot to learn about heating. Between coal, oil, gas, electric, even kerosene and some odd types of heating, there was more variety than in AC systems. Fortunately they didn't have to learn everything at once, and besides, they had Kevin. But now they had access to experts in boilers, radiators, sheet metal and duct work. It turned out to be a memorable Christmas.

* * * * *

On January 28, 1958, baby Catherine was born, and On March 1, JJ turned 18. Family life at the Robinsons was busier than ever, and JJ could now get his driver's license. Once again there was a large birthday crowd and Baby Catherine added to the noise level. And once again JJ's birthday turned into a planning session. This time, for a wedding. The Kurzmanns were hoping for a wedding at their house. It seemed there would be quite a number of people, and it was evident that their house and yard would be too small. They thought of their little church, but Anna had always wanted an outside wedding. After Kevin and Patty's wedding, she was sure of it. While they were talking, Laura, who had been sitting off in a corner nursing the baby, said, "I've got an idea." Everyone stopped to listen. "What about the farm? Aunt Beverly's farm?"

JJ looked at Anna. It would be her decision. "I've never seen it," said Anna. "But I like the idea. Can you take me there?"

"How about tomorrow, Dad?" asked JJ.

"Probably," said Tom. "Let me phone the renters and see if they would mind."

The Kurzmanns were getting a little concerned about the cost of all this when Gloria asked to speak to them outside. "Howard has asked me to talk to you about this wedding," said Gloria. "I'm sure you have a lot of family and friends you want to invite, and Howard wants to invite many of our business associates who know JJ. Howard has asked if he might be allowed to pay for the wedding expenses. He wants to have a catered wedding so none of us have to do anything. He's terribly fond of JJ and Anna. He doesn't want to interfere, but he'd really like to do this."

"I don't know what to say," said Mrs. Kurzmann. "That would be wonderful."

"That would be very generous," said Mr. Kurzmann.

"Well, let's plan this together," said Gloria. "When Anna decides what she wants to do, we'll figure it out. We're together in the office every day so it will be fun."

And so, the wheels were set in motion for Anna to have the wedding she always wanted. The next day was Sunday. In the afternoon Tom, JJ, Anna, and her parents drove out to the farm. The young couple renting the house was happy to see them. Anna thought it was a pretty place and knew it meant a lot to JJ. She quickly decided that Aunt Beverly's old farm would be an ideal venue for the wedding. Gloria and Howard started working on arrangements. Anna now had another dress to make, this time for herself.

* * * * *

April 12 was Anna's 19th birthday. This year her party was a crowd, and the Kurzmann house was barely able to contain it. In addition to Anna's school friends, the whole "family" was there, and Anna was a full-fledged member. Besides being almost married to JJ, she was a key employee at the company and had become good friends with Gloria. The only people missing were the folks from Tutu House. When Anna blew out her birthday candles, JJ asked what she wished for. Anna had a big smile on her face and looked around the room. She held JJ's hand, and said simply, "I didn't wish for anything."

* * * * *

The end of May brought JJ's high school graduation, and he began his work as a full time employee. Between the work schedule, and the Kurzmann's schedule, the wedding day was set for Saturday, September 20, 1958.

The Kurzmanns had saved money for a wedding and since Howard was paying for pretty much everything, they wanted to give Anna an extra nice wedding present. They had mentioned this to Tom and Laura at the 4th of July party. Tom said he and Laura were trying to think of something, too. They decided to pool their resources and get a car for JJ and Anna. It would be a great surprise.

JJ and Anna loved going to the Mills Movie Theater where they had their first date. They went to see a show almost every weekend. They watched "The Blob," "The Fly," "South Pacific," "Attack of the 50 Foot Woman," and many others.

Anna worked hard to finish the pink bridesmaid's dresses and her own dress. It was a job she really enjoyed. It was doubly fun for Gloria. Not only was her job easier with Anna's help, but what could be more fun than planning a wedding? Before long, it was September.

Friday night before the wedding, Anna didn't go to sleep right away. She was excited about her wedding day, but she wanted to remember the way her room looked on her last night at home. Everything would be different starting tomorrow. She loved her parents for all they had done for her, for her room and her things, and for the nice little house she had lived in for these past years. Her cat Princess was resting on the bed, and she was glad Princess would not be a problem for JJ. On one hand, she was sad to be leaving her home, but she was happy to be marrying the best man in the world.

On Saturday morning, the weather was cooler than normal, with fog and light drizzle in the morning. Mrs. Kurzmann had to smile when she heard Anna singing "Oh What a Beautiful Morning." By afternoon the sun was mostly out from partly cloudy skies, and a light breeze was blowing. The chairs were set up on the lawn facing the back of the yard in ten rows, six on each side of the aisle, arranged so JJ and Anna would be married under a tree like Anna wanted. A large tent covered the entire area.

The guests included Miss Nancy, Mrs. Barclay, and all the kids who lived at Tutu House. Laura had arranged to have Miss Nancy represent JJ's past and sit next to her on the front row. Even Sheriff Doug had been invited.

Kevin, Uncle Howard and Tom were JJ's ushers, and Kevin was JJ's best man. Anna's friend Lauren was the maid of honor. Gloria and Patty were bridesmaids. Little Lois was a flower girl. The catering company brought a record player for the music, and an extension cord was run from the house.

They brought Anna's wheelchair to make it easier for her to get around, but when it was time to walk down the aisle, she used just the one crutch and had her father help her in the same way JJ always did.

Laddie had been put in the farmhouse, but escaped just as the wedding was about to start. He ran to JJ, who was already standing in the front. JJ picked up Laddie and was about to carry him back to the farmhouse when Miss Nancy held out her arms. JJ paused, then turned to Miss Nancy and handed Laddie to her. Miss Nancy sat back down with Laddie on her lap while many chuckled. Everyone there knew Laddie or knew about him. Tom said, "Well, it makes more sense to have Laddie here anyway." Laddie sat contentedly on Miss Nancy's lap.

Just after 2 pm little Lois walked down the aisle, dropping pink flower petals. Anna followed with her father as the wedding march played on the record player. Anna's smile couldn't have been bigger. Her mother and many others wept with happiness. JJ beamed, thinking how lucky he was. He was proud of Anna and the gorgeous wedding dress she had made, and how beautiful she looked.

Anna walked with her father's help to JJ, who took her from her father, and supported her while they said their vows. Even Kevin had to wipe his eyes. Who could have imagined eight years ago that he would be the best man for a wedding like this, with a good job and a wife of his own? Miss Nancy and Mrs. Barclay both cried. Mrs. Kurzmann was happy to see her little girl all grown up and married, but sad at the same time, knowing that Anna would not be coming home to them anymore.

All in all, it was a simple, short, but beautiful wedding ceremony. Howard was immensely pleased with how everything turned out and felt his money was well spent. Gloria was thrilled and looked forward to a nice wedding for her daughter. Tom and Laura hugged Mr. and Mrs. Kurzmann and wished they didn't have to move to Pittsburgh. Anna and Gloria laughed about Gloria's daughter Evelyn catching the bouquet. "At this rate," said Anna, "I'll have to go into the wedding dress business!"

"You're not kidding," said Gloria, and nodded to her oldest daughter who was there with a fiancé.

Laddie ran around to see everyone and had a good time. He was happy when anyone spilled food.

After visiting and eating, taking pictures, opening wedding gifts and having the wedding cake, it was after six. The Kurzmanns, Tom, and Laura walked with JJ and Anna to the area where all the cars were parked. There was one decorated in traditional wedding vandalism, but neither JJ nor Anna recognized it. Tom let Mr. Kurzmann present the keys of the new car to JJ and Anna. It might not have been the exact model JJ would have picked himself, but the car was chosen for its legroom in the front and the wide and easy access for Anna. JJ and Anna couldn't have been happier or more grateful.

It was time for JJ and Anna to begin their new life. They didn't have far to drive since they were heading to the little house in back of Tom and Laura. There was no time for a proper honeymoon.

Laddie spent the night in JJ's old room as usual, but JJ and Anna spent their first night together in "Aunt Beverly's" house. From then on, it was JJ and Anna's house.

That day, JJ gained a lifetime of love and affection. Anna secured her true love. Tom and Laura gained a beautiful daughter. Lois and Catherine gained a sister. The Kurzmanns gained a son and were granted their lifelong wish. Laddie and Princess gained permanent play partners.

The next day, Anna brought Princess to their new home, and the cat quickly adapted. Laddie stayed with JJ and Anna after that. Princess thought it was splendid. Princess liked to stay close to Laddie and Laddie liked to stay close to JJ, so it was not unusual to see JJ walking, followed by a dog, followed by a cat. At night, Laddie would jump onto the bed and settle by the footboard. Princess imitated Laddie and curled up next to him. It was a good arrangement.

Anna and JJ moved Anna's things to the little house and moved Anna's sewing and painting supplies to the office above the theater where there was plenty of room. The elevator that Gloria and Anna had cleaned up came in handy.

It was a sad affair to help the Kurzmanns move to their new home in Pittsburgh. There were more tears as goodbyes were said, and the Kurzmanns began their new adventure. Laura said to Mrs. Kurzmann, "We'll all take good care of Anna."

"I know you will," said Mrs. Kurzmann.

It was hard for the Kurzmanns to leave their family and friends behind. The Kurzmanns had family there, but it would be different now. JJ and Anna began a new tradition of traveling to Pittsburgh nearly every Saturday for dinner.

Gloria's oldest and second oldest daughters were planning weddings. Howard had set up a sewing area in the office for Anna, in one of the upstairs rooms with two windows facing the street. It was becoming a tradition for Howard to buy the wedding dress material and have Anna make the dresses.

During the day, when JJ and Anna were at work, Laura and the kids watched Laddie and Princess. Sometimes, when Lois was at school, and Catherine was napping, Laura would sit on the couch and look at Laddie and think about their lives. Laddie would come over and jump up next to her, and she would pet Laddie on the head. "You have no idea what you started, do you?" she would think with a smile.

At the office, Anna now answered the phone saying, "Mills and Robinson, Anna Robinson speaking."

Gloria joked that Anna never made a mistake. "I'm surprised you haven't slipped up with your new name," she said with a smile.

Anna smiled back. "I've been practicing for a long time."

14

On the Other Hand

Shortly after her parents moved to Pittsburgh, Anna began working on a wedding dress for Gloria's daughter. It was a pleasure being able to work on her sewing projects during work hours when things weren't too busy.

Life was different, though. Sometimes Anna would pause, look out the window, and think about her mom. Once, when it was late in the afternoon, and the phones were quiet, Anna was feeling just a little melancholy. She stared out the window in the direction of her old home. Gloria walked in and said, "It takes time to adjust. You'll be fine." She walked over and gave Anna a hug. "That dress is looking very nice," she said. "Why don't you give your mom a phone call?"

"Oh, but it's long distance," said Anna.

"I'm sure we can afford a few dollars for you to say hi to your mom," said Gloria.

* * * * *

Over time, everyone adapted. Mr. Kurzmann now had a short drive to work at the steel mill. Mrs. Kurzmann volunteered at two junior high schools, helping kids with polio do their physical therapy.

Anna still rode to work with JJ and Tom, but now had breakfast with Tom, Laura, JJ and the girls. Most days Anna waited for JJ to come back to the office to bring her home, and sometimes she would let Gloria or Tom bring her home. When JJ was working late on a job, Anna was glad to be able to visit with Laura and the kids.

* * * * *

Soon it was Halloween. Lois wanted to go trick or treating. She dressed as a cute little witch, and everyone walked around with her. Anna used her wheelchair and held Baby Catherine all bundled up. JJ pushed Anna while Tom and Laura walked along with Lois. They only walked around the block, but it took them an hour. It was a strange feeling to walk by Anna's old house and see it occupied by strangers.

The day after Halloween was Saturday. Lois was tired and didn't feel well. Probably too much candy, they thought. By Sunday, Lois had a temperature, a sore throat, and a cough. Laura was starting to panic, and Tom was worried. Those were the symptoms Baby Karen started with years ago. They called the doctor who told them to go to the hospital, and he would meet them there. Laura bundled up Lois and Tom drove them to the hospital. JJ and Anna stayed home to take care of Baby Catherine. While they were waiting, Howard called to ask Tom about something. JJ answered the phone and told Howard what was going on. Howard called Gloria and Kevin. Then he drove over to Tom's house just as Kevin and Patty arrived. Gloria called to ask if they knew anything. After a few hours, Tom came home. "They think it's just measles, but they don't want to take any chances," said Tom. "I came to pick up Catherine and bring her to the hospital for Laura."

They all decided to drive to the hospital. Howard called Gloria to let her know what was happening. Laura burst into tears when she saw everyone. "I'm just so worried," she said. "She's sleeping now. They're watching her and doing some tests."

After a while, the doctor came and spoke to them. "At this point, we're almost positive it's measles. I'm pretty sure she's going to be just fine. It's going to be important to keep your other child away from Lois for next couple of weeks. Let us know if she comes down with symptoms."

Tom spoke to Laura: "Why don't you let JJ take you home? Get some rest and take care of Catherine. I'll stay here for a while."

"Let me know if you need anything," said Howard.

The next day Lois went home. It was a horrible scare, but everything was fine. They kept Lois isolated as best they could and worried about Baby Catherine, who never did get sick.

At Thanksgiving, everyone was especially thankful for their health, and for the full recovery of little Lois. At Tutu House, it gave them something to talk about.

It gave them even more to talk about when Tom and Howard showed up to make an announcement. Mills and Robinson Air Conditioning and Electric was now the proud owner of Tutu House, a state historical landmark. "We still have some things to take care of," said Howard. "But one way or another, this place will be an orphanage for the rest of our lives."

Mrs. Barclay had the biggest smile anyone ever saw. Miss Nancy nearly collapsed in tears of joy. She had to leave the room for a while but came back and told Howard he had no idea how much this meant to them. Howard felt really good, even though he wouldn't be able to get any publicity for it. In fact, it would be better to keep the whole thing quiet. At least they were able to buy the place for a good price. The designation of historical landmark had kept other bidders away.

It was an extra good Thanksgiving. The Kurzmanns came from Pittsburgh and spent the next two nights in a motel close by, and spent the days with Anna, JJ, and their new friends.

On December 24th, Howard, Kevin and Patty made another trip to the orphanage in Pittsburgh. It was toasty warm, and the kids were excited to see them again. Howard had managed to create some publicity by replacing the old furnace and adding air conditioning. There were several orders that came in as a result of the publicity, but Howard would have been happy regardless. The December 24 visit became a tradition lasting for thirteen years until Mrs. Adams retired, and the orphanage closed.

* * * * *

The next few years kept everyone busy. Kevin and Patty had twins, a boy named Timmy and a girl named Sue. JJ and Anna were saving money to buy their own house. They often had dinner with Tom and Laura, and sometimes ate by themselves. They had their own TV and enjoyed watching Laddie and Princess play together. Animals were funny, they thought. The cat and dog would entertain themselves by doing the same thing every night. Princess was slowing down, though. She was 14, much older than Laddie. You would think Laddie, seeing Princess every day, wouldn't be interested in Anna's old house anymore. But every time they walked past, Laddie would go up to the fence and look for the cat. JJ and Anna would laugh at Laddie and wonder if he was looking for another cat.

There were numerous trips to Tutu House, and Miss Nancy and Mrs. Barclay were always happy to see them. Miss Nancy loved to hear every detail about the business and what was going on with Tom and Laura and the kids. She and Anna often played the piano together. She no longer had to worry that JJ would slip out of her life, or that she would have to leave Tutu House.

Going to the Mills Movie theater was always fun, and became a family tradition. They enjoyed movies like "Ben-Hur," "Sleeping Beauty," "The Time Machine," and many others. Sometimes they took Miss Nancy. She especially enjoyed "Pollyanna" and "Swiss Family Robinson."

* * * * *

By 1961, business was doing better than ever. They were able to work with the guys at Christianson Heating and trained two of them to be full-fledged air conditioning technicians. This reduced the number of trips they needed to make into Pittsburgh and allowed them to start working in some of the other small towns around Indiana. Gradually, as their trucks needed maintenance or painting, they replaced the words on the trucks with "Mills & Robinson Heating and AC," the new company name. The office manager for the old heating company retired, and Gloria and Anna took over that job. They installed a direct phone line to Pittsburgh, which gave them a local number so people there could call without having a long distance charge. Gloria and Anna had learned how to do payroll and prepare data for the accounting firm that now did their books and taxes. Howard was pleased with the business. The theater business was beginning to show signs of changing. The small downtown theater was losing ground to the new multiple screen theaters.

The "Friends Ladies" still came by once in a while, but the Grace Hope Home for Children was now the responsibility of Mills and Robinson. It was funded partly by money from the state and partly by Mills and Robinson. Mrs. Barclay managed everything.

At the end of 1961, Alex Stewart died, and within a year the hardware store was closed.

* * * * *

By 1963, Kevin and Patty's twins were four. Patty loved to read children's stories to the kids, and Kevin loved to watch her do it. Over time, Kevin realized he could recognize almost all of the words, and he began reading to his children. Perhaps it was the repetition of the stories. As Patty bought new books for the kids, Kevin was able to read them. Maybe not as fast as others, but it was something. For the first time in his life, Kevin looked forward to reading, especially to the kids. It seemed the more he enjoyed reading, the easier it got. Or maybe it was just practice. Patty noticed it, too. She wasn't teaching in school now and wouldn't be teaching again for another few years. She knew something important was happening.

One evening after Timmy and Sue were put to bed, Patty casually mentioned how the kids enjoyed Kevin reading them a story. "Yeah, it's strange," said Kevin. "I seem to be able to see the words easier now."

Whether it was age, interest, or something else, Kevin read to his kids almost every night. He started reading the newspaper. It was harder to read, but no one was pushing him. He looked forward to reading the headlines, captions beneath the pictures, and the weather forecast.

Timmy and Sue loved their bedtime stories. Timmy developed quite an imagination and invented his own stories. One was quite a tale about a magic forest he and his sister had visited.

* * * * *

One morning in early spring, JJ and Anna were having breakfast with Tom, Laura, Lois, and Catherine.

"Dad," said JJ. "Anna and I have been thinking. We'd like to buy Aunt Beverly's farm."

"That's interesting," said Laura.

"That old house is in terrible shape," said Tom.

"We're thinking of building a new house there. It's a huge piece of property."

"You mean tear down the old house?" asked Laura.

"Yes," said JJ.

Tom thought for a moment. JJ wasn't sure how Tom would feel about that.

"I agree," said Tom. "It's time to move on."

"Actually," said Laura, "We've also been doing some planning."

"Yes," said Tom. "We've been thinking about remodeling this place."

Tom spoke to Laura: "If the kids moved out, we could tear out the little house and expand this place."

Then he spoke to JJ: "What kind of time frame are you thinking?"

JJ looked at Anna, and then back to Tom. "As soon as possible."

"How big?" asked Tom.

"Big," said JJ. "Five bedrooms. Enough for kids."

"I'll tell you what," said Tom. "You can have the house on one condition."

"Ok," said JJ.

"After you build your new house," said Tom, "You let us come and stay with you while we do construction work on our house."

"Of course!" said Anna.

"All right," said Tom. "Let's do it."

Kevin and Patty also made changes. They moved into a larger home further out of town. Grandma Connor was a great grandma now and getting older. She moved in with Kevin and Patty. Grandma Connor sold her house and put the money she made toward the new home. Uncle Howard helped Kevin and Patty find a three bedroom house with a fourth extra room in the back, with its own bathroom. It was perfect for them. Grandma Connor was able to watch the kids so Patty could go back to teaching.

JJ took several pictures of Aunt Beverly's farm house and had one enlarged and put in a frame. It was the view of the farm from the road, the view he had seen when he first spotted it twelve years ago. JJ and Anna had worked up a nice plan for a five-bedroom "ranch style" home with four bathrooms. That would make it easy to host guests, like Anna's folks. They also thought it would be a good place for kids, even though no children had shown up yet for them.

It was with mixed emotions that they watched bulldozers take down the farmhouse and barn. In one week, there was nothing left but the field where JJ and Anna had been married.

While this was going on, Anna's cat Princess got sick. They took her to the vet and discovered she was in kidney failure. She was suffering and had only a short time to live. It was quite a shock, but there was only one decision a kind person could make. Princess died gently and peacefully in Anna's arms. JJ got the wheelchair from the car and brought it inside so he could wheel Anna out holding her old friend. They drove home, and then went with Tom, Laura and the kids to the farm. Everyone tried their best to comfort Anna. JJ wheeled Anna, carrying Princess in a blanket, to the far left corner where they had buried Aunt Beverly's ashes, and dug a little grave. They stood sadly for a while in the August afternoon and didn't say much. Anna sobbed quietly. "I was ten when I got Princess."

JJ put his arm around Anna and said, "If it hadn't been for Princess I never would've met you."

JJ was glad they were building a new home here, but he couldn't help wondering when they would have to bury Laddie. It was a sad thought for a sad day.

A few months later, the entire country was shocked and saddened when President John F. Kennedy was shot and killed.

* * * * *

By 1965, JJ and Anna had been living in their new home for almost two years. They now brought Laddie to work with them each day. Aunt Beverly's house was gone, but JJ could look out the back door and see the fireflies in the summer. There was also a sliding glass door in JJ and Anna's bedroom that provided a nice view to the backyard. The field had been planted with grass, and it looked like a park. A fence was added to the little area where Princess was buried next to Aunt Beverly's ashes. The only thing missing now were children. JJ and Anna didn't think about it too much as they were both busy with the business. They visited Tutu House often, now that they were practically in walking distance. They took Laddie on a walk nearly every day. Sometimes it was a short walk and in the winter it was a very short walk. Once when they were visiting Tom and Laura for dinner, JJ took Anna and Laddie around the old block where they used to walk. Laddie stopped at Anna's old house and looked through the fence for Princess. It made Anna cry.

Tom and Laura had demolished the little house in their backyard and renovated the main house, adding two bedrooms, another bathroom, and a large family room. They also installed a new whole-house heating and air conditioning system. For a few months during construction, Tom, Laura, and the girls stayed with JJ and Anna in their new home. When Tom, Laura, and the girls finally moved back home, they loved their new, bigger house. But something was missing.

"I miss Laddie," said Catherine.

"Me too," said Lois.

Both girls had known Laddie their entire lives. Lois was now thirteen, and Catherine was seven.

"I think we need a little dog," said Laura to Tom. "Or maybe a cat."

"I can't believe I'm saying this," said Tom. "But I think you're right."

They made a visit to the local animal shelter. It was not a large facility, and there weren't many choices. Tom had thought maybe they would find a puppy. It didn't take long for Lois and Catherine to explore all over. They came back asking about one dog in a cage apart from the rest.

"That little dog is already six years old," said the attendant. "She's been abused and is blind in one eye. No one wants those kinds of animals. We have to put them to sleep. We'll be putting her down later today."

For some reason, Lois and Catherine wanted the quiet little black and white dog. It was mostly black with white patches.

"I want her," said Lois.

"Me, too," said Catherine.

And that was that. Lois and Catherine rescued a sweet little dog. They held and loved the little dog while Tom and Laura did the paperwork. They carried little Maggie home in the car. Maggie was dirty and needed a bath, and the girls were eager to do it. Maggie was quiet and afraid of almost everything. JJ and Anna came over to meet the new family member and brought Laddie. Laddie wasn't as bouncy as he used to be. He seemed to be able to tell that Maggie was nervous. He approached Maggie carefully, much like when he had met Princess many years ago.

It can take time to adapt. Like many adopted pets, Maggie was quiet for a long time. Eventually, they heard her bark at the doorbell. The girls each had their own room and took turns having Maggie sleep with them. Over time, Maggie gravitated to Catherine but enjoyed the whole family.

* * * * *

Laura joined Gloria and Anna in the office during the time when Catherine and Lois were in school. Howard had been advertising in the Yellow Pages for several years, and it was paying off. They were handling a lot of service and repair calls for old heaters, and even air conditioners. Howard had taught every employee that each service call was also a sales job; that sometimes this was a customer's first experience with Mills & Robinson. "Always be thinking long term," he repeatedly said, and "never let a dispute lead to the courtroom." Gloria and Anna spent a fair amount of time dispatching and scheduling service technicians, mostly in Pittsburgh but some in Indiana and other small towns in the area. Laura was able to help with the bookkeeping. It was quite a different business from 1950. Laura spent the mornings working in the office and usually brought Maggie with her. Laddie looked forward to seeing Maggie at the office.

* * * * *

In the fall of 1965, Kevin and Patty drove out to her folk's farm in Greensburg with their kids to spend the weekend. Timmy and Sue were six years old and loved to visit the farm. They always had something interesting to talk about in school after visiting the farm and this trip would be no exception.

The drive to Greensburg only took an hour. Kevin and Patty arrived around noon. Patty's dad came in from the field for lunch. Kevin asked what he was working on. He said they were bailing hay, but the bailer jammed. "Usually I get it unstuck in a second," he said, "But the doggone belt slipped, or something's jammed the gearbox."

"I'm sure Kevin can fix it," said Patty. "He can fix anything, right honey?"

"No problem," said Kevin. "Let's go take a look."

The two men walked off to the field where the hay bailer was sitting, and Kevin examined it. Kevin was able to size up almost any kind of machine just by studying it for a moment. Patty's dad had removed a cover plate so you could see the pulley and belt inside the gearbox which powered the bailing apparatus. Kevin looked at it for another minute and concluded the problem must be down inside where the belt ran around the lower pulley. He reached his hand down inside and could feel a piece of wood or branch or something tangled in the belt. He tried to wiggle it lose, but it was really stuck. He told Patty's dad to start the engine and run the bailer for a second and then stop, but keep the engine running. Patty's dad did this, and then Kevin reached down again to try to remove the blockage. It still wouldn't budge.

"Ok, hit it again," said Kevin. Patty's dad ran the hay bailer for a second and then stopped.

Kevin felt that the blockage was beginning to budge. As he tried to pull on the stuck piece, his other arm slipped. It looked to Patty's dad like Kevin was signaling to run the bailer again. The bailer lurched, and Kevin's left hand was dragged into the pulley. He instinctively yanked his hand out. Patty's dad looked in horror at the blood all over Kevin's arm. He turned off the machine, jumped out, and ran to Kevin. Kevin had a shocked look on his face. His hand seemed to be missing fingers. Patty's dad tore off his shirt and wrapped it around Kevin's hand as tightly as he could. He held Kevin's hand as they walked back to the house.

Patty was leaning against the kitchen sink, sipping a cup of coffee and talking to her mom. She looked out the window and saw Kevin and her dad heading to the house. Her dad was shirtless and holding Kevin's hand, wrapped in bloody cloth. "Oh my lord!" exclaimed Patty and ran outside with her mom.

"We've got a serious injury here," said Patty's dad. "We need to get to the hospital quick. Patty, get the car ready. Mom, stay here with the kids and phone the hospital to let them know we're coming in with a bad hand injury."

Patty helped Kevin into the car and held his hand tightly. He was now in shock. Her dad drove to the hospital, about twenty minutes away. It was the first time she had ever seen Kevin appear weak and helpless.

Patty phoned her mom from the hospital. "He's in surgery now," said Patty. It was difficult not to be hysterical. "He's lost at least two fingers. They're doing what they can to save his hand."

Within a few hours, JJ, Anna, Tom, Laura, and the girls arrived, along with Uncle Howard and Gloria. Patty's mom had brought the twins to the hospital. Patty was a wreck, and her mom and dad were upset. When JJ and Anna came in, Timmy said, "My dad got his hand chopped off."

"They don't allow too many in at a time to see him," said Patty. "He lost three fingers on his left hand. His thumb's ok."

JJ and Anna walked in with Patty to see Kevin, who was resting in a hospital bed with his hand wrapped up. He was still sleepy from surgery and pain medication.

"Hey, Kevin," said JJ.

"Hey," said Kevin slowly.

It was hard to think of something to say.

"I'm so sorry," said Anna.

"Well, I won't be washing dishes for a while," Kevin joked. "On the other hand…"

*****

Kevin gradually got back to work. He was a strong guy and wasn't going to let something like a mangled hand get in the way. It was a major nuisance not to have those fingers, but he did have his thumb and the little finger. Within a week, he was back on the job, but mostly as a supervisor and inspector. He was used to being the workhorse of the company. He had already experienced being a supervisor with his soldering methods and other techniques he had invented. This took supervising a step further. Kevin was well liked by the heating guys, and they didn't mind having Kevin double check their work. Kevin always helped when technicians faced a difficult problem.

It was amazing how quickly he adapted to the new shape of his left hand. By Thanksgiving, he was thankful it wasn't any worse and especially thankful for his "family."

"You don't know how much your family means to you until you have something like this happen," he said. "On the other hand, this wouldn't have happened without my family," he joked with a smile.

* * * * *

By 1968, things were changing.

Handheld calculators were now available. Mills and Robinson bought one for each of the workers. Kevin didn't need his but Patty had fun with it.

The war in Vietnam was a big problem.

In New York City, they were building a new office building. It would be two towers, higher than the Empire State Building, and needed lots of steel. Pennsylvania made the strongest steel in the world, but the steel contracts were given to other states. It was a disappointment for the Pennsylvania economy.

Uncle Howard was concerned and had a frank talk with the employees of Mills & Robinson about being prudent.

1968 was to be another year of tragedy. In April, Martin Luther King was killed, and in June, Robert Kennedy was killed. "What is wrong with people?" asked Anna.

"I don't know," said JJ.

Times were changing.

* * * * *

Everyone was getting older. At the beginning of summer, on a Friday afternoon, JJ got a call from Mrs. Barclay at the orphanage. It was about Miss Nancy having a hard time getting up and down the stairs. JJ said he would come over the next afternoon. As they got ready for bed, JJ and Anna talked about Miss Nancy.

"She's 66," said Anna. "We've got plenty of room here, and no stairs."

"I know," said JJ. "I've thought about that too."

The next day they drove over with Laddie. The children always liked to see Laddie, but he was a quiet dog now. He mostly liked to lie on the floor or the big chair and watch everyone. His fur had been gray for some time. Miss Nancy always had a treat for him, and the younger kids would often come over and sit and pet him. Laddie liked that.

"JJ and I were talking," said Anna. "We think it's time you retired. Why don't you come and live with us?"

"Thank you, sweetie," said Miss Nancy. "That would be nice, but I wish I could stay here."

JJ looked at Mrs. Barclay and said, "How about moving down to a room on the first floor?"

"I suppose I could," said Miss Nancy, slowly.

"You like your room, don't you?" said Anna to Miss Nancy.

Miss Nancy's room had become a gallery of photographs. Between school pictures, graduation pictures, weddings, and photos from children long since grown, photographs were everywhere. JJ and Anna had contributed plenty of them.

"I really do," said Miss Nancy. "But I admit the stairs are getting harder. I've fixed some lunch if you're hungry."

They had a nice visit like they always did. JJ took Miss Nancy and Laddie outside. Anna spoke with Mrs. Barclay.

"I'm looking for a replacement for Miss Nancy," said Mrs. Barclay. "It's hard. She's been my friend for so long. I just don't know what to do. She would be heartbroken if she had to leave."

"Is there any rule against her staying here?" asked Anna. "I mean, it's our house now. JJ and I will be happy to take care of her living expenses. We would love to have her come and stay with us, but she seems attached to this place."

"And that room," added Mrs. Barclay. "She would love to be able to stay here. I'm certain this is where she wants to die."

JJ decided to install a chair lift for Miss Nancy. He ordered the equipment and Kevin helped install it. At first, the kids played on the chair lift and Mrs. Barclay would scold them, sort of. Within a few weeks, it was ordinary. It became a common sight to see Miss Nancy riding up or down the stairs, often with a child on her lap.

* * * * *

By 1969, there were eleven kids living at Tutu House. Mrs. Barclay's own children had grown up long ago. Many orphanages were closing down, but Tutu House was well funded. It was now known as a "residential education facility." A new aide was hired, named Lisa. She was chosen partly because of her love for animals. Mrs. Barclay had taken advantage of the fence that had been installed many years ago and picked up two mutts from the animal shelter. The children loved having the animals around. Mrs. Barclay had decided that having the children take care of pets was beneficial. Miss Lisa worked out wonderfully and adapted quickly.

Miss Nancy helped here and there but was officially retired. She did some of the cooking and read stories to the children. She was enjoying her life. She relished visits from JJ and Anna and Tom and Laura. She loved the children, and she loved being where she was. She could often be seen sitting outside in a chair, under the shade of a certain tree, eating an apple, reading a book, or just keeping an eye on the children.

Tutu House now had four television sets, thanks to JJ and Anna. Mrs. Barclay and Miss Nancy each had their own TV, and there was a TV in each of the two main areas for the kids. Miss Nancy didn't watch TV much, but liked having it to watch the "Lawrence Welk Show." She also loved the Christmas programs that came on each year.

On July 20, 1969, Mrs. Barclay, Miss Nancy, Miss Lisa, and all the children at Tutu House were able to watch men land on the moon. The older kids were glued to the television set, amazed.

"Wow," said Miss Lisa.

"Incredible," said Mrs. Barclay.

"Can you imagine that," said Miss Nancy.

15

Old Age

Time has a way of slipping by. Things and people change slowly, often unnoticed. Last year the roof at Tutu House had leaked. When JJ checked it out, he realized it was in need of repair. This year, other things were wearing out.

One April evening in 1970, a few days after Anna's 31st birthday, JJ arrived home from a job in nearby Blairsville and found Anna upset, and holding Laddie. "What's wrong, honey?"

"Laddie can't jump up on the bed. I hadn't paid attention, but he hasn't been on the bed lately. The last time was the day before yesterday when you were carrying him around and put him there."

"Hey, what's a matter, old boy?" said JJ to Laddie.

"I picked him up because I saw him trying to get up."

JJ looked at Laddie, who was comfortable and happy lying in his usual spot on the bed, by the foot, right in the middle. Now that he thought about it, Anna was right. Last night, Laddie slept under the bed. Laddie had been slowing down for some time now. On their walks, JJ had been carrying Laddie earlier and earlier into their walk. When Anna went with them in her wheelchair, Laddie almost immediately wanted Anna's lap. It was a somber thought. Laddie was quite old for a dog, and he couldn't live forever.

"I'm worried that he might hurt himself jumping off the bed," said Anna.

"Maybe I could build a ramp." Said JJ.

"I don't know," said Anna.

JJ was trying to figure out a way to make a ramp, but the footboard was in the way. He thought of lowering the bed, but that would make it hard for Anna.

"We're just going to have to help him up and down," said JJ.

From then on, Laddie's condition was on their mind. Laddie spent most of his time resting or sleeping. He was a contented little dog, and always seemed to have a smile on his face. Who could know what he was thinking? Did he still remember Princess? *You're just like me,* thought JJ. *No one knows where either of us came from.*

"Laddie's nineteen," said Anna.

"I know," said JJ.

"That's awfully old for a dog," said Anna.

JJ held Laddie on his lap like he had done thousands of times before. JJ was a grown man, and Laddie was an old dog. Anna stroked Laddie, who seemed more gray than brown. Anna and Laddie had formed a deep relationship after many years of spending the day together at the office. Kevin, Gloria and Uncle Howard were all used to seeing Laddie there. On their last visit to the veterinarian, Dr. Roger had said that Laddie was doing well for a dog his age. "Usually, when an animal is suffering, you'll know it."

For several more months, Anna and JJ took special care of Laddie. They continued to bring Laddie to work where he stayed with Anna. In the first week in September, Laddie began to show signs he wasn't comfortable. By the middle of September, Laddie had lost his smile. He even whimpered once when Anna picked him up. His tail rarely wagged. On the night of September 22, they made the decision that all pet owners dread. They stayed up the entire night taking care of Laddie and enjoying what they could of their last moments together. The next morning JJ asked Anna to call Dr. Roger's office.

"I want to take Laddie by my old house," said JJ. They stopped at Tom and Laura's house and got out Anna's wheelchair. JJ put Laddie in Anna's lap. Tom and Laura came out with Lois and Catherine, who had stayed home from school. Maggie came over to see Laddie. Both of JJ's sisters were crying and pet Laddie for the last time. Laura gave Laddie a sad little hug and said goodbye. Even Tom had a hard time.

From Tom and Laura's house, Dr. Roger's office was only five blocks away. JJ pushed Anna and Laddie for their last walk together. They walked by Anna's old house, but Laddie paid no attention. When they reached Dr. Roger's office, the front door was open, and Dr. Roger was standing there with one of his assistants. Putting an animal to sleep was Dr. Roger's least favorite part of being a veterinarian, but he knew it was important to give an animal as much comfort as possible in their last moments. Laddie died peacefully in JJ's arms, with Anna's hand on his head.

September 23, 1970, was the saddest day in JJ's life. Tom, Laura and the girls came with JJ and Anna to bury Laddie with Aunt Beverly and Princess. Kevin and Patty, Gloria, and Howard Mills came to say goodbye. It was the end of a long story that had affected everyone there. Still, it seemed to end too soon. The stories of our pets always end too soon.

Afterward, everyone left but Laura, who tried to console JJ and Anna. "The little animals we love teach us that life is short, and we need to love and enjoy those around us because you can't know when they'll be gone."

Laura stayed with them for a while. "Why don't you come back with me and have dinner with us?" she said. JJ and Anna agreed.

"We should get another dog," said Anna.

"Yeah, we should," said JJ.

During the next few days, they worked as usual. They kept meaning to go to the animal shelter, as it was now being called, but never got around to it. Anna rode home from work with Laura nearly every day now and waited for JJ to pick her up. It was much better visiting with Laura and the kids after work than sitting in an empty house. Little Catherine would sometimes ask "When are you going to get another dog?"

Anna would say "Maybe this next weekend. We'll see how it goes."

Several weeks passed without getting around to it. Sometimes it was hard to do even the smallest things, like vacuum the furniture, and watch the last traces of Laddie slowly vanish.

* * * * *

On a Monday morning in October, JJ got a call from Mrs. Barclay. "It's Miss Nancy. She's not doing well. She wants to see you. I think you should come."

JJ had Gloria cancel his appointments and picked up Anna. They arrived at Tutu House, and Mrs. Barclay met them at the front door. "She's upstairs in her room." They could see concern on Mrs. Barclay's face.

Anna used the chair lift, and JJ walked up the stairs alongside her. Miss Nancy's door was open. She was lying in bed and turned to look at them. As soon as she saw JJ and Anna she smiled.

"Oh, it's so good to see you," she said. She spoke slowly, with a tired voice. "I'm sorry to hear about Laddie. He was a special little dog."

Anna sat down in a chair next to Miss Nancy's bed, and JJ sat on the edge of the bed. "How are you feeling?" asked Anna.

Miss Nancy held Anna's hand and said, "I'm feeling very tired, but I'm happy. Thank you so much for sharing JJ with me."

"He has adored you his whole life," said Anna.

Miss Nancy smiled again and closed her eyes for a moment.

"You know," said Miss Nancy. "The day JJ ran away was one of the worst days of my life."

"I'm so sorry," said JJ.

"No," said Miss Nancy, looking at JJ. "Look at all the good that came of it. You and Anna are together. You saved your Aunt Beverly, and you saved Tom and Laura. That saved Kevin and who knows how many others? You met Howard Mills and helped build a company that saved this house. You've made me so happy watching you grow up and do all these things. It's been a wonderful life, JJ, just like the movie." She paused for a moment. "Just think of all the people affected by this. I remember when you used to hate Kevin."

"I know," said JJ. "It's hard to imagine that now."

"You never really know someone until you know their story, do you?" said Miss Nancy.

Mrs. Barclay came in and stood in the doorway.

"I wish I could know your story," said JJ.

"I do have a story, and I'm ready to give it to you," said Miss Nancy. "Over in my desk, in the lower right-hand drawer is my story. I want you to have it."

It was a tall drawer. JJ pulled it open. In the drawer were fourteen diaries. He grabbed each one and handed some to Anna.

"I was ten years old when the Titanic sunk you know," said Miss Nancy. She paused, like she was thinking about something. JJ could see that she was holding an old photograph in her hands, pressed against her chest. She handed the photo to JJ and said, "A few pictures, my diaries, and this house are all that I have left of my past."

Mrs. Barclay came over and sat on the bed next to JJ. Miss Lisa was downstairs watching the children. JJ and Anna looked at the photograph and could see that it was a picture of a young Miss Nancy standing in front of a house with a handsome young man. It was dated September 17, 1924.

"This is you in front of Tutu House!" said Anna.

"Yes," said Miss Nancy. "Back then we called it Colonial House. My Arthur built it for me. We were going to have a family. This room was going to be the nursery. Then there was the depression. We lost everything, including this house. Arthur got sick and died. That was the worst day of my life. Eventually, I came back here to work. It's a long story, but you have it now."

The room was silent as JJ and Anna contemplated the photograph. Miss Nancy reached out her hand again, and JJ and Anna held it. Mrs. Barclay wept silently.

"Is there anything I can get for you?" asked Anna.

"I would love to hear some music," said Miss Nancy. "If you could just help me down to the big chair..."

JJ gently handed the picture back to Miss Nancy. He stood up and put his arms under her and carefully lifted her, along with her blanket. As he carried Miss Nancy slowly down the stairs, he thought how different she was from the person he had known all his life. She was now frail, weak, and dependent on him.

Miss Nancy smiled, thinking how JJ was so different from the little boy she used to carry when he was sad. Now he was big and strong, married, and working in a successful company he'd helped create.

Mrs. Barclay helped Anna to the chair lift and went down the stairs with her. JJ carried Miss Nancy to the big chair next to the piano. It had been repaired and reupholstered but was still the same chair JJ remembered as a child, the same chair Miss Nancy had sat in countless times, reading and telling stories, and comforting children. He tenderly made Miss Nancy comfortable while several children gathered around. Anna came in with Mrs. Barclay and sat down at the piano.

"What would you like?" asked Anna.

"Could you play some of the songs we used to do together?" asked Miss Nancy.

One by one, Anna played all the songs she knew Miss Nancy liked. Mrs. Barclay brought over another chair and sat with JJ next to Miss Nancy. She put her hand on Miss Nancy's arm while JJ held Miss Nancy's other hand.

When Anna stopped, Miss Nancy smiled and thanked her for playing so nicely. Then she spoke to Mrs. Barclay. "Thank you for everything, Margaret. You've been as dear a friend as anyone could want."

Next, she spoke slowly to JJ. "I'm sorry I won't get to see your children, but I seem to have run out of energy. I want to be buried by my Arthur. Can you take care of it for me?"

"Of course," said JJ with a lump in his throat.

"You and Anna have been so precious to me." She squeezed JJ's hand ever so slightly. "You've done well, and made a good life. That makes me happy. I wish Arthur could have been this happy."

There was silence. Then Miss Nancy continued, speaking softly. "Anna, would you play 'Danny Boy' for me?"

Anna tried to hold back tears while she played several verses. Miss Nancy looked at JJ, Anna, Mrs. Barclay, and the children. She smiled and closed her eyes, thought about another place and another time, and went to be with her Arthur.

JJ gently placed Miss Nancy's lifeless arm on her chest. He carefully took the photograph from under Miss Nancy's other hand and gave it to Mrs. Barclay. Mrs. Barclay kissed her friend on the cheek and said goodbye. Then she covered Miss Nancy with the blanket.

It was a chilly afternoon with a light breeze outside, and a day no one there would ever forget. Mrs. Barclay lost her best friend, the children lost their story teller, JJ lost a part of his life, and a careworn soul got to rest.

The next day, Mrs. Barclay took JJ and Anna to see where Arthur was buried. "We hadn't realized Miss Nancy was a widow," said JJ, as they stood by Arthur's grave.

"You'll be learning a lot about her from the diaries," said Mrs. Barclay, "and me too, I'm afraid."

"I wonder why she never talked about Arthur," said JJ.

"Sometimes people aren't comfortable talking about some things, or they just don't know how," said Mrs. Barclay. "There was a time when Miss Nancy didn't want to live."

After a moment she continued. "Miss Nancy wouldn't want a fancy grave marker. Just a simple one, like Arthur's."

After returning to Tutu House, JJ and Anna picked up Miss Nancy's diaries. "Have you read them?" asked Anna.

"Yes I have," said Mrs. Barclay.

"I wonder why Miss Nancy wants me to have the diaries?" asked JJ.

"Of all the children who lived here," said Mrs. Barclay, "you were the one who felt like her own child."

Mrs. Barclay handed the picture of Nancy and Arthur to JJ. "I think this should belong to you, too. You'll understand better when you read her diary."

During the next few days, Tom, Kevin, and Uncle Howard helped JJ make the arrangements that Miss Nancy wanted. Mrs. Barclay notified as many people as she could. JJ and Anna began reading Miss Nancy's diaries.

The funeral was held the following Saturday, at 10:00 in the morning. It was a graveside service, under a tent. The temperature was mild, but the sky was cloudy, and there was a light rain off and on.

JJ gave the eulogy. He started to speak, but many memories were playing in his mind, and he was having a hard time. Anna stood up and worked her way over to JJ and put her arm around him. It was inspiring to see Anna supporting JJ. He talked about how Miss Nancy had been a good friend and teacher to so many, about the stories she read and told, how she cooked for them, played the piano, helped them with their school work, and so many acts of caring and kindness. Mrs. Barclay also spoke, struggling with tears. She said Miss Nancy was her dearest friend. She thanked Tom and Laura for their friendship, and for keeping JJ in Miss Nancy's life. "We were Miss Nancy's family," she said.

Miss Nancy was laid to rest next to her Arthur, as she had requested. Her grave was marked with a simple stone:

Nancy Quinn Kappel
January 12, 1902 – October 19, 1970
Beloved Wife, Mother To Many
Cherished Friend

She was buried next to a grave that also had a simple marker:

Arthur Joseph Kappel
March 5, 1897 – May 20, 1931
Beloved Husband

There was a lunch reception at Tutu House. Tom and Laura hired the catering company used for JJ and Anna's wedding. Past orphans came from all over. One lady traveled all the way from California. JJ was sadder than he thought possible. He was a grown man but felt like a little boy. He greeted others who had lived at Tutu House in the past and wished Miss Nancy could be there to see everyone who came. Mrs. Barclay was just as sad as JJ. Her own children, Jon and Shannen, were there, all grown up and married.

When JJ and Anna got home that afternoon, they continued reading Miss Nancy's story. They read all afternoon and into the evening. After dinner, they went to bed and continued reading. They read late into the night and hardly slept. About eleven o'clock the next morning they got a phone call from Laura inviting them for lunch.

"I'd like to stop at Tutu House on the way," said Anna, "and see the tree."

"Me too," said JJ. "I never paid any attention before."

They hugged each other for a while, got dressed, and drove the short distance to Tutu House. They knocked on the door, opened it, and stepped inside. Mrs. Barclay walked over, gave them both a hug and asked if they had read the diary.

"Yes," said JJ. "We're almost done."

"We came to see the tree," said Anna.

"I figured you would," said Mrs. Barclay, with a gentle smile. The big house seemed emptier, just knowing Miss Nancy was not there. Mrs. Barclay led them out the back door and to a tall tree in the backyard. It was the tree closest to the house and had grown nearly ten feet since Arthur had carved the words "Arthur and Nancy Forever" so many years ago. The growth of the tree had made the words illegible, but they were clearly there, high up in the tree, the same height as Miss Nancy's window. The three of them stood for a while in the chilly late morning air, and each touched the tree.

"You all suffered so much," said Anna.

"Yes," said Mrs. Barclay. "Those were hard times. I don't know what we would've done without the children and this wonderful place. I don't know what Miss Nancy would have done if you hadn't come into our lives. In many ways, you rescued her. And me, too."

"Just think," said JJ, as he looked up at the tree. "If Arthur hadn't brought Miss Nancy here, none of this would have happened. No Tutu House, no Robinson family, no Mills and Robinson company. I would never have met Anna."

"It's so nice, all the things you've done for us," said Mrs. Barclay, "especially helping us stay in this house. You can see why it was so important to Miss Nancy. When you ran away and found Tom and Laura, it turned out to be the best thing for all of us."

"It was serendipitous!" said Anna as she and JJ hugged Mrs. Barclay again. They both said goodbye and walked toward their car.

"Let us know if you need anything at all," said Anna.

Mrs. Barclay stood outside and watched as JJ and Anna drove away.

They were glad to see Tom and Laura.

"Are you reading Miss Nancy's diary?" asked Laura.

"Yes," said JJ.

"It's very sad," said Anna. "But it's a beautiful story, and we're all in it."

"I'd like to read it too," said Laura.

"I brought the first diary," said JJ. "After all these years it turns out I knew hardly anything about Miss Nancy. Or Mrs. Barclay."

"Most of the time we only see a tiny part of a person's story," said Laura.

They ate lunch and talked. Lois was out with friends and Catherine was doing homework in her room. The house was sure different now. It was bigger and nicer, but different. Everything was changing.

"This has just been a terrible year," said JJ. "First Laddie and now Miss Nancy. For so long everything was fine, and we were all happy."

"At some point we all face our mortality," said Tom.

"That's what's making me so miserable," said JJ. "Someday I'll lose you, and Uncle Howard, and Kevin. All the people I love will be gone. Sometimes I think I don't ever want another dog. I don't know if I can face this kind of pain again."

There was silence for a few moments. Then Tom said, "Would you really want to trade all the memories you have of Laddie and Miss Nancy so that you won't feel pain now?"

"No, not really," said JJ softly.

Laura said, "You'll have Anna for a long time, I'm sure, and someday there might be children. And we're not going anywhere soon."

"That's for sure," said Tom. He spoke quietly and continued, "When I got back from the war, your mom and I had nothing in common. Who knows what would have happened if you and Laddie had not come into our lives? We probably would have gone our separate ways, and your sisters would never have been born."

He paused and then continued, "The only way not to have pain is not to love anyone or anything. I'll tell you this, JJ, one of the best ways to deal with sadness is to find someone else who needs help, and then help them. When we took you, Laddie, and Aunt Beverly into our home, it was the beginning of a new life for us and frankly, I believe it saved my soul."

"That is so true," said Laura.

JJ thought about everything as they sat in silence with each other. He thought about how lucky he was to have such a wonderful mom and dad. He thought about his good times with Laddie and growing up with Miss Nancy. He thought about his wonderful wife, Anna.

Little Maggie came over and sat by JJ's feet. He instinctively reached down and patted her on the head. Then he picked her up. He sat for a moment, petting Maggie. Anna reached over to pet her too.

"You know what?" said Tom. "You and Anna ought to go to the pound and find some little dog who needs your help. I'm going to insist on it. Tomorrow, noon. You, me, Anna, and Mom. What do you say?"

"Ok," said JJ.

16

Part 1 End

Seven months after Miss Nancy died, on a Friday evening, JJ got a phone call from Mrs. Barclay.

"Hello, JJ, how're you and Anna doing?"

"We're doing ok."

"I was wondering if you and Anna will be dropping by tomorrow on your way to Pittsburgh?"

"Yeah, I think so."

"Good. I need to speak to you about something."

"Is there a problem?"

"Not a big problem. I need to show you."

"Ok. Do you need us to bring anything? Bread? Milk? Eggs?"

Mrs. Barclay laughed. "No, we're fine, thank you. We'll see you tomorrow?"

"Yeah, right after lunch, if that's ok."

"That would be fine," said Mrs. Barclay.

"What was that?" asked Anna.

"Mrs. Barclay wants us to come by tomorrow and show us something."

"I hope she's not having trouble with the new dishwasher," said Anna.

"I'm not sure. She wants to show me."

Anna laughed. "I should have spoken to her. You men never ask enough questions! Better bring the truck. She probably needs something fixed."

The next afternoon, JJ and Anna drove over to Tutu House. It still seemed strange to be there without Miss Nancy. Miss Lisa was a wonderful replacement. She was 28 and good with kids. She also loved the animals that lived there now, and she liked reading stories on Saturday nights.

It was a sunny but cool day in early May. JJ helped Anna out of the truck, and they made their way into the house.

"Hi, Mrs. Barclay. What's cookin'?"

"Come on in. It's always nice to see you both." Mrs. Barclay reached down to pat JJ and Anna's new dog on the head. "I've got a chance to fix a problem right now, and I need your help." She walked over to the window overlooking the backyard where most of the kids were playing. JJ and Anna followed. Mrs. Barclay pointed to three children — a boy and two girls, sitting under Miss Nancy's tree, watching the others chasing the dogs around the yard.

"What cute kids," said Anna. "When did they arrive?"

"They got here on Tuesday," said Mrs. Barclay. "Their parents, Oleg and Lena Dzbinski, were killed in that car crash that was on the news last week. They were immigrants from Poland. I don't know how we'll find a home that could keep these kids together."

JJ stared out the window as Mrs. Barclay continued talking. Inside was a swirl of emotions and a pit in his stomach. In his mind, he asked himself "What's wrong with living here?" but he knew what Mrs. Barclay was getting to. This was not exactly the kind of thing he and Anna had been considering. It was twenty years ago when Tom had faced similar feelings about JJ.

"The boy just turned eleven, the one girl is seven, and the little one is four."

"Oh, JJ!" said Anna, and grabbed his hand.

JJ opened his mouth but couldn't find words. There was a lump forming in his throat. Anna gently held his hand as they stood silently watching out the window.

"It won't be easy," said Mrs. Barclay. "They've been through a lot, those kids." She paused for a moment and then continued. "Every situation is different, isn't it? They could stay and live here, but I really think you should go out and meet them. I promised Miss Nancy I would help you build a family, and I feel you are just right for these kids."

JJ and Anna looked at each other. "It's like what Miss Nancy wrote in her diary," said Anna.

"I know," said JJ. He took Anna's hand, and they walked toward the back door. They made their way down the back porch stairs, JJ helping Anna as usual. Two young girls ran over yelling "Hi Mrs. Robinson!" They gave her a quick hug and ran off. Mrs. Barclay smiled as she watched out the window.

At the same time, the two dogs who lived at Tutu House came over to greet JJ and Anna's dog. All three dogs ran around the yard.

As JJ and Anna approached the tree where the kids were sitting, the two older ones stood up to greet them.

JJ spoke first. "Hi. My name is JJ. What's yours?"

The older boy answered "My name is Eryk. Nice to meet you, sir."

JJ answered back, "Nice to meet you, Eryk."

Eryk continued, "This is my sister Janina, and my sister Anatola."

Anna smiled and said, "Hi, Eryk and Janina and Anatola. My name is Anna."

"That's like my name," said little Anatola.

"Yes it is!" said Anna with a smile.

JJ said, "I see you are new here."

Eryk told JJ about the car accident. The girls didn't say anything.

JJ paused, and then he said, "I remember when I used to live here."

Eryk and Janina's eyes widened.

"Yeah, I used to be an orphan. I lived in this house for a long time. I was eleven when I got adopted."

JJ helped Anna sit down on the grass next to the kids, who looked at Anna's leg braces.

Their dog came running and jumped into Anna's lap and tried to lick her face. All three kids smiled.

Janina, the seven-year-old, asked, "What happened to your legs?"

"I had polio when I was a little girl, just about your age," said Anna as she looked at Anatola. "I got better, but my legs didn't. These braces help me stand up and walk. You can touch them if you want." She handed the dog to JJ.

Janina reached out and touched the metal brace. Then, Anatola reached out and touched it also.

"How old are you?" asked Anna, trying to think of something to say.

"I'm eleven," said Eryk. "I'm seven," said Janina. "I'm four," said Anatola. "How old are you?"

Anna laughed cheerfully. "I'm 32. Here, do you want to hold our dog?"

Janina asked, "Is it your dog?"

"Well," said JJ. "She's going to be a family dog."

"What's her name?" asked Janina.

Anna smiled and said, "Her name is Lassie."

Part 2

1918 - 1970

Miss Nancy's Diary

The following chapters are excerpts from Miss Nancy's Diary.

From the day she got her first diary until a few days before her death, Miss Nancy wrote almost daily. For the sake of our story, only selected entries are included here.

1

Anthracite Coal

<u>*Tuesday, April 30, 1918*</u>

My name is Nancy Quinn. I am 16 years old. I go to school here in the mining camp. Mr. Kappel is our teacher. He is very nice. I have been going to school here since I was 7. We didn't have many books and things until Mr. Kappel came last year. That's when we got books for everyone and papers and pencils that we could keep and take home.

Today I got this diary. It is a book to write in about my life. There are 5 of us who got them today from the school. Mr. Kappel gave them to us because we are the best students. He wants us to practice writing. I am already pretty good at reading.

I lived here all my life. My mom died when I was 3 years old. Mrs. Barrett lived next door and took care of me during the day. She has 2 boys named Patrick and Andres and a girl named Darcy. Her name is Janis. When I was 13 my dad married Mrs. Barrett because her husband died in a explosion. The mine is very dangerous. All us kids are like brothers and sisters. Darcy is a year younger than me. Patrick is 13 and Andres is 11.

I was born in January when it was very cold. It was 1902. My mom was sick for a long time afterward. I don't remember much about her except the song she used to sing to me. It makes me feel good when my stepmom sings it. It's the Ballyeamon Cradle Song. I only remember my mom lying in bed and her holding my hand. I wish I could remember more. When I turned 14 Pa gave me my mom's things. That's when I got the nice brush and comb and mirror that I love.

189

My dad and mom came from Ireland. My dad's name is Martin Quinn. He lived in Ballingarry and worked in the mines there. They had the same kind of hard coal that we have in this mine. Pa says it's the best kind of coal. In 1899 he left on a ship to America by himself when he was 19 years old.

My mom's name was Margaret Dunne. She came with her brother who was my uncle Fergus but I never met him. They came by themselves because my other Uncle Seamus and Aunt Mary were just children and got sick before the ship left. If you get sick they won't let you on the boat. So my Grandmother and Grandfather Dunne stayed in Ireland with Seamus and Mary.

My dad made friends with my uncle Fergus while they waited in Ireland for a ship and that's how he became friends with my mom. They had to wait in Ireland for more than a month before they could get on a ship because of all the people waiting to go to America. The ship was not a big one and it was crowded and stinky. It took 8 days to cross the ocean. On the last day my dad and mom got married on the ship by the captain. When they got to America my Uncle Fergus went to New York but my dad came to the mine here because he already knew how to be a miner. My uncle Fergus did boxing where they bet on who would win the fight. Somehow he got killed but my dad doesn't know why.

My dad and mom settled in this mining camp. After a while my mom had a baby boy named Brian that died a few days after he was born.

We can always tell when things are going good in the mine. That's when Pa plays his harmonica after dinner and we have a good time. He says we're lucky because not everyone has a job. I'm glad to have my pa and my stepmom.

Pa gets a little sad when he talks about my mom. He says I look just like her. Someday when he saves enough money he wants to take us all back to Ireland but I don't think we will ever have enough money for that. Besides, I'm used to living here.

I like a boy named Hugh Braeden. He is a year older than me and already works in the mine. He thinks it's funny that I like to read, but he likes it when I tell him stories I read. Last month we kissed on the way home from the dance. It made me happy that he likes me. Pa says Hugh is a good worker and has a good future.

Mr. Kappel says I am his best student and lets me take books home. Pa doesn't like me to stay up and read because it wastes candles but Mr. Kappel gave me extra ones. His family runs the mine and they are rich. He even has a automobile. He lives in a big house way down the road. Mr. Kappel told us his grandfather came from Germany many years ago.

* * * * *

The Kappel family emigrated from Germany in 1840. They settled in North Eastern Pennsylvania where the anthracite coal mines were being developed.

The Kappel family worked hard building the canals needed to transport coal to the local rivers and on to eastern cities. They became prominent building contractors, and as the coal mining operations expanded, became mining contractors. In 1864, Werner Kappel was born and by the time he was a man, the Kappel family owned the coal mine. Werner married Louise and they had three children, all boys, named Lars, Oswald, and Arthur. Arthur was the youngest by ten years. Werner and Louise were proud of their achievements and made every effort to gain status in the world of the affluent.

Lars, being the oldest, got the brunt of parental worry. Oswald had it a little easier, and by the time Arthur was born he could do pretty much whatever he wanted.

Lars and Oswald were absorbed into the family business early on, but Arthur went to boarding schools in Boston and then attended Boston University where he graduated in three years at the age of twenty.

During the summer, when Arthur was a teenager, he roamed all around the family estate, the city, and even the coal mine. The life he saw in the mining camp was very different from Boston and his home.

After Arthur graduated and returned home, he often complained to his father about the working and living conditions of the coal miners. Werner grew tired of arguing and put Arthur in charge of the company school. Arthur was given an allowance of $150 per year for books and supplies. It would be the first time the company school had enough books and other materials. Arthur Kappel now had an occupation, and he took it seriously.

* * * * *

Saturday, May 11, 1918

It's night now but this has been a good week. The weather has been fine and it was easy to do our washing today.

In school we have been learning about the big war across the ocean. Some of the men have had to leave the mine to go and fight. I don't know if Hugh will have to go.

Mr. Kappel is a good teacher and makes history and other subjects interesting. Mrs. O'Boyle is the other teacher and she mostly helps the younger kids.

Sunday, June 9, 1918

It has been windy the past few days but it was quiet and warm today. Hugh walked me home from church and we held hands.

Last night was a dance at the school. Afterward when everyone was going home we kissed again. There was no moon and it was dark outside. My family likes Hugh and his family likes me.

After Hugh walked me home I lit one of the candles that Mr. Kappel gave me and stayed up for a while reading a book called The Adventures of Tom Sawyer. It's harder to read than the books I learned on but the story is interesting. This is the longest book I ever read.

Thursday, June 13, 1918

After breakfast Pa left for work and I saw Hugh walking to the mine with the other men. He smiled and waved at me.

I have been enjoying the book about Tom Sawyer. School is over for the summer but Mr. Kappel is always around to help anyone who wants to practice reading or numbers. I like to go there after lunch when our chores are done. Also I sometimes have questions about some of the words in the book I am reading.

This past week Mr. Kappel has been telling us stories about history. Today there were 7 kids who showed up.

Mr. Kappel told the story of Abraham Lincoln. He was poor like us but he studied hard and became an important person. He grew up and became a president of our country and helped free the slaves. We learned about the Civil War and how Abraham Lincoln was killed. It made us all sad when Mr. Kappel told about President Lincoln being assassinated. It was a sad word to add to my words list.

Sunday, June 23, 1918

It has been another nice week. It gets warm during the day but in the morning it is cool and makes doing our chores easy. I enjoy working with my stepmom. I'm glad Pa married her.

Sunday, June 30, 1918

Hugh's team won the contest they were having this past week for mining the most coal. Mr. Kappel's father even came over and gave all the miners on his team an extra dollar.

Thursday, July 4, 1918

It has been a fun holiday. There were some fireworks and firecrackers. For the box social I made 2 sandwiches and put in an apple. Hugh used the extra dollar he got from winning the contest to buy my box dinner. We had fun eating together outside on the blanket with his family.

It was fun that Mr. Kappel has been around. All us kids like him. The rest of his family are never around except for business.

Sunday, July 14, 1918

This past week Mr. Kappel told stories about how our country got started and why we had the 4th of July celebration. We don't have any tests at school because of summer but it is fun to learn.

Church was nice and afterward me and Hugh walked over to the meadow and picked flowers. I told him about the history we have been learning. He told me about the tools he was using in the mine. Even though he had a bath last night you can still see coal dust here and there. That's the way all the miners are. My stepmom always said at least it's clean coal.

Sunday, July 21, 1918

It's very hot and everyone is sweating all the time. I hate to say it this way but everyone is a little stinky. I'm glad for the extra candles because it is easier to read at night when it's cooler.

It's been fun this past week hearing the stories about how our country got started. We learned about Benjamin Franklin and how he invented things, like the stove we use to cook our food and also warm the house in winter. He lived in Philadelphia that is about 150 miles from here. We did a fun problem to see it would take about 7 days of walking to get to Benjamin Franklin's house from here.

I'm almost done with the Tom Sawyer story.

Sunday, July 28, 1918

This past week the moon was out and we did some of our washing at night when it wasn't so hot. I finally finished the book about Tom Sawyer. I really liked it. I gave it back to Mr. Kappel. I've been learning my times tables even though it's not school.

Wednesday, July 31, 1918

Hugh got hurt today. A coal car that was being loaded bumped into some of the men but Hugh was hurt the worst. When the whistle started blowing in the middle of the afternoon I knew something was wrong. They took him to the hospital in Carbondale. I haven't seen him. I am so worried. Everyone is worried.

Thursday, August 1, 1918

Both of Hugh's legs are smashed and part of his hip. I sure hope he is going to be ok.

Friday, August 2, 1918

I don't understand it. They said Hugh died. I just don't understand it.

Saturday, August 3, 1918

We had a funeral today for Hugh at the church. I cried a lot and so did many others. His mom cried the worst. His dad was getting worn out and Hugh was helping to make extra money for the family. I thought maybe we would get married someday.

Sunday, August 18, 1918

It is so hot. Between being sad and the heat I haven't done any reading or numbers. I haven't been by the school for a while, just doing the chores like usual. Everyone is depressed because of Hugh getting killed. It makes me sad just to write these words. I miss him and think about him all the time. It's just not fair. I didn't get to see him or say good bye.

Sunday, September 1, 1918

Everyone sang and prayed for the miners. I don't know if I can ever stop being sad. I went by the school yesterday and Mr. Kappel was there. He was very sorry about the accident. He gave me another book to read called The Hunchback of Notre Dame. Since I was sad he said I should read a sad book. It's a really big book, bigger than the Tom Sawyer book.

Most everyone gets up early to do the washing before it gets too hot. Sometimes I wake up in the morning because I can hear other ladies getting their wash tubs ready and I know I need to get started. Most of the time we start when it is barely light, before the sun is up.

Serendipitous Rescue

<u>Sunday, September 22, 1918</u>

School has started and even though it's hot it's nice to be back in school. I've been able to read about 8 pages each night and I'm not even half way through the book. It's a very long book, the most pages I've ever seen in a book. It's in France. I like this story but it sure is hard to read sometimes. There are so many words that I have to learn but I like to learn them. At school we have been learning about other countries and other places.

Last night I had a dream about Hugh and me walking in the meadow.

<u>Sunday, September 29, 1918</u>

This past week Mr. Kappel gave us an assignment to write about a small thing that happened to us in the past that still affects us. It was for us older students. I thought about writing about my mom dying or Hugh dying but those are big things so I wrote about the time I lost my favorite blouse. It was when I was 11 years old before my dad married my stepmom. It was summer time and we had washed some clothes at night and put them on the line next to our house to dry. During the night it got really windy and when we went outside in the morning the clothes were everywhere. Mrs. Barrett lived next door and helped me look for the clothes. She always said if the clothes were clean a little dust wouldn't hurt anything. We just had to shake the dust out. The problem is that we couldn't find my favorite green blouse anywhere. We looked all over but it was gone. Now, every time I put clothes on the line by our house I think about losing our clothes in the wind and especially my green blouse.

<u>Sunday, October 13, 1918</u>

My dad said it would take time and I wouldn't be as sad about Hugh. I'm still sad but he is right. Another boy wanted me to go to the dance last night but I didn't feel like it. The story about Notre Dame is sad. I still have lots more pages to read. I have used so many candles but Mr. Kappel says it's ok. I don't know how he gets so many but he is rich.

It's getting colder now. It's much easier to do our cleaning and cooking but I dread when it gets really cold.

Some people have been getting sick. More than usual.

Sunday, October 20, 1918

Mr. Kappel got sick. He hasn't been at the school for 2 days. After we got back from Mass my dad started getting sick. The other kids have gone off to play. My step mom is worried about pa.

Sunday, October 27, 1918

I haven't had a chance to read any books or write in my diary this whole week. Pa has been really sick and now my step mom isn't feeling well. Patrick and Andres started to throw up and now Darcy has a fever. I haven't been to the school all week. Lots of families seem to be getting sick. I have been doing all the cooking and cleaning.

Tuesday, November 12, 1918

My step mom seems to be doing better but it's hard to say. Pa is not doing well at all. We can't get the doctor to come by because so many people are sick. Everyone says they have never seen anything like it. I heard that the whole Kappel family has gotten sick. I went by the school on the way to the store and Mr. Kappel was there but he didn't look good. He asked about my family and I told him about everyone being sick. He gave me some more candles and told me the whole country was getting sick and it was one of the worst diseases ever and was going all over the world. He gave me some medicine and told me not to tell anyone because they don't have enough to go around. The candles come in handy for taking care of everyone during the night. Mr. Kappel says he is working on getting electricity for the houses.

Thursday, November 14, 1918

Pa died. Patrick and Andres are very sick. The fever is bad. The priest came by and did the last rites. I am so tired.

Serendipitous Rescue

<u>*Sunday, November 17, 1918*</u>

Patrick and Andres have died. Now it's just me and my step mom and Darcy. My step mom is sick but not all the way sick. Darcy has a fever and hasn't eaten. I gave her some of the medicine that Mr. Kappel gave me. We are desperate. I'm worn out from taking care of everyone. My step mom has a fever but hasn't gotten sicker. There is so much to worry about. Now we won't have a way to pay for the house we live in and we have no where to go.

<u>*Wednesday, November 20, 1918*</u>

Mr. Kappel came by to see how we are doing. He said his dad died and his mom is sick but getting better. No one knows what is going to happen at the mine. He told me and my step mom not to worry that he would make sure we wouldn't have to leave the house. He was surprised that I never got sick. He asked if I took the medicine and I told him no I gave it to Darcy. He says I might have a natural immunity. He had to explain it to me and spell it for me. I added it to my words list. It might keep me from getting the sickness that is going around. It is true that not everyone got sick but a lot did. He said one of these days he will explain about germs and how they work.

He has the school going again but lots of kids don't come because of the sickness.

I gave him back the book about the hunchback. I can't finish it. Every time I look at it I think of my dad and everyone being sick. Mr. Kappel said it was too bad but it was normal for me to feel that way about it. He is so smart about things. It's like he knows about everything.

<u>*Sunday, November 24, 1918*</u>

Yesterday Mr. Kappel drove around the coal truck for people to get their coal. The regular drivers are busy working in the mine. Anyone who is not sick is working in the mine. A lot of the people who are in charge are sick and it makes things confusing. Mr. Kappel came to our church today. He seems worn out and still sick a little.

Sunday, December 1, 1918

Mr. Kappel didn't come to our church today but it has been busy. He brought around some new blankets to people who needed them. Many people burned the clothes and bedding of sick people. I think my step mom is going to be ok.

One of our neighbors is a man who works in the mine and has a 5 year old boy named Josh. His wife died a few weeks ago. I think he wants to marry my step mom.

Sunday, December 8, 1918

This has been another hard week. Some other people got sick but some are getting better. Mr. Kappel says it's news everywhere how bad it is. They are calling it the Spanish flu. Mr. Kappel drove the coal truck around again this week to deliver coal to everyone. He had more blankets for people and even brought some food from the big store in Carbondale.

Saturday, December 14, 1918

It's very late but I must write about the Christmas tree. It is the most beautiful thing I ever saw. Mr. Kappel brought a pine tree for a Christmas tree to the school. He had some ornaments and we each got to put one on the tree. He had small electric lights that he put on the tree and had wires that went a long way to the machine that makes the electricity for the mine. When he turned on the Christmas Tree there were red and green lights. It is so beautiful I can't describe it.

Sunday, December 15, 1918

Our neighbor, Mr. Allen, walks with us to church. My step mom has been watching his boy during the day.

Monday, December 23, 1918

At school Mr. Kappel had extra candles for everyone, even some holly. We learned about Christmas traditions in different countries, including Germany with the Christmas Tree. I got to tell about our Irish tradition *of having holly and putting a candle in the window for the Christ Child. I was excited to take my own candle home for my own window.*

<u>Wednesday, December 25, 1918</u>

They shut down the mine today for Christmas but that's not the best thing. Mr. Kappel drove over the delivery truck and it was loaded with food. He brought meat and bread and eggs and all kinds of food from Carbondale. All the people who work here like him.

He wants to take his mom and brothers to Boston but they are too sick to travel. It sure is hard to believe but he said millions of people have died.

<u>Sunday, January 12, 1919</u>

Today is my birthday and I am now 17 years old. It is cold and windy. I'm glad we have this kind of coal because when we get home from church the stove is still going and nice and warm. I feel sorry for people who don't have good coal to keep them warm.

Mr. Kappel came to our church today. After church he had a birthday present for me. It was a dictionary and is my very own. It has all the words and now I don't have to write words down in my word list any more. He said I was his best student. He said that before. It made me feel warm inside.

2

Family Business

Sunday, January 19, 1919

School has been good. For the younger kids, it's all day but for the older ones like me is only for a short time because we have work to do. My step mom is feeling better and lets me go to school for 4 hours a day. Mr. Kappel brought in a newspaper for us to read. We are also learning more about history.

Sunday, January 26, 1919

My stepmom and Mr. Allen got married yesterday. It's very practical because he needs us to watch Josh during the day and we need money to live.

Church was nice today but it was even nicer to come home to a warm kitchen. It was so windy and cold outside. Mr. Allen sits with us in church now. My stepmom is in a better mood now that everyone is not so sick. My stepmom said I can be at the school for 5 hours every day because we are getting our work done. Mr. Kappel set up 2 electric washing machines inside the school toward the back for everyone to take turns using. It makes the laundry go much easier but if people don't get their laundry done early they have to wait until school is over to use them. They also put electric lights in so we can do laundry at night. They also added lights to the school room. It would be easier to do laundry at night if we had lights where we hang up the clothes to dry. I don't like leaving the washing out at night, especially in the wind.

Serendipitous Rescue

Wednesday, January 29, 1919

I've been spending a lot of time at the school and it is wonderful. We are learning more about the history of America and Ireland and Germany, and why we had the big war. There are still a lot of sick people but things are getting better.

People are talking about the arguments that are going on at the mine. I asked Mr. Kappel about it and he said since his dad died his brothers can't agree about who's in charge.

Sunday, February 2, 1919

It's really cold. The snow is hard and crunchy and it is not fun doing the laundry, even with the electric washing machines.

Thursday, February 6, 1919

It was an interesting day today. It started yesterday when Mr. Allen, my new stepfather, said I should spend more time working and less time in school. I told Mr. Kappel and after work when Mr. Allen was home from the mine, Mr. Kappel came to our house and talked to Mr. Allen. Mr. Kappel talks very nice and smiles a lot but he said it wouldn't be good for his job if they didn't let me go to school. Then he gave my mom and Mr. Allen 5 dollars and told them to buy food for a nice dinner for next Sunday. They shook hands and it seems everyone is in a good mood, especially me.

Tuesday, February 11, 1919

It's easier to write in my diary now because I can do it at school if I want. It's nice not to have to work so much during the day. Besides there's plenty of time after school to do the cleaning and help with cooking and we can't do laundry anyway during school if we want to use the electric washing machines.

Mr. Kappel says that he may have to go to Boston next week because of the family trouble. He wants me to help other kids in school while he is gone. I'm getting good with my numbers and writing and I'm a pretty good reader. I will do my best to help out.

Monday, February 17, 1919

Everything went good at the school today. Mr. Kappel is in Boston and will be gone for the rest of the week, probably. My stepmom is happy that I am doing an important job and I still can do my chores. Mr. Allen has been nice and saying things like the dinner was very good and things like that.

Saturday, February 22, 1919

Mr. Kappel got back today and came by to see how things went. I told him that it went very well at the school. He said he already talked to some others and they said the same thing. Mrs. O'Boyle has been sick a lot and Mr. Kappel said to my stepmom and Mr. Allen that he wants me to be a helper at the school and he will pay me some money that I can use for my family. Everyone was very agreeable especially me. Now I can be at the school all day.

Monday, February 24, 1919

Today was my first day of working at the school as the helper. Mrs. O'Boyle was not here so it was good that I can help the kids with their reading and numbers. It's good practice for me, too. Mr. Kappel wants me to read to the kids each day and maybe they will learn to like reading like me. Tomorrow I will start reading The Swiss Family Robinson book to them. We will read a few pages each day.

Friday, February 28, 1919

The school job is going good. Mr. Kappel says the kids are learning their numbers better from me than Mrs. O'Boyle. That made me feel good. They like the time that we spend in the afternoon reading the story.

Mr. Kappel had to leave early today. He walked all around the mine with some men with and also his 2 brothers.

Serendipitous Rescue

<u>Sunday, March 2, 1919</u>

At church today more people said hi to me than usual. I'm still getting used to Mr. Allen being my stepfather and sitting with us in church. I miss pa and Patrick and Andres so much. Everything is changing. I feel sad. I try not to cry. I'm glad for school.

<u>Tuesday, March 4, 1919</u>

Yesterday was busy and so was today but Mr. Kappel said the school is doing well. For reading time the kids are using the beginning books that Mr. Kappel brought last year and I help the kids when they are learning a new word. Some kids are working on the very easy words and some others are working on harder ones. Everyone is different and it makes me feel smart to be able to help them. In the afternoon I've been reading to the kids and they like it. We're still on the Swiss Family Robinson story.

<u>Friday, March 7, 1919</u>

It has been interesting this past week. People around here are calling me Miss Quinn and saying good morning Miss Quinn and hi there Miss Quinn. I really like being a helper at the school. It makes me feel happy and important.

<u>Sunday, March 9, 1919</u>

Yesterday was Saturday and more people came around to see the mine. Mr. Kappel was with his brothers again and this time his mom came along. They came by the school and everyone said hello but his mom seemed grumpy. I felt embarrassed. Everyone was dressed in fancy clothes and looked at me in a way that made me feel bad.

It's funny how one day you can feel important and the very next day you feel dirty and small.

<u>Wednesday, March 12, 1919</u>

School is going ~~good~~ very well. I get to be a teacher and I also get to learn a lot. Mrs. O'Boyle is back teaching the younger kids and I still help but now I can spend more time studying. I still read in the afternoon to the kids and now I am reading a book called "The Secret Garden" to them. Mr. Kappel says it's a new book.

I am learning to write and speak better. Sometimes after most of the school is done for the day Mr. Kappel helps me learn the right way to say things. It's nice because it's just him and me and I learn more quickly that way. I showed him what I have been writing in this diary and he was very happy and said I'm doing a wonderful job. The way he said it made me happy. He also showed me how to write things better, like the name of a book.

It has been bothering me about how the people made me feel last Saturday. The funny thing is that Mr. Kappel is rich and smart and has nice clothes but he doesn't make me feel dirty or small.

The electrician men started working on the houses today. They are putting in wires to each house so we can have lights.

Saturday, March 15, 1919

I did my laundry in the school room today. Mr. Kappel was there working on some papers and we were able to talk about things while my laundry was in the washing machine. I will say that the electric washing machine is sure a lot easier than washing the clothes by hand. Mr. Kappel said that some more men will probably be coming to see the mine in a few days or a week. I asked him if his mom would be coming too and he laughed and said no she was on her way to Florida for a few weeks. I must have made a face or something because he said not to worry about his mother. He said his mother does not like me working in the school with him but he doesn't care.

The electricians put lights in our house today. The house we live in has 2 bedrooms and a kitchen and a main living room. We have 4 lights, one in each room. There is a switch on the wall for each room. You can see the wire that goes to the light and to the switch. At night we turned on the light and it is so much brighter than the candles. You can tell when the machines are running in the mine because the lights will flicker or get dim for a second and then get bright again.

Serendipitous Rescue

<u>Sunday, March 23, 1919</u>

After church today we had a nice dinner. I helped my stepmom cook and with the extra money from me working in the school we had extra food. My stepmom said she was proud of me and how smart I was. It gets harder and harder to remember my mom that died.

I still use candles when I read at night. The electric lights are good for cooking and eating but they are too bright at night and it keeps people awake if I don't use candles. I'm used to the candles anyway.

<u>Wednesday, March 26, 1919</u>

It's very late and I'm so worried I can't sleep. A man came by the mine this morning. He didn't stay very long and Mr. Kappel and his brothers showed him around. Afterward his 2 brothers went off with the man and he came back to the school. At the end of the day when we usually talk, I asked Mr. Kappel why people were coming to see the mine. He said that since his dad died his family can't decide on how to run the business and it's causing trouble. He said that his family wants to sell the business to someone else and that means that his family wouldn't be running the mine any more. I asked if he would still be the teacher and he said no. I couldn't help myself and started crying. He took both of my hands and said it would be ok and I don't have to worry and that it wouldn't happen for a while. He said he needed to leave right away but we will talk about it tomorrow and not to worry. But I do worry. Things will change. What if the new people are mean?

3

Romance

<u>*Thursday, March 27, 1919*</u>

Today was the biggest shock of my life and a day I will never forget. After school when people started coming in to do the laundry, Arthur asked me to go for a walk so we could talk in private. He asked me to call him Arthur instead of Mr. Kappel. He asked me if I liked him. Of course I did but what he meant is if I liked him like love. He said that he loves me and wants me to think about it. I said I didn't need to think about it and he kissed me on the lips. He told me that it will take a while before they sell the company but when they do he wants to take me away with him and go live in Pittsburgh.

I can't describe how surprised and happy I am. Arthur says we shouldn't talk to other people about it because it would be a problem with his family. It will be our secret for now. Arthur told me now because he didn't want me worrying about the business. It's hard to think about regular things knowing that I will be leaving this place. Arthur says his mom will never like me but it doesn't matter because we will be far away from her and he will probably never see his family again once they sell the business.

It's late again and I can't sleep but now it's because of being excited instead of worrying. Just saying or writing <u>Arthur</u> makes me shiver and be warm inside.

Serendipitous Rescue

<u>Friday, March 28, 1919</u>

Nothing seems the same anymore. I had a hard time looking at Arthur and not thinking about the walk we took. It was hard to concentrate. We went on another walk today after school. He told me he admired me for a long time and if you admire someone you can fall in love easily. It must be true because I sure admire him but that's easy because he is smart and rich and looks very nice. I am plain and poor and I can't think of anything special about me. He said that probably around the time it's my 18th birthday he hopes the business will be sold but it's hard to say exactly. One reason they are putting electricity in the houses and doing other things is to make the mine look as good as possible so they can get the most money when they sell it.

There are still lots of sick people but not many people are dying. I don't know how long this will keep going. At least there aren't as many sick as before.

<u>Sunday, March 30, 1919</u>

At church today all I could think about was Arthur and what is going to happen. Arthur said we must try to pretend that we are just good friends working together at the school. He said it was his idea to sell the company because once they do he can get his part of the money and leave his family to start a new life. It's sad that he doesn't like his family but he is very different from them.

I think about him resting in his nice big house. He said he is still not over being sick and needs to rest all day on Sunday. That worries me but he said sometimes when people get real sick it takes a long time to get all better.

<u>Friday, April 4, 1919</u>

I'm getting used to being at the school and trying to be normal but it's hard. Arthur and I look at each other and smile. Tomorrow is Saturday and Arthur wants me to ride with him to Scranton to get some more paper, pencils, candles, and other supplies for school. He told me to ask my stepmom if it was ok to go with him to the store in Scranton. She said it would be fine and seemed very pleased about it. Once again I have a hard time sleeping. I've never been in an automobile before. I washed myself pretty good tonight. Sometimes I wonder why Arthur ~~likes~~ loves me.

Saturday, April 5, 1919

It was such a delightful day today, probably the best day of my life. About 10 o clock he came over to our house. I can tell by the way my stepmom looks at me that she is thinking something. She smiled and told us to have a good time. Then we walked over to his automobile.

It was exciting to ride to Scranton. I've never been there before and we went so fast. Arthur said we were going 40 miles per hour sometimes. It took us a little more than an hour to get there but we weren't driving that fast all the way.

We went to a big store that was really big. Everything in Scranton was bigger and nicer than the mining camp. There were so many people and cars everywhere. And so many roads and houses and buildings. It's like everyone was rich there.

At the store ~~Mr. Ka~~ Arthur bought several packages of paper, some notebooks, 2 cases of candles, pencils, some chalk, and some boxes of laundry soap. The store had many rows of shelves and while we were back in one corner he gave me the best hug I ever had and kissed me on the lips again. He didn't say anything and neither did I. We just looked at each other and then he kissed me again. Then he said he will be happy when we can leave this place. He said he was glad that I loved him.

After putting everything in the car I thought we would go back to the mine but Arthur asked if I was hungry. I was still thinking about kissing in the store but when I thought about it I was hungry so he took me to a restaurant. Arthur said it wasn't a fancy one but it sure seemed like one to me. We went in and sat down at a small table with 4 chairs. A person came and gave us a piece of paper with a list of the different foods you could get there. Outside the windows you could see everyone walking and driving cars. I was having a hard time figuring out what food to get and Arthur said why don't we both get hamburgers. That sounded good to me so that's what we did. We got Coca Cola, too. I had it before but not for a long time. That was the best tasting meal I ever had. The hamburger was big and I had a hard time eating it. I felt awkward being there and eating the big hamburger but Arthur didn't seem to mind. I had to go to the bathroom and they had one inside the restaurant that was a flushing toilet. I found out that his birthday is March 5. He is 23.

After we ate our dinner we got back in the car and rode back to the mining camp. I wished it would take all day to get back. Along the way we talked and when the road was straight Arthur held my hand.

When we got back I helped carry the things we bought to the school. The whole camp looked different to me now. The school and all the buildings were not painted and nice looking like in Scranton. There are only a few roads here and not fancy. At least we have trees. The school seemed small and the houses seemed small. Everything was the same but different. People were using the electric washing machines and Arthur brought over the laundry soap and put it on the shelf in the corner for everyone to use.

Arthur said thanks for your help and said good bye. I just said you're welcome and left but we looked at each other and smiled and I don't think anyone noticed.

My stepmom asked how it went today since we were gone for so long. I told her about the big city and the supplies we bought for the school and eating the hamburger for lunch. She smiled and said she was glad I could do that. Darcy teased me about being away with Arthur.

I took the laundry over to the school to wait my turn with the washing machines. Arthur was not there which made it feel empty. A lady was just finishing and said she would hurry up and get out of my way. I said not to worry but it made me wonder if people were thinking about me different.

When my washing was done I carried the clothes back to my house and put them on the line to dry while my stepmom was cooking dinner. I could hear her arguing with Mr. Allen about me going with Arthur today. He doesn't like that Arthur didn't ask his permission.

My candle is almost out and everyone is asleep but I'm much too excited about the day to go to sleep.

Monday, April 7, 1919

At school today, after the lessons, I told Arthur about the lady wanting to get out of my way and how people say hello Miss Quinn and other things like that. He smiled and said we weren't doing a very good job about our relationship. He asked me if that bothered me. I said that in one way I liked it but in another way it did bother me. He said that's what he liked about me. He said the best thing to do was to help people in little ways, like help them carry their laundry or do little things for people. He said to talk to everyone and just be nice. That way they won't think I'm special or better than them. Once again I could see that he was so smart about things.

Sunday, April 13, 1919

This past week I helped at the school like usual and worked on my grammar and writing. Also I like reading to the kids each day in the afternoon. After school was out and the ladies started bringing their laundry in, I helped them load the washing machines and asked them how they were doing. It's surprising how many ladies liked to talk about things. I've learned about other people who lost family to the Spanish flu, husbands with injuries, and so many other problems. I'm getting to know people that I've seen many times but never talked to before. At church today people are still saying "hi Miss Quinn" but now it seems more like they are happy to see me and not just being nice.

Monday, April 14, 1919

After school I talked with Arthur again. He always seems rested and healthy on Monday. When he is resting he has a chance to think about things. He told me today that it's possible things might not go well and would I still like him if he ended up being poor. Of course I would still like and love him. He is a nice person and very smart and I admire him.

Sunday, April 20, 1919

I've kept busy this week but told Arthur I'm having a hard time concentrating and that it's hard to read and think because my mind is always thinking about him and what might happen in the future. He gave me a book to read "Anne of Green Gables" which is a mostly happy book about an orphan girl. I'm kind of an orphan. Arthur said I should keep myself busy and distracted for the next few months. Of course he is right as usual and that's what I plan to do.

Saturday, May 3, 1919

I have been keeping busy and reading. I'm back to reading at night with my candles. Arthur gave me another book "Little Women" and I'm getting so I can read easier and easier and I like these stories. I've also been busy with chores. I'm getting along better with Mr. Allen. I think he likes it that other people are always saying "hello Miss Quinn."

Sunday, May 11, 1919

It's Sunday and things have been pleasant. The sickness seems to be going away and there aren't that many sick people any more. Arthur said more miners were killed by the influenza than from all the mining accidents that ever happened.

Some of the kids are singing a little tune when they are playing outside, especially when they jump the rope. It's about the Spanish Flu:

There was a little bird and its name was Enza.
We opened up the window and in flew Enza.

I finished the "Little Women" book.

Monday, May 12, 1919

Last Saturday I told Arthur that I finished the book and he said it was time to read a really big book and today he brought in the biggest book ever called "Les Miserables" by the same man who wrote about the hunchback. It's another story in France. Arthur said it will take me a long time to read it but we can talk about it each day.

Friday, May 16, 1919

I've been talking to Arthur about the story. I've read about 20 pages. It's not as easy as the other books. I can tell Arthur likes it so I will read it even if it's hard.

Arthur is going to Boston again and will probably be coming back Tuesday or Wednesday and asked me to help take care of the school for him.

Wednesday, May 21, 1919

Arthur got back today and he has a man with him who is an attorney that is going to help Arthur sell the business. Arthur says he is too young and his brothers aren't much help. He needs someone who is important and who knows how to convince people. Arthur brought him by the school and he shook my hand. His name is Mr. Johnson. He was smiling and jolly but you could tell by the way he talked that he was very smart. Arthur said Mr. Johnson will get to keep 10 percent of the money for selling the business. Arthur said that if he tried to sell the business he would probably only sell it for 200 thousand dollars or so because he doesn't know how to sell better. That sounded like a lot of money to me. But Arthur said if Mr. Johnson sells the business he can probably sell it for more than 400 thousand dollars so even if they have to give him 10 percent they still get more money that way. I would never have thought of that. I can't believe so much money.

Serendipitous Rescue

The fun thing is that Arthur brought a beautiful stained glass window for the church that he got from Boston. It is a little bigger than him. It is a picture of Jesus being a shepherd and the hills are green and everyone says it looks like Ireland. The priest is very happy. Arthur said he will pay some men to get it installed in the church. The priest likes Arthur even though his family goes to the Lutheran Church.

Sunday, May 25, 1919

I have a hard time concentrating because of thinking about everything and selling the business and leaving to go off with Arthur. I like the "Les Miserables" story but it's harder to read but I will keep reading it.

Sunday, June 1, 1919

The men have finished working on the new window Arthur brought for the church. It is even more beautiful in the church. Arthur came to our church again today. Everyone loves the new window.

I'm enjoying helping people by doing little things. It makes me feel good and I'm making more friends. People still think I'm important because I work at the school but they seem more friendly now and I'm always talking to someone. I have to say that Arthur has really changed my life.

Sunday, June 8, 1919

It's getting hot again. They started church an hour earlier so it wouldn't be so hot.

This past week Mr. Johnson came around with some people. Arthur was with them but Mr. Johnson did most of the talking. He kept talking about different numbers about this and that. When they came by the school I could hear him talking and it sounded like he was describing a different place than where I was. Later I asked Arthur about it and he said it was more like a little exaggeration and that mostly what he said was true.

Sunday, June 15, 1919

Arthur didn't come to our church today. It's hard to sit in church and think of God and Jesus with everything that's happening. That is so much money. Would I be living in a nice house and have a car if I get married to Arthur? Will I have nice clothes? What will happen? Will Arthur still like me if he gets rich from that money? It's not a good thought for church but I couldn't help it. I have to remember that Arthur does not like vanity.

Arthur has to go to Boston again for the business. I don't like it when he's not here.

Sunday, June 22, 1919

Arthur didn't get back till yesterday. It makes me nervous when he's gone and I'm hoping that nothing is wrong. I worry about the pretty ladies there dressed all nice. It's hard to sleep at night and I'm glad for my chores otherwise my imagination gets the best of me. It seems I'm either excited or worried. The business deal is complicated. Arthur said they are almost done.

It's really hot now. I feel sorry for the miners. I told Arthur and he said he was worried about them too and what would happen after they sold the business to someone else.

The past week has been nice, though. School is done for the summer but some kids like to come anyway and I read stories. There's a young boy who is interested in reading and he likes to come by the school.

Most people wait until it's dark and cooler to come by and use the electric washing machines. The only trouble at night is the bugs that fly around the light by the washing machines.

Thursday, June 26, 1919

Today is another day I will never forget.

Arthur left the school this morning and went to talk with Mr. Johnson. He came back this afternoon and waited while I finished the story to the kids. When I was done he was smiling and asked me if I wanted to go to the 4th of July picnic with him. I was shocked and couldn't say *anything. Arthur said the deal was done and there was nothing his family could do to change it. He hugged me right there in plain sight and kissed me again. A lady coming in to use the washing machine was quite shocked. The people here all like Arthur but this will be a big surprise for everyone.*

He explained that for the deal to work out he would have to remain for 2 more months to train the new people and explain things to them. The Kappel family would get 450 thousand dollars but not all at once. I can't remember the rest of it but we don't have to be secret any more.

Arthur walked with me back to my house and told my stepmom that he intends to marry me and does she have any objections. She said she wasn't surprised and would miss having me around but seemed very happy for me. Arthur visited for a while until Mr. Allen got home and we told him the news. At first he didn't seem happy or mad or anything. Then later I heard him talking in the other room with my stepmom. He said Arthur should have asked his permission to marry me. But Mr. Allen isn't my real kin. He does not like Arthur. I wish my stepmom didn't marry him.

Sunday, June 29, 1919

Arthur came to our church and sat by me. He said it would be best if we didn't hold hands and just acted proper. For one thing Mr. Allen is mad at Arthur and another thing it was only last year that Hugh died. I never thought my life would be so complicated. But Arthur is always smiling and nice to people. Afterward he talked to the priest about something.

Friday, July 4, 1919

It was an interesting day but it was fun. I liked being with Arthur and seeing how surprised people were. I felt bad for my stepmom. Mr. Allen was not in a good mood today. He didn't want to play any of the games but Arthur did. Even Darcy and Josh had fun.

I felt a little bad seeing Hugh's family but they were nice to me. Arthur made the Kappel family give them some money because of Hugh getting killed.

Even though I love Arthur I feel bad about Hugh. I still think about the nice time I had last year with him. Arthur said it's perfectly natural to feel that way. It seems life gets more complicated all the time.

Sunday, July 13, 1919

Arthur came to our church today. I wish Mr. Allen liked Arthur. Then we could have Arthur come to our house and eat with us.

Sunday, July 20, 1919

It was nice to have Arthur at our church today. He said he didn't like going to church with his own family.

I've kept busy doing chores and helping fix nice dinners for the family. I've been trying to be nice so Mr. Allen won't be grumpy.

Sunday, July 27, 1919

I had a good time with Arthur today. We walked around after church and held hands. Arthur even came to dinner. Yesterday he brought 2 pounds of fine beef and a sack of potatoes. My stepmom said it would be rude not to invite him for Sunday dinner so Mr. Allen agreed. Arthur doesn't seem to let things bother him. He is trying to get along with Mr. Allen. After dinner Arthur went back to his big house to rest.

Now everyone is in bed. While I was reading, I could hear Mr. Allen talking and he said he'll be glad when I'm gone and I'm not their real child anyway. I couldn't hear what my stepmom said. It made me sad but I have never felt like Mr. Allen was family to me.

Monday, July 28, 1919

After school I took a walk with Arthur and told him what I heard last night. He hugged me so nice and kissed me. He said we should get married soon because it's creating gossip about him and me and no chaperone.

I feel much better tonight. I only worry about my stepmom and Darcy.

Serendipitous Rescue

<u>Saturday, August 2, 1919</u>

I walked over to Hugh's grave today with his family. It's been a year since he died. I put flowers on his grave that I picked from the meadow. Sometimes I feel bad that I love Arthur.

<u>Sunday, August 3, 1919</u>

Today has been interesting and exciting. I will have a hard time going to sleep tonight.

Arthur came to our church again and sat with me. People are always nice to Arthur even though he doesn't belong to our church. Everyone has been extra nice because they love the beautiful window that Arthur brought.

After Mass, Arthur and I talked with the priest. We talked about us getting married. Arthur said Mr. Allen won't give his blessing and we want to get married in this church and we want to get married soon. The priest said since I don't really have any kin he could give his blessing to us. The only trouble is that since Arthur is a Lutheran we can't get married in the church. The priest said how about if we get married at the school. Then Arthur said how about if we get married at the dance at the school in 2 weeks.

Arthur went to rest at his big house. Mr. Allen was mad that I wasn't helping get dinner ready. He said I was dishonoring our Irish traditions. All I know is I love Arthur and he is a good man.

Arthur said his mom was mad. She said he was throwing his life away. Arthur said he will be glad to leave his family and is looking for an apartment in Carbondale.

<u>Saturday, August 9, 1919</u>

Arthur took me to Scranton today and we got a nice dress for me to get married in and rings for each other. A lady helped me get the right size and it was fun. We got lunch again at that same place. It was another good day.

Arthur said he found an apartment for us in Carbondale. We have to stay in town for a few more months so Arthur and his family can teach the new people how to run the mine.

When I got home Mr. Allen said I shouldn't be marrying a Lutheran and that Arthur bribed the priest by getting things for the church. I wish Mr. Allen didn't live here. I'll be glad to leave.

Sunday, August 10, 1919

Arthur came to our church today and sat with me. We talked to the priest about getting married next Saturday. Arthur said we should both just go to our own houses today and not cause trouble.

Wednesday, August 13, 1919

It's been fun with me and Darcy doing our chores together. She is happy for me to get married. It's been nice at the school to be there with Arthur. Not many kids come because of summer and Arthur has family business to take care of but I like to be there. I like reading to the children and I like helping the ladies who come in to use the electric washing machines. I just feel so happy. Everyone is in a good mood except for Mr. Allen.

Sunday, August 17, 1919

Yesterday was the best day of my life and another day I will never forget. Arthur came over with the priest right after lunch and we signed the papers for us to get married. Then he went back to his big house. Fortunately Mr. Allen was working all day.

My stepmom was happy for me and Darcy was happy to see me in my new dress. It seems that our wedding is not following my customs or Arthur's customs.

About 6pm me and Darcy and my stepmom walked over to the school where they were still getting ready for the party. It was strange walking there in my wedding dress. People were coming out of their houses and waving at me. Some were also coming over to the school for the dance. About the same time I heard Arthur's car arrive. He looked especially handsome. People were gathering around and talking and the fiddlers were getting ready and practicing and then the priest came in. The priest announced that we were going to have a short wedding ceremony but everyone already knew it. Everyone got quiet and the priest talked to us about love and marriage and we said our vows. My stepmom and Darcy were happy and so was everyone else. Mr. Allen was not there and I was glad of that. Everyone clapped and then the fiddlers started playing so it was like the dance was our wedding celebration. Arthur opened the company store and brought out some wine and sodas. It had been a hot day and the evening was warm and the dance turned into a big party. The person who is in charge of the store was worried and talked to Arthur and Arthur said to charge everything to the Kappel family and he would take care of it. By 10 o clock everyone was having a good time and it was probably the best dance party ever. I was just happy to be with Arthur. The dance party was still going on when we left. My stepmom hugged me and said good bye. We walked over to my house and gathered all my clothes and things and put them in Arthur's car. We got my books and papers and my diary but Arthur said I won't need the candles any more. Then we drove to Carbondale to the apartment that Arthur got.

The apartment has a bedroom and a kitchen and a sitting area and a bathroom with a bathtub and a flushing toilet. Arthur said it's not a fancy apartment but it sure seems nice to me. Arthur's things are already here. He has a bed and a desk and a chair and a big chair and a small table with 4 chairs. He also has lots of boxes of books and things from when he went to the university.

He said I looked beautiful. He hugged me and kissed me and asked me if I was happy and I said yes of course I am. We went to bed and snuggled for a long time.

Now it's Sunday afternoon and here I am in a strange new place. We cooked some eggs for breakfast but Arthur says we need to get more cooking things and more food. We have a nice ice box here.

After we had breakfast we closed the windows to keep the heat out. Arthur rested for a while. It's very quiet. I'm tired too and am going to lie down beside Arthur and rest. I am happy.

4

A New Life

<u>*Monday, August 18, 1919*</u>

It's night time now and Arthur has made a place for me to do my writing at this desk. He is lying on the bed watching me while I write. He likes that I am still writing in this diary. There is an electric lamp on the desk which is very bright and it makes it easier to write and look up words in my dictionary. I had a bath and it was nice. I was thinking it would be cold water but you can turn on hot or cold water and make it be however you want. It felt nice to be all clean. Arthur said I can have a warm bath any time I want.

Yesterday after Arthur rested we made some dinner together and it was fun. After we ate dinner we talked. Arthur asked me what I wanted to do, stay here until the business was over or keep working at the school. I said I would like to keep working at the school and I could tell that it made him happy. Besides, he would have to be spending some time there with the new people to show them how everything worked.

Arthur said he saw me go to the graveyard a couple weeks ago and asked how I was doing. I said I felt bad about being happy since it's only been a year since Hugh died. Arthur said Hugh was a nice person and it was tragic that he died. He said I should always feel love for him, and it was normal to feel guilty about being happy. I admire how Arthur always knows the answer to things.

Today we made breakfast again and then we drove back to the mine and walked by my house. I said hi to my stepmom and Darcy and went to the school. This afternoon after I finished reading to the kids people came in to do their laundry. Some people were saying hi Miss Quinn and then saying I mean Mrs. Kappel. Others remembered that I was married.

Tuesday, August 19, 1919

I started reading a new book to the kids today. It is very hot again and everyone is sweaty but the kids like this new story. It's called "The Wonderful Wizard of Oz" and I like the story too. Another story about an orphan girl. People sure do like to tell stories about orphans.

After the end of school I helped Arthur fix the clothes line in back of the school. One line had been broken and yesterday another one broke so Arthur brought some new wire and we put it up so now there is enough for more clothes to dry.

Then we went back to the apartment. Arthur asked if I was hungry and I sure was so we walked over to the store to get more food. It is bigger than the company store but not as big as the store we went to in Scranton. We bought cheese and eggs and butter and milk and potatoes and some sausages and some hamburger meat. We also bought some more knives and forks and spoons and a can opener and a frying pan and a pot. Across the street from the store is the bakery and we bought some bread. We had four bags of food and things and each carried two. We put the food in the ice box and cooked dinner again and it was fun to do it together. We fried some potatoes and hamburger meat and it was very good. We forgot to buy a sharp knife to cut things with so we had to use the eating knife but we laughed and had fun. Out the back window you can see trees and out the front you can see the street. Arthur says not to get too used to it because we will only be here for a few months. We had to open all the windows to let the air move through the rooms. Arthur said we need to buy an electric fan. It rained and made the air muggy. On the good side, we can see the fireflies easy at this place.

Wednesday, August 20, 1919

We got up early this morning and hugged and kissed a lot. Then we made breakfast using the eggs and sausage we bought last night. We didn't wash the dishes yet because for one thing we forgot to buy some soap and another thing we forgot to get a dish rag. I asked Arthur if he did any cooking before I got here and he just smiled and said no he was waiting for me.

The man who is buying the business came to the mine today so we had to get over there so Arthur could talk with him. His name is Mr. Oppenheimer. I went to the school to get things ready. Quite a few kids have started coming in and it's easier to teach them when it's cooler in the morning. Arthur introduced Mr. Oppenheimer to the foremen and walked around and then they went into the little mining office for a while. I read more of the Wizard of Oz book and the kids seem to really like it.

Everyone around here now just says "Hi Mrs. Kappel" and I smile and say "Hi" back to them. Arthur says I'm one of the smartest persons in the mining camp. That's something to think about.

We drove back to Carbondale and went to the store and got a sharp knife and some dish soap and a dish rag and some more towels and a dish drainer. We also bought an electric fan. It uses electricity to make the air blow. Since it's so hot tonight we can have the fan blow air on us while we're sleeping in bed or just sitting or while we're eating.

It's strange to go to the store and be able to buy anything I want.

We washed our dishes from before. Then we made dinner again and it was easier with the things we bought. After dinner we washed our dishes again and set them in the drying rack.

Thursday, August 21, 1919

I really like the electric fan. I wish we had one at the school but it has to be plugged in to the electricity. Arthur says that most all the houses in the cities have electricity.

It's not really school because of summer but Arthur still teaches like he did last year and I help. In the afternoon Arthur's brother Oswald came by and he was mad at Arthur for getting married to me and taking his furniture out of the house. Arthur said there was nothing they could do about it and pretty soon they would have to sell the house and share the money. I can see why he doesn't like his family. They make me nervous. Arthur said that was one of the reasons he got

Mr. Johnson to sell the business so that there was a contract that his family couldn't change. I'm glad Arthur thought of all this.

Tonight I cooked dinner while he rested. I can cook pretty well. After dinner we went for a walk and went over to the store and bought another electric fan. We have one blowing air on Arthur while he rests and another one on me while I write in my diary. Arthur says it's a good thing that I am writing and he thinks I'm doing a very good job and someday I'll be glad.

Friday, August 22, 1919

It was another hot day at the mining camp school. At least the kids like the story I'm reading about the Wizard of Oz.

Arthur had to leave for a while to talk with Mr. Oppenheimer. I think they are getting along good. Arthur wants to be friends so he can give Mr. Oppenheimer his ideas on how to run the mine.

When we got home Arthur took a bath and rested in his big chair while I made dinner. I had one fan in the kitchen and the windows were open and it was much nicer that way. It is so hot and humid that you can sweat by hardly doing anything.

I cooked some spaghetti with meat sauce that came from a can and that sure was easy. The only problem was that somehow when I dumped the spaghetti into the pan with the sauce it tipped over and spilled. Most went on the floor. I started crying while I was cleaning it up. Arthur came in when he heard the pan spill and me crying and helped me clean it up and said not to worry there are worse things. He said think of the miners who got killed or injured or the sick people and spilling spaghetti was nothing to worry about. He made me feel better and he is so right. I admire him even more and that makes me love him more. We walked over to a little place that sells hamburgers and hot dogs. There's no place to sit. You just get your food and pay for it and leave. We got a hamburger and a hot dog and took it back to the apartment and cut the hamburger and hot dog in half and each had a half of each. We had some 7 up in the ice box from yesterday.

While we ate I thought of the spilled spaghetti and said the reason I was upset is that where I came from spilling the dinner meant eating the spilled food or going hungry and I need to remember that life is

224

different now. Then Arthur said it was a good point and he needs to remember that to other people different things are important. Then he said he admired me for teaching him something and that we were good for each other.

I took a bath and then we snuggled for a long time.

Saturday, August 23, 1919

Today we had laundry to do. I said let's use the electric washing machines at the school so we did. We got there right after we ate some lunch and people were using them so we waited for our turn. The funny thing is that after we did our laundry and said hi to my stepmom we went back to the apartment and the electricity wasn't working. Arthur says that happens sometimes so I said that we might need candles after all and he laughed and said I was right. We walked over to the store while it was still light and bought a box of candles. We also got some more milk and ice and some Oreo cookies and some bread from the bakery. It got dark and we used the candles but then the electricity came back on and that was good because I was getting used to the electric fans and without electricity the fans don't work.

Tonight I let Arthur read my diary again. He likes what I have written and asked if I'm still interested in learning and I said yes. He said he will use what I am writing to help me learn to write better. He said he doesn't want it to be like he is in charge of me but I like it when he teaches me things so I think it will be fine.

Sunday, August 24, 1919

It's Sunday afternoon and Arthur is sleeping. We had a nice breakfast. I showed Arthur how I fry the bread in a pan to toast it. Then I cooked eggs and we ate it. I'm glad the electric fans are working. One is blowing air on Arthur on the bed and the other is blowing air on me but I'm going to lie next to Arthur and rest too. I love him so much and I worry about him but it seems that once he has rested he is ok.

Wednesday, August 27, 1919

The past few days we have gone to the school in the morning, then Arthur meets with Mr. Oppenheimer, then I read to the kids, visit my stepmom and Darcy, and we go back to the apartment.

We have been going for walks around the area and exploring. We hold hands and talk about things. I asked Arthur why he is so nice when the rest of his family is not. He said that when he was a teenager he used to ride his bicycle to the mining camp. He made friends with a boy who lived here named Billy. For several years they were good friends. Sometimes he even ate dinner with Billy's family. Billy eventually started working in the mine. One day he was killed in a cave in. It was many days before they found the body. Arthur said he could never stop thinking about it. He said it's hard not to care about people when you get to know them. He said his family didn't care and didn't understand why he was friends with the mining people. That's when he realized he liked the mining people more than his own family. Later when he went to the university in Boston he had a class about philosophy and there was a professor who said that you should study all the religions and find the best parts. I'm glad Arthur is the way he is because if he was like his family I wouldn't have met him.

Friday, August 29, 1919

I love living in this apartment with Arthur. He said if I really like it we can stay for a while. He wants to move to Pittsburgh but says there's no hurry and we might want to wait till after winter because he still has to sell the big house. I asked him what if his family doesn't want to sell it and he says they have no choice. I asked him what if they don't share the money and he said that Mr. Johnson takes care of that and they will probably be mad but there's nothing they can do about it. I'm glad I don't have to worry about it.

The boy who is doing well at our summer time school is named Jimmy. Maybe he will be able to help the kids when I leave. When I think about leaving I feel sad that I won't be able to help the kids and read to them. Then I feel sad thinking about leaving my stepmom and Darcy. But if I had to choose between them or Arthur I would choose Arthur. Sometimes I wonder why he chose me but I'm glad he did.

<u>Saturday, August 30, 1919</u>

It was a very fun day. Mr. Allen was gone to Scranton and won't be back for a few days so we invited my stepmom and Darcy and Josh to spend the day with us at the apartment. We drove in the car to my old house and they all got in and we all drove back to the apartment. They had fun riding in the car. My stepmom and Darcy helped me fix a nice dinner while Arthur showed Josh some pictures of animals from one of his books. We only had the 4 chairs and the small table and the chair from the desk so it was hard to eat but we had a good time.

We spent the afternoon visiting. My stepmom enjoyed the electric fan. It made me feel bad that she doesn't have one but they only have electricity for the lights and don't have the places to plug in the fan.

Later we all walked over to the store and got Oreo cookies and more milk. It was fun. When it started to get dark we drove them back to my old house. On our way back to our apartment I felt a little sad but being with Arthur always makes me feel better.

<u>Sunday, August 31, 1919</u>

I'm deciding that Sunday afternoon is just about the best time, especially when it's quiet. We have the windows open so the breeze can get in the apartment and the fan is blowing air and I can hear the cars go by and people talking when they walk by our apartment. It's a pleasant sound and I look at Arthur sleeping and feel so good inside. I wonder if he ever watches me when I sleep.

School is almost ready to start. I like talking to the ladies using the washing machines and try to help them and they seem happy to talk to me. Everyone calls me Mrs. Kappel now. Sometimes people say hi Mrs. Kappel and I forget they are talking to me.

I have noticed lately that it seems like people are more stinky or maybe I am just noticing it more. I told Arthur and he said it's because I get to have a bath any time so I smell nice. I asked him if I was stinky before and he laughed and said yes I was a little but you have to be nice to people even if they're a little stinky. Otherwise we would have never been friends and then we would never have fallen in love. It's more things for me to think about.

Serendipitous Rescue

<u>*Sunday, September 7, 1919*</u>

This past week the weather has been cooling down a little and regular school has started and Mrs. O Boyle is back. Since it's cool at night, Arthur put one of the electric fans on the kitchen table and pointed it to blow air out the kitchen window. He closed all the windows except the bedroom window and the fan blowing air out the kitchen window made outside air come in the bedroom window. We have been doing it this past week. I would have never thought of that.

After being at the school and the mine during the day we have been coming home to our apartment and having some food or sometimes we walk to the little place that sells the hamburgers and hot dogs. Then we go for a walk. We hold hands and walk all over the town. We found a little restaurant on the other side of town that Arthur didn't even know was there. He said we will go there one of these days. As far as I'm concerned I could live here forever.

<u>*Wednesday, September 10, 1919*</u>

We got some shocking news today. When I went by to say hi to Darcy and my stepmom she told me that they are moving to a new mining camp by Scranton. Arthur said Mr. Allen can't be happy here at our mine because of his pride.

<u>*Sunday, September 14, 1919*</u>

I finished reading "The Wonderful Wizard of Oz" at school. I let Jimmy read parts of the story out loud and he did ok. Arthur got me a new book to read for the kids called "Pollyanna." It's another story about an orphan girl.

Yesterday we bought a laundry tub and a washboard. The reason is that we went to the school to do our laundry but there were several ladies waiting to use the washing machines so I told Arthur let's do it back home. It's easier to use the electric washing machine but I wasn't in the mood to wait and we didn't have that much laundry. Besides, I'm good at washing clothes with a wash board. Arthur says that when we move to Pittsburgh we'll have a house with our very own electric washing machine.

Arthur had to go over to his big house while I was washing the clothes. He said his mom is back to help with selling the big house and she is mad about everything. When he was telling me about it he was laughing and said I wouldn't believe the things she was saying about me. I tried to laugh too but it hurt my feelings the way his mom doesn't like me. Then I got a tear and Arthur gave me a hug. He said his mom has been that way all her life. He said it was her loss because she will never get to know me. Sometimes I don't understand why Arthur is so nice.

Wednesday, September 17, 1919

Arthur said the transition to Mr. Oppenheimer is going well and that I'm not really a teacher any more at the school. He said that if I want I can still help out at the school. I said I did. Arthur said he has agreed to help Mr. Oppenheimer until October 31 but will probably help longer if needed. He wants to be sure that Mr. Oppenheimer will be nice to the miners.

We had a very nice walk again today. It's not as hot as before and it's getting dark earlier. While we were walking I talked to Arthur about the stories I have been reading to the kids and also the ones I have been reading myself. There are so many different stories and I wonder how people think of them. Arthur said that some stories are true but the ones I have been reading are made up and you can get an idea for a story anywhere. He said behind everything is a story. So I stopped and pointed to a tree and asked if there was a story about the tree. He thought for a moment and said once upon a time a girl was being chased by a bad wizard from a broken rainbow. She tried to throw rocks at the bad wizard but when she threw a stick it hit the wizard in the head and killed him. The stick started growing and turned into a beautiful tree that was big and strong and protected the girl for the rest of her life.

I thought it was a silly story and laughed. I picked up a rock and said is there a story about this rock? He thought for another moment and said once upon a time this rock lived dark and deep under the earth and wished it could see the sky and feel the sunshine. One day a miner was looking for coal and as he was digging he came across the rock. The miner was annoyed that the rock was in his way and threw it away but the rock landed in the mining cart and was pulled out of the mine. When the loaders found the rock they threw it away and it rolled down the hill and rested and now it could see the sky and was happy.

I laughed again but he was right. I said I wished I had an imagination like that. He looked at me and said someday I will. I looked at him and squeezed his hand and he squeezed my hand back and we both smiled.

By then it was starting to get dark and the lights were on in the houses as we walked by. We ate some cookies and milk and got ready for bed. I said Arthur was a good story teller and said he should tell a story about me. He said he would think of one and now I'm going to go to bed with my Arthur.

Thursday, September 18, 1919

I'm writing about the story Arthur told me last night. I can't remember the exact words but it is morning and we will be leaving soon.

Once upon a time there was a poor girl who lived in the mining camp. She was a princess but didn't know it. A witch had disguised the princess with coal dust and raggedy clothes. One day a king named Arthur came looking for the princess. He knew the princess was disguised so he asked a wizard to help him. The wizard created a magic candle that could tell a real princess and the flame would turn pink when it found one. The king traveled everywhere, looking for his princess. When he visited other lands, the flame of his magic candle turned pink whenever he was by other princesses. But they weren't his princess. He traveled to the sea and didn't find his princess. He traveled to the mountains and even the desert, but could not find the princess. One day he was visiting the coal mine and to his surprise, the flame of his magic candle started changing color. The king walked all over the mining camp, watching the magic flame. The closer he got to the princess the candle flame turned more and more pink. In this way the magic candle guided the king to the house of the poor princess and once he found her, he carried her away to his castle far away and they lived happily ever after.

Saturday, September 20, 1919

My stepmom and Darcy and Josh and Mr. Allen all moved to Scranton today. Arthur tried to be nice and asked if he could help them but Mr. Allen said no thanks. My stepmom seemed sad. Maybe someday my stepmom and Darcy can come to Pittsburgh.

Sunday, September 21, 1919

It's Sunday and Arthur is resting like he usually does.

I have been thinking about the story Arthur told me. He is very clever. This morning after we had breakfast, I asked if he was going to take me to his castle. He said he would but he needs to build it first. I said are you going to build a castle? And he said he has been thinking about it and that's what he wants to do. He looked through some books and boxes and pulled out a drawing of a beautiful house. He said a friend of his in college had drawn it for a class and gave it to Arthur because he admired it so much. Arthur said he will build that house for me and we will have our very own electric washing machine and an electric refrigerator too. The house looks huge and I said I didn't need a huge house like his family had but Arthur said he will build me a castle and I am his queen and we will have lots of children.

I don't know what to think about that. It's the afternoon now and I will wash the dishes and fold the laundry while he rests and then I will lie down by him and when he wakes up we will snuggle.

Sunday, September 28, 1919

I miss going to the little church in the mining camp but being here with Arthur and watching him rest is peaceful.

At school the kids like me reading stories like Pollyanna but I sometimes have to stop and explain things about the story. It's been strange to walk past my old house that is empty now.

Between helping Mr. Oppenheimer at the mine and helping with selling the big house Arthur has been busy and I'm glad I have been able to help him by cooking and taking care of the apartment. I asked him if he missed living at his big house and he said the apartment was the best place he ever lived. It sure is the best place I ever lived. He said any building can be a house but a home is where love and happiness abide. He said his big house was just a house.

He brought more books from his family's house in several boxes and said we should give some books to Mrs. O Boyle at the school.

It's been getting colder at night and we don't open the windows or use the fans at night. Arthur said pretty soon they will be starting up the boilers for the radiators. There are 2 radiators in the apartment that will get warm when they start the heating. I wondered about that since there is no fireplace here and the stove is just for cooking. Arthur says they burn the coal from the mines and the fire heats the water into steam and the steam goes to all the radiators in all the apartments.

Sunday, October 5, 1919

Arthur says that by the end of the month we will be all done with the mine and do we want to move right away or stay in our apartment until after winter. I asked what about the school and Arthur says we can help if we want to but no one will pay us to work there anymore. Arthur says we have lots of money now so it's up to me what we do. We don't have to decide today.

Sunday, October 12, 1919

We finally ate dinner at that restaurant we found a few weeks ago that Arthur didn't know about. We walked there yesterday after I did the laundry. We had to have our coats on because it's getting cooler now. This is a very nice time of year and I love it. The trees have been turning red and yellow for a few weeks and now the leaves are blowing all over the place in the wind. It's not too hot and it's not too cold. The sky was cloudy and we brought an umbrella. It rained a little.

There were only 4 tables inside but one was empty and we sat down there. It smelled really good, like stew cooking. They didn't have pieces of paper with the food on it but a woman came out and Arthur asked what they had and they said they had soup and salad and bread. So we said that was fine. They brought some bread and butter right out and it was fresh baked and warm and soft and very tasty. Then they brought out the rest of the food that they had already made. We could see people coming in and getting food in bags and leaving. We learned that lots of miners come in and get food from this place. There are many other mines around here besides the one we go to and lots of miners live around here in Carbondale. The soup was really good. I can see why people come here. It had vegetables and potatoes and meat and gave me a good idea for fixing food. They also had a salad that was tasty. With the soup and the bread, it was a good meal and we were full and it didn't cost much, only 20 cents each. Arthur asked about the people coming in to get food. They told us that if you bring in your own pail they will fill it for 5 cents.

Today is Sunday. It has been a day to just rest and do my writing. Arthur is resting again but he didn't seem as tired this week.

Sunday, October 19, 1919

We had a good week at the school and the kids really like me there. I told Arthur that I'm hoping we can stay here as long as possible and I love the kids. We finished the "Pollyanna" story and Arthur said maybe we could find a book that wasn't about an orphan girl. He said he had one called "The Jungle Book" that might be fun to read. It was about an orphan boy.

Saturday, October 25, 1919

Mr. Oppenheimer doesn't want Arthur to keep coming to the mine anymore so we decided I would stop at the school, too. We went by there and I said good bye to Mrs. O'Boyle and I cried a little. She is a very nice lady and was also sad. We took 2 boxes of books and some boxes of paper and pencils and gave them to her. We barely started reading "The Jungle Book" but we left it there too in case Mrs. O'Boyle wants to read it to the kids. Arthur and I both felt bad but we knew this day would come.

Arthur said let's walk to the little restaurant and have some dinner even though it's only 3 in the afternoon so we did. Walking with Arthur and holding his hand always makes me feel better. We were the only ones there at the restaurant. We got the same thing again, soup and salad and fresh bread. We bought an extra loaf to take back with us. We walked back to the apartment and the leaves are almost gone from the trees and the breeze is cold. The radiator was on and made the apartment cozy and warm.

We were both feeling a little sad and he said he had an idea. He got out some maps and said let's look at where we will be moving to. We looked at the maps and Arthur said that Pittsburgh was about 300 miles away and how long would it take to get there if we averaged 30 miles per hour in our car. I started doing the dividing and could see that it was an easy problem and it would take 10 hours. We talked about what it might be like and looked at the map to see what cities we would be travelling through. We talked for a long time and relaxed and ate some of the bread we brought back. Arthur took a bath and the apartment was nice and warm and then I took one too. Talking about our future made us feel better. We went to bed early and snuggled.

<u>*Sunday, October 26, 1919*</u>

While we were eating breakfast Arthur said he had another idea and let's go on a trip and see where we would be moving. We cleared off the kitchen table and put the maps on the table and looked at them again. Arthur said we could leave tomorrow morning. He said we should take 2 days because driving for 10 hours would be hard for him. We looked for places to stop along the way and decided we would try Bellefonte. It's about half way. I'm excited to think about it, going so far away. Arthur said let's start packing some clothes and things to take with us. Arthur has two suitcases from his big house that he used for going to Boston. We put our clothes together in the big suitcase and we will put shoes and other things in bags and some boxes in the car. We put our underwear and socks and things in the smaller suitcase. Arthur said it was the first time he ever had girl clothes in his suitcase. It will be hard to sleep tonight.

5

A Trip

We are at a small hotel in Bellefonte. I am so excited and this has been a wonderful day. Arthur has been to many places but I've never been farther than Scranton. We got up a little after 6 am and got some breakfast. We put the suitcases in the car trunk along with some bags and boxes. We stopped in Scranton for gas and water for the car and tried to find the place where my stepmom lives but no one knew about them. I was disappointed but Arthur says we will look again when we return.

Next we drove to the city of Bloomsburg. We went across a huge river on a bridge. It was almost noon and after we got more gas and water for the car we ate lunch in a small restaurant by the highway. Then we drove to Bellefonte. That took almost 3 more hours but sometimes we went 50 miles per hour. There are so many hills. It seems like we barely get through with one and we go up another hill. The car slows down if the road is steep but then we go fast on the way down.

This is a very cute and beautiful town. The people in the hotel were happy to see us. Arthur said we were newlyweds and everyone was very nice to us and helped us get our suitcases and things into room 105. They showed us where we can go to get food and we took a walk around the town and found a restaurant to eat in. Then we walked around some more and came back to the hotel room. It has a tiny bathroom but it does have a bathtub so we took baths. Arthur is already asleep and I'm so excited that I can't go to bed yet. We have the maps out and it's fun to look at them and see where we have been *driving and where the mining camp is. The hotel room has a radiator for heating just like our apartment in Carbondale. I feel bad that I'm having so much fun and the miners are working hard and the ladies are cooking and cleaning.*

Tuesday, October 28, 1919

We are in a hotel in the town of Indiana. We got here by accident. This morning we ate breakfast at the restaurant and then got gas and water for the car. We were supposed to take the highway to Youngstown but when we got to Dubois the highway was closed for construction and wouldn't be open for several hours. There was a detour to Punxsutawney and Arthur checked the map and said it would be ok. We kept having trouble with the car and had to keep putting in water. When we got to Indiana we stopped at a service station to get gas and the man said our radiator was leaking and needed to be fixed. I didn't know a car had a radiator but it does. Lucky for us we're not in a hurry. Arthur said let's spend the night here because they weren't sure how long it would take to fix the car so that's what we're doing. The service station man showed us where a hotel was and he rode with us over to the hotel and we took our things out of the car and the man took the car back to the service station. This is a very pretty town and I don't mind that we had to stay here. By the time we got our room figured out it was time for dinner and they showed us where there were 3 different places to eat. One was a place that had hamburgers and since we both like them I said why don't we go to the hamburger place. It reminded me of the first time Arthur took me in his car. On our way back to the hotel it was almost dark and windy and cold. This hotel room is a little bigger than the one in Bellefonte and also has a bathroom with a bathtub. I brought the book "The Call of The Wild" with me and I will start reading it again while Arthur rests.

Wednesday, October 29, 1919

It has been a very nice day. The sun has been out all day but the air is crisp and cool and breezy. We are still here in Indiana. Not the state, the city. I am so far away from home and yet we are still in Pennsylvania. On the maps I can see that we are only a tiny way across the country and the world is so much bigger than the country. I wonder how the kids are doing at the coal mine school.

They worked on the car today and it is finished but since it was dinner time when they finished we decided to stay another night here.

We walked around a lot today. It is very beautiful here and there are lots of trees. We looked at different stores and ate at a restaurant that had tasty sandwiches and Coca Cola. This town is smaller than Carbondale.

I forgot to say that we had breakfast at a restaurant and had eggs and ham and toast and orange juice. I never had orange juice before but I really like it.

I love walking with Arthur and holding his hand and seeing all these places. He has been to Pittsburgh before but not this town so it was fun to explore together. Because of the big breakfast we didn't eat lunch until after 1pm. The restaurant where we had lunch was right down town and you could look out the window and see the people and cars just like when we were in Scranton. They had a telephone at the restaurant where you put in a dime and you can call someone else who has a telephone and Arthur called the service station to see how the car was doing and that's how he knew it would be ready. Then we walked by a clothing store and went in and Arthur bought me 2 new blouses, a white one and a green one.

We carried our things back to the hotel and then walked to the service station. The people there were very friendly and the man in charge explained what he did to fix the radiator and Arthur paid him the money. They also put gas in the car.

Since we weren't hungry yet we rested in the hotel for a while. Arthur said we will get a telephone when we build our house. I took a bath because the gusty winds blew dust around and I felt dusty. Around 7 pm we got in the car and drove around the town to find a restaurant. We found one that looked nice so we went in and it was fancy. They had white table cloths on the tables and it was very quiet inside. We had steak and potatoes and bread and vegetables and even some wine. When we were finished the dinner cost almost 5 dollars. I couldn't believe it was so expensive. Arthur said don't worry and once in a while we have to enjoy it.

Serendipitous Rescue

Now we're back in the hotel and tomorrow we'll go to Pittsburgh. According to the map it should take us less than 2 hours to get there.

Thursday, October 30, 1919

We are finally here in Pittsburgh and this is a really big city. I have never seen anything like it. There is no end to the streets and houses and buildings. There are giant steel mills and you can see them off in the distance because of their smokestacks. Arthur said they make half of all the steel in America here. He said they have every type of store and big schools and libraries and theaters.

We slept in and had a late breakfast in Indiana and got here just after noon. We went to a hotel that Arthur already knew about and our room is on the third floor. They have an elevator so you don't even have to walk up the stairs. The room is nice and big and you can look out the window and see people and cars down below. I can't even see the edge of the city. Besides, there are too many hills. Arthur says there are more than a half a million people living here.

We went to lunch at a restaurant that Arthur has been to before and it is a fancy one. I thought the restaurant in Scranton was fancy but it is nothing like the one we went to last night and for lunch today. We drove all around the city looking at different places to build a house.

Tonight we went to a picture show. I've never been to one before and it was interesting. We saw a movie called "Male and Female." It was about a rich lady and poor man, just the opposite of Arthur and me. The poor man was the butler. He worked in the rich lady's big house. She fell in love with the butler while they were stuck on an island but they got rescued. Her family was vain, also like Arthur's family, and she didn't end up marring him. The story bothered me that she would choose vanity over love. Arthur said vanity makes people choose wrong all the time and not just about love.

Friday, October 31, 1919

Today was another new experience. We slept in late and Arthur said let's have room service for breakfast. I didn't know what that was and he said they bring the food to you. He pushed a button on the wall by the door and after a while a man came and knocked. Arthur told him we wanted eggs and sausage and toast and orange juice. By the time we got dressed he came back with a cart with the food on it. I can't believe it. We ate the food in our room.

Arthur took me for a ride in the car and we drove all over the city again. We went by where the steel mills were to show me where lots of the coal was going. We looked at many places where people can build houses. We saw so many buildings and bridges and houses.

In the middle of the afternoon we saw a hot dog stand by a park and stopped to eat there. We got some hot chocolate in a paper cup because it was starting to get cold.

Today is Halloween but I was tired after all that and Arthur was too so we went back to the hotel. By then it was almost dark and it's fun to look out the window at night and see all the lights and everyone moving around down below.

Tomorrow we're going to the zoo.

I finished my writing while Arthur was resting and he said let's go downstairs and get a snack. So we went down to where the hotel has their own restaurant and got some ice cream. Now I'm finally finished for the day. I just don't know what to think of everything.

Saturday, November 1, 1919

We had room service again this morning for breakfast. Then we drove over to the zoo and walked around and looked at the animals. I've never seen such a thing. We were at the zoo for several hours and it was quite interesting.

We spent the rest of the afternoon driving around some neighborhoods where there were houses. There were lots of areas toward the outside part of town with empty places for houses. I just can't believe how big this city is.

Arthur asked me if I wanted to go see another show and I said this place is so busy it's making me tired. He said he was tired too so we went back to the hotel and had dinner in the little restaurant there and went to our room.

Arthur asked me if I wanted to go looking for more places to build a home tomorrow. For some reason I started to cry. I was thinking about all that has been happening lately and just felt overwhelmed. I said I missed our little apartment in Carbondale and going for walks and holding hands. Arthur hugged me until I stopped crying and said he wasn't thinking very smart. He said he liked Pittsburgh when he was here before but didn't think how I would like it. He said he liked our apartment too but wants go get away from that area. Then he said how about the town of Indiana where we got the car fixed and where we got the blouses at the store. I loved that place and said let's go back there and look. We will stay here one more day and then leave. The room service people took our dirty laundry and will have it back to us sometime tomorrow so then we will pack up and go back to Indiana and look around.

Arthur said that everything in my life has changed so much that it's a lot to get used to.

Sunday, November 2, 1919

We had room service again this morning and it was gloomy outside so I'm glad we didn't have to go out. It looked windy but was nice and warm inside.

I thought about people making wrong decisions because of vanity and told Arthur that I'm sure we can find a nice place to live in Pittsburgh. We did see lots of nice houses and places to build houses. He said he woke up in the middle of the night and thought about things and he also was thinking that Pittsburgh was too busy. He said if we lived in the city of Indiana we could visit Pittsburgh because it's not that far away.

When they brought us our breakfast they also had our clean clothes so we looked at each other and Arthur said lets pack up and go. Arthur went to pay the money for being in the hotel and they came and got our suitcases for us. I will say it was fun riding in the elevator. We got some gas for the car and it doesn't need water because the radiator is fixed.

It took less than 2 hours to get to Indiana and we went back to that same hotel we stayed in before and Arthur got gas at the same service station. They gave us the same room we were in and we brought our things in. We weren't hungry yet so we drove around the city. There were so many pretty places and it didn't feel so busy. We found several places that seemed ideal for building a home. We like the southern part of town and on the west side of town. We got some lunch at a small restaurant that wasn't too fancy and then we kept looking around. I like it more and more.

It started raining as we drove back to the hotel and by the time we got there it was raining hard. We stopped right before the hotel at the little restaurant and ate some dinner. I told Arthur I was getting tired of the restaurants and I can't wait till we're back in our apartment. Arthur says we'll look for an apartment tomorrow. It's raining hard and we can hear the rain and it's cold and windy. I love him so much.

Monday, November 3, 1919

It was wet outside and the sun was shining and very cold but not freezing. We got some breakfast and it was delicious. I guess we were hungry.

We went downtown and Arthur had an idea to go to the store where we bought the blouses and ask the lady where was a place that could help us find an apartment. She was very nice and said there was a bulletin board at the town hall where people put notices of houses for sale and apartments and things like that. We went there and Arthur wrote down the addresses of some apartments on the south and west side of town. We spent hours going from one place to another and only looked at 4 places but it takes time to check things out. We decided on one and I am excited. It is about the same size as the one in Carbondale with 2 bedrooms and a kitchen and a living room and the bathroom is bigger with the same size bathtub. It seems a little newer and has a radiator in each room. It's close to the downtown area so we can walk around. The only thing is that it cost more than the other ones we looked at and will be 52 dollars per month but Arthur says not to worry about it. Arthur signed a contract with them that says we will stay there for at least a year. They have a laundry area that is a room with 2 electric washing machines, just like we had at the school. They gave us the keys to the apartment and my stomach was rumbling because I was starving and Arthur was hungry too so we just walked from the apartment over to a restaurant and got an early dinner. We took a long time eating because we were talking so much about everything. Now we know where we will be moving to so we are both anxious to get going back to Carbondale and get our things.

Tuesday, November 4, 1919

We got up very early and took our boxes of shoes and some of our clothing and took it to the empty apartment and put it inside. Then we got some breakfast and started driving back to Carbondale. We are here in the town of Bellefonte like before and at the same hotel. Driving makes Arthur tired especially when they are working on the roads and we have to stop and wait, and some of the roads are not smooth. I'm tired too. I wish I could drive the car and help Arthur. He said he will teach me some day.

Wednesday, November 5, 1919

We are back at our apartment in Carbondale and we're both just worn out from everything. I never thought I would get tired of riding in a car. We forgot about everything in the icebox. The iceman did keep ice there but the milk was spoiled and the bread was moldy but we'll worry about it tomorrow. I'm too tired to write any more about today.

Thursday, November 6, 1919

We didn't get up until almost 11 am. We walked over to the little store to get some fresh milk and bread from the bakery. It was nice to cook breakfast and eat at our own table. Being here makes me think of the miners and the kids at the school and I feel bad about leaving but excited too. I dread driving again. After eating and washing the dishes, Arthur took a bath and then I did too. We had to drive into Scranton to make arrangements with a company that can move our furniture and clothes to Indiana. We decided on next Monday so we won't be here that long. Everyone just hopes it won't rain.

We didn't see my stepmom or Darcy but we found out the mining company where they live. We can send a letter to them.

I feel overwhelmed again and I don't know why I'm so emotional.

Friday, November 7, 1919

It's morning and I just wanted to write that last night I cried and couldn't even understand why. Arthur hugged me and when we got in bed he hugged me and talked about everything. There's a lot going on and everything's changing and on top of that I'm tired. Arthur has traveled a lot but I haven't. I feel much better this morning. We will take it easy for a few days.

This morning we made breakfast and went out for a walk. The trees are bare and it felt like it could snow but it didn't. We had spaghetti for dinner and it was fine.

I am so lucky to have Arthur. It seems like he knows how to fix every kind of trouble. I will do anything for him and will be happy to live wherever he wants.

Saturday, November 8, 1919

We drove to Scranton today and managed to find where my stepmom and Darcy live. Mr. Allen wasn't there. We were glad of that. We all went in the car to the restaurant that Arthur took me to my first time there. We had such a good time. We told them about our trip to Pittsburgh and about moving to Indiana. It was sad to take them back to their house and say good bye.

I keep getting sad and then happy. I think part of it is that I will be leaving the mining camp forever and even though I'm glad, I'm also sad. The only friends I ever had besides Arthur were at the school and the church and my family. I am ready for my new life but Arthur says I may be sad for a while but he will try to help me. As long as I have Arthur I will be fine.

Sunday, November 9, 1919

This morning Arthur asked me if I wanted to go to the mining camp church to say good bye and at first I did and started putting on a dress and then I couldn't do it. I thought I would cry again but Arthur said don't worry and hugged me like he does. Instead we made breakfast together and I really liked cooking and not having to go out. Besides, the sky was all white like it might snow so we stayed inside all day. We spent the day resting and I finally started reading "The Call of the Wild" again.

Monday, November 10, 1919

We're back in Bellefonte again. It's funny how you can feel like you get to know a place when really you only have been here a few times.

The people with the truck are also here but are in a different room. They wanted to drive all the way but Arthur said he would pay them the extra money to stay here tonight and finish tomorrow. We all went to the little restaurant for early dinner. There are two men named Mark and Eric. They are nice and were glad to go to the restaurant with us.

I don't know if I will feel like reading tonight. I'm more excited now that we are on our way. I feel sad leaving my stepmom and Darcy behind. Arthur said we'll visit them again after we get settled.

Tuesday, November 11, 1919

We left early this morning but didn't get here till almost 4 pm. The truck can't go as fast as the car and it has a hard time going up the hills. Eric said it was a good thing we didn't try to drive all in one day. It rained quite a bit after we left Bellefonte so it was a good thing our things were all inside the truck. It only took Eric and Mark a half hour to unload the truck. Now our bed and the desk and its chair and the big chair and table for the kitchen is in our new apartment with all our clothes and it feels wonderful. Arthur gave the men their money and they will stay in that hotel tonight and go back to Carbondale tomorrow. I had a bath and it's a little different but it's nice. Since there is a heat radiator in the bathroom it's nice and warm in there.

6

A New Home

<u>*Wednesday, November 12, 1919*</u>

Today was our first day in our new apartment. We had to go to a restaurant for breakfast but then we walked to the store and got food for lunch and dinner and food for tomorrow. We also got milk and ice for the icebox. We talked to the people in the store and told them we live here now and they asked about us and where we came from and it was nice getting to know them. It made me a little sad because it reminded me of talking to the ladies at the washing machine in the school. We cooked soup for lunch and then walked around to explore some more. We walked by the store where we bought the blouses and the lady remembered us and said hi and we said that we moved here and will be living here now. She was happy to hear that and said welcome to Indiana.

The fun thing is that we walked across the street and down a ways to a hardware store. It's where they sell tools and machines and other things separate from the food store. It's called Stewart's Hardware and Arthur talked to the man there and said we want to buy a refrigerator. I was shocked but happy. The man took us to another man who is in charge and said he could order us one from Pittsburgh. Arthur paid him some money and the man was happy and we told him about moving here and we talked for a while. He also said welcome to Indiana.

Now that this is our home I feel even better about everything. After being out today and talking to people it seems that the mining camp and the school and the people there are already getting harder to remember.

The nice thing about this apartment, just like the other one, is that it has the places where you can plug in the electric fan for the electricity, and that's what we will use for the electric refrigerator.

Thursday, November 13, 1919

We ended up snuggling last night in our nice warm apartment. It tried to snow a little this morning but then the sun came out. It's been a very beautiful day and I am happy. We've been tired and this afternoon we just rested. The helper from the hardware store came over and knocked on our door and told us the refrigerator will be here tomorrow and they will bring it to our apartment and will we be around. We said yes and now we're excited for that.

I wrote a letter to my stepmom. Arthur and I walked into town to the post office.

Friday, November 14, 1919

About 10 am this morning Mr. Stewart came over with a flat bed truck with the new electric refrigerator on it. The helper man was with him and they lifted the refrigerator down and wheeled it into the apartment. He plugged it in and that was all there was to it. At first it didn't seem cold at all but later it was. After dinner it was all cold and you could see ice in the freezing part. The freezing part can actually make ice. We moved our food from the ice box to the refrigerator and now we won't have to keep buying ice. Then I told Arthur remember when the electricity stopped working in the other apartment and we had to use candles? He thought about it and said since it took a long time to get cold today maybe it will take a long time to get warm if the electricity stops but it was something to worry about.

Saturday, November 15, 1919

I love the electric refrigerator. It makes a humming sound sometimes. That's when it's working on the cooling. When I'm lying in bed and it's all dark, I can hear the humming and it sounds nice.

We walked over to the store to get some eggs and went by the little restaurant to get some more orange juice.

We were being lazy today and resting. I asked Arthur what we should do now that we are settled in our new home. We are away from the mining camp and his family so we don't have anything to do like working. Arthur says he will think about it and for now it will be like we are on a vacation. I said well for now he could start teaching me more things and he said that was a good idea and hugged and kissed me. We decided to go to the church tomorrow that is close by here. That way we can meet some more people. So far the store people that we have met have been friendly.

Sunday, November 16, 1919

We went to a church this morning. It was very different from what I'm used to. It was a Presbyterian Church. For one thing the people were all dressed nice and another thing they had different songs and it was different from the mining camp. The whole time I kept thinking about my other church at the mining camp. On the good side we did meet nice people. Since we're new, a lot of people came to talk to us afterwards. One of the people we met was a man and wife who live in the same apartment area as us named Susan and Scott. They are a little older than us and have a girl named Stefani that is 3 years old.

This afternoon Arthur fell asleep in the nice big chair he likes. He told me that his grandmother bought the chair soon after she came to America. He used to sit on her lap when he was a young boy and she would read stories to him. Later when he was older and away at boarding school his grandmother died. His mom wanted to get rid of the big chair because it wasn't fancy. Arthur wanted to keep the chair so his mom let him keep it in his room. I like that chair too.

I started reading "The Call of the Wild" again. I started over since I've been interrupted so much. I like the story.

We were about to start cooking a late dinner and Scott and Susan knocked on our door. They brought over some fresh baked bread. We were happy to see them and invited them in. We realized that we didn't have a lot of places to sit so we got the kitchen chairs out and we sat and talked for a while and learned about each other. They were very interested to hear how we met and got married.

I said that I liked orange juice from the restaurant and they said we should buy oranges and make the juice ourselves and it would be cheaper. They explained about getting a juice squeezer and we can get one at Stewart's hardware store. They said at this time of year you have to go to Pittsburgh to get oranges. I wasn't ready to go back to Pittsburgh yet but they said they would be going next Saturday and they could get some for us if we wanted. Arthur gave them some money and said if they would buy a whole bunch of oranges for us and them he would pay for all of it. At first they didn't want to take the money but Arthur says he wants a lot of oranges so they said ok. I'm excited about getting the oranges and Arthur says we will go get a squeezer tomorrow. Their little girl Stefani is cute. She's the age I was when my mother died.

We ended up having fresh bread for dinner and I said we were blessed for going to church and Arthur said yes we were.

<u>Monday, November 17, 1919</u>

We made a nice big breakfast and I did most of it myself. I missed having orange juice but I keep thinking about getting oranges next Saturday.

We went to Stewart's hardware but they weren't open yet so we went back to the apartment and got in the car to drive around. Arthur says we need to get busy finding a place to build his castle for me. We saw lots of nice places and I'm excited about it but I like the apartment just fine. We went back to the apartment and then walked over to Stewart's store but on the way we decided to stop at the little restaurant (not the fancy one) and get some lunch. I tried a new thing that was a toasted cheese sandwich and I really liked it. Arthur had it before and knew I would like it. Then we went over to Stewarts's Hardware and asked him for a juice squeezer for oranges. He had to look in the back for a while but found one. It's pretty heavy but we carried it ok back to the apartment. It has a big lever and when you press down on the lever it squeezes these 2 things together. You cut a orange in half and squeeze each half and the juice comes out into a glass. They said it's good for lemons, too. I can't wait to try it.

Wednesday, November 19, 1919

We have been driving around looking for places to build a house. We have found a few good ones. Some of the prettiest places don't have water or electricity yet.

We did find a nice neighborhood that is very new. There aren't many houses yet but they do have electricity and they are putting water pipes in the ground. It's over on the west part of town and we like that area.

I'm enjoying "The Call of the Wild" book. It's more true than some of the books I have read.

Friday, November 21, 1919

We've been driving around looking at other areas. We only spent a few hours driving because it gets tiring after a while. We are taking it easy and Arthur has not been worn out for a long time.

This afternoon we drove back over to the one neighborhood that we saw on Wednesday and got out and walked around. We found one place that has a park in the back yard. It's on a street named Colonial Drive and Arthur likes it because probably no one will ever build any houses in the back because of the park. I liked it because the whole area is very pretty. It's just dirt roads right now but you can see markers where the edges of the road will be.

We saw our neighbors again today. It was the first day I used the electric washing machine and Susan was there and showed me how the washing machines worked. They are different from the ones at the mining school but not too different. The washing machines are in a small room and next to the room are 3 sets of clothes lines. It's very handy. I told Susan that I'm excited about getting the oranges and she seemed happy that they could get them for us.

Saturday, November 22, 1919

After breakfast we walked over to the store for more food. One nice thing about the electric refrigerator is that it has more space inside than the icebox.

We drove around some more but the more we look, the more we like the area by Colonial Drive.

Scott and Susan didn't get back till dinner time. That's a long way to go back and forth in one day. They brought over a whole box of oranges. Arthur asked if they were hungry and they said yes they just got back and Arthur said why don't we all go to the restaurant for dinner. Scott didn't look like he wanted to but Arthur said he would pay for dinner and it's the least he could do since they went to Pittsburgh and back. Susan looked really happy and said yes so we all walked over to the not fancy restaurant and we sat at a table that was big enough for us and Stefani. It was really fun and was a lot different than when Arthur and I eat by ourselves. They told us about their trip to Pittsburgh and the big food market where they had the oranges. It was a whole different area than when Arthur and I were there last week. Pittsburgh is so big.

Scott works for the water department that gets the water to all the houses. Susan is expecting a baby in about 6 months. When we said good bye they said they would see us in church tomorrow so I guess we'll go again tomorrow. I wonder when I will be expecting a baby.

<u>*Sunday, November 23, 1919*</u>

We got up early and made eggs and toast and orange juice for breakfast. It was really fun cutting the oranges and squeezing them into juice. I did some and so did Arthur. We squeezed 9 oranges and had a little juice left over that we put in the refrigerator.

It was nicer at church today because I recognized some of the people and of course Scott and Susan were there so it didn't seem so strange. We sat with them. We saw Mr. Stewart from the hardware store with his wife and 3 kids. The minister talked to us afterward and we told him about our plans to build a house. Arthur asked the minister if he knew a carpenter who could help us. He said Mr. Ranta was a good carpenter and was looking for work. The minister introduced us to him and Arthur told him about wanting to build our house. He used to have a company that was ruined because somebody embezzled and he had to go bankrupt and lose all his money. Arthur said to come over tonight and have dinner with us and we'll talk about it.

In the afternoon Arthur and I walked around the neighborhood and held hands but we didn't stay out long because it was pretty cold and the wind was blowing. We saw Scott and Susan and Stefani and they said what are we doing for Thanksgiving next Thursday and we hadn't thought about it and they said let's have Thanksgiving together and that sounded good to us.

Mr. Ranta came over with his wife and we had a nice dinner and they seem like very nice people. We had spaghetti because it was easy to do and it's tasty. Arthur said we are going to have to get more furniture because we have the 4 chairs for the table and the one big chair that he likes to sit in and the other chair that I'm using at the desk.

The way they looked reminded me of the people in the mining camp but the minister said Mr. Ranta has a lot of experience. I think he's about 45 years old. Arthur got out the picture of the house and also some other papers that told how to build the house. Mr. Ranta said it's going to be a very big house and he will study the plans but it will cost a lot of money. Arthur said it's ok and does he have any helpers. Mr. Ranta's name is Jannik and he said he can find people to help him that were his friends before his trouble. His wife's name is Aileen and she seemed so happy I thought she was going to cry. They came from Finland a long time ago and lived in Minnesota before they lived here. He said this would be the finest house he ever built. He said he will build it strong and sturdy and it will last for our grandchildren's grandchildren. He kept looking over all the papers and Arthur said to take them home and study them so we can figure out how to get started and to come over tomorrow and we would all take a drive over to where we would like to build it.

It's been another very nice day.

Monday, November 24, 1919

Mr. Ranta came over in the afternoon and we all drove over to the place on Colonial Drive that Arthur and I liked. Mr. Ranta walked around and said it would be a good place because the house is going to be so big. Then we said let's go to the restaurant for dinner. Mr. Ranta's wife Aileen wasn't with us but we went and got get her and we all went over to the restaurant that was nice but not the fancy one. It was very jolly.

Arthur is already in bed and we are both very happy but next we need to go and see if we can buy the land for the house.

Tuesday, November 25, 1919

We saw Scott and Susan in the morning and said we would buy the food if they will make the dinner for Thanksgiving.

Then we went over to the office of the company that is selling the land in the neighborhood that we like. Arthur told them we want to buy lot number 5 and the man looked in a book and said that it would cost 1650 dollars because that was the best one. Arthur said we want to buy it and the man asked if we already talked to a bank or a savings and loan and Arthur said no but we want to buy it right now for 1600 dollars. He pulled a whole bunch of money out of a bag he was holding and counted it out on the desk. The man was very surprised and so was I. He brought in another man who was very happy and he wrote things down and had us sign papers. It took a long time to take care of everything, not like buying milk. Afterwards we went over to Mr. Ranta's house to tell him.

Wednesday, November 26, 1919

We drove over to Colonial Drive to see lot number 5 again and it was different seeing it and knowing we could now walk around on the ground we paid for and would be our home.

Thursday, November 27, 1919

Today is Thanksgiving and it has been a wonderful day. First of all it has been trying to snow but not much. The sky has been cloudy all day but not real dark, just a little. We both took a bath and put on nice clothes and went over to the apartment of Susan and Scott. I helped Susan finish doing the cooking and getting dinner ready. Their kitchen table is bigger than ours and has 6 chairs. We had a good dinner and a good visit. Scott and Arthur talked about how we're building a new house. Scott knew the place because the water department had been working in that area putting in the pipes. Their little Stefani is cute and has toys and a baby doll to play with.

Arthur says we will get a big table for our house.

<u>*Friday, November 28, 1919*</u>

We did our laundry today.

I finished reading "The Call of the Wild" and cried. Arthur asked how I liked the story and I liked it a lot but it was sad how people can be mean to each other and animals. Arthur said there are lots of mean people but there are lots of nice people too. I was glad that Buck was able to have a good life in the end after all his trouble.

I asked Arthur why some people are mean. He said lots of people are unhappy about their life and when you're unhappy for a long time you can become mean. I said I hope I don't become mean for being sad about missing my stepmom and Darcy. He said being sad isn't the same thing as being unhappy. If you are thankful for what you have you can be happy no matter what. He said Mr. Allen was mean because his pride made him jealous of other people. He said his mom was mean because she would never have enough things to be happy.

I have Arthur and that's all I need.

<u>*Saturday, November 29, 1919*</u>

It has been a strange day. Mr. Ranta came over today to talk to Arthur about the building plans. He was so excited to go over everything with Arthur and they figured out what to start with but when Mr. Ranta left Arthur was shocked at how much it was going to cost. Arthur checked the numbers with Mr. Ranta. I guess Arthur didn't realize the house was going to be so big and cost so much to build. I asked if we were going to be poor and he said no but we would have to be careful with our money and not have a maid or other helpers in the house. I said that was fine because I can cook and clean and take care of a house. Arthur said we need to think about this before we get started and we might need to think of making new plans for a smaller house. Arthur is in bed but the way he is thinking about all this worries me.

Serendipitous Rescue

<u>Sunday, November 30, 1919</u>

We walked over to church today with Scott and Susan and Stefani and everyone at church was extra friendly, including Mr. and Mrs. Stewart and Mr. and Mrs. Ranta and the minister. I guess word got around about the big house and everyone is glad because it will help the businesses in town. Even the minister said thank you Lord for bringing the Kappel family to our town when he prayed. Afterward we smiled and shook everyone's hand.

This afternoon we sat in our apartment and thought about everything. This is the first time I ever saw Arthur in a worrying mood and after lunch he was at the kitchen table writing things down on paper and doing a lot of figuring. I said I was worried and I don't care if we're poor or if we can't build the big house but Arthur said we can do it. We won't have much money left after we pay the tax on the money we got and build the house but we get money each month from the mining contract and will keep getting it for 5 years. He said the mining contract payments will give us time to work out things. I said I hope this doesn't mean we're vain. He said if we don't act like vain people we won't be vain and building the house will be like we're giving money to the people in the town for helping us. He said he has wanted to build that house for a long time and if there is a way to do it that's what he wants. It's a lot to think about.

7

Colonial House

Monday, December 1, 1919

Arthur, me, Mr. Ranta and a man named Mr. Korhonen drove over to lot number 5 on Colonial Drive and walked around. Mr. Ranta and Mr. Korhonen talked about the house and walked here and there and placed little markers on the ground. They were figuring out where to start building parts of the house. I guess they have to dig a basement first. In the basement will be the furnace to heat the house.

Mr. Ranta talked to Arthur about money and schedules. After we walked around the house area we went back to Mr. Ranta's house and Arthur gave him 500 dollars to get started. That made Mr. Ranta happy because normally they don't get money until after they have done some work. We will meet with Mr. Ranta every Saturday night to go over the expenses and see how things are going.

Tuesday, December 2, 1919

They started digging the basement today. Mr. Ranta used some of the money to buy shovels and digging tools and wheelbarrows. Mr. Stewart brought everything over on his truck. There are 5 men working on the basement. They also built an outhouse toward the back.

Friday, December 5, 1919

The men have been digging all week and have a great big hole dug. There are 12 men working now. It's very cold outside but it's a good time to be working hard. It reminds me of the miners working. Arthur

255

and I go there every day at noon to bring them hot chocolate and coffee and lunch.

There are no other houses on this street yet.

Saturday, December 6, 1919

Mr. and Mrs. Ranta came over tonight and had dinner with us and Arthur went over the things the men bought to work with plus how much he paid the men. Mr. Ranta wants to order some bricks and concrete and cement and lots of other stuff.

Saturday, December 13, 1919

It's been a busy week and Arthur and I have been there every day. After lunch we stay for a while in case Mr. Ranta needs something from a store. The big hole for the basement is almost done. Some of the men don't have a good way to get to the house so we pick them up in the car in the morning and take them home at night.

We got a Christmas tree after breakfast and put it in the apartment. Then we went to the store and got some ornaments for the tree. Arthur wanted some electric lights but they didn't have any at the store. That made me sad but then we went to Stewart's Hardware store and he had Christmas tree lights for us. Mr. Stewart said they were free and was full of the Christmas spirit. He had to order the lights special. Arthur had been teasing me at the store to make me think there wasn't any lights but all along he knew Mr. Stewart had ordered them.

We put the lights and the ornaments on the Christmas tree tonight and it is so beautiful. It reminds me of the one last year at the mining camp and it almost made me cry. This one has red, green, blue and yellow lights so it is different but I would say it is even more beautiful. And here it is in our very own apartment. The lights are on right now and while I'm writing I can't stop looking at the Christmas tree.

Saturday, December 20, 1919

Another busy week. I get tired just helping out and I'm not doing the hard work. The holes are all done but it has snowed 2 times this week and there is snow at the bottom of where they have been digging. Bricks and other things have been delivered and are stacked in different piles around the yard.

I got a letter from my stepmom. She said they are happy where they are and Mr. Allen has been nicer. She was glad for me to be away from the mines and was happy that I was with Arthur. I wish she was with someone nice. Arthur says maybe Mr. Allen will be nicer now. I wrote another letter telling her about building our big house and getting a Christmas tree. I love the Christmas tree.

Sunday, December 21, 1919

At church we sang lots of Christmas carols and everyone was very merry. You would think we were important people the way people say hi to us and shake our hands and say they are happy to see us. Of course, I am happy to see them, too. My life is so different now. This year we have our Christmas Tree and our candle for the window.

Thursday, December 25, 1919

It's been a very nice Christmas day. Last Christmas Arthur was just my friend and now I am Mrs. Kappel and living far away.

Even though Arthur says we must be careful, he got me some more diaries for Christmas. He says the way I'm going I'll need more and he wants me to keep writing. He also got me a new dress from that store and it was all wrapped up nice. I said I didn't have anything for him and he said it's ok and we'll figure it out next year and that I need to have my own money. He said all he wants from me is a Christmas kiss and he would be the happiest man in the world. That was easy to do but I do wish I had a present for him.

We went over to Scott and Susan's apartment for dinner. We sang Christmas carols. It makes me a little sad thinking about the people I used to know at the mining camp. I wonder what Darcy and my stepmom are doing. My new friends are wonderful and I like everyone here and I'm glad I moved here with Arthur.

Saturday, December 27, 1919

Mr. Ranta came over to review the expenses. It snowed again yesterday and they are deciding not to do any work for a while because it's too cold and snowy.

Sunday, December 28, 1919

Lots of people at church say hi to us. Mr. Stewart and his kids were there. We met Jimmy and Virginia and Mary. He told us how happy everyone was that we're building the big house. He said he hoped Jimmy would someday take over the hardware store like he had from his father. Jimmy is 11 and seems shy.

Wednesday, December 31, 1919

We went by the post office today and got the address for our new house. It will be 22. That will be easy to remember.

We celebrated New Years Eve with Scott and Susan and Stefani. Susan is barely starting to look like she will have a baby. We brought some Champagne that we bought and we all drank some. We played poker and used toothpicks for betting. I never played it before and Scott won all the toothpicks. It was a fun night.

Today was the last day of a strange and wonderful year. My life is so different from when this year started.

Sunday, January 4, 1920

Even though nothing is happening with the new house, people at church talk about the great house we are building. I guess some of the people had a better Christmas because of the money we paid them.

Arthur said he has settled himself about the house. He said the house will cost more to build than it will be worth, but he doesn't want to disappoint the workers who are already planning on getting the money for working on such a big project. Besides, he really wants to build the house. He said it's his one vain thing. He said it doesn't matter how much the house is worth because we will never sell the house and hopefully we'll both die here and pass it on to our children.

We had dinner after church with Scott and Susan and they were talking about women getting the vote. They all said it was a good idea and it sounded like a good idea to me. Arthur said it will probably happen this year and I should have a vote in our family decisions like money, too. I trust Arthur and I don't care about the money but he makes me feel important and that's the best thing.

Wednesday, January 7, 1920

Everyone is talking about the prohibition law that starts soon. We won't be able to get wine at the restaurant any more. I don't really care and Arthur doesn't drink it that much, but he says it's a silly law. Lots of people have been getting extra bottles of wine for when they can't buy it any more. Arthur was going to buy some to save, but the stores are all out.

Monday, January 12, 1920

It's my birthday and I'm eighteen years old now. Arthur got me a purse from that store. The purse is black and is beautiful. I've never had such a nice thing. I hope this doesn't make me vain but I love it so much. I put all my things in it that I need to carry around. Susan and Scott came over and brought cookies and we were very merry.

Sunday, February 1, 1920

It's been very cold. I'm glad for the radiators in the apartment. I like reading but I get tired of being in. I like going to church just to get out but it made me think of the ladies back at the mining camp washing clothes in the cold and my stepmom living in Scranton.

Saturday, February 15, 1920

I'm saving my money for a birthday present for Arthur. I've been looking at different things but I'm having a hard time deciding on something.

Serendipitous Rescue

<u>*Saturday, February 28, 1920*</u>

I still haven't decided on what to get Arthur for his birthday. I talked to the lady in the store today while Arthur was across the street at the hardware store and she suggested either a hat or a wallet and to think about it and come back on Monday.

<u>*Sunday, February 29, 1920*</u>

It's leap year so we get an extra day. I don't remember leap year last time. I didn't even know what it was until today.

<u>*Monday, March 1, 1920*</u>

I've decided on the wallet and went to the store today and told the lady and she helped me wrap it. It's the first time I ever bought a wrapped present for anyone. I'm nervous and excited. Arthur wanted to come with me but I told him it was a surprise and to wait at home. When I got back with the present I told him he had to wait till his birthday on Friday.

<u>*Wednesday, March 3, 1920*</u>

We divided up our money for the month and I took my part to the store because I didn't have quite enough for the wallet and the lady said I could bring the rest later so that's what I did.

<u>*Thursday, March 4, 1920*</u>

I'm worried that maybe I should have got something else for Arthur's birthday. I hope he likes the wallet. He keeps looking at the present all wrapped up sitting on the desk where I do my writing.

<u>*Friday, March 5, 1920*</u>

I gave Arthur his birthday present. He is 23 now. When he unwrapped it he almost cried and said it was the best present he ever got from anyone. I know it's not the most fancy present he ever got but I'm sure he said that because he loves me.

Susan and Scott came over and we had dinner. Susan helped me bake cookies and showed me how to do it. After dinner we had milk and cookies. Susan is getting big and it won't be much longer before the baby is born. I hope it won't be long before I'm expecting a baby.

Sunday, March 7, 1920

After church we went over to Scott and Susan's apartment to see the radio they bought yesterday. During the big war no one was allowed to have a radio and now everyone is talking about getting a radio. They went to Pittsburgh yesterday and had to wait in a line of people getting radios. The radio has people and music from Pittsburgh and other cities. They talk and sing and it comes out on the radio. I can't imagine how it works. It's like a telephone except everyone with a radio can hear at the same time and there are no wires and you can't talk back.

They also brought back more oranges.

Monday, March 8, 1920

The men started working on the house again. They are building a shack where they can keep papers and also eat lunch. They have the shack almost finished just in one day.

We went into town to get hot chocolate and coffee from the restaurant and stopped at Stewart's hardware and ordered a radio. They will deliver it later this week or next. Arthur said we should have a radio even though we are being careful.

I got a letter from my stepmom. They are glad for the warmer weather and are able to walk into town.

Tuesday, March 9, 1920

They finished the shack and started working on the house. It gets pretty windy sometimes and they can keep the papers and things in the shack while they are working. The shack even has one window. So now there is an outhouse, a shack and a hole in the ground. There aren't any other houses on the streets yet except for one house being built on the street next to us and one other house being built on a street in the other direction. It's exciting to see them actually start working on our house.

Serendipitous Rescue

<u>*Saturday, March 20, 1920*</u>

The radio we ordered still hasn't arrived yet. The prohibition law started this week.

There are posts and things all over the house area now and it's looking busier and busier with all the men working. They are putting bricks down in the basement for walls.

<u>*Saturday, March 27, 1920*</u>

The radio finally came today. We've been learning how to adjust it for different stations. There aren't very many in Pittsburgh yet but there are several more planned soon. When Mr. Ranta came over to talk about the status and money we showed him the radio and had some music while we talked. It's been cold and windy this week and the shack has come in handy. We've been bringing hot chocolate and coffee there about 11 am and we also have water for the men.

I asked Arthur why it's taking so long to get the basement done. He said it's not just the basement, it's the foundation for the whole house and it's no use building a big house if the foundation isn't solid. They have finally started working on the floor that goes over the basement so that's good.

<u>*Saturday, April 10, 1920*</u>

Mr. Ranta came over as usual. He seems like he really knows what he is doing. Arthur says we made the right decision to have him be in charge of building the house. He knows how to find the right people to work on things. They have been putting in wires for the electricity and pipes for the water for the bathrooms and the kitchen. There will be two small bathrooms downstairs and two big bathrooms upstairs. It's very complicated and I don't know how they think of everything. They have also started working on the floor for the second story which is also the ceiling for the main floor. Mr. Ranta says the plans for the house don't have the details for how to put in the water and electricity but it's ok because he knows how to make everything work. Arthur said it's lucky for us that Mr. Ranta can work with the plans we have.

I asked Mr. Ranta who the most important worker was and he said every job that does something useful is important.

Arthur and I have kept busy this week. In addition to being at the new house most of the day and taking men home when needed and going to the hardware store, we've also been helping Scott and Susan at night. She is really big with the baby and we help them get dinner. It's nice because we talk about the day and have music on the radio. The radio also has people that talk about the news. They talk a lot about the prohibition law and the vote for women.

This evening Arthur said Mr. Ranta was the most important worker on our house, but what Mr. Ranta said was also true, and we're fortunate that Mr. Ranta was available. It's like his bad fortune in the past was good fortune for us, but now we're helping each other.

Sunday, April 18, 1920

After church Arthur and I drove over to the new house. It's all quiet and we walked around to check things out. You can see where the rooms are on the main floor and where the front door will be and the back doors. There are steps down to the basement and the furnace has been put there. It's a boiler that heats up water into steam to go to the radiators but there are no radiators yet. There are pipes and wires everywhere. I don't know how they keep track of everything. There is a stairway to the second floor but it's not finished yet and I wouldn't want to try to go up it but the men do.

Sunday, April 25, 1920

It's been another busy week. After church we both went back to bed and slept for a few hours. It's nice out and we can open the windows and let the fresh air go through and hear the birds outside and sometimes kids playing. I love the house we're building but I like this apartment too. Later we went over to Scott and Susan's apartment as usual to help with dinner and also visit.

This past week they have been working on paving the street where our new house is. It's interesting to see how they do it. It's much nicer not to have so much mud everywhere. It's a lot easier to drive the car on a smooth road.

We got a letter from my stepmom. Darcy has met a man that she likes. I'm not surprised. She is very pretty and always had lots of attention at our dances. His name is Mr. Walsh and he is about the same age as Arthur. He works for the trolley company that runs the electric street cars in Scranton. My stepmom said he makes good money. The funny thing is that Mr. Allen doesn't like him.

Sunday, May 9, 1920

The house now has a wood frame all the way to the roof. It looks like a skeleton house. It really seems big now. Sometimes cars drive by and people stop and look and sometimes talk to us. At church people ask how the house is doing. Mr. Ranta likes to talk about the house and he is getting lots of attention. Yesterday when Mr. Ranta came over to go over the expenses he said someone else wants him to build a house but they will have to wait. Arthur says this house will be good for Mr. Ranta and maybe he will be able to get his company going again.

Sunday, May 16, 1920

Susan had her baby this evening. We went over to see if they wanted to walk to church and she was getting ready to have the baby. Arthur and Scott drove the car over to get the midwife and I stayed with Susan and Stefani. I stayed with her all day and helped. I helped many times at the mining camp and they were glad I was there. I also made lunch and dinner. She had another girl and they named her Mary. Everything worked out well and little Mary is doing fine and so is Susan. I'm too tired to write any more, but it was a good day.

Sunday, May 23, 1920

This past week I've been helping Susan with the new baby. After we take lunch to the workers at the new house, Arthur drives me back to stay with Susan. She's doing pretty good. I've been cooking dinner for all of us. Even little Stefani helps out. Everything is working out well.

Saturday, May 29, 1920

The second floor has been done for a while and the attic floor is done. They are working on the roof. There are still no walls on the higher parts of the house but on the lower part the outside walls are getting done. I climbed up to the top and looked over the edge and it's scary being up so high. There's going to be several nice windows in the attic room so you can see all over.

Sunday, June 13, 1920

It's rained off and on during the past few days. It's nice having the roof done but it will be nicer when all the walls are done. Arthur looked all over the house and said Mr. Ranta is doing a good job.

The money from Mr. Oppenheimer at the mine was late and finally got here. Arthur has been concerned and that makes me anxious.

Some of the men have started working on the garage. They put concrete down for the garage floor and are building the garage big enough for two cars.

Sunday, June 27, 1920

It's getting warm out. Most of the men are working with their shirts off. The garage is done and they tore down the shed and now we have the table in the garage for lunch and for the water to drink. The outside walls are up all over the house and it really is looking like a real house now except there's just holes for the windows and doors.

Sunday, July 4, 1920

It's been a day to celebrate. This past week they took down the outhouse because they have the flushing toilets working in the downstairs bathrooms. The electricity is working and we can turn on lights in some of the rooms.

In the evening we did fireworks with Scott and Susan and their kids and some other people who live in the apartments. The firecrackers were very noisy and Scott burned his fingers but not bad. Our clothes smell like fireworks.

Serendipitous Rescue

<u>Tuesday, July 6, 1920</u>

I had an idea to bring the radio with us to the new house and now everyone can listen to music and radio programs and news while they're working.

I've gotten to like the sound of hammers and saws and the people working. It's a very pleasant and happy sound.

<u>Tuesday, July 13, 1920</u>

This house will have a sleeping porch. It's like a regular porch except it has walls made of screen material so the bugs can't get in. Because of the screen material the air can blow through. I've never heard of this before but Arthur says lots of houses do it to make it easier to sleep on hot summer nights. I really love this house.

The big surprise was the letter we got from my stepmom. For one thing Darcy got married. She is a year younger than me. The other shock was that Mr. Allen abandoned the family, even Josh, his own boy. Mr. Walsh said my stepmom and Josh can live with him and Darcy. They had a nice traditional church wedding a few weeks ago. I could tell that my stepmom was happy but I'm surprised it happened so quickly. Arthur thinks it's very practical because Mr. Allen is gone.

<u>Friday, July 23, 1920</u>

It was interesting today because this afternoon a car came by and the people got out and came to talk to us. They wanted to know about the big house and who was building it because they want to build a house down the street from our house. It won't be as big as this house but they are impressed with how our house looks and that so many people are working. They want to start next spring and would we be able to help them build it. Mr. Ranta is excited about having more work for next year.

<u>Sunday, August 1, 1920</u>

They put the windows in because they need to do the finishing on the outside of the house. There are lots of windows and it lets in lots of light. Outside, the house looks almost done but there's still a lot to be done on the inside. At least we won't have to worry so much about rain. They have the shingles on the roof and have started painting on the outside.

Sunday, August 15, 1920

We had a summer rainstorm today which was nice for a while but in the afternoon after church it was warm and muggy.

The outside of our house is all painted and looks wonderful. It looks very much like the picture Arthur showed me when we lived in Carbondale. He really has built me a castle.

Monday, August 16, 1920

We celebrated our 1ˢᵗ wedding anniversary today. I said let's go get hamburgers like we did last year so we did. We ate lunch at the not fancy restaurant and it was fun.

Arthur said we should do something special for our anniversary. He said let's go see a picture show at the Film-O-Rama here in town. That didn't sound good to me and I said let's just walk into town and hold hands and walk around and go to dinner at the restaurant again so that's what we did.

First we stopped by the store that sells the clothes. They were just getting ready to close for the day but they let us in. Arthur said I should get something and so we got me some new shoes. We said we would come back tomorrow to pick them up.

Then we walked all around like we used to do in Carbondale and it was fun. We finally went back to the restaurant for dinner but they were getting ready to close so we had to go to the fancy one. They were also getting ready to close but still had some food left and so we shared a pork chop and a steak. They said they were sorry they didn't have more to choose from but when I'm with Arthur I always have a good time. The one advantage Pittsburgh has is that places stay open later. But I like that it is quiet and peaceful here.

After we ate our dinner we walked around for a long time but not fast. It has been a wonderful day.

Serendipitous Rescue

<u>*Thursday, August 26, 1920*</u>

This morning the men we bought the property from came by to see how we were doing. They looked all over the house and said it was very fine work. They wanted to know how we were paying for building the house and Arthur said we had the money to do it. They asked if we would be interested in helping other people build houses. That was a surprise to Arthur but he said he would think about it. They said it would be easier to sell their properties if they could also recommend a builder like Mr. Ranta and someone who could help finance the construction. They said we could all make money that way. More things to think about.

We got a letter from my stepmom. They are all doing well and are happy. They still haven't heard anything about Mr. Allen. Arthur says hopefully they never will.

<u>*Sunday, September 5, 1920*</u>

They have been working mostly on the inside of the house and cleaning up the yard. The fireplace is done and they have been finishing hooking up all the pipes for the water and for the heating radiators. They turned on the furnace to test the radiators which was kind of funny since it's still warm outside.

This afternoon after church Scott and Susan came over to have lunch with us. We went for a walk around the neighborhood. Susan had the baby in the buggy and Stefani walked along and held her dad's hand. It was cute. We saw an old dog lying in someone's yard and I asked Arthur if there was a story about the dog. Susan and Scott looked at me funny and I said behind everything is a story, right Arthur? So Arthur made up a story about the dog:

Every day the old dog comes to the front of the yard and waits. He walks slowly because his bones are old and stiff. He used to be a puppy and bounced all over the place and ran fast and played with his owner every day. When his owner came home from school the dog would be happy to see him and they would run around the yard and play. His owner grew up and went off to the big war and never returned but the old dog comes out every day to wait.

I said the story was too sad and so did Susan. Arthur said he thought it was a nice story about how the dog loved a boy. Arthur said for me to tell a story about the dog so I said:

Once upon a time there was a puppy who played with a little boy. They both grew up together and loved each other. When the boy went to school, the dog would wait for him to come home. Every day after school the dog would jump all over the boy to greet him. The boy grew up and married a nice lady who is inside cooking dinner for everyone. The dog is old now and moves slowly but is waiting for the man to come home and is thinking about how nice his life is.

Arthur said my story was a good story too, and who knows what the true story is. Maybe the true story might be even more interesting.

When I see kids outside playing or people sitting on their porch it makes me wonder what their stories are.

Sunday, September 19, 1920

The walls are all done on the inside and they have started painting in the upstairs. The main bedroom is done. It's a big room with its own bathroom. The bathroom has a bathtub and a shower. The shower is interesting. There is a bathroom at the other end of the house and it also has a bathtub and a shower. The bathrooms downstairs only have a flushing toilet and a sink but there's one at each end of the house. They finished the stairs and now they look nice and safe.

Wednesday, October 6, 1920

Today was exciting. The new refrigerator came today and it is a nice one and bigger than the one in the apartment. Arthur says we'll give the one in the apartment to Scott and Susan when we move. All the sinks in the bathrooms and kitchens work. Even the hot water heater is working. It's been interesting to see how all these things are connected.

We got a cheerful letter from my stepmom. Darcy is expecting a baby. I am happy for her.

Serendipitous Rescue

Sunday, October 17, 1920

All the floors are finished and they have done the painting. We have ordered some furniture, including a large dining room table that has 14 chairs. We should have plenty of room now for when people come to visit.

We drove over to the house after church. It's always quiet on Sunday. We walked around and hugged and kissed in the back yard and looked at the house. It's almost done. Arthur picked up a knife that someone had left on the ground by the house and got an idea. He walked over to the tree closest to the house and carved our names into the tree and it said, "Arthur and Nancy Forever." I asked if there was a story behind this tree and he said:

Once upon a time there was a sad tree that grew all alone. Far away were the woods with lots of trees. Eventually some other trees started growing close by and the tree was happy to have some friends. One day some people started making a road and building houses close by. The tree was happy thinking that it would have people around and maybe children. It took a long time but after a while Arthur and Nancy came along and built a fine house. They loved the tree and carved their names into it. Every day they came out to see the tree. After a time there were children around who played by the tree. The tree was so happy that it promised to protect them and their house, and said it would watch over them forever. When Arthur and Nancy die, the tree would be their landmark and guide them to each other so they would always be together.

I told Arthur now that is a good story.

Sunday, October 31, 1920

This past week some of our furniture came and we've put some chairs and couches where they will be going. The walls have been painted and the inside doors are almost all installed. We need some carpets because the empty house echoes when you talk. Arthur said we need a piano but neither of us knows how to play a piano. Arthur said we could get piano lessons. We drove to Pittsburgh yesterday to a piano store and also got a bunch of oranges. Pianos cost a lot of money and I said we are trying to be careful with the money and Arthur said ok we'll get an upright piano instead of a grand piano. We decided to think about it and came back home but at least we had two boxes of oranges.

It's Halloween. We got some candy to hand out at the apartment with Scott and Susan and the children. There were lots of kids around and it was fun. There were mostly witches, ghosts, and clowns.

Wednesday, November 3, 1920

We got news in the mail today that Arthur's mom died. Mr. Johnson, the attorney who did the contract for selling the business, sent us a check for Arthur's share of his mom's money. Arthur said it's a sign we should buy the piano and what did I think. I said it's his money but he said women have the vote now and even if they didn't we both need to agree on important things like this. The money from his mom dying was more than enough to pay for the piano so we told Mr. Stewart at the hardware store to order the piano for us from that store we were at in Pittsburgh. Next Arthur says we need to get our own telephone at the house.

I asked Arthur if he was sad that his mom died. He said no, he was only sad that his mom was a mean person. She would never like me even though I was the most important person to him. I think my own mom was a nice person. I'm sure my mom and my dad would have liked Arthur. I miss my stepmom and Darcy.

Friday, November 5, 1920

We talked to the telephone company people and they said we're lucky that we are building the house in that area because they are already putting in the telephone lines and we should be able to get a telephone in a week or two.

Wednesday, November 17, 1920

We called Mr. Stewart at the hardware store using our new telephone and told him our number, 365. Everyone with a telephone has a number. When you pick up the phone there is a person who answers and asks what number you want and you tell them. Then they connect you to that number and you can talk to them. It's exciting to be able to talk to someone far away from our own house. Next we called the piano store in Pittsburgh to check on when the piano will be ready. That costs more money because it's long distance. They told us they will deliver the piano on Saturday if we'll be home and we will. Also, the electric washing machine is ready and Mr. Stewart will have someone bring it over tomorrow.

Thursday, November 18, 1920

It was exciting today to get the electric washing machine. I can't wait to use it. The helper from the hardware store connected the pipes and plugged it into the electricity and checked it and said it is working. He showed me how to use it and it is similar to the ones here at the apartment.

Saturday, November 20, 1920

We got the piano today. We came over to our new house early and waited for the big truck to arrive. The piano is really heavy and it was handy that we still had a few people working on the house so they could help carry the piano into the living room. It's not even the great big kind of piano and it's too heavy for me to move even a little bit. They said to let the piano sit for a week or so and they will send out a man to tune the piano. I don't know what that means but the piano won't sound right until they tune it.

Sunday, November 21, 1920

At church today we talked with people about finding a piano teacher and one of the ladies told us about Mrs. Cummins, who goes to a different church. On our way home we stopped by Mrs. Cummins house to see if she would be able to teach us the piano. She said she would be happy to.

We also arranged to borrow Mr. Stewart's truck to move our furniture from the apartment to the house. I'm so excited it's hard to sleep.

Wednesday, November 24, 1920

Mrs. Cummins came over this afternoon to see us at the new house. Her name is JoAnn and she has two boys and two girls. One boy and girl are married and the other boy and girl are in high school. She inspected the piano and sat down and played a song called "Schubert Serenade." It was so beautiful it made me really want to learn how to play music like that. Mrs. Cummins said it will take a long time and lots of practice to learn that. She also said it was a nice piano but needed to be tuned. We told her that a man will be coming out to do that soon. She asked when did we want to start lessons and I said right now. She showed us some finger exercises and how to properly hold our hands and to start practicing finger exercises. She was very nice and told us it takes patience and we have to start with simple songs. We decided she would come over on Tuesday and Thursday starting next week.

Thursday, November 25, 1920

We had Thanksgiving with Scott and Susan and the children again. Next year we will have Thanksgiving in our new house. We are thankful that the new house is almost done and we are thankful for our friends. I am extra thankful for Arthur.

Saturday, November 27, 1920

Today was the big day we have been waiting for. We had some of the workers help us move the furniture using Mr. Stewart's truck. There are only 3 men working on the house now because it's mostly finished and they are putting some lights in the attic and doing some other finishing up things. Mr. Ranta and the others are already working on a building in town and also helping repair a house. There are two more houses that people want to build starting next year so Mr. Ranta is very happy.

Mr. Stewart's truck isn't as big as the other truck that moved us so we had to make two trips but it isn't that far. While we were moving our furniture into the new house, the piano man came to tune the piano. His name is Mr. Olsen. It's strange to see how he does it and it takes time. He has special tools and a thing called a tuning fork that always plays the right note. Arthur knew all about it.

By the end of the day everything was moved and arranged. We also moved the electric refrigerator in our old apartment to Scott and Susan's apartment. Then they came over to our new house to help and to see how everything was going. Arthur said let's all go to the little restaurant for dinner so we all went including the workers and the piano tuner man. We all had a jolly dinner. Afterwards we took the men home.

Now it's just Arthur and me and the house is quiet. We have the radio on and we're in our new bedroom on the second floor and I am writing and Arthur is in bed watching me. Arthur tried out the new shower but I took a bath. I'll try the shower tomorrow. The radiators are working fine and the house is warm.

8

The Prosperous 20's

Saturday, December 4, 1920

Mr. Ranta came over to the new house today to go over the expenses. There won't be much more expenses with the big house since it's all done but now he and Arthur are talking about the other houses. Mr. Ranta is excited about having more work. The people who sell the property are also happy to have our nice big house done because it makes everything look good around here. Arthur is excited because he says this will be his first real job that earns money.

Mrs. Cummins came by on Tuesday and Thursday and I have learned to play a very simple song. It's only 4 different notes but it's a start. It's hard to be patient. Mrs. Cummins played "Schubert Serenade" again and it sounded even better now that the piano is tuned. She said the piano was very nice and there are thousands of different songs to play once I learn the rules.

Sunday, December 12, 1920

It's different going to church by ourselves and not walking with Scott and Susan and the children. Sometimes it feels lonely here. Not everything about living in the new house is happy.

The piano lessons are going well and I love to have Mrs. Cummins over. We decided to concentrate on me learning because Arthur is not as patient and he has been spending time with Mr. Ranta and talking to bank people about the houses to be built. I've been practicing a lot when Mrs. Cummins is not here. I am learning how to read the notes on the music that tell which keys to press for each note. It's like learning to read all over again but I like it.

Monday, December 13, 1920

We got a Christmas tree today. It was so much fun. We got a big one, bigger than me, and put it in the living room. This house is so big there's plenty of room for a large Christmas tree. Arthur says we need to invite people over for dinners and parties, especially since it's Christmas time. We put our decorations and lights on the tree and I love it so much. We need more lights now that we have a big tree. We also bought a new candlestick holder for me to put in the window. It will be special, just for Christmas time.

Tuesday, December 14, 1920

I learned how to play "Jingle Bells" on the piano. It's not fancy like how Mrs. Cummins plays it, but it makes me happy to be able to play a real song.

Thursday, December 16, 1920

We told Mrs. Cummins to stay and have lunch with us after the piano lesson and she said ok. I really like her. She is very smart and plays the piano so nicely and doesn't get mad when I make a mistake. She says I'm learning pretty well.

The only problem so far with the big house is that it gets lonely because we aren't close by to anyone. It's nice that Mrs. Cummins can stay and have lunch and visit. At least we're not too far from town. I love it when people can come over. I'm glad we have the radio.

We plan to have a Christmas party on Dec 23 and invited Mrs. Cummins and her family to come.

Saturday, December 18, 1920

Scott and Susan and the kids came over to have dinner with us. They came early in the afternoon and Stefani had fun running all around the house and exploring. We don't have a lot of furniture yet but we do *have lots more places to sit than we had before, especially at the big dining room table. Scott and Susan really like having the electric refrigerator from our apartment. I miss seeing them all the time. We told them to bring their laundry over and use our electric washing machine and that's what they did. We even have an inside clothes line in the washing machine area. It's not as big as the one outside. We told them to come to our Christmas party on the 23rd.*

We had a nice dinner and visited for a long time while the clothes dried. The house is quiet now and we are getting ready for bed.

Sunday, December 19, 1920

We invited Mr. Ranta, the Stewarts, and anyone else who wants to come to our Christmas party on the 23rd.

I wrote a letter to my stepmom to give her our new address and tell her about our house being done.

Tuesday, December 21, 1920

Mrs. Cummins said she will come to our party and said I should just call her JoAnn from now on.

Arthur and I went to the food store and got lots of food and cookies from the bakery for the party. We also got some holly for decorating. It is looking very festive.

Thursday, December 23, 1920

Our Christmas party was fun but I am tired now. Scott and Susan and the children came over early and helped us get ready. We had so many people it was quite jolly. On the radio they were playing Christmas music. Then JoAnn Cummins played the piano for us to sing Christmas songs and that was fun. I hope I can do it next year. Everyone had a good time walking around the house and going up and down the stairs and seeing how the house looks. The funny thing is that Mr. Ranta brought 3 bottles of Champagne that he had saved for the prohibition. He really likes Arthur. It is quiet now that everyone has left.

Serendipitous Rescue

<u>*Saturday, December 25, 1920*</u>

Arthur got me a nice coat for Christmas and a little wooden music box. I got him some nice work boots and also a coat. We put our new coats on and walked around outside. The snow outside is not deep but it's cold and the new coats were fun to wear.

The little music box plays a very pretty song that I never heard before. I have listened to it over and over. It came from Switzerland.

<u>*Friday, December 31, 1920*</u>

Scott and Susan came over for New Years Eve with the kids and so did Mr. and Mrs. Ranta. It's nice to have people here. Another year is over and once again my life is so different from how the year started. It's different for Susan and Scott, too, since they have two children now.

I got a letter from my stepmom. She was happy to hear about our new house. They are excited because they are making a trip to Ireland. Mr. Walsh is going there to talk about electric trolley cars and he is taking the family with him. They will be leaving sometime in March.

<u>*Saturday, January 1, 1921*</u>

It snowed a lot last night and the new year is starting off all white. Arthur and I went up to the attic room to look out the big window. You can see all around. It reminds me of when we stayed at the hotel in Pittsburg and we could see everything down below. Everywhere is white with the snow.

<u>*Sunday, January 9, 1921*</u>

I'm getting better with the piano lessons but it seems like I have such a long way to go. After each lesson JoAnn Cummins and I fix a nice lunch. She's also showing me different things about cooking.

Yesterday Scott and Susan and the children came over and spent the day with us visiting and doing the laundry. It's so dry inside that the clothes dry faster than outside in the summer time.

Wednesday, January 12, 1921

I'm now 19 years old. Arthur got me a necklace and some earrings for my birthday. It's cold and there's so much snow outside. There's not much to do but it was a good day for snuggling.

Sunday, January 16, 1921

Scott and Susan were here again yesterday with the kids. We told them to come every Saturday to do the laundry.

Sunday, January 23, 1921

Mr. and Mrs. Ranta came over yesterday afternoon and had dinner with us and Scott and Susan and the children. The people who are selling the property talked to Mr. Ranta and they have another house they want him to help build. That's three houses now. Arthur is excited about it too. At church Mr. Stewart was also happy about what's happening with the house building.

Sunday, February 6, 1921

At church we prayed for a little boy who got polio. I don't know them very well but I feel sorry for them.

Sunday, February 13, 1921

Church was sad because the little boy with polio died. It made me sad just thinking about it and remembering the kids and my dad who died from the Spanish flu. It made us all worry about Stefani and Mary getting polio. Arthur says anyone can get it and not just children.

Sunday, February 20, 1921

Another big snowstorm this past week. We're sure glad for the radio. We've learned where all the stations are on the radio dial and when the different programs come on. Some radio stations play music and some tell stories and one in Pittsburgh is like a church.

Serendipitous Rescue

Sunday, February 27, 1921

It's starting to warm up a little so hopefully Arthur and Mr. Ranta will be able to get working soon. Scott was telling us about all the problems they have when it gets cold and some pipes freeze and break. No one likes working in the cold.

Sunday, March 13, 1921

It rained this week and melted a lot of the snow. Now it's wet and muddy. Arthur went out with Mr. Ranta to mark off some work areas and used the boots I got him for Christmas. The boots got all muddy so we had to clean them but he said they worked really well and he loves them.

JoAnn Cummins got a telephone this past week. She said that with the money we pay for the piano lessons they can afford it. Her number is 382.

Sunday, April 3, 1921

The rain today made everything very wet but Arthur and Mr. Ranta have been starting on the different houses. Arthur handles the business and Mr. Ranta handles the building. Now we're back to having Mr. Ranta come over on Saturday night to go over the expenses and plans for the houses. Scott and Susan still come over with the kids so it's like we're a big family.

I got a letter from my stepmom. They were getting ready to leave for Ireland. They will be there for a few months so Darcy will have her baby in Ireland. That is something to think about. It makes me think of my dad. He always wanted to take us to Ireland. Arthur said maybe someday we'll take a trip across the ocean and visit Ireland and Germany.

Sunday, May 1, 1921

I'm getting better with the piano. We have been working on rhythm. JoAnn says I'm a good student. We have lots of practice things I have to do but also we're working on learning a new song and as soon as I *learn how to play it really well we learn another new song. Yesterday after dinner I played two songs that I have learned.*

The money from Mr. Oppenheimer at the mine was late again but it finally came and we bought a bed for one of the rooms in case we have overnight visitors or children some day.

Arthur rested again all day. He said he likes to listen to me doing my piano practicing while he sleeps in bed upstairs. Arthur said he should probably go see a doctor one of these days.

Sunday, June 5, 1921

We hardly have the radiators on any more and soon it will be hot. Mr. Ranta has been busy with the other houses and has hired more workers. More people want to build houses in this area and even in other areas. Sometimes Mr. Ranta brings people by our big house to show them what he can do. Even the property people come by sometimes. They call our big house "Colonial House" because it's the biggest house in the area and it's on Colonial Drive. Mr. Ranta finally got a telephone. Arthur said we all need one since we're working together. His telephone number is 397.

Monday, July 4, 1921

Scott and Susan and JoAnn and her family came over for dinner and fireworks. Mr. and Mrs. Ranta also came. It was a lot of fun.

Scott and Susan have a telephone now. Their number is 290.

Friday, August 5, 1921

We listened to a baseball game on the radio. Arthur said it was the first time a baseball game was on the radio. Scott and Susan came over with the kids. I don't know anything about baseball but Arthur and Scott did and they were interested in listening to it.

I'm doing well with the piano lessons. I showed JoAnn how we blow air out the window downstairs with the fan and it brings air in through the bedroom window and she said she would try it at her house. She doesn't have a sleeping porch. It sometimes makes me feel bad that I have these nice things and others do not.

Tuesday, August 16, 1921

Today we have been married for two years. It seems I have known Arthur my whole life and yet it seems like yesterday we were living in Carbondale.

We invited Scott and Susan to go to dinner with us to celebrate our anniversary. It was fun but little Mary was fussy for a while. Arthur and I had hamburgers and a Coca Cola again. I love doing things with Arthur and I also love doing things with our friends. I love my life with Arthur.

Sunday, August 28, 1921

We bought another bed for another room. We also bought a rug for the two bedrooms that have beds now.

Mr. Ranta got another request to build a house.

Yesterday we got a letter from my stepmom. Darcy had her baby last May. It was a girl and they named her Irene. I am happy for them and I really miss them. They are going to stay in Ireland and live in Dublin. Mr. Walsh got a good job working there with trolleys. Arthur said we can be glad they are having good fortune and so are we.

Sunday, September 25, 1921

We had a celebration at the one house that is now finished. It's for a family with 5 kids and they are all happy and excited. Now that the house is finished the bank gave them a loan and paid us the money for the construction. Arthur got most of it because he has been paying Mr. Ranta and the workers and for the lumber and other supplies. The extra money is the profit and Arthur and Mr. Ranta share it. After getting the money we had our own celebration. Arthur said it was too bad about prohibition but Mr. Ranta had one last bottle of Champaign and this was the time to drink it.

We had Stefani's birthday party at our house this past week because she loves it here. She is now five years old. I played the "Happy Birthday" song on the piano and we all sang.

Sunday, October 16, 1921

This past week they finished another house and we should be getting the money from the bank again in a few days. We're all happy because the bank people said they like working with us and told one of their customers to talk to us about building another house. Scott and Susan also want to build a small house. It's very exciting.

Friday, October 18, 1921

We got some shocking news in the mail. Mr. Oppenheimer at the mine is going bankrupt. We don't know why because business has been good everywhere. We can go back there to see if we can get anything out of the mess but Mr. Johnson, our attorney, says it won't be worth the trouble. The problem is that now we won't get the rest of the money. Arthur says we have enough money to keep the business going but we will have to be extra careful. The good thing about us building houses is that each time we build a house we get a more money than it took to build the house. Arthur says we are making our own money now, and we have learned an important lesson that you can't always count on things.

Monday, October 31, 1921

We did Halloween at Scott and Susan's apartment because there aren't enough houses around here that have kids. We finished another house this past month and are almost finished with another. Arthur says we're slowly getting ahead with the money so that's good.

Tuesday, November 15, 1921

I learned a new song for my piano lesson today that reminded me of my dad and mom. It's called "These Are My Mountains" and I remember my dad used to sing it. It kind of made me sad to hear it but it brings back nice memories of my dad. It's an Irish and Scottish song about going back home. Many miners came from Ireland and lots of them wanted to return some day. JoAnn could see that I liked it and said she would get me a book of Irish songs.

These are my mountains:

For fame and for fortune I wandered the earth,
And now I've come back to the land of my birth,
I've brought back my treasures but only to find,
They're less than the pleasures I first left behind.

The berm by the road sings at my going by,
The lark overhead wings a welcoming cry,
The loch where the scart flies at last I can see,
It's here where my heart lies it's here I'll be free.

Kind faces will meet me and welcome me in,
And how they will greet me my ain kith and kin,
The night by the ingle old sangs will be sung,
At last I'll be hearing my ain mother tongue.

For these are my mountains and this is my glen,
The braes of my childhood will know me again,
No land's ever claimed me tho' far I did roam,
For these are my mountains and I'm going home, and
I'm coming home.

Thursday, November 24, 1921

Thanksgiving was at our house. We just had Scott and Susan and their children because everyone else had family to go to. Scott's family is in New York and Susan's family is in New Jersey somewhere so they are glad to be with us. Our house is warm and we have the radio and the kids are playing and Arthur and I have each other so it's a lot to be thankful for.

I played some songs on the piano. I played the "Schubert's Serenade" song and also "These Are My Mountains" which I have been practicing. I am learning "O Tannenbaum" for Christmas. It's a German song. Arthur likes it because his family came from Germany. Scott brought a harmonica and played along with me. It was a very fun day and reminded me of when my dad played his harmonica.

Sunday, January 1, 1922

It's hard to believe another year has gone. Last night we had a New Year's Eve party and it was very grand. Scott and Susan and the children were here along with Mr. and Mrs. Ranta and Mr. and Mrs. Cummins and three of their children. JoAnn and I played tunes on the piano and Scott did his harmonica again. Mr. Cummins brought a guitar and played along too. I like the guitar and think I would like to learn how to play it. The Stewarts came by for a while.

Thursday, January 12, 1922

We celebrated my 20th birthday today.

Sunday, February 5, 1922

Yesterday Mr. Ranta came over to go over plans for the houses we're building. We're on our own now. No more money from the coal mine or the Kappel family but Arthur seems happy. I think he is happier than ever because he is earning his own money. Mr. Ranta is always happy now. He even looks different than when we first met him.

We had a really big snow storm yesterday. Mr. Ranta left before it got really bad but Scott and Susan were here late doing their laundry as usual and got stuck and spent the night with us. It was very fun and we stayed up late and did games and music. The kids had a hard time going to bed since it wasn't normal. The snow was piled high this morning and we didn't go to church. Arthur and Scott worked for more than an hour clearing snow away from the driveway and garage. They had breakfast and lunch with us which was really fun.

It's the afternoon now and Arthur is fast asleep.

Sunday, March 5, 1922

We celebrated Arthur's 25th birthday.

Thursday, March 23, 1922

I showed JoAnn my music box and asked if she knew the song. She said of course and it was a Brahm's Waltz. She played it on the piano and it was beautiful. I wish I could play the piano like JoAnn but she has been playing the piano longer than I have been alive.

Sunday, April 9, 1922

Everyone's busy working on the houses. It's barely warm enough to work but it's a good time for digging basements. Two more families have signed up with us to build houses. They aren't big houses but it's exciting to see more business. Mr. Ranta has had to hire more people.

Tuesday, May 29, 1922

The president of the bank that we have been working with came over to our house today. His name is Mr. Thompson and his father who lives in Harrisburg has retired and wants to move to our city. Mr. Thompson wants to build a nice home in his neighborhood for his father. We showed him all around our house and he was very impressed. Arthur is very excited. He said it's good to have a bank president as your friend.

Sunday, June 25, 1922

The bad news is that the doctor thinks Arthur has tuberculosis. Arthur seems healthy but coughs too much and gets tired easily. He might have had it for a long time, ever since the Spanish flu. The doctor said he is surprised that I haven't gotten sick because I kiss Arthur a lot. It might be because I got used to it and built an immunity or it might be my natural immunity that kept me from getting the Spanish flu. Hopefully as long as Arthur gets plenty of rest it won't get any worse.

Sunday, July 30, 1922

They started working on the house for Mr. Thompson's father. Mr. Ranta has four crews of men working on different houses now. The good thing about this new house is that Mr. Thompson has plenty of money and we don't have to wait for the house to be done before we get the money. It's not going to be a big house like ours but it needs to be fancy so it will take lots of work.

Wednesday, August 16, 1922

We have been married for three years now. Arthur has been busy with Mr. Ranta and I told him let's have hamburgers at home so that's what we did. Arthur didn't get home until after 6 and he looked tired. I was in the middle of cooking the hamburgers when he got home and he hugged and kissed me and the hamburgers got just a little burned but not bad. Arthur said they were the best hamburgers he ever ate. He always says things like that.

Sunday, September 3, 1922

It's been very hot and we have enjoyed the sleeping porch. We told Scott and Susan to come over whenever it gets too hot and spend the night with us and they have done it several times. We have more beds and places to sleep out there and it's fun to have them here. We do lots of singing and I play the piano and sometimes Scott plays the harmonica. I'm getting pretty good now. If I practice a song beforehand I can play it with hardly any mistakes. Also, I'm getting better at playing poker with toothpicks.

Sunday, September 10, 1922

Yesterday Scott and Susan left Stefani and Mary at our house and drove to Pittsburgh. They like to go there and shop and see shows. They spent the night in Pittsburgh so it was like we had children. We had a lot of fun. The kids are used to being at our house. We put an extra bed in our room and Stefani and Mary slept in our bedroom. Scott and Susan brought back lots of oranges. They didn't get here till the afternoon and we didn't go to church today.

My stepmom and Darcy are doing well. Darcy is expecting another baby. I hope we can visit them someday.

I was feeling sad that we are not having a baby. I talked to Arthur about it and he said it's normal to take time sometimes and not to worry. He always makes me feel good.

Serendipitous Rescue

Monday, January 1, 1923

It's been quite a year. There are more radio stations to listen to on the radio.

We had a grand party for New Year's Eve. Besides all our friends, Mr. Thompson, the bank president, and even the property people came.

We have more orders for houses for this next year. We're all excited that this has become a real business. I have been helping by keeping track of the expenses.

Thursday, August 16, 1923

Today was our fourth anniversary. My life is so wonderful. JoAnn brought over some cookies that we had with lunch after the piano lesson. She has been married for a long time and has a nice family.

Arthur is always happy and loves the house building business. Scott and Susan are planning a new home and Arthur and Mr. Ranta will build it. Everyone is in a happy mood.

Saturday, November 24, 1923

We had a celebration today because they started work on Scott and Susan's new house. They got approved for a loan from the bank that we work with and Mr. Ranta has a crew digging a basement. It's not too far from this house and we're all excited. We had a nice dinner and lots of singing and music. Scott and Susan stayed the night. Stefani is seven now and has her own room at our house and likes staying here. Mary is three and stays in the same room as Scott and Susan. Susan is expecting another baby.

Monday, March 10, 1924

Susan had a baby today. It was a boy and they named him John. Once again I helped out. The girls will stay with us for a few days while Susan gets her strength back.

I haven't heard from my stepmom for a while.

Sunday, August 17, 1924

We celebrated our 5th anniversary yesterday. I told Arthur we should go to Pittsburgh and see a show and spend the night. He was very surprised but I said we should do it. Before we left we used our telephone to call the hotel and make a reservation. Then we packed a few things and got in the car and drove there. We went to the same hotel we were at five years ago and then walked to the restaurant. After we ate we walked to the picture show. We saw a movie called "The Hunchback of Notre Dame." It was about the book I started reading back in the mining camp. It was interesting to see it as a movie.

Being in Pittsburgh didn't seem so bad and I had a wonderful time with Arthur. After the show we held hands and walked around. It's very different because the stores and places stay open late and there is lots of activity. We stopped at a shop that sells ice cream and had some. It was a very fun night and I could see that Arthur really enjoyed it.

Sunday, September 14, 1924

We all helped Scott and Susan move into their new house. It was fun moving our friends into a house that we built. Their house is about a half a mile away from our house so we can easily walk if the weather is not bad.

Wednesday, September 17, 1924

Scott got a camera to take pictures. It's exciting that their house is finished and they have moved in. We took pictures in front of their new house and then we all came over to our house and took pictures. I can't wait to see them. Afterwards we all went to the little restaurant that we like and had a jolly dinner. It's different now because we almost always see someone at the restaurant we know.

Saturday, September 27, 1924

Scott and Susan came over as usual and Scott had the pictures developed that he took last week. He gave me the one of me and Arthur standing in front of our house and it is a very nice picture. I will treasure it forever.

Thursday, Jan 1, 1925

What a wonderful year this has been. We have been so busy building houses and we have had parties for nearly every occasion.

Our New Year's Eve party last night was especially nice. I am so blessed to have so many friends.

Darcy has three children now. They live in a nice house on the outskirts of Dublin. My stepmom is happy. I'm glad for them.

It's times like this when I feel a little guilty for the wonderful life I have with Arthur. I think of the miners back in Carbondale and the little school there. I sometimes wish that Arthur's family had been nice and perhaps we could have remained there. But life in our big house here is wonderful and Arthur enjoys building homes. I have learned about so many things and I'm glad I can help with the business. I keep track of all the money and the materials and the schedules. Arthur says I am his partner in the business.

Saturday, April 4, 1925

Arthur and Mr. Ranta drove the car to Pittsburgh this morning to check on the workers who are building two houses there. When they got back we all went to the picture show at the Film-O-Rama. Scott and Susan got a babysitter and came too. We watched a movie called "The Big Parade." It was about the big war. A young man from a rich, vain family went to fight and fell in love with a poor girl in France even though he had a girl in America. It was sad to see all the things that happened in the war but it had a happy ending and the man went to live in France with the poor girl. It made us all glad we aren't having a war.

Friday, January 1, 1926

Once again I look back on a wonderful year. Our huge Christmas tree has been so much fun. Our Christmas party with all our friends has made for a wonderful holiday season. Last night we did New Year's at

Scott and Susan's house. Tomorrow we are going to Pittsburgh with Scott and Susan and the children. We'll spend the night at a hotel. I've learned to enjoy our trips to Pittsburgh. Sometimes I feel bad that we didn't make our home there but then we wouldn't have met Scott and Susan and all our friends here.

I got a letter from my stepmom. They are happy in their life. Josh has left for America to try to find his father.

Arthur is happy working with Mr. Ranta and I am happy working with Arthur. He really has a purpose now and I admire him so much. He is the most wonderful man in the world.

* * * * *

The next few years were a time of plenty. Nancy mastered the piano and could play almost any song from memory. JoAnn Cummins continued to come twice a week for piano lessons, lunch, and a visit. They often played the piano together for holiday parties.

Scott and Susan visited often. Their own home was only a half mile away, an easy walk that Arthur and Nancy made often. Sometimes Scott and Susan's kids would walk over to Colonial House to spend the night so Scott and Susan could go to Pittsburgh, always returning with plenty of oranges.

9
Crash

<u>Tuesday, January 1, 1929</u>

Last night we had another grand party. It has been such a good year. I don't know how I could be any happier. I love the huge Christmas tree. This next weekend we will take it down. We had to use the ladder again to decorate so we will be using the ladder again to remove the lights and ornaments. I'm always sad to see the end of Christmas.

We have built many houses this past year, some for people who have made money in the stock market. We have been careful with our money but we have enjoyed it as well. People love to come to our house for parties and we love to have them. Scott and Susan are here frequently with the children and we also visit them at their house. It's fun that we live close to each other.

Darcy sent a letter about my stepmom passing. It made me sad that I couldn't be with her. At least she had a good life with Darcy and her family. Darcy has four children and is expecting another.

Next week we're going to Pittsburgh to talk to the people at the adoption agency. I had hoped we would have children by now but some things aren't meant to be. Arthur said he had a dream that our house was full of children.

We have started getting the room at the top of the stairs ready to be a nursery. It's just across from our room so it's ideal. I do worry about Arthur's tuberculosis.

Serendipitous Rescue

Saturday, February 2, 1929

Scott and Susan were over today. Scott is a little worried about how the steel mills in Pittsburgh have been slowing down. That makes Mr. Ranta and Arthur a little worried too. We are working on eleven houses right now and three of them are for people who work at the steel mills. The bank president was concerned because new cars are not selling well.

On the radio we heard that the famous gunfighter, Wyatt Earp, died.

Saturday, March 30, 1929

There has been a panic about the stock market. It's been the news on the radio and everywhere. People are trying to sell their stocks and are losing money. We bought some stocks the year before last. Everyone is worried. One of the families who signed up to build a house wants to delay.

Sunday, April 7, 1929

Things have calmed down and everyone believes the panic is over. The bad news for us is that two of the people who signed up for us to build them a house canceled and said they want to wait till next year.

Sunday, May 5, 1929

Things seem better now and people aren't worried so much. Arthur said he is still concerned because the bank president is worried and the steel mills are still not making as much steel as usual. Scott and Susan were over yesterday and Scott said he might be transferred to another city. All these things are a worry.

Two more people have canceled their houses to be built but another family signed up.

Thursday, June 27, 1929

The news is tragic. Stewart's Hardware store burned down. We went into town to see. It was very sad. The Stewarts have been good friends and we do business with them. Jimmy Stewart is away at college. Mr. Stewart says he will rebuild the hardware store.

Friday, August 16, 1929

We celebrated our tenth anniversary but the world seems uncertain. The adoption agency is concerned that we don't have regular jobs. Scott and Susan are worried about being transferred to another city.

Sunday, September 29, 1929

Things have gotten worse. The stock market news has been bad. So many people are taking their money out of the bank to pay for margin calls that the banks are running out of money.

Another person canceled the house for next year. Mr. Ranta and Arthur are worried. Mr. Stewart has been rebuilding the hardware store and said he can get us anything we need for building.

Saturday, October 26, 1929

It's more bad news. On the radio they have been talking about how the banks and the government have been trying to fix the problem. Many people are panicking because their stocks dropped and they bought on margin. Sometimes they can't get their money from the bank because of the panic. That makes the panic even worse.

Sunday, November 10, 1929

Things are very worrisome now. On October 29 there was a big stock market crash but then seemed better the next day. Then it got bad again. Many of our friends are deeply in debt because they borrowed money to buy stocks and the stock price has dropped so much. The banks can't give them their money to pay for the margin calls and some banks have closed altogether. I'm glad we didn't borrow money to buy stocks but I feel bad for everyone.

Serendipitous Rescue

<u>*Sunday, November 24, 1929*</u>

This has been a very bad week. We stopped working on two of the houses because the people told us they are bankrupt and cannot afford the house now. It's bad for us because we have spent money on the materials and Mr. Ranta's workers. Hopefully we can work with the property people and the bank to find someone else to buy the houses. The problem is that the bank is having a hard time with their money and might not be able to get our money to us and they aren't making new loans right now.

<u>*Thursday, November 28, 1929*</u>

This has probably been the worst Thanksgiving ever and it's been hard to find things to be thankful for. Another person canceled the house we were supposed to start working on and Scott is getting transferred to Harrisburg. They will only be here a few more weeks, until the end of the year. Susan and I cried a lot and Scott and Arthur were not happy. Harrisburg is a long way from here. They are lucky that Scott has been working for a long time because many younger men where he works have lost their jobs. Besides being sad Arthur is worried about the money. Most of our money has been spent building houses but if we can't finish the houses we won't get our money back. Mr. Ranta has had to tell half the workers they don't have a job anymore. I have never seen him look so sad.

<u>*Saturday, December 14, 1929*</u>

We bought a small Christmas tree today. We're worried about money and we probably shouldn't have. We had decided not to buy one this year and Arthur found me crying in the bathroom and said let's just go get a small one that doesn't cost much money so that's what we did. It's not big. We put it on the piano.

We aren't planning on a Christmas party, just Scott and Susan and the children. I haven't felt like playing the piano for a few weeks and JoAnn Cummins doesn't come by anymore because they had to sell their car. The problem is that everyone who lost money in the stock market is trying to sell things and with all the people selling things no one can get a good price for anything. Arthur said it's the wrong time to try to sell our stock. It is worth hardly anything right now.

Wednesday, December 25, 1929

Scott and Susan came to our house for a Christmas dinner. They brought some food with them and we had a nice dinner. It was sad because they are almost all packed up and ready to move. We didn't sing but did listen to the radio. The Christmas tree was nice and I'm glad we got it. The kids played on the stairs and ran around the house. It was the only happy sound today. It's hard to believe that Stefani is thirteen years old. Where does the time go?

Sunday, December 29, 1929

Yesterday we helped Scott and Susan load up the truck and waved goodbye to them. I cried and cried and so did Susan and even Scott and Arthur had tears. They have been our best friends and I don't know if I'll ever see them again. Hopefully when times are better we will go and visit them.

Arthur says we should start being careful with the electricity and turn off most of the radiators to save the heating cost.

Sunday, January 12, 1930

Today is my birthday. I'm twenty-eight years old. Arthur and I have agreed not to spend money on birthday presents but we did have orange juice. Arthur says we have enough money for a year or two if we're very careful and by then things should be better.

It's been a sad birthday for me without my friends. Arthur has done his best to cheer me up. I don't know what I would do without him.

At church people aren't as happy as they used to be but it is nice to be there. So many people have troubles. We also prayed for Mrs. Ranta who has gotten sick.

Arthur is resting as usual and I am crying again about Scott and Susan moving away. There is so much to worry about and I miss my friends. I miss seeing JoAnn. Two of her married kids have come to live with her and her house is very crowded and she is busy.

We canceled our telephone to save money. We did get a letter from Scott and Susan and they are back living in an apartment. Harrisburg is a big city but not as big as Pittsburgh. Their apartment is downtown and is not as pretty as living here. On the plus side they are very close to the Hershey chocolate factory. Susan said she misses us and that's partly why I am sad this afternoon. I sent them a letter and told about canceling the telephone and how we're saving money.

Sunday, February 9, 1930

It was nice to go to church today. We haven't gone anywhere besides church and the store for the past few weeks to save money. Arthur has been in a good mood and has been figuring out our situation. He gets so much rest now he doesn't need to sleep all day on Sunday.

Wednesday, March 5, 1930

We did Arthur's birthday today. We had hamburgers and Coca Cola for dinner because that's what he wanted. It's lonely with just the two of us but we can go for walks around the neighborhood and meet people. And of course, we have each other. I started playing the piano again. Arthur says he likes hearing the music in the house. He has been teaching me about science and astronomy. The stock market seems like it might be doing better so people are hoping the money situation will improve. Some of the men have gone back to work on two of the houses. We have moved lumber and materials from the houses that have canceled to the houses that need it.

Sunday, April 20, 1930

The good news is that the stock market has been doing better and everyone is thinking that the worst is over. Even Mr. Ranta is looking happier. Mrs. Ranta is still not feeling well.

Scott and Susan are doing well in their new life but I sure do miss them. I remember back in the mining camp when I was sad about Hugh getting killed and my dad said it would take time and he was right. It takes time to get over sad things and sometimes I still cry about Scott and Susan being gone but I'm getting used to it.

Sunday, May 18, 1930

The day has been bright and cheerful. Church was nice. We walked all the way there instead of driving. It took a while but we had plenty of time. Mr. Ranta wasn't there but others were. Mr. Stewart has been rebuilding his store.

This afternoon we were out in the back yard and Arthur noticed that the carving in the tree that said, "Arthur and Nancy Forever" was getting hard to read because of the tree growing. He got a knife and carved over the letters again so you could read it. He had to get a small ladder because the tree has grown and the letters are up higher now.

I have been doing a lot of thinking lately. I worry what will happen to us in the future. I worry about Scott and Susan, JoAnn, Mr. and Mrs. Ranta and all our friends. I worry about Arthur. He said the way things are going we will be poor but we must deal with what life gives us and do the best we can.

No matter what happens in the future, I have everything I could ever want.

Friday, June 20, 1930

Arthur had to go check on the houses that we are still building. It's sad that we're only working on two houses now.

The other day we bought a small picture frame from some people at a house that were selling things outside in their yard. We put a picture of Scott and Susan and their family in it. We got another letter from them today.

Friday, July 4, 1930

We didn't do any celebration today. It's bad news again. The stock market has dropped again and more people are panicking. More banks have closed down and more people have lost their money. That makes other people want to take their money out of the banks that are still open. But if everyone takes their money out, more banks will fail. It's a mess.

Friday, July 25, 1930

The news is worse than ever. The stock market has dropped again. Arthur was in town today and visited the bank president. He told us to stop working on the houses because we were wasting our money. He said everyone has canceled their house or has gone bankrupt. Arthur is very worried now. The bank president reminded us that on a few of the houses we actually were the property owners because of how we had made the loans. Arthur said he will try to sell four of the properties to get us some more money. It seems things are not going to be good for a while. It makes me worried to see Arthur so worried.

Sunday, August 17, 1930

We went to church and found out that Mrs. Ranta died a few days ago and Mr. Ranta killed himself yesterday. They were bankrupt from the stock market and I guess he didn't want to live without his wife. It seems our whole life has turned upside down.

I have been beside myself with sadness and worry today. Usually, Arthur can cheer me up but he is taking things pretty hard. Arthur really liked Mr. Ranta. I don't think I've ever seen Arthur so upset. I don't know what to do.

Tuesday, September 2, 1930

We got some money from selling one of the properties. We sold it for $115 even though we paid $900 for it. At least that helps us pay our property tax on our house. Arthur is very worried about the situation.

The stocks are even worse. Arthur said to put the stock certificates away and not think about them. They are practically worthless now but there could come a time in the future when they might be worth something.

We are still depressed about Mr. and Mrs. Ranta. They were one of our first friends here along with Scott and Susan. Only two years ago we were all happy.

Arthur has nothing to work on. Sometimes he takes the hammer that Mr. Ranta gave him and uses the claws to pull weeds. This morning he walked all around the yard looking for weeds to pull.

Friday, September 19, 1930

We sold another property. We only got $75 for it. At least it's more money. We decided to splurge and go to the restaurant since we were already in town. We hadn't been there for a long time. We were shocked to see boards covering the doors and windows. It felt like one more friend was gone. Arthur put his arm around me and we walked home. Arthur said he has never seen anything like what is happening and neither has the bank president or the property people. It's not just here, it's all over the country and even the world. It's like the Spanish flu but this time it's money.

When we got home there was a letter from Scott and Susan and they said the same thing was happening in Harrisburg. It's lucky for them that Scott has a job. They had some stocks but not on margin.

Friday, October 31, 1930

It's Halloween but we turned off all our lights because we forgot to get candy. A few kids came around but not too many. Some of the new houses here have been abandoned. It makes the neighborhood seem spooky at night.

I don't know how I can be any sadder. I miss Scott and Susan and the children. They used to have so much fun running around the house and Halloween was fun with them. I miss the kids' birthday parties and playing "Happy Birthday" on the piano.

Arthur is sad. I wish I could do more to help. He has tried to find a job in town. The problem is that stores and businesses are getting rid of people, not hiring anyone.

We have canceled our plans for adoption. Everything is so uncertain right now. We haven't talked with the agency people for a long time.

Serendipitous Rescue

Every time I go upstairs I can't help myself looking at the room that is ready to be a nursery. I think of Scott and Susan and the children spending the night and how much fun we used to have.

Sunday, November 16, 1930

I don't know how things can get worse. At church people are talking about some who are losing their jobs and asking if anyone can hire them. People are starting to go hungry and it's scary because we don't know how we'll survive if this keeps up. We did sell another property but only got $80 for it. Arthur is resting because he said he was tired. That worries me too.

Thursday, November 27, 1930

It's Thanksgiving but we don't have a lot to be thankful for. We got a letter from Scott and Susan on Monday so we're thankful for that. I envy that they have three children. I hope they're all healthy. We're all alone this year, so different from years past. I would give anything to be back in that little apartment next door to Scott and Susan.

I am thankful for Arthur. He is the best thing that ever happened to me.

Monday, December 8, 1930

I have started reading "Les Miserables" again. Perhaps I'm older or perhaps because of the situation I'm in I seem to be able to relate to the story better now. It seems that all we do now is wait. Our only hope is that things improve before we run out of money. Arthur is hoping that maybe things will improve next year and maybe he can find a job. Our business is ruined. Maybe I can find some sort of work. Maybe we will sell our house.

Wednesday, December 31, 1930

It has been a horrible year. At least I have Arthur. I have tried to play the piano but it's hard to get in the mood. Mostly I have been reading. I have enjoyed cooking and doing the laundry. Arthur sometimes helps because he doesn't know what to do with himself. We play games and I have gotten pretty good at playing poker. Sometimes we just listen to the radio. I'm glad we have it.

Arthur said he should learn how to play the piano. I started showing him the easy lessons that JoAnn taught me long ago.

Monday, January 12, 1931

It's my 29th birthday and all I have is Arthur but that's enough. I just wish our future wasn't so uncertain. I wish Arthur wasn't coughing so much. He's getting plenty of rest but our financial situation weighs on him heavily. We both look older than when we first built this house.

Sunday, January 25, 1931

We didn't go to church today because Arthur didn't want to use the gas and it's too cold to walk. It worries me that he doesn't seem to have energy. We stopped the piano lessons. He can't seem to get in the mood. I played for him while he rested in the big chair. It's one thing I can do that makes him happy.

Tuesday, February 10, 1931

Arthur is not well and I want to call a doctor but he says not to waste money and there isn't anything a doctor can do anyway. He says he just needs rest.

Thursday, March 5, 1931

Arthur has perked up for his birthday so maybe he will be fine. Winter can be depressing. I baked some bread and we had spaghetti. It would be more fun if we had people around but we love each other. I have finally finished reading "Les Miserables."

Sunday, March 29, 1931

Arthur and I walked to church today. We haven't been for a while and the minister was glad to see us. Mr. Stewart was glad to see us too and wanted to know how we were doing. His hardware store has mostly been rebuilt but business is very slow. It was nice to see everyone.

Serendipitous Rescue

We took our time walking home. Arthur said we should enjoy the nice weather and walk slowly but I think he was out of energy.

Wednesday, April 15, 1931

Arthur has not been feeling well again and has been resting. It makes me feel sad to see him this way. I haven't felt like playing the piano but today Arthur asked me to play some music while he rested in his big chair.

Sunday, May 3, 1931

The money situation has only gotten worse. The future seems bleak. We have been going to church every Sunday. I play the piano every day, not because I want to, but because it makes Arthur happy.

I have had to face the fact that Arthur is dying. I have seen enough sickness in the past to know that I can no longer pretend that he will get better. I am terrified of the future but I must be strong for Arthur.

Arthur has again refused to see the doctor. He asked me to read him a story. I asked him which one he would like. He asked to hear his favorite story, my diary about how we met. Those were such good times. It's my favorite story too.

Monday, May 18, 1931

We didn't go to church yesterday. Arthur sleeps downstairs in his big chair now. It's easier for him to breathe that way. I have moved a couch next to his chair to be with him. I worry that he won't survive the night.

I fixed dinner and brought it to him and he was crying and said he has failed me. I cried too and said it wasn't so. Here I am practically educated and we have had a good life together, better than lots of people get. I hugged him and he said I was the best thing to ever come into his life. I told him he was the best thing in my life as well and I have no regrets. I hugged him and kissed him and he was happy that I loved him.

<u>Tuesday, May 19, 1931</u>

I fixed breakfast for Arthur and he seemed a little better. By afternoon he was out of energy again and his breathing was labored. I played all the songs I could think of, even Christmas songs. Arthur rested in the big chair and smiled. Afterward he talked to me very seriously. It was hard for him to talk. He told me not to pay the property tax and to stay here as long as I could and only pay for the electricity and the gas. He said we will lose the house. I sat with him for a long time in the big chair. He made me promise that I would never become a mean person.

<u>Wednesday, May 20, 1931</u>

This has been the worst day of my life. Arthur seemed good this morning even though he had a hard time breathing. We talked about plans for the future. It got cloudy and started raining. I played the piano again for him. After a while I stopped and he was smiling. He asked me to play "Danny Boy" and so I did. When I finished, he was still smiling but he had died. I held him and wept. I knew he had been suffering and was glad I could give him comfort in his final days.

It was about two in the afternoon and the rain had stopped so I put on my coat and walked to the church. I don't remember anything except weeping and arriving at the church. The door was open and I walked in and looked around for the minister. I found him in his office and before I could say anything I started crying again and he got up and hugged me and said he was so sorry.

10
Depression

Sunday, June 7, 1931

The past couple weeks have been a blur and I don't remember much. They came and took Arthur away and we had a funeral on Saturday, May 23. I didn't have a lot of money for a burial, but some of the people in the church donated money. The minister said that the Stewart family gave the most. I have been sadder than I ever thought possible. I had to write a sad letter to Scott and Susan. It seems that all the good things in my life are now gone. I asked the minister if I was being punished for having the big house. He said no, there was bad fortune all over the country, and the big house had been good for many people. He said lots of people were worse off than me and at least I didn't have any debt. I just don't know what I'm going to do.

Sunday, June 21, 1931

I have some money saved but it won't last long. I haven't had much of an appetite lately and haven't needed to buy much food. I have gone to church and it helps a little. People are sorry for me but there is trouble and sadness everywhere. Several families have left town and moved to Pittsburgh.

Dear Arthur, I miss you so much. I'm so very lonely. I'm glad for church and afterward I go by to see your grave. Then I walk home and go stand by our tree and hope that you are lingering by. I don't play the piano anymore and have covered it with a cloth.

Serendipitous Rescue

I don't sleep in our room and have moved a bed into the nursery and moved the baby things up to a room in the attic. I don't know how I'm going to cope.

I told the minister that I need something to do and would be happy to volunteer to help anyone or do anything.

Sunday, June 28, 1931

Dear Arthur, it's getting warm now. After church I walked over to JoAnn Cummins' house. She was glad to see me and we both cried. Her house is chaotic with everyone there. I told her to send someone by our house and they could have another electric fan. I could tell they are struggling as well. No one is doing piano lessons. JoAnn is looking like an old woman.

The minister told me they are setting up a weekly dinner for people who are struggling and asked if I could help with the cooking.

Saturday, July 4, 1931

Dear Arthur, I have really missed you today. I walked over to the church in the morning and spent the day there. There are so many people suffering. I helped cook stew and we made bread. It was a lot of work and is hot. There are lots of people who still have jobs and they are contributing money to help out people who are hungry. It made me feel better to help but in the evening they did a few fireworks and it made me cry because I wanted to give you a hug. Afterward I started walking home. It was dark but not cold at all. A car came by and it was Mr. and Mrs. Stewart and they gave me a ride back to the house. It's so lonely being here without you.

Sunday, July 12, 1931

Dear Arthur, I spent the day yesterday at the church helping again. At least I have something to do. I told the minister and Mr. Stewart that I need to sell the car. I guess I should have learned how to drive but it saves money to walk. Mr. Stewart told me he and Mrs. Stewart will take me home on Saturday nights. I did walk to church today and back home again. I'm in no hurry and it gives me something to do. The only problem is I keep reaching for your hand and you aren't with me.

Sunday, July 26, 1931

Dear Arthur, It's quite warm now. I tried sleeping out on the porch but that made me feel extra lonely. I put a fan in my bedroom like we used to do in our apartment and opened the window.

I am going to the church on Wednesdays as well as Saturday to help out. It makes me feel better to help other people and get my mind off of my troubles. Everything is different. There are so many who are having a difficult time. There are some stores in town that have closed down. I worry about the future. If things don't get fixed soon I don't know what I'll do. Perhaps if I'm lucky I'll get sick and die and we can be together.

Sunday, August 23, 1931

Dear Arthur, I do miss you so. It seems that Sunday is the only day I feel like writing. It rained while I was walking home from church but I didn't mind. It's hot and the rain felt good. It's hard not to have tears. Every change in the seasons or the weather reminds me of being with you. There was a breeze this evening and I put a chair out by our tree and ate an apple. The breeze made me feel like you were close by.

Sunday, September 20, 1931

Dear Arthur, there was another letter from Scott and Susan this past week. Also, the property tax people sent another letter that we're past due for the tax on our house. I started playing the piano at the church to make some music for the people who come to eat.

Sunday, October 11, 1931

Dear Arthur, we're getting a new minister. He seems to know all about my situation. He talked with me after church and thanked me for helping out. I still have a hard time talking about you without getting a tear.

Serendipitous Rescue

<u>*Sunday, October 25, 1931*</u>

Dear Arthur, Halloween will soon be upon us. It was bad enough last year without our friends but this year I won't even have you. I don't know how I'll get through Thanksgiving and Christmas.

I talked to the new minister about my worries and he said he would look into some possibilities.

I walked by to see JoAnn Cummins again this afternoon on my way home. Her husband lost his job but one of her boys who is living there got a job. They are struggling. It breaks my heart to see so much suffering. She was glad to see me and gave me the longest hug. We visited for a while but it's getting dark early now. It did lift my spirits to see her.

I finally sold the car for $75. Mr. Stewart said he could use another car but I believe he was just being nice.

<u>*Thursday, November 26, 1931*</u>

Dear Arthur, on this day of Thanksgiving, I can only say that I'm thankful for the years we had together. I would be happy to die now and join you but it doesn't seem to be my time.

<u>*Sunday, December 20, 1931*</u>

Dear Arthur, our castle is cold and dark. It is just a house.

In the past we would have had a Christmas tree by now. I have the heater turned down and all the radiators are off except in the living room and in the bathroom upstairs. The kitchen gets warm when I bake dinner, but I'm not cooking much here anymore. My only joy is helping at the church and reading letters from Susan. It made me feel better to play Christmas songs for the people who come for food. The Stewarts are nice enough to give me a ride back and forth as it is cold and slippery now.

<u>*Thursday, December 31, 1931*</u>

Dear Arthur, the worst year of my life is past. I spent the day yesterday helping at the church but today has been loneliness and sorrow. Susan said that they are struggling because Scott doesn't make as much money now but at least he has a job. They were able to get a few things for the kids and had a merry Christmas.

Tuesday, January 12, 1932

Dear Arthur, I am finally thirty years old. I thought you would be with me for this birthday but it can't be so. I fell asleep on the big chair with a blanket. The sun is out and shining on the snow. It's such a beautiful day that it seems impossible that there is so much trouble everywhere.

I finally heard from Darcy. She said she was sad to hear about you. They are doing ok but are being very careful. She has five children.

I have been feeling extra sad today. Having my birthday without you seems unbearable. I'm glad for the time we had together but I feel cheated. I don't know what's going to happen to me. Life doesn't seem worth living. I wish I could join you.

Saturday, March 5, 1932

Dear Arthur, you would be 35 years old today. I worked at the church today helping. I played the piano for them, too. When I got home I stood by our tree and had the most wonderful feeling. I don't know if it was you or not but I felt such comfort and peace. I will try to deal with what live has given me and do the best I can.

It's late and I can't sleep. I'm going to read our favorite story now. I'm glad you gave me the diaries.

Sunday, March 20, 1932

Dear Arthur, I got another letter from the property tax people. It was the final notice and I will have to leave soon. I talked to the minister about it and he said I have been very helpful to them and there is a big operation in Pittsburgh that could use my help and I could stay there. It wouldn't cost anything to live there and I would be helping people every day. I don't like the idea of moving away from here and living in Pittsburgh but I have no choice.

Susan said they are being transferred to Allentown. It's even further away from here but it's closer to where the mines are where we used to live.

Sunday, March 27, 1932

Dear Arthur, I've realized that if I leave this house I won't be able to take much with me. That makes me sad but I don't know what else I can do. I am saving my money to try to get enough to go to Ireland but I don't know if I really want to do that.

I have moved your clothes, some of my clothes, my music books, and my Christmas things to the farthest room in the attic with a note begging whoever comes to live here to please keep my belongings until I can return and collect them someday, if ever.

The minister has worked things out for me to get a ride to the food distribution center in Pittsburgh. I will be leaving soon. I sent a letter to Susan and told her to send me her new address care of the church here. I sent Darcy a letter and told her what is happening.

Sunday, April 3, 1932

Dear Arthur, I'm much more upset than I thought I would be. I'm leaving in the morning for Pittsburgh. I've said goodbye to my friends at church and walked over to see JoAnn Cummins. I thanked her for teaching me the piano and for the many food lessons. I stopped by your grave and then walked home and took in my last view of this place. I will be leaving our castle and who knows if I will ever see this place or any of my friends again. I have walked all around the house and the yard and will miss everything here. I hope your story about our tree is true and that someday we will find each other. I removed the cloth from our piano and played "Danny Boy" one last time.

I pray that the next people who live here will be a nice family with lots of children.

11

Pittsburgh

Wednesday, April 6, 1932

My Dearest Arthur, how I do miss you. I find myself in a strange place and my whole world is so very different. At night I stay in a room with three other ladies who cook and help take care of people. Everyone seems nice enough. I helped with dinner and there are so many people who come here for meals. Many people have no place to live. There are some places here for women and children to sleep at night. Lots of different churches collect donations and food to help out. It's sad to see so much suffering but it's good to see how many people are trying to help.

Sunday, April 10, 1932

Dear Arthur, it has been a busy week and I'm thankful for that. I shall never stop being sad that you aren't with me but helping out is a good distraction.

The three other ladies who stay here are also widows like me but they are all older. One lady named Diane lost her husband last year and has no family either. She is 54 years old and very nice. We have been working together and when the day is done we talk about our lives. Lucile is 64 and Helen is 59. There are other people who live in the city that come here each day to help, so there are a lot of people helping.

Serendipitous Rescue

We are not far from the steel mills. It reminds me of when you and I came here so long ago and saw the steel mills off in the distance. Now I live here.

There is lots to do, including the laundry and taking care of people who stay here at night. Some people are sick and stay here during the daytime. I'm glad for the work because it keeps my mind off the trouble. We mostly have soup or stew or anything that is quick and easy to dish out. We serve food at lunch and dinner. The biggest crowds are at dinner. We also have fresh bread for everyone, but not butter. During the night a few ladies come in to bake bread for the next day. Sometimes they work most of the night in order to have enough. It's a never ending job.

Sunday, April 24, 1932

Dear Arthur, I have been so busy. I'm getting used to the routines here and they keep us working from early morning till late at night. I am thankful for the work because I'm able to sleep soundly at night, and I don't have to worry about having a place to stay. I have the two suitcases with a few clothes, my diaries, the little music box, and some pictures. I have my nice purse that you got me and in it is the wallet I gave you. I keep them in my suitcase so I won't appear vain. Sundays are nice because other people come to help and we get the afternoon to rest.

I have been playing my little music box at night when we are getting ready for bed. The other ladies love to hear the song it plays. It's very soothing after working all day. It makes all of us think of better days. Last night I had to wind it up three extra times because Lucille was sad and wanted to keep hearing the music. None of us have any living children. We all have sad stories and we help each other.

Sunday, May 15, 1932

Dear Arthur, it's getting warmer and I am not looking forward to working in the summer. It gets hot working in the kitchen. I wish I could have brought one of the electric fans with me.

Sunday, June 5, 1932

My Dearest Arthur, I have spent the last week working in a hospital. They wanted to know if anyone would volunteer to help with patients who have tuberculosis like you had. I said I had experience with it and they took me. I'm ashamed to say that the reason I volunteered was the hope that maybe I could get sick from someone else and die. Sometimes just when I think I'm going to be ok something reminds me of you and I just want to leave this world.

The job situation has gotten worse than ever. Everyone is very discouraged. It doesn't look like things will get better for a long time, maybe never. So many men are out of work.

Sunday, July 3, 1932

Dear Arthur, I'm still working at the hospital but I find it rewarding. This past month two men and one lady died and I was the one who sat with them and held their hand while they died. I'm not afraid of getting sick. I do miss you so, but at least I am doing something good for others.

It is very hot and humid. They have some electric fans for people but not enough.

Sunday, July 31, 1932

Dear Arthur, there are so many sad and sick people. Two more people died and I was glad to help take care of them. I have learned so many stories from talking to sick or dying people. Some who are dying are all alone and they talk to me about their lives. It's interesting to hear about the different things people have done and the places they have seen.

The people in charge like me and I like them. They are happy that I can do so many different things. I can cook, do laundry, clean, help the sick, play the piano, and scrub floors.

Serendipitous Rescue

Thursday, November 24, 1932

My Dearest Arthur, how I do miss you on Thanksgiving. Once again I'm thankful for my memories. I was able to play the piano today. There were extra ladies here to help cook the Thanksgiving dinner and while I waited to do the serving, I played some hymns from the church music book. There is an old piano in the corner of the room where everyone eats. Everyone liked it and told me to keep playing the piano instead of working in the food line. It seemed to make people happy. I also played some Irish music that I knew by heart.

Sunday, December 18, 1932

Dear Arthur, what a nice surprise it was yesterday when a man from one of the churches brought in a Christmas tree. We had a few ornaments but no lights. We made popcorn and then used thread to make strings of popcorn and decorated the tree with it. I played Christmas music on the piano again. They always like me to play music. I'm glad I can. I still help out in the hospital. I am really keeping busy.

Sunday, December 25, 1932

Dear Arthur, how can I ever not be sad at Christmas time? I will say that this Christmas was better than last year. Having this job and a place to live keeps me from being so depressed. I finally got a letter from Susan. There was a mix up when she sent the letter to the church in our town and they sent the letter back to her. So she wrote another letter to the church and asked for my address and they sent her my information. They live in Allentown now and have an apartment on the south side of town where it's not quite so crowded. They like it better than where they lived in Harrisburg. Now that I have her new address I wrote a long letter telling her about my new life. I also wrote to Darcy.

Sunday, January 1, 1933

Dear Arthur, the new year reminds me of our good times and makes me sad. I don't know what I would do if I wasn't busy.

A lady named Mrs. Thaw spoke to us yesterday. She is friends with Helen Keller, the famous deaf and blind lady. She had such inspiring stories to tell. When I think about not being able to see or hear I am ashamed to be complaining at all.

I received a letter from Darcy. Things have gotten worse there. Her husband had to get a different job because they aren't building any trolleys now. She is busy with her family.

Sunday, February 5, 1933

Dear Arthur, I received a new assignment this past week which is to take care of children in the afternoon. They asked if I could play songs to help entertain them. There are fourteen kids and they like to sing songs while I play the piano. They also wanted to hear stories. We did Cinderella and then I remembered some of the books I read and told them a short story of the Wizard of Oz from my memory. They loved it and so did I. It reminds me of when we were teachers in the mining camp.

Sunday, March 12, 1933

Dear Arthur, I am doing ok. There are so many different things to do that it keeps my mind off my troubles. My favorite thing is the children. They ask for me to come and tell them stories. I am trying to remember the story of Pollyanna from memory. I think I can tell it better than reading from the book. There isn't enough time to tell the whole story at once but that's ok and the kids look forward to hearing the next part. I'm also thinking up stories and learning how to use my imagination. I think of the little stories you told me and I am going to expand them for the kids. Now when I go to bed at night I try to think of new stories. It's much better than crying myself to sleep.

Sunday, April 2, 1933

Dear Arthur, you would be proud of me. The past few weeks I have made up several stories for the kids. They like that I have stories to tell that they have not heard before. Most of the kids that stay here have parents who are working or are trying to find jobs. They're all poor.

Serendipitous Rescue

More banks have failed. For a long time many people have had trouble getting their money and now they have lost their money forever. People are hopeful that the new president, Franklin Roosevelt, will help the situation.

Even though we're close to the steel mills, it's very nice because we're near the river. I'm getting used to living here but I miss our big house.

Sunday, June 11, 1933

Dear Arthur, the good news is that the stock market has improved a little. Everyone hopes that means the depression will be over soon but for now things seem worse.

There are seventeen kids that I watch in the afternoon. They love my stories. I have also told the story of "The Call of the Wild." I wish I had the book with me. I can't remember it exactly so I made parts of it up. I have done that with "Tom Sawyer" and other stories.

I have been working in the hospital in the evenings. I have taken care of people with cancer, fevers, and even polio.

Yesterday was a slow day and I walked down to the river. There is a place that sells hamburgers and I used some of the money I saved to get a hamburger and a Coca Cola. It was so yummy and reminded me of the first time I went to Scranton with you. I'm not so sad all the time but I still miss you terribly. I ate a little more than half the hamburger when a skinny dog came by and just looked at me. I felt so bad that I let it have the rest of my hamburger. It made me think of your sad story about a dog and wonder what its story was. Even the animals are suffering.

Sunday, January 12, 1936

Dear Arthur, can you imagine that I'm 34 years old today? The winter has been hard with lots of snow. They are saying it's a record snowfall almost everywhere. It's very hard on people with no place to live. We have been letting people stay in every place we possibly can. The churches have been asking anyone with extra room to help out. The children get bored from being inside and I do my best to help out with stories and music. We will all be glad when it warms up.

Darcy and her family are getting by. I don't hear from her often. She has seven children now.

Thursday, March 5, 1936

Dear Arthur, you would be 39 years old today. I am no longer sad and weepy all the time but it doesn't stop me from missing you.

I had an interesting experience this past month. A very nice man kept spending time around here and wanting to help. His name was Michael Callaghan. I realized after a while that he was trying to court me. I told him that I appreciated his attention and help but I had a break in my heart that could never be healed. He was very nice and polite and I didn't see him after that. By all reason I should have entertained him. It might have meant some security for me.

It's gotten very warm lately, much warmer than usual. Everyone likes that the weather is pleasant and the kids can go outside. You should see all the water from the snow that is melting. It is quite something and the rivers are clear to the top.

Sunday, March 15, 1936

Dear Arthur, everyone is worried about flooding. The snow is rapidly melting and it looks like it might rain tomorrow. The sky is dark and foreboding. The river has flooded over its banks and water is on some of the streets.

Sunday, March 22, 1936

Dear Arthur, it has been a disaster. Our food distribution area has been ruined by the flood. Worst of all, when they started loading everyone into cars and trucks, everyone was in a hurry and I only got one suitcase. I was helping everyone and thought I had both of my suitcases loaded but didn't notice the one with my purse, your wallet, and my other pictures wasn't in the truck. The water was already around our feet by the time we left. It was raining hard and we were all in a panic. I am just sick about it. I had some money in that purse. I can't find my little music box. People everywhere are crying over things that have been lost or ruined. At least I got the one suitcase with some clothes and my diaries.

The steel mills have been flooded and thousands of people that had jobs are now out of work. There have been explosions and fires. It seems like God has condemned this whole area. The water has been contaminated and the National Guard is here. The trains aren't running and electricity is out. We are staying in a relief area until they can figure out what to do. The Red Cross has been helping and I do what I can.

<u>Sunday, April 5, 1936</u>

Dear Arthur, I'm having to adjust to life again. We are in a different area that is run by the Quakers. They have been very nice to us and we are all working to help. People have been working to clean up the city and still have a lot of work to do. I was hoping I would be able to go back and try to find my other suitcase but that is impossible. On the radio they are calling it the Great Saint Patrick's Day flood.

I have the one picture we took in front of the house because I had it in the pages of my diary. It's my only picture and I will guard it with my life. Everything else is gone. It seems like my past is being erased, piece by piece. I would feel worse if it weren't for all the suffering of other people.

<u>Sunday, April 19, 1936</u>

Dear Arthur, I really like the Quaker people. They let us have our church service after they are done with their service. They do things differently from what I'm used to and have different songs. There is also a nice piano in the large room where we feed people and I have been learning some of their songs on the piano. The hospital didn't get flooded but we are too far to walk so I have been getting rides when they need help there. I have made friends with a lady named Helen Bradshaw. I learned that Pennsylvania was founded by a Quaker named William Penn. You probably knew that.

The nice surprise was that I ran into Diane from the old place that was ruined in the flood. She had my little music box and gave it to me, safe and sound. It's surprising how a little thing can make you feel so good. She is working in a relief area on the other side of town.

Sunday, May 17, 1936

Dear Arthur, I have adjusted to my new way of life again. I sent letters to Susan and Darcy, telling about the flood and what has been happening to me. I like working with the Quakers just fine. I have been working with children again. I'm glad they like my stories. It makes me feel good that I can help them.

Sunday, Jan 3, 1937

Dear Arthur, another year is gone. Scott and Susan are doing well and their children are growing.

It seems the money situation has improved somewhat. There are still a lot of people without jobs but there isn't so much panic anymore.

Sunday, Jan 2, 1938

Dear Arthur, it has been quite a year. I have talked with many interesting people while working in the hospital. One man who was dying was once shipwrecked on a small island and was stuck there for several weeks before getting rescued. He said he almost died and it wasn't fun like in some stories and books. We talked for many days before he died. He enjoyed my company and liked talking with me. He was a sailor who worked on many different ships and went all over the world. He had lots of stories to tell. His name was Mr. Rasmussen. He said he was content and ready to die. He said life is like the ocean with many waves. Sometimes life is good and sometimes bad. One wave passes and another comes along. He said he was finished sailing on the sea of life. He gave me many things to think about and in some ways reminded me of you.

Another man had worked in the Wright Brothers bicycle shop and knew Orville and Wilbur. One lady worked in a hotel in New York where Susan B. Anthony often stayed. That's the lady who helped with the votes for women. There have been many others needing my help who kept their stories to themselves.

There is always something for me to do and I have kept busy. I've learned how to do many different things.

Scott and Susan are doing well and I'm glad for them. It seems unlikely I'll ever see them again but I'm glad we have stayed in touch.

I often think of Darcy and her family. I'm sure I will never go to Ireland. My only dream is to someday return to our little town and be buried next to you.

There are signs of improvement and more men are working. At least things aren't getting worse. There are fewer people who come here for food. That's a good thing but it makes me worry about what is to become of me in the future.

This past year saw the death of my friend Lucille who worked with me here. She was often sad. I'm glad her troubles are over.

12

Arabella

Sunday, April 3, 1938

Dear Arthur, this past week has been interesting. The Quakers want me to go work in a house and help take care of a family with three children. The mother has consumption like you had and needs help. They have been unable to find someone willing to work in their home because of her sickness. They have asked the Quakers for help and the management people knew I would be willing to go and live there. I will miss the people here but I am excited at the same time. The father works in a steel mill and is a manager. They live in a nice home with no money trouble.

Saturday, April 9, 1938

My Dearest Arthur, today has been quite an experience. I arrived at the home of Mr. and Mrs. Linden this afternoon. I am to take care of the children and to cook and clean. I will actually get a small amount of money for doing this.

When I got to the house, I introduced myself and Mrs. Linden was very surprised to hear that my name was Nancy Kappel. She asked if I was related to the Kappel family from Carbondale. I told her I married Arthur and you should have seen the look on her face. It turns out she knew you from Boston. Her family used to be rich but they lost almost everything in the crash. She said your mother wanted you to marry her and she thought you were handsome but you weren't interested. Her name is Arabella and she wanted to hear all about me. She was sad to hear that you have died and felt sorry for me. She said she always wondered what happened to you.

She showed me where everything was in the house and introduced me to the children. She has a boy Charles, who is twelve, Helen who is ten and Dorothy who is seven. They live in a very nice house, but not as big as Colonial House. I fixed dinner and Mr. Linden came home and after dinner he went into a little office to work on some things. They have a telephone and a few times the phone rang and he talked to people who had questions for him to answer.

After dinner she turned on the radio and while the children were listening to the radio she asked me lots of questions. She wanted to know everything about me. She said I was the mystery woman who took you away. She wasn't angry or anything like that, she was just curious. She even laughed and said she used to be much too vain for the likes of you. Her name was Arabella Schwartz when you knew her.

It has been a strange day but she seems like a nice person. I have my own room to sleep in and there is a bathroom that I can use. Everyone has gone to bed and I am tired.

Sunday, April 10, 1938

Dear Arthur, it will take time to get used to this place. Mr. Linden took the children to church this morning and I stayed home with Arabella. She didn't seem like she was too sick to go to church but I think she just wanted to talk to me while everyone was gone. I have told her our whole story and she wanted every detail. Later in the day she was very tired, though.

I got to know the children a little better today but they are shy to me. My first impression of Mr. Linden is that he seems busy and important.

Sunday, April 17, 1938

Dear Arthur, it has been an interesting week. On Wednesday Arabella was feeling well and while the kids were at school she took me to a store and got me some new clothes. She seems to like me and we have talked about everything you can imagine. She sleeps a lot in the afternoon and when the kids come home she is happy to see them. I cook all the meals and do the cleaning. Mr. Linden doesn't get home until 6pm or so and I have dinner ready. The children are getting used to me and are curious. Mr. Linden always seems to be busy.

I showed Arabella the only picture I have of you, in front of our big house with me. She said it was you all right. She showed me some of her pictures. She was quite attractive. We are both feeling the effects of age.

I sent Susan a letter telling about my new job and got a letter from her. She is happy for me. Stefani is almost 22 years old and is married and expecting a baby. Can you imagine that?

I also sent a letter to Darcy.

Sunday, May 1, 1938

Dear Arthur, I have been enjoying my work here. Arabella has a piano and knows how to play really well. The children like to hear songs and she has lots of music books. Other people don't want to be around because of her sickness and she seems to really enjoy my company. When the kids come home from school we have a snack. I've started telling stories for them and even Arabella seems to enjoy my stories. It has been so nice to talk to someone about you. She has told me stories about you and her in Boston that I never heard before. Sometimes it almost feels that you are alive again. I have a feeling that Arabella is a very different person than when you knew her. Perhaps if she was this way back then you would have married her. From my experience, it seems that she doesn't have long to live, perhaps a year or so.

Saturday, May 21, 1938

Dear Arthur, it's starting to get warm again. I have been keeping so busy that the seasons seem to come and go quickly. I don't think I like Mr. Linden and I'm glad he is not around here much. The sad thing is I don't think Arabella likes him very much either and he doesn't seem to like her. He doesn't seem mean, though, and always says "thank you" for the dinner. Arabella says he is unhappy because they used to be rich and he doesn't like working in the steel mill. He has a nice job compared to some people.

Serendipitous Rescue

I have been reading to the children. They have lots of books here and we have been reading "The Wonderful Wizard of Oz." Next they want me to read a new book called "Mary Poppins." Mr. Linden likes to go into his office room to study or work by himself. The children and Arabella listen while I read stories. It is so nice to be here with children and someone who knew you that I forget about the suffering all around and the people who are working hard to take care of the poor people. In this neighborhood you wouldn't even know there was any money trouble. I have heard that more people are working, thank goodness.

<u>Saturday, June 4, 1938</u>

Dear Arthur, we had such a pleasant day today. I took the children on an outing. I needed to go to the store for some bread and Arabella said to take the kids and get some food. She gave me extra money and that's what we did. The weather was very fair and just a little cloudy but there was no rain. The children and I walked to the hamburger place first and it was a like the one in Carbondale except they had a few tables outside where you can sit and eat. I had a hamburger and a Coca Cola. It has been a long time since I had one and it always makes me think of you. Then we walked across the street to the store and got bread. On our way home we passed by an old woman with dirty clothes sitting on the curb of the sidewalk. I felt so bad thinking that could easily be me. I had twenty seven cents left from shopping and gave it to her and she was very thankful. When we got home the kids told Arabella about the old lady and I said I was sorry but she smiled and said it was fine.

We had a good time doing stories tonight and the kids went to bed happy. They wanted one more story in bed so I told them a short story about a rock that was buried in the ground and wished to see the sky.

I have really missed you today.

<u>Sunday, June 26, 1938</u>

Dear Arthur, the children have been out of school for the summer and it keeps me busy finding things for them to do. We go for walks a lot. The neighborhood where we live is pleasant.

I got a very nice letter from Susan yesterday. She even sent a picture of her and Scott and the children. It was a shock to see how they have changed. I could barely recognize Stefani. It made me cry to see the picture and realize that I have missed out on their life. Arabella was curious about the picture so I told her about our friends. She hugged me and said life has been very hard. I wish I had the pictures of when we were all together.

<u>*Saturday, July 9, 1938*</u>

Dear Arthur, we had fireworks on the 4th and it reminded me of our good times. The food store has a freezer now and they sell ice cream already made. I took Charles, Helen and Dorothy on an outing and we brought back ice cream to the house. We had so much fun eating it. Arabella said the ice cream reminded her of good times when they used to make it in Boston. It made me happy to see her happy.

Arabella wanted to read our story. She saw that I like to write in my diary and she asked if I had kept it long. I showed her my diaries, all 6 of them. She was surprised and spent several days during the week reading. Yesterday she finished and gave me a hug and said she could see why you chose me. I don't know what she was like before but she is very nice now. Some days she is fine and other days she is weak and tired. She and you would have lots in common now with her sickness.

<u>*Saturday, August 6, 1938*</u>

Dear Arthur, I shall always love you and treasure our life together. Being around these children makes me wish we could have had our own. They have gotten to like me and love to hear stories. It seems their favorite ones are the ones I make up. They also like it when I tell my own version of stories, like "The Call of the Wild." Sometimes I read from the book but tell it my own way.

Today I took the children to a movie. We walked over to the theater that isn't too far away. It was a cartoon movie of "Snow White and the Seven Dwarfs." It was in color and had the sound of people talking and even music. Little Dorothy got scared at the end but ended up having a good time. I love doing things with the children.

Serendipitous Rescue

<u>*Wednesday, August 17, 1938*</u>

Dear Arthur, what a nice day we had today. I took the children on an outing to a park not far away. It gave Arabella a chance to rest this afternoon. After we were there for a while it rained and we had to take shelter in the gazebo. Some other children and another lady were also there. We all thought it was jolly fun and saw a rainbow. The children took turns running out into the rain and then back under the gazebo. It wasn't cold at all. When it stopped raining we went home because the swings and slides were all wet. Arabella was happy to hear about the adventure from the children. It has been a happy day.

We were married 19 years ago yesterday.

<u>*Wednesday, September 7, 1938*</u>

Dear Arthur, I had a fun day today. While the children were at school, Arabella said I should go see a picture show. She was reading in the newspaper about the movies and said there was one I should go and see. I asked her what it was about and all she said was the name, "You Can't Take it With You." She was smiling and said I would probably like it. She gave me fifty cents and told me to hurry and not be late.

I walked to the same theater that was not too far away where I took the kids. The movie was about rich, vain people but this one had a good ending. One of the main people in the show was little Jimmy Stewart. He is all grown up and is famous now and lives in California. Arabella says you would have liked the story and I agree.

<u>*Sunday, October 30, 1938*</u>

Dear Arthur, we had a bit of a scare this evening. On the radio was a program that pretended to be an emergency broadcast about the whole earth being invaded by people from Mars. We could tell it was for fun but some people outside were panicking and we wondered if it were actually real. The children were getting nervous but Arabella insisted it was all in fun. I agreed but still it was unnerving. In the end Arabella was right.

It seems the real threat to earth is growing in Germany. The news from Europe is not good. People are talking about Hitler and what is happening there.

Monday, October 31, 1938

Dear Arthur, we had a fun Halloween. Arabella was too tired to go out so I took the children trick or treating. Mr. Linden didn't get home until late. This was the most fun Halloween since Scott and Susan moved away.

I found out that Arabella is sick because she kissed another man a few years ago who was sick. Mr. Linden doesn't know and she made me promise to keep the secret. I don't know what to think about all this. They have enough money to be perfectly happy but they are not. Arabella thinks that Mr. Linden likes another lady and I think she is probably right.

Thursday, November 24, 1938

Dear Arthur, it was the best Thanksgiving in years. I feel like I should have been helping the other ladies feeding the poor people but it was nice to be here where it was quiet and comfortable and clean.

Yesterday I got a letter from Susan. After all these years Scott finally got a small increase in his salary and they are quite happy. It's good that we're both doing better.

I'm sad to say that Arabella is not. She has gotten worse but at least she is comfortable. I take care of everything for her and am glad to help. I have come to love her.

The work here is not at all difficult. They even have a vacuum cleaner that plugs into the electricity.

Saturday, December 17, 1938

Dear Arthur, I can't tell you how happy I am today. Arabella told me to take the children for a walk and try to find a Christmas tree. I was just as excited as the children. We found a medium sized tree that was just a little shorter than me. Charles grabbed the top of the tree and I grabbed the bottom and we carried the tree back to the house. Our hands got cold and sticky but we had fun.

When we got back there was a package from Sears and Roebuck and another from Montgomery Ward by the door. I brought them in and Arabella had me put them in her room. She said they were special presents for the children.

While I got dinner ready the children worked on decorating the Christmas tree while Arabella watched. They even have electric lights for the tree. The children were very happy and it was a noisy dinner. I would have been melancholy this time of year if it weren't for all the commotion.

Sunday, December 25, 1938

Dear Arthur, you won't believe what happened today. When everyone was opening presents, there was a present for me. I was surprised but even more surprised to unwrap a brand new purse. I was so happy I cried and cried. It was a nice black purse. Arabella must have read about the one you got me from my diary. She seemed very pleased and I hugged her and thanked her. She said I have been a good friend to her. After dinner I played Christmas songs on the piano and the children sang along. Arabella seemed so happy. We both know this will be her last Christmas.

Saturday, December 31, 1938

Dear Arthur, what a strange year this has been. You just can't tell what is going to happen in life. Being with this family has been good for me but who knows what will happen when Arabella passes on. It seems that in life, happiness is followed by sadness. Soon I will have to say goodbye to these children and it will break my heart again.

Arabella and her husband are making arrangements to have the children move to Philadelphia after she passes. He has family there. I believe the children will stay with his sister. I've not met any of his family.

It's very late and has gotten noisy outside as people are celebrating the new year. There's lots of trouble in Europe but more people have jobs. Folks are beginning to think that better times are ahead.

Thursday, January 12, 1939

Dear Arthur, it has been another wonderful day. Right after I cleaned up the breakfast dishes, Arabella gave me some money and told me to go buy something for my birthday. She would like to have gone shopping with me but didn't have the energy. She insisted that I go and so I did. I didn't want to leave her and was very quick about it. She was very generous and gave me more money than I needed for a dress and when I got back I showed her what I bought. She said to put the extra money in my new purse. I thanked her and then she said she had something for me and gave me a nice suitcase that she had. She said she won't need it any more. I gave her a hug and kissed her on her cheek. She hugged me back and I could tell she really liked me. I have to help her with everything now, including getting dressed and going to the bathroom.

Thursday, January 19, 1939

Dear Arthur, I have been feeling depressed these past few days because of Arabella. She is often scared and afraid, and wants me close by. Her love is her children and she doesn't want to die. I would gladly trade places with her if only I could.

The children know their mother is very sick and are sad as well. Mr. Linden has been nicer lately.

When I put the children in bed at night we talk or I tell them stories. Charles asks me questions about life for which I have no answer.

Monday, January 23, 1939

Dear Arthur, it's been another sad day in my life. Arabella passed away just a little while ago. The children are at school and we are alone. We talked for a while and I held her hand. She coughed and cried a lot. She said she was a better person than she used to be but that I was always a better person. She thanked me for being with her and for being a friend. I held her hand and she said, "Arthur made the right choice." We sat together for a while and didn't say anything. I put my arm around her as she struggled to breathe. Shortly after that she died. I couldn't help but be sad. It was an odd and unexpected friendship. I don't know why so many people get sick and die and I have to stay alive.

I called the Quaker people on the telephone and they said they would handle everything but I need to pack my things. It's not proper for me to be in the house with Mr. Linden. His sister is on her way and is expected to arrive this evening.

I dread when the children get home. At least they didn't have to see their mother die. I'm glad I could be here for her. I wish she could have lived longer. I wonder what will happen when it's my time. Will there be anyone for me?

13

Home

<u>*Sunday, January 29, 1939*</u>

Dear Arthur, it is a strange feeling to be back with the Quakers, but I feel good about helping the poor people around here. It seems that more people are working but it's cold now and there are still folks who need help.

I have been weepy lately because of leaving the Linden family. The children were crying for their mother when the Quakers came to pick me up. It was a very sad situation. I don't know how much more sadness I can bear. At least I had a few months of joy.

The management people were very pleased with how I handled things. They talked to me for a while and asked questions about how I liked working with the children and what we did together. I told them I enjoyed being there and how I told stories to the children and played games. They said I was one of the best workers they ever had. I'm glad for that, but I wonder if I was just not meant for happiness. At least some of the kids are still here from before. I'm glad to see them.

I sometimes wonder if I should have married Michael Callaghan. I just can't imagine loving someone else.

<u>*Sunday, February 12, 1939*</u>

Dear Arthur, I had an interesting experience this afternoon. The management people talked to me again and asked if I liked working with children. I said yes, I love working with children. They wanted to know about my education. Of course, I didn't have a formal education like lots of people but I have read lots of books and am good with numbers. I told them about how I used to help out at the school in the mining camp and how I helped the kids there with reading and numbers. They told me about a home for orphans back in our town of Indiana they had started and asked if I would be interested in working there. I told them I would love to return and live in my town again. They said I would have to live at the orphanage and help take care of children and help with schoolwork and things like that. They wouldn't be able to pay hardly anything, but I would have a place to stay and food to eat. They wanted to know if I was interested in finding another husband. I told them I had no interest in a husband. Besides, I am 37 years old now.

I must have answered their questions well because they said they would like me to start work soon. I hope I will be able to visit our big house someday and get my things if they are still there.

Sunday, March 5, 1939

Dear Arthur, I always think of you on your birthday. It's too bad Arabella didn't live long enough to celebrate your birthday with me. I know she wanted to. I really miss her.

It's different being back here and working with the poor people and the helpers. There are lots of groups of volunteers who help people, and I'm proud to be able to help.

I keep thinking about going back to Indiana to work in a home for children. I wonder where it will be and what it will be like.

Sunday, April 2, 1939

Dear Arthur, there's more trouble in Europe and Japan is having a war with China. Lots of people think we are going to have another big war.

Sunday, April 23, 1939

Dear Arthur, I am shocked and nervous about tomorrow. They told me I would be going to the orphan home. I was curious about where it was and asked if they knew the address. They told me it was 22 Colonial

Drive. I couldn't believe it! I am nervous and excited at the same time. I don't know what to think. I don't know how I will sleep tonight.

<u>*Monday, April 24, 1939*</u>

Dear Arthur, this has probably been the strangest day in all my life. The ride to Indiana after lunch seemed to take forever. I had my suitcase from you and my suitcase from Arabella. I wore the dress I got for my birthday from her.

My heart was beating so fast as we came into town. When we got to the house, I thought I would burst. The trees are all bigger. The house seems old. As we walked toward the front door, I could hear the muffled sounds of children inside. It was a strange feeling. The driver knocked on the front door of what used to be our home. A lady named Mrs. Barclay opened the door and welcomed us in. It was a curious thing to step inside and see everything. The driver introduced me as Miss Nancy Kappel, but I didn't say anything. Then Mrs. Barclay's husband came in to greet us. We only talked for a few minutes. The driver and the other lady walked back to the car. When they left, it was quiet, and the children came to see me. There are five children living here but one is a baby. When Mrs. Barclay said she would show me around, I told her I knew this house very well and that I used to live here. She was quite surprised. She knew the previous people had lost the house and said she was sorry for me. I told her I was just glad to be back and was happy that children live here now.

My dearest Arthur, it is nothing short of amazing. The dining room table, the refrigerator, the beds, and even your big chair, and the piano and the electric washing machine are all here. Things are arranged differently, and Mr. and Mrs. Barclay live in our room, but I don't care. The radio and one of the electric fans that we bought are gone, but they have a different radio. Mrs. Barclay showed me where the children sleep. I was disappointed that Mrs. Barclay's children are using my favorite room but that is ok. Two of the kids who live here are Mrs. Barclay's own children. She has a one-year-old girl and a three-year-old boy. She is using my room as a nursery, which is what we intended anyway.

Mrs. Barclay seemed to feel awkward with having me there. She is younger than me, but I told her not to worry, and I have no problem with her being in charge.

It has been seven long years since I have seen this house. I can't tell you how happy I am. I walked around the back yard, and our tree is still there and has grown even taller. I know it can't be so, but I like to believe that our special tree has brought me home.

I told Mrs. Barclay I was used to working hard, and I was ready to help get dinner ready. It was easy helping fix dinner since I was familiar with everything. There is a telephone here again.

It was a little odd having dinner with them and the children. It will take time to get used to each other. Mr. and Mrs. Barclay both wanted to hear about what I had been doing in Pittsburgh. I also told them about you and how we built this house. The children didn't say much but after dinner they played outside for a while.

I took care of the dishes and told Mrs. Barclay to relax. She turned on the radio. There are more stations to listen to now. The news about war is bad everywhere.

After the children had been put to bed, Mrs. Barclay was curious to hear my story. We talked for quite a while until I could see she was tired. I am exhausted but am too excited to go to sleep. I am in the room at the end of the hall where Scott and Susan used to sleep. I will finish writing and go to bed, even if I can't sleep. I feel that a new life is beginning for me. Our big house is a home again.

Tuesday, April 25, 1939

Dear Arthur, I woke up early today and for a moment I thought I was dreaming. I am so happy I can't describe it. The sun was out for a while, but it's turned into a rainy day. I was up before anyone, but Mr. and Mrs. Barclay were soon up to take care of the baby.

I asked Mrs. Barclay what we should have for breakfast. She said they usually have oatmeal today, so that's what I got ready. I took care of the dishes and Mrs. Barclay appreciated it.

After lunch, I asked Mrs. Barclay if I could go up and check in the attic. She said it was fine and walked with me up the stairs to the room in the attic where I had put my things. Before we even opened the door, she said it was still there. I walked in, and there were my things with my note still on it. I couldn't help myself and starting crying. It was like meeting an old friend. She hugged me, and I hugged her. I left my things there and closed the door and thanked her over and over.

We went downstairs, and I talked with the children. Mrs. Barclay's three-year-old boy is named Jon, and her baby girl is named Shannen. Shirley is five, and Mark is four. The oldest boy, Bobby, is seven and goes to school.

The children were shy about me, but I asked if they wanted to hear a story, and they did. We sat on the couch and I told a short story that I made up about a lady who was travelling on a great ship that sunk in a storm and she was the only one left and floated for days on a piece of wood and came to an island. On the island were magical people but they didn't know how to swim. The lady taught the magical people how to swim and they were very grateful. They wanted to do something nice for the lady and could see that the lady was very sad. They asked her why she was sad and she said it was because she missed her home and family. They said to think very hard about her home and they would do magic. So the lady closed her eyes and thought very hard about her home. Suddenly she was flying, and flew through the air until she was back at her house.

Mrs. Barclay said she never heard that story before. I said I just made it up. She smiled and seemed amused.

I walked over to the piano and lifted the cover over the keys. Shirley asked if I knew how to play the piano. I asked Mrs. Barclay if she minded, and she said no go right ahead. I sat down and played "Schubert's Serenade." It felt so good to play and hear that song in this room again. When I finished, little Shirley said it was pretty and wanted another song. I played "These Are My Mountains" and sang the words about coming home. I got a lump in my throat, and I could see Mrs. Barclay was touched. By then Mr. Barclay came in. I played the Brahms Waltz from my little music box and also Fur Elise. Then I played some children's songs. Mrs. Barclay said it was nice to hear music from the piano.

We talked more and Mr. Barclay went outside to work on the yard. He used to work in a big store and lost his job in the crash. They are poor like me, but she had been a school teacher and was certified to take care of orphans. I told her about the mining camp and how I used to help out at the school.

I got out my little music box and let the children hold it carefully while it played its music.

Bobby came home from school, and Shirley told him about my story and playing the piano. So I had to tell my story again, and you would think it was the best story in the world. Then I played the piano again. The kids named different songs that they wanted to hear, and I knew all of them. We had a very jolly time, and then I noticed that Mrs. Barclay was working on dinner, so I stopped and said we would do more later and went into the kitchen to help.

We had a nice stew for dinner and bread that came from the farm. I helped cut up potatoes and carrots, and Mrs. Barclay sliced some meat. As far as I can tell everyone here seems very nice.

After dinner, the children wanted another story. I told my long version of the rock who wanted to see the sky. The children wanted more songs so I played songs like "London Bridge" and other children's songs that they could sing along with. Mrs. Barclay got the children ready for bed while I did the dishes. She said I was very clever and that made me happy. I told her about how you taught me these things.

The children wanted more stories and songs but Bobby needed help with arithmetic, so I told the kids we would do more tomorrow, and I helped him practice like I did at the mining camp.

Shirley has been calling me Miss Nancy, Jon calls me Mrs. Apple, and Bobby calls me Mrs. Kappel. I told the children they can just call me Miss Nancy if they like. Mrs. Barclay smiled and said it was fine and would be easier to say than her name. When the children got ready for bed, they said, "good night Miss Nancy." It seemed just right.

After the children were settled in bed, I looked through my things in the attic. It was so much fun seeing everything. Mrs. Barclay came in and saw the Christmas ornaments and said she hoped we could get a Christmas tree this year. When we went downstairs, I got my new purse and showed her the money I got from Arabella. I also had some money from working there and said let's save it for the holiday. She smiled and agreed.

I had so much fun today, but now I'm exhausted. It's different taking a bath in this other bathroom, but I don't mind at all.

Wednesday, April 26, 1939

Dear Arthur, it has been another interesting day. After breakfast, Mrs. Barclay and I got ready to drive to the market. As we were walking from the house to the garage, she explained that a man named Mr. Stewart had donated a car when he found out they were starting an orphanage. It was the car he bought from me! Life has been strange, but it has been made nice by good people. Mrs. Barclay knows how to drive. As we rode into town, I told her about the car. She asked if I wanted to drive, but I told her I never learned. She agreed that life was strange and was happy that we had a nice car to drive. She was glad the car didn't need a crank to start. She told me how hard it has been for her husband to be out of work and how everyone believes that this is the way life is going to be from now on, and we just have to get used to it. The town looks mostly the same as before. Many buildings need paint. Most people are just getting by.

At the store, Mrs. Watson recognized me and asked how I was doing. I told her I had been living in Pittsburgh. She was sorry to hear about everything. I walked over to Stewart's hardware to see if Mr. Stewart was there but they said he wasn't. I asked Mrs. Barclay if we could stop by JoAnn Cummins' house. We did, but she had died right after this past Christmas. Mrs. Barclay was nice and asked if there was any other place I would like to see. We stopped for a short time at your grave.

After lunch, I washed the dishes and sat in the big chair. We turned on the radio, and before I knew it, I was asleep. I had a dream that you came home, and I was showing you around to see all the changes.

I woke up to the sound of Shirley trying to play notes on the piano. Mrs. Barclay came in and asked her to please be quiet. I said it was okay and didn't mean to fall asleep. I'm glad I woke up because we needed to start working on dinner. We had another nice meal. We are so fortunate to be able to get food from the farm that is run by the

Quakers. Things like butter are so expensive, and lots of people don't have any at all and we have almost as much as we want, as long as we're careful.

Thursday, April 27, 1939

Dear Arthur, it has been another pleasant day. The newness is wearing off, and I almost felt a touch of depression after breakfast, but then everything was fine. Mrs. Barclay got a telephone call from the management people, and we will be getting another child sometime next week. There are lots of orphans in Pittsburgh, and they want to move some of them here.

Mrs. Barclay is very nice, and we talked for a while after lunch. She said she felt bad about having our old bedroom, and I said not to worry, and I didn't want to sleep there anymore. I told her I was so happy to be back here I didn't care if I slept in the garage with the car. She smiled and said she was glad I was here, and we all have to look out for each other. She talked about how they are worried that there might be another big war.

Saturday, April 29, 1939

Dear Arthur, it's funny how life is. I'm so glad to be back here but I've had times when I feel happy and other times when I feel depressed. I like Mrs. Barclay and I love having the children here but it's so different, and so many things bring back memories. Sometimes I hear something from the other room and for a moment I think it's you and then realize it's just a child or Mrs. Barclay. Last night I had the most wonderful dream about when we lived in Carbondale and you and I were walking in the cold, holding hands, laughing and talking and telling stories. Then I woke up.

It's going to take some time to adjust but it's a lot better than where I've been. Sometimes I feel guilty being here when there is so much suffering all around. The good news is that more people are working. The bad news is about the wars. Mr. Barclay is worried about what will happen if we have another big war.

We did our laundry after lunch. Mrs. Barclay said she was glad that you and I bought the electric washing machine.

Saturday, May 6, 1939

Dear Arthur, there's nothing like a busy week to make you forget your troubles. We received two little girls this week, on Tuesday. One is a seven-year-old named Patricia, and a six-year-old named Barbara. They are sisters and their mother got a fever and died. They were staying at the shelter when their mother died and I remember them. They have been sad little children, and I have been taking care of them as best as I can. Since they don't know Mrs. Barclay any better than they know me, Mrs. Barclay said I might as well take the lead with them. They remember me and I have sat in the big chair with both of them and talked about their mother and told them stories. I found out their favorite songs and played the piano with them sitting next to me. I helped them set up their room but then decided to put a bed in my room for them until they are used to things. At dinner, I sat between them. They helped me get the food ready. Mrs. Barclay said I'm very good with children, but I've never had this kind of experience before. One time little Barbara was crying and Shirley who is only five walked over and hugged her and said, "it's ok." It was very cute.

It's nice to be working with children again. Mrs. Barclay says it's our job to take sad children and make them happy. This is a serious business, and I will try not to ever feel sorry for myself again.

Sunday, May 14, 1939

Dear Arthur, Margaret and I have been getting along very well. We agreed that I should call her Margaret, and she would call me Nancy. I told her she has the same name as my mother.

We've kept busy over the weekend. It rained quite a bit. I'm glad we have this big house. Patricia and Barbara are doing better. The children all stayed up late Saturday. Margaret made popcorn while I was telling a story. We did some singing, and little Patricia and Barbara joined in. We didn't even use the radio.

Saturday, June 3, 1939

Dear Arthur, it's amazing how children can adapt. I have done my best to help them by telling stories, holding hands, sitting them on my lap, making popcorn, going for walks and playing games. Little Patricia decided she wanted her own room. We moved the bed out of my room and into a room with two beds. I asked Barbara if she would like to sleep in her own bed next to Patricia, and she said she would. We found some old trunks at the charity store so the girls can put their things there. Patricia and Barbara didn't come here with much. They each had a rag doll and one extra dress. Each child now has a trunk in which to keep their things and some more clothes that have been donated.

Tuesday, July 4, 1939

Dear Arthur, it seemed last year that the bad times were starting all over again but this year things seem a little better. There are still many people out of work.

A man and some boys from a church came by today selling sparklers. They were going to all the houses. We bought a few for the children with my money. Holidays are very hard for me. You and I used to have parties here on special occasions, but those days are gone. The children had a lovely time with the sparklers.

Wednesday, August 16, 1939

Dear Arthur, today is our twentieth wedding anniversary. I am happy to be back living in our castle with these nice people. So much has happened these past years. I don't know what the future will bring. I cherish the time we had together.

The sleeping porch has been working out well. Several screens have been tearing at the bottom, and Mr. Barclay has managed to secure them. Last night was very warm but after we turned out the lights, you could see the fireflies. I must think of a story about fireflies.

Wednesday, September 6, 1939

Dear Arthur, Margaret and her husband saw a movie tonight. You'll never guess what the movie was. It was "The Wizard of Oz" and they went to see it at the little theater we used to go to. The Film-O-Rama is now the Mills Movie Theater. I took care of the children while they were out.

Little Jimmy Stewart is in a movie about a politician. He isn't little anymore. He will never work in the hardware store but I think Mr. Stewart is proud of him.

Margaret is turning out to be one of the best friends I ever had. It's different from Scott and Susan because Margaret and I are together all the time. I still miss Scott and Susan and their children. Their little baby John is fifteen years old now. I haven't seen them for so long it's hard to remember what they look like. Probably only Stefani would recognize me. They have new friends now, and I'm just fading away.

Last Sunday we had a fireside chat on the radio. President Roosevelt talked about the wars in Europe. It's very serious.

Saturday, September 30, 1939

Dear Arthur, it was a lovely day today. I do wish you could be here with the children and me and the Barclays. The ladies from the farm came by today with fresh milk, bread, eggs, and other items.

When it got dark and time to get ready for bed, we all gathered around like we do now for a story. I made up a story of the last firefly since they are almost gone now. The children liked my story, and so did Margaret and her husband. After that, I played the piano, and the children sang songs. It was a very nice night. You would have been proud of me.

Tuesday, October 31, 1939

Dear Arthur, it has been a fun Halloween. I was a little sad thinking about Arabella's children, but the kids here kept us busy. It was quite a commotion getting everyone ready but we had fun going trick or treating. There are still some vacant houses all around, and it made things extra scary. It's like there's a haunted house on every street. Margaret and I walked the kids around, and Mr. Barclay stayed home to give out candy.

I wish you could be here. You would have had so much fun. It's very late now, and everyone is asleep. There is a breeze blowing, and it's dark and cold outside.

Serendipitous Rescue

Thursday, November 23, 1939

Dear Arthur, we had a nice Thanksgiving today. Mr. Barclay was hoping to have a job by now, but we are all thankful for each other and for the orphanage and the children who live with us. Margaret and I worked all morning and afternoon. Even Patricia and Barbara helped. We had dinner about 4 pm. Our big table has been very useful here with all the children.

While the ladies from the farm were here, they asked if we would be able to take another child. Margaret looked at me and I said of course we would.

Thursday, November 30, 1939

Dear Arthur, the ladies from the farm brought a boy named James today. He is seven. He has been an orphan since he was five and has been living in Pittsburgh. They will bring us another bed next week and for now he will sleep with Mark. You would be happy to see all the children here. It gets noisy sometimes in the evening, but it has been a good thing that we built this big house.

Saturday, December 16, 1939

Dear Arthur, we got a Christmas tree today. I'm so happy, but it does make me miss you so. Margaret has been just as excited as me. We have also been trying to find presents for the children. We will have some presents that are donated, but we want to see if we can get one new toy for each child. We used my money and ordered a crystal radio set from Sears and Roebuck for Bobby and James. For the girls, we ordered a bracelet and necklace set.

We put the presents we have been collecting in the room where my things had been kept. The children already knew that was an off-limits area. I can't help but feel excited.

We had so much fun decorating the Christmas tree. We brought down the ornaments and lights that I had saved. Margaret made popcorn to string up as well. Everything was merry. I played the piano, and we all sang carols.

I often think about Arabella and her children. And of course, Scott and Susan. I wish I had been able to get a picture of me and Arabella.

<u>*Monday, December 25, 1939*</u>

Dear Arthur, it has been such a nice day. Last night we were up late getting things ready and before that we spent the evening singing songs and telling stories. I told the story of "A Christmas Carol" about Scrooge and the three ghosts. Before that, I read "A Visit from St. Nicholas" for the younger kids. I played the piano, and we sang songs again. Once the children were in bed Margaret, her husband, and I retrieved the presents from the attic and brought them down to where we had the tree. We wrapped them and put names on. By the time we were done with all that, it was after midnight.

Christmas morning was such a joy. Oh Arthur, I wish you could have been with us. The children were so surprised and happy. There were no presents for me this year and yet it has been my best Christmas since you died. I wish there were a way for me to earn extra money so that I could help the children. Bobby got his radio put together quickly and helped James put his together. It's a radio that you can only hear by putting an earphone in your ear so only one person can hear the radio. The girls all had fun dressing up in their jewelry. They also got dolls that were donated, and Bobby got a toy car and a football, and James got a toy sailboat.

We cooked a nice Christmas lunch and ate the popcorn that had been strung on the tree. There was quite a snowstorm last night, and it's still snowing so they boys can't play with the football or the sailboat, but they are playing with the other toys. All the children got some clothes and shoes.

Now that it is night, all is quiet. My day was so full of fun and activity, but now I feel the emptiness from you not being with me. I go to bed alone, once again. At least it is in a house full of children and love.

<u>*Sunday, December 31, 1939*</u>

Dear Arthur, it is now the end of a year that has been very different from anything in the past, and once again everything is so very different from how the year started. I am thankful for the Barclay family and the children here. In the past, I have met others that would be difficult to live with. I'm glad Margaret is a nice and thoughtful person. As the year ends, and the house is quiet once more, I can't help but think of my father, my stepmother, you, Arabella, Scott and Susan, JoAnn Cummins, Mr. and Mrs. Ranta, and all the people who are no longer in my life. I wonder what the future holds and how long I will be able to live in this house. I found out that we can stay here in our big house for twenty more years. That's a long time from now and a lot can happen between now and then. It makes me sad to think that someday I'll have to leave this wonderful house again. Hopefully, I will die before that happens.

14

War

<u>*Friday, January 12, 1940*</u>

Dear Arthur, I had a very nice birthday today. I played the birthday song on the piano, and everyone sang "Happy Birthday" to me. We had a cake that Margaret baked with the help of Patricia and Barbara. Those two seem to have adapted very well and like to be in the kitchen with me.

We have begun a tradition of having stories every Saturday night. What's cute is how Margaret and her husband like this. I've told the children about what you said about there being a story behind everything. I even play a game where one of the kids picks something to make a story about, and I try to come up with a story. It's a lot of fun and sometimes I have to stop and think, and the children will start making suggestions about what should happen next in the story. Sometimes I say "what do you think happens next?" and the children will call out ideas. It's very fun. Usually, when I'm done, I play some music for them. The little ones start falling asleep, and it gets everyone in the mood to go to bed.

The news is not good. Germany has invaded Poland. Russia has invaded Poland and Finland. There are other problems with other countries. Japan and China are still fighting. Jewish people are being rounded up. I don't understand it. President Roosevelt says we will not go to war, but it is a worry.

Serendipitous Rescue

<u>Tuesday, March 5, 1940</u>

Dear Arthur, I always think of you on your birthday and what I would be doing if you were alive with me. The good news is that Mr. Barclay was able to get a job working at the lumber yard. It's only fifteen hours a week, but it pays thirty cents per hour. The extra money will come in handy.

<u>Friday, April 19, 1940</u>

Dear Arthur, it's been nearly a year since I came back to our big house. We have more children now, and everyone is a little older. We may get another child soon. The management people have sent a little extra money for us to buy another bed so we'll be ready. Bobby and James now sleep in the attic rooms. They think it's jolly fun to be up there. Also, their crystal radios work better up high.

Today was Margaret's birthday. It was my turn to make a birthday cake. Patricia and Barbara helped me, and it was fun. Mr. Barclay gave her some earrings, and it reminded me of when you gave me some.

I'm sorry to say that you would not be proud of your homeland. Germany has invaded Denmark and Norway. We've had all these money problems for so long and now it seems the world is being ruined by wars.

<u>Saturday, May 25, 1940</u>

Dear Arthur, we had such a nice story night. Someone donated a book called "The Story of Doctor Dolittle" and I started reading it to the children. It's about a Doctor who takes care of animals and can talk to them. Everyone quite likes the story.

Yesterday I got a letter from Susan with anther picture of their family. I was so happy to see it but now I'm getting into a mood, and I don't know if I can keep the picture up. Scott and Susan are so much older. It's almost hard to recognize them. Stefani is almost twenty-four and has two boys. Mary is twenty and married, and John is sixteen. They are all in the picture. I don't recognize the children at all, and certainly not the men they are married to. I don't know why this disturbs me so. I wish I had the pictures we took when they moved into the house we built for them. Those were good times. I got the one picture out of you and me in front of this house. I will put it away in the morning to keep it safe.

The news about the wars is bad. Germany has taken over France and other countries in Europe. Many people are worried that we will be fighting soon even though the President says we will stay out of it. Tomorrow will be a fireside chat, and the President will be talking to us on the radio.

<u>*Sunday, June 23, 1940*</u>

Dear Arthur, we have been reading the stories about Dr. Doolittle. There are quite a few books written. Margaret and I tried to find more at the little library here in town, but they didn't have any so we talked to the management people, and they found a few more for us to read.

I put the picture of Scott and Susan and their family away. I am ashamed to say that I have been feeling sorry for myself. When I think of the suffering of families who have lost children, and children who have lost their parents, and people who are blind, and so many other terrible problems I have no right to complain. I know if you were here you could put me straight.

I'm afraid it's more bad news about the wars. Now Italy is fighting. It's turning into another big war. President Roosevelt says we will stay out of the war but is rebuilding the navy just in case, and we're sending lots of supplies to England. There is good news about the jobs, and more people are getting work. Fred (Mrs. Barclay's husband) even got a small raise.

<u>*Thursday, July 4, 1940*</u>

Dear Arthur, we had a nice celebration today in spite of bad news in the world. Fred bought some sparklers and also pictures of Hitler to burn with the sparklers. It's been nice having extra money and Fred has been happy to be able to earn it. He is a good man, and you would like him.

Serendipitous Rescue

<u>*Saturday, July 27, 1940*</u>

Dear Arthur, I enjoy our Saturday evening story night. I am feeling much better now. I am so fortunate to be here with the Barclays and the children. It's warm now, and we are all trying to sleep on the sleeping porch. The fireflies are out, and the crickets are chirping. It makes the stories about Dr. Doolittle more fun. The children can lie on the beds we have out here and listen to the stories.

We received a new child this past week, a girl named Alice, who is eight, like Patricia and James. She hardly speaks at all. I told Patricia and Barbara to be my helpers and let Alice sit with me with me when I tell stories or play the piano and to be extra nice to Alice. She came here with no toys or extra clothes. We found a doll and some clothes for her.

The war news is not good, and people are worried. We do enjoy the music programs and on Sunday mornings there are programs that are like being in church. There is a very nice program from Salt Lake City we like to listen to.

<u>*Saturday, August 17, 1940*</u>

Dear Arthur, it has been quite a week. Yesterday was our twenty first anniversary and today we had a celebration for my certification. I completed the paperwork and tests and am now certified to take care of orphans like Margaret. She says I am a natural but Alice will be my big test. We had a very merry story night and I was full of good cheer. Fred even bought Oreo cookies and oranges for breakfast tomorrow. I feel you would be proud of me. I have really missed your hugs tonight.

<u>*Sunday, August 25, 1940*</u>

Dear Arthur, we are keeping busy here. I can't remember when I was at your grave last. Our tree has grown taller. I can't reach your words to touch them any more without a stool, but that's ok. They are safely out of reach, and I can see them just fine. I enjoy our tree more than being at your grave. Sometimes I pretend you are here at the tree waiting for me.

Little Alice hardly says anything and just looks at me without smiling or crying. I try to give her love the best I can.

Saturday, September 21, 1940

Dear Arthur, it is cooling down somewhat and has rained a few times and been windy, so we are back sleeping in the house. I have Alice sleeping on a bed in my room. We put her in school, and she seems to handle it ok. She's very quiet.

The bad news is that starting in October Fred will have to register with the government. All men who are older than twenty-one and younger than thirty-six have to sign up. The government will start randomly picking men who have registered to be trained as a soldier for one year. It sure seems like we will be going to war and Margaret is starting to show signs of worry. The bad news is that the wars in Europe are not getting any better, and Germany is stronger than ever. When we go into town, everyone talks about Hitler.

Thursday, October 31, 1940

Dear Arthur, we had a nice Halloween, but the trouble in Europe is on everyone's mind. Thanks to Fred, all the children were able to have Halloween masks this year. We had witches, Snow White, skeletons, and other ugly faces.

Little Alice has stayed by my side almost all the time and sits on my lap when I play the piano. She has started to smile now and then. I helped her play "Chop Sticks" on the piano and I believe she had fun.

Fred went to register for the selective service and for the first time I saw Margaret cry. I did my best to comfort her. The chances are slim that Fred will get picked and even if he does, it's only for one year. If there isn't one thing to worry about, it's another.

Thursday, November 21, 1940

Dear Arthur, there has been much to be thankful for on this Thanksgiving Day. For one thing, Fred has not been chosen to be a soldier. Another thing is that jobs are getting easier and easier to find. Fred got a different job and is making thirty-seven cents per hour now.

Another thing to be thankful for is that the children are all well and mostly happy, even little Alice.

We had a wonderful day. The ladies from the farm brought us another turkey and with Fred's money we bought plenty of food and even ice cream. I haven't been sad for a while and feel like we are a big family here. I get along with Margaret just fine and let her be in charge of everything. She is not bossy and does almost anything I want to do. We respect each other.

With all the children living here now, the house is very warm and noisy. It is so different than when you and I lived here by ourselves. You would really like it. We don't have parties here, but we don't need to because there is always so much activity.

I have been helping the children with their reading and numbers like I usually do, but I had a wonderful experience this past week. Barbara, who is now seven, was practicing her reading. We have some beginning reading books like the ones you brought to the mining camp school. I asked Alice if she could help Barbara with some words, and it was like a miracle. Alice started helping Barbara read and soon Alice was talking up a storm. Barbara kept talking to Alice after they finished, and I couldn't believe how happy Alice seems tonight. We have moved her into the room with Barbara and Patricia. I think she will be fine.

<u>Saturday, December 21, 1940</u>

Dear Arthur, it has been another happy day. Fred has not been called by the government, and we got a Christmas tree. Fred has been so nice to share his money with the children. We have managed to get a few presents for the children and are excited for Christmas. We got a big tree like the ones you and I had before. It was a splurge for us. Fred and Margaret were pleased. We had some trouble getting the lights to work because of the burned out light, but we have a few spares now from Stewart's hardware. It was very jolly decorating the tree. I played Christmas songs on the piano while Margaret and the children decorated the tree. Sometimes the kids would sing along when they knew the words to the songs.

I work hard and keep busy. When the day is done I can fall asleep with no trouble. My life is good but I wish you were with me.

<u>*Wednesday, December 25, 1940*</u>

Dear Arthur, what a nice Christmas we had. The children were happy with their new things. The boys all got flashlights and toy cars. The girls got more pretend jewelry and some aprons. We got new dolls for Alice and Shannen. All the children got their own bag of marbles. Fred bought a Tinkertoy set to be shared by everyone. It's interesting what the children have put together. Bobby got a set of pencils and paper. The surprise was that Fred and Margaret got me a fine new pen for writing.

My money is gone. The one thing I can do is make everyone happy with stories and music, and that's what I did. Last night I read the Christmas stories like last year, and even a new one called "Rudolph the Red-Nosed Reindeer" from the Montgomery Ward store.

If it weren't for the bad news about the wars life would be nearly perfect. We have very little money, but we have enough to get by, and we are like a big family. Sometimes there are quarrels but nothing bad. Almost all the children have a sad memory somewhere. I had to adjust to sharing the bathroom with the children, but it's not been difficult. It's almost like you built this house to be an orphanage.

<u>*Tuesday, December 31, 1940*</u>

Dear Arthur, it's been such a nice year. Here I am writing in my diary using this fine new pen given to me by people I did not know a few years ago. Now they seem like family. I wrote a letter to our friend Susan and told her the latest news about my life. Scott didn't have to register with the government because he was older. This has been an interesting year. I love taking care of the children and helping them. I've not been back here two years yet, and already they seem like they could be my own children.

Darcy is doing fine and is happy for me. She has a big family and is busy. They are struggling but are doing ok.

Serendipitous Rescue

<u>*Sunday, January 12, 1941*</u>

Dear Arthur, it's hard to believe it's my birthday again. Next year I'll be forty years old. You're almost forty-five. I wonder what you would look like now. I've developed a few gray hairs lately. Scott and Susan are grandparents.

<u>*Wednesday, March 5, 1941*</u>

Dear Arthur, once again it is your birthday, and I pause to think of you and how we loved each other. It doesn't seem that I am to die anytime soon so I will make the best of it. I miss snuggling with you and how you would teach me new things and tell me stories.

The good news is that I moved back into my room. Little Jon (Margaret's boy) is five now and wants to be in a room with Mark. Shannen has moved into the big bedroom with Margaret and Fred. I can look out the window and see our tree.

There's lots of bad news on the radio. The Navy has been reorganized, and it seems like we are getting ready for the war.

<u>*Saturday, April 19, 1941*</u>

Dear Arthur, we had a nice birthday party for Margaret. Fred saved up some money and got her a necklace. It makes me happy that they love each other.

There is more bad news on the radio. We have had some fights with Germany even though we are not at war.

I am enjoying being back in this room. I have a better view of the back yard and can see the children when they are outside. I can look down and see your words on our tree.

More people are working in the factories building ships, and others are becoming soldiers. It makes more jobs for people, but it's sad that we are going to join the big war. The steel mills in Pittsburgh are busy. People are thinking that the money troubles are over, but now we have war troubles.

<u>*Tuesday, May 27, 1941*</u>

Dear Arthur, there has been another fireside chat on the radio. President Roosevelt talked about how we have a national emergency. I wish you were with me. I always felt like you could figure out what we should be doing. Now I just have to do the best I can.

The children play outside pretending to be soldiers shooting at each other and shooting at Hitler. Hitler is a very bad name around here. The children have no idea how serious this is.

<u>*Sunday, June 15, 1941*</u>

Dear Arthur, it has been terrible news today. Fred has been selected to be a soldier. Margret has been so upset. He has to report on July the 21st. After the children had gone to bed, we talked about how we'll cope and handle things. Margaret couldn't hide her tears. At least it will only be for one year.

In town, they have been talking about Jimmy Stewart. He has joined the Army. It's also on the radio.

<u>*Friday, July 4, 1941*</u>

Dear Arthur, we had a lovely July fourth today in spite of the looming sadness. Fred made sure we had plenty of sparklers and even some small fireworks. We've moved our beds to the sleeping porch. When we look out and see the fireflies, it is so peaceful and pretty. It's hard to imagine the wars all over the world.

Fred will soon leave us. It creates a pall of sadness over everything we do.

<u>*Wednesday, July 9, 1941*</u>

Dear Arthur, Margaret took Fred and their two kids to the photographer today. They wanted a picture that Fred can take with him. They all came back here, even the photographer with his camera. The photographer's name is Mr. Roberts. His son has already left to be a soldier. He said we should have a nice picture of all of us together and didn't charge any extra.

Serendipitous Rescue

<u>*Monday, July 21, 1941*</u>

Dear Arthur, Fred got on the train to Pittsburgh this morning. It was very sad. He will be travelling to California. The army will pay about $160 per month because he has a wife and two kids. He will be sending some money to us each month. We don't know how all this will work, but we would rather be poor and have him with us. All the children were sad to see him leave. Margaret drove him to the train station in Blairsville and took the two kids with her to see him off. A year will be a long time to be gone. At least he has three nice pictures, one in a studio and two at our big house.

<u>*Saturday, July 26, 1941*</u>

Dear Arthur, it was very difficult to have our story night. None of us were in a cheerful mood.

Margaret stays close by me now most of the time unless she has something to do. We cook together, we clean together, and when we relax we are together. I don't mind at all and, in fact, I enjoy that we spend so much time together. At night, I sometimes hear her weeping in her room. Last night I got up and sat with her for a while. I told her I was an expert on being sad at night.

<u>*Saturday, August 30, 1941*</u>

Dear Arthur, there has been the most dreadful news. President Roosevelt announced that the men will have to stay in the Army for eighteen months, not just a year.

Margaret got a letter from Fred. Fortunately, there was no bad news in the letter. She let me read the letter and cried on my shoulder. She was just sad.

A few days ago Margaret got a book from the library "The Swiss Family Robinson." It's been so long since I read that story to the children in the mining camp. What nice memories that gave me. We all gathered out on the sleeping porch for the story. Because of the younger children, I don't read the words exactly, and tell it in my own words. I have gotten pretty good at reading ahead and telling the story my way.

Afterward, we turned out the lights and the children went to sleep. There was a half moon out and the night was very pretty. It would have been so nice if Margaret could have had Fred with her, and I could have had you with me.

Margaret was asking about my diary so I asked her if she would like to read it. She said she would love to read it and I'm happy to let her.

Sunday, August 31, 1941

Dear Arthur, Margaret has been so sad today. The news yesterday about the men staying away for eighteen months has really upset her. I don't think she slept at all last night. She thinks things are just going to get worse, and Fred will probably have to go to Europe and fight Hitler. I told her I'm sure things will be ok, and we will stick together.

Saturday, September 20, 1941

Dear Arthur, the children are back in school. Margaret is doing better. I know how hard it can be to adjust. She has been reading our favorite story. We have become closer than ever. We keep our bedroom doors open at night. Sometimes I can hear her walking around, so I get up, and we talk.

We keep busy helping the children with reading and numbers. Bobby is doing well in school and is learning multiplication and division. We brought the beds in from the sleeping porch. The older kids are good helpers. I know how important it is to keep busy, and that's what we do here.

Saturday, October 25, 1941

Dear Arthur, we finally got some money from Fred. He sent us $100. We are fortunate to have most of our needs provided for and are saving the rest of the money for Christmas and Thanksgiving. Once again I dread the holiday season but this time for the sake of Margaret.

Serendipitous Rescue

Friday, October 31, 1941

Dear Arthur, how I do love these children. I took them out this evening in our neighborhood trick or treating. Margaret stayed home with the little ones and handed out candy. It has been a busy evening fixing dinner and getting everyone dressed in their costumes. They are oblivious to the trouble in the world. There are still some vacant houses but not like when I first got back here.

Margret is still reading my diaries. Being busy is good. The more we learn about each other, the more we like each other.

Thursday, November 13, 1941

Dear Arthur, the good news is that we got more money from Fred. I feel so bad for him being away from his family. I hope he is not sending us too much. At least Margaret and I have each other and the children. I can't imagine how lonely and sad he must be. I'm sure they are keeping him busy but he is a nice man, and it makes me sad for him.

We have ordered some toys from the Sears and Roebuck catalog for Christmas.

The bad news is on the radio. Some people want the country to go and fight, and others don't. Margaret and I just want the wars to be over and have the men come back home.

Thursday, November 20, 1941

Dear Arthur, we had a lovely Thanksgiving, but it was bittersweet. Fred's money helped us have a very merry time, but we would much rather have Fred instead. We both felt sad thinking of Fred having Thanksgiving without us.

Margaret and I are thankful for each other and for the children. She has finished reading my diary. We are both looking forward to Christmas and decorating the house. We will get a few more things for the children and see what comes in from the donations. We know it will be hard without Fred, but we want the children to be happy.

Saturday, December 13, 1941

Dear Arthur, it's the worst news yet. We have gotten into the big war. First we were attacked by Japan. It was on Sunday, and the government has declared war with Japan. Then on Thursday Germany declared war on us. It's a worse mess than the last big war. We have been listening to the radio constantly. We are so worried. Now Fred will probably have to go fight. He's just a nice man who worked in a store and helped us with the orphans. It's very sad, and Margaret hardly sleeps at all. I haven't slept much either. I stay with Margaret all the time.

Saturday, December 20, 1941

Dear Arthur, we received a letter from Fred and also some more money. He will be going with the Marines to fight the Japanese. We can't help but be worried. He said not to worry because he is being trained as a radio operator and a driver so he will be safer then the younger men. We have decided to save Fred's money so that when he gets back we will enjoy it together with him. We will only use a small amount of it to help the children with school, birthdays and clothes. He said to be sure to get a Christmas tree, and we did that today. He said he misses us very much but he hopes we will use the money for a good Christmas, and that will make him feel good. We already did get a few things for the children.

The children had fun decorating the tree, and I played music. We are trying to be as cheerful as possible, but it's very hard for Margaret. After the children went to bed I had an idea and told Margaret that we need to have the nicest Christmas time as possible and then we can all write letters to Fred and tell him we miss him but thank him for the money he has sent. Then she can tell him in her own letter how sad she is not to be with him but she should let him know that his sacrifice is being put to good use. She liked that idea.

Wednesday, December 24, 1941

Dear Arthur, I'm happy that we are able to have presents for the children. It's sad not to have Fred helping us get ready for Christmas tomorrow. I've put my candle in the window for Christmas. I put an extra candle for Fred.

Friday, December 26, 1941

Dear Arthur, what a difficult time this has been. I have spent every spare moment with Margaret. We had a wonderful Christmas morning yesterday with the children.

In the afternoon yesterday we all sat down to write letters to Fred and thank him for sending the money and for fighting for our country. I helped some of the children write their letters. Bobby, Alice, Patricia, and Barbara wrote such nice letters. It almost surprised me. Alice is doing so well now.

Today was easier but since the kids are out of school for the holiday, it kept us both busy. It was very cold but sunny, so we took the children on an outing by walking into town to mail the letters. Alice and Patricia took turns pushing the buggy and the baby did fine. There was snow on some of the sidewalks, but we had a good time. It was good to get out. We stopped at the store so the children could each get some penny candy. The walk did us all good, including Margaret.

Wednesday, December 31, 1941

Dear Arthur, What a year this has ended up being. We have no money problems, but our family has been torn apart.

Jimmy Stewart and other famous people have been on the radio talking about the war. I still think of him as a little boy.

We also received a letter from Fred. He said he has friends and is not lonely but misses us all terribly. He talked about how everyone is ready to go and fight, and they will be getting on a big ship in a few days. He said the government will be sending his money to us, or part of it, I'm not sure. The letter was dated right before Christmas so by now he is on a big ship headed to the war.

15
Lost

<u>*Monday, January 12, 1942*</u>

Dear Arthur, things are settling down. Margaret is getting used to how things are, and we have a plan to cope. I can't help but feel just a little jealous that she can write to Fred and when he returns she will be so happy. It's been so long since I had you with me. I almost dread the celebration we will have when Fred comes home. I wish you could come home. It's hard to believe I am forty years old today. I think back from where I was when I met you and what I am now. I'm glad I can be of use to others, but it would be so nice if I could tell you a story, or play the piano for you again.

I feel oddly out of sorts. It's likely the weather. As usual we've had a lot of snow, and the children can only play outside for so long in the cold. Most of the kids spend a good part of the day at school so there is time to relax now and then. I think I'm just tired. The news is always bad.

<u>*Saturday, January 24, 1942*</u>

Dear Arthur, the day has been good. There was more snow yesterday, and the children have built a large snowman. I tried to make up a story about a magic snowman, but my imagination wasn't working.

Margaret read a letter from Fred. He described riding on the ship and the huge guns and where he slept and what they do during the day. The children found it quite interesting. He has not seen any fighting yet.

Margaret was at the store yesterday and heard that a little girl who lives here in town died from scarlet fever. How sad that would be. I dread if anything bad were to happen to any of these kids. Scarlet fever is probably what made Helen Keller deaf and blind when she was a baby.

I'm just tired. I don't know why but I just feel worn out. Margaret is doing fine now, it seems. The one thing I miss about this arrangement is our nice bathroom. I'm glad you made the other one nice and big.

Sunday, January 25, 1942

Dear Arthur, for some reason I felt like playing "Danny Boy" this afternoon. Margaret mentioned how nice my song was and that she had never heard me play it before. I shouldn't have played that song. I've been melancholy all afternoon.

Bobby and James had homework to finish so I helped Bobby and Margaret helped James. I was glad when the day was over. Writing helps me think about things.

Saturday, February 14, 1942

Dear Arthur, I had a good cry last night, and I feel better now. I think Margaret can tell that I'm struggling. I'm ashamed to say that if it weren't for her and these children I don't know what I'd do. After Arabella died I almost gave up.

Margaret surprised me tonight after the children went to bed. She asked if I would like the big room back. I told her no, of course. It is her room now. Besides, I left that room after you died. She emphasized that if I need to use her bathroom for any reason I was welcome to do so. She is a good friend.

Saturday, February 21, 1942

Dear Arthur, I've felt so much better today. I even had a good story about a magic snowman for story night:

Once upon a time there was a house full of happy children. They loved the winter time because they could play outside in the snow. One winter it was especially cold, with lots of snow. They made the best snowman ever. It was as tall as Bobby. They got a carrot for the nose and found small stones for his eyes. They used a piece of a shoelace for a mouth. The children danced and sang around the snowman. After dinner, it was getting dark but the children hated to leave. They loved their snowman. Each one kissed the snowman good night. What the children didn't know was that those kisses worked magic that night. The next morning they all saw that the snowman was smiling. That made them happy, but they wondered who put the shoelace in the shape of a smile? Each child said, "it wasn't me." The tallest boy said he would take the shoelace off and examine it. The other children all shouted "no, no. Leave it there." So they did. All winter long the children enjoyed their snowman and every morning they got up to see the snowman's smiling face. The children built snow houses and other smaller snowmen, but the big smiling snowman was their favorite. He watched the children as they played. As winter ended, and spring came, the children were sad to see the snow slowly melting. Each day more snow was gone. After several weeks, all the snow was gone, but to everyone's surprise, the snowman was still there! The mom said it was probably because it was so big it would take longer for the snow to melt. But no snow melted from the snowman, and he continued to smile each day. Every morning the children were delighted to see that their snowman was still there. It was now truly a surprise to everyone. By the Fourth of July, it was still there, and the children could give the snowman a hug when they got too hot. By the end of summer, the snowman was still there, smiling each morning, and still cold to the touch. People came from all around to see the snowman who never melted. When summer was over, the children started back to school. Everyone was curious about the magic snowman. One day, a few of the children started getting sick. Soon, all the happy children were sick with a bad fever. The doctor came to their house and examined the children. He said it was very serious and was scarlet fever. Everyone was very worried. When they looked outside, they could see that the snowman's smile had changed to a sad frown. That night, as the children tried to sleep, his magic started working. By morning, everyone was well, and good as new. When they went outside, the snowman was gone, and the ground was wet. The snowman had taken the fever from each child, and all those fevers had warmed him so much that he finally melted. All that was left on the ground were the small stones used for eyes, the carrot, and the shoelace smile.

Everyone liked my story, and I feel much better. Bobby sits off in the corner now, reading or drawing or writing, but I can tell that he still likes hearing my stories.

Sunday, March 1, 1942

Dear Arthur, we've had another nice week but soon it will be your birthday, and I've gotten into a sad mood again. I keep it to myself, but I cried myself to sleep last night. I don't know what's wrong with me. I feel lost. I'm not deaf, blind or crippled. I live in our nice house. We have no money worries. The children here love me, and I have a good friend in Margaret. But living here is different from the good times I had with you. I don't know why it bothers me, but it does. I'm mad at myself for feeling this way.

Margaret got a letter from Fred. He has been to Pearl Harbor and saw the destruction from the Japanese attack.

The good news is that nearly everyone has a job now. There are factories all over the country building ships and airplanes and trucks and all the steel mills are working. Even women are working in factories.

Thursday, March 5, 1942

Dear Arthur, I had a nice chat with Margaret today. I told her that I get depressed on your birthday, and she said that was normal. She said I will never get over you dying, but I must find a way to cope and get by. We had a nice talk about how our life is good because it keeps us busy doing things. I can't help but wonder if she is telling me this to help with her own worries.

Sunday, March 22, 1942

Dear Arthur, we had a restful day and tried to listen to cheerful music and church music. We haven't heard anything from Fred for some time, but we did get more money. The news is very discouraging, and we have lost some battles where Fred is. We don't know if he is fighting or not. In Europe, the news is sometimes good but mostly bad.

We're tired of the cold weather, and we're all glad it's getting warmer.

Yesterday I walked with Bobby, Patricia, James and Alice into town. We brought all the metal things we could find in two wagons for the war effort. We put some old wire and pipes and some junk that I don't know what it was into the wagons. It was pretty chilly but not bad. The sun was out, but it was breezy. Lots of people were there bringing in small amounts of metal. It doesn't seem like it would help much, but I guess if all the little cities everywhere are bringing in scraps of metal it could help build ships.

Next we walked over to the store so the children could get some candy. They really like to go to the store and get a treat. They got some Cracker Jacks. We talked with some people and heard that the police were there Friday because of a little boy that was lost.

For story night last night we talked about knowing our address in case anyone ever got lost. They call our big house "Tutu" house because our address is easy to remember. We also started reading "Dr. Doolittle" again.

Monday, March 23, 1942

Dear Arthur, we've had a very strange day today. This morning the police called on the telephone and wanted to know if we could help take care of the little boy we heard about. They can't find anyone in town who knows who the little boy is and want us to watch him while they investigate. He seems to be around two as far as we can tell. Margaret called the Quaker people to let them know. The little boy doesn't speak much and is still in diapers. He cries incessantly. He didn't want to eat, so Margaret got out a bottle for some warm milk. He can walk just fine. I put him on my lap and sat at the piano and started playing like I did when we got Patricia and Barbara. The piano seems to soothe him and he finally fell asleep. My back was aching from holding him. He slept all afternoon. I hope they find his parents or family soon as I am not fond of diapers.

When the older kids came home from school, they were surprised to see the baby and did a good job of being quiet.

Margaret and I were getting dinner ready and the baby woke up and started crying again. Fortunately, Margaret has baby things like diapers and bottles. She warmed some milk, and we gave him a bottle. He is probably too old for that, but it seemed to comfort him. After he finished the bottle, he started crying again. The girls tried to comfort him, but it didn't work. Margaret told me to take care of him and she would finish dinner. I changed his diaper and put him on my lap again and played songs. Then I sat in the big chair and started singing songs. That seemed to work as well as the piano. After everyone else ate dinner Patricia came over and sat in the chair and held him and sang but it didn't work so I brought him to the dinner table and he sat on my lap while I ate my food. We had stew tonight, and the cooked potatoes and carrots were nice and soft so I fed him small bites, and he seemed to like that.

The Quaker people called on the telephone after dinner to ask how we were doing. They have called the police to talk about the boy and if the police can't find any relatives by Thursday they will come and pick him up and take him to Pittsburgh where they have an orphanage that is better prepared to take care of babies. For now, it seems I am the only one who can give peace to the little boy. I have played the piano again and been singing songs and am worn out. He is sleeping now in the crib that Shannen used to use. We moved it into my room. It is very late. I hope I get some sleep.

Tuesday, March 24, 1942

Dear Arthur, it has been another exhausting day. The little boy woke up in the middle of the night and started crying. I picked him up and put him in the bed with me after I changed his diaper. With the light out and resting next to me he went back to sleep. In the morning, he didn't cry much but just seemed bewildered. Margaret's little Shannen is almost five and has been very interested in the boy. He held on to my hand wherever I walked. It was difficult helping with breakfast and getting the children ready for school. Shannen is not in school yet, and it has been helpful for her to play with the baby. After the children left for school we called the sheriff's office to see if there was any news but there wasn't. It's quite a mystery. Margaret and I fed him some oatmeal and a bottle, and he looked like he was getting sad again, so I sat down at the piano with him and played "Fur Elise." He seems to like that song. For a while, I walked around the house holding his hand and Shannon held his other hand. I sat in the big chair with Shannen and the baby. Shannen asked for a story, so I told my simple stories like the one about the rock and the magic tree. The little boy seemed to like that as much as the music from the piano. He also likes listening to the little music box.

I carried him while trying to help Margaret get dinner. She is better with babies than I am, but this one won't let go of me. At least Margaret can help and tell me what I need to do. I held the baby on my lap while helping others with homework. I played the piano again as well.

The baby didn't want to sleep in the crib, so I put him on my bed and lay down until he went to sleep. Then I got up and talked with Margaret for a while. We'll both be glad when they can pick him up on Thursday.

<u>*Wednesday, March 25, 1942*</u>

Dear Arthur, we made it through the night ok. He wakes up now and then but goes back to sleep. He cried a little today but I sat in the big chair, and he put his head on my shoulder for a while. It sounded like he was trying to say something, but we couldn't understand him.

It's been helpful having Shannen here. She tries to play with him and talks to him. She was already talking at his age. Sometimes he has the saddest little face. He ate better today. This afternoon Shannen asked him what his name was. He said something that we don't understand.

He seemed sad again this evening, so I played the piano. This time, I had him sit in the big chair with Shannen while I played. We moved the chair next to the piano so he could see me and be close by.

I put him to bed and lay down next to him for a while until he went to sleep. He held my hand for a while. He looks like a little angel when he is sleeping.

I got up and talked with Margaret. We talked about the war. I didn't hear the news myself. She said things were bad with Germany, and it was horrible what they were doing to people. I don't know why people have to be mean. Your family is from Germany, and my family is from Ireland and we got along just fine.

Thursday, March 26, 1942

Dear Arthur, the Quakers from Pittsburgh called on the telephone this morning and asked if we could keep the little boy until Saturday as they won't be here on Thursday this week. I said it was ok.

He slept better last night and ate well at breakfast. After the children left for school, he walked over to the big chair by himself and climbed in. He was waiting for me to play the piano, so I did. It was very cute. Margaret had already washed the dishes and I asked if he would like a bath in the sink. It seems like he can understand quite a few words. Margaret and I gave him a bath in the big kitchen sink. I couldn't tell if he was going to cry or not but he did ok. After we dried him off, we sat in the big chair again and did the same stories as yesterday. Then we put on warm clothes and went outside. The little boy held my hand the whole time. Shannen came out too, and we walked around the yard. The snow is gone except in some places where the sun doesn't reach. We walked over to our tree as I often do and the little boy let go of my hand and touched our tree and said the word "tree" and I could hear it quite clearly. I said, "yes, that's right" and he almost had a smile.

He and Shannen were both enjoying being outside, so I held their hands and we walked down the sidewalk and back the other way and then went back inside the house. I removed the extra clothes and picked him up, and he hugged my neck. He seems to be fine as long as he is right next to me, especially holding my hand.

In the afternoon, I did most of the laundry. Sometimes I carried him in one arm and sometimes I had to put him down. Margaret did most of the cooking for dinner, but I helped a little. The little boy seems interested in everything we do but still has a sad face.

After dinner I was helping the children with homework and Shannen was holding the little boy's hands and looked right in his face and said, "what's your name?" and he said something like "Bark" or "Jared" or "Jark." We couldn't really tell. Patricia brought over a toy car and said, "Jark – do you want to play with this?" and I think he nodded.

She gave him the car, and he took it but just held it and didn't really do anything.

I said, "Jark, do you want to hear some music?" and he started getting off my lap and walking to the big chair. Whatever his name is, "Jark" seems to be close enough. I played "The Bear Went Over the Mountain" and a few other songs but when I played "Fur Elise" he smiled and sat back in the chair. Little Shannen climbed in with him and it was very cute. I held him while the other children got ready for bed, and we walked into each room to say good night and I said, "do you want to go to sleep" and he looked like he did so I put him in my bed and lay down with him again. He held my hand and looked at me and I looked at him. I sang a few children's songs and he fell asleep holding my hand again.

It was only a little past nine, so I got back up and visited with Margaret. We talked about the little boy and Margaret asked how I was holding up. I didn't quite know what to say. Then she asked me if I would like her to try and see if we could keep the little boy here until they find out more about him. They were short-handed anyway in Pittsburgh. I was surprised to hear myself say that it would be fine with me if he stayed here longer.

Friday, March 27, 1942

Dear Arthur, we may very well have the little boy for a while. After breakfast and sending the children off to school, Margaret called the office and talked to them and explained that we would be happy to keep the little boy here. She explained that we have plenty of baby things like clothes and diapers and a high chair because of her own children. They agreed and said they would check with us every few days to see how we were doing. I am surprised at my feelings and am glad he will be staying. I have become accomplished at changing diapers, but I'm not fond of washing them. I told Margaret that every situation is different, isn't it.

We moved the crib out of my room. Little Jark won't sleep in it. When the kids returned from school we told them the little boy will be staying with us for a while, and we don't know for how long, and we will call him "Jark." Most everyone seems to want to help little Jark adapt to our life here.

Serendipitous Rescue

We had a story night tonight, and I said we will have one tomorrow as well. First we listened to a program on the radio that the children like and then some music. Jark sat on my lap and watched the other children. I'm sure he didn't understand the program, but he liked the music. Then I read from the "Dr. Doolittle" book. I kept Jark on my lap the whole time. It must have been boring for him because he fell asleep while I was reading.

Saturday, March 28, 1942

Dear Arthur, it has been such a nice day. Little Jark woke up early but waited for me to get up. It's some effort to sleep because he pushes himself against me constantly and kicks in his sleep.

It rained all morning and the children played in the house. We had a late breakfast and had eggs and even some bacon. We haven't had that for a while, and Margaret surprised me with some orange juice.

I sat with Jark in the big chair after breakfast and watched the others run around and play hide and seek. He seemed interested in watching them run here and there and laughing and playing but didn't want to leave my lap. It's very sweet the way he wants to be with me.

The sun came out after lunch, and it stopped raining. The ladies from the farm came over with eggs and bread, and were interested in little Jark. He had an awful reaction to them. Margaret said it will take a while for him to get used to things.

After that, we all walked around the neighborhood. It was wet everywhere from the rain, and the trees and grass and bushes all glistened in the sunlight. I let Jark hold my hand and walk now and then, and I think he likes being with the other children. Margaret and I both feel that it will be good for him to be around the other children, especially the younger ones. I'm glad for the experience I've had with other children, but this is very different for me.

The cute thing is that when I played "Fur Elise" on the piano Jark actually smiled again. The only thing we can think of is that he heard it before.

Margaret and Alice and Patricia made popcorn. Then it was time for bed. When I picked up Jark to take him upstairs, he was getting sleepy and hugged my neck. He seems so sweet.

Sunday, March 29, 1942

Dear Arthur, we had another nice day, except little Jon (Margaret's boy) came down with a fever. Margaret mostly took care of him. It wasn't severe. Now and then I would get a wet rag for her, and Jark seemed interested in what I was doing. Shannen started crying and was worried about Jon's fever because we didn't have a magic snowman. We told her it was not going to be serious, and Jon was fine.

Sunday, April 5, 1942

Dear Arthur, little Jark is doing so much better. I don't need to carry him so much, but he still follows me everywhere, often holding my hand. He is curious about washing the clothes and fixing the meals. He carries the little toy car with him but doesn't play with it or the other toys. He smiles off and on, so we know we're making progress. He likes to sit in your big chair, especially when I play the piano. Still no resolution from the police about him.

The news about the war makes us worried. I wish we could get mail more often from Fred.

Sunday, April 19, 1942

Dear Arthur, I made a birthday cake for Margaret, and the children helped. It was difficult keeping little Jark happy and making the cake and letting the children help, but we all had a good time. Margaret's only birthday wish was to have the war be over and have Fred back.

Saturday, May 2, 1942

Dear Arthur, we finally got a bunch of letters from Fred all at the same time. He doesn't say anything about the war at all. They aren't allowed to, but it makes Margaret nervous. He did say that he has not seen any battles yet. Margaret read the letters and then had me read them to the children for story night.

Little Jark is doing well now. He is playing with toys and likes to play with the younger children. He loves to go outside for outings. He likes the radio and has tried to play the piano. The authorities have said that we will keep him indefinitely. They apparently have no clues at all as to how he came to be here or who he is. The doctor came by to check on everyone and said Jark is in good health and appears to be a little older than two years old. We are setting his birth date as March 1, 1940. For all we know, he might very well have been born on your birthday. His records now name him as Jark Jackson.

16

A Different Life

<u>*Saturday, June 27, 1942*</u>

Dear Arthur, you would just love little Jark. I know I shouldn't get so attached to the children, but I can't help it. We are getting him potty trained and it is going well. Jark is playing with the other children more and is playing with the toys. Bobby gave Jark his old flashlight that doesn't work well and Jark carries it around. He says quite a few words now and I believe he understands well. He is much happier than at first. He uses the high chair for meals that Margaret had for Shannen and Jon. Margaret and Fred hope to have more children when he returns from the war.

The news on the radio about the war is very unsettling. There have been some big battles in the Pacific where Fred is and Margaret hasn't heard anything from him.

<u>*Saturday, July 4, 1942*</u>

Dear Arthur, we had a very nice 4th of July tonight. Margaret bought some sparklers and Bobby helped the others with them. The news on the radio was encouraging. They said we won the big battle that we had last month, and it means we are doing well where Fred is. We got some mail from him, and it is always a relief to hear that he is okay.

Little Jark was fascinated with the sparklers. He was also interested in how we moved some beds out to the sleeping porch. He was a little resistant about getting in bed out there but he also wanted to copy what the other kids were doing. The older boys prefer to remain in their rooms in the attic. They can listen to baseball and other games on their crystal radios that work better when they are up high. They open all the windows and often get a good breeze. We were able to see the fireflies, and I had to tell my story again.

The children are out of school for the summer. In the afternoon when it's very warm the children wish we had a magic snowman.

Thursday, July 16, 1942

Dear Arthur, we had a sad experience today. After breakfast, we all walked to the store for an outing to buy candy. It hadn't warmed up too much, and there was a light breeze out. Little Jark walked most of the way, holding my hand. On our way back we were about half way home and passed by a house where the Western Union messenger boy was just leaving. The front door was open, and you could hear someone inside crying. It made everyone sad, including the children. For the rest of the day Margaret was very busy doing laundry and cleaning. She even swept out the garage and washed and cleaned the car. We are all hoping the war ends soon. By dinner time she was worn out. I told her to relax and turn on the radio and listen for news, and I would take care of dinner. We had another late night together.

Monday, September 7, 1942

Dear Arthur, we all listened to the President on the radio tonight. We got a letter from Fred just today, so we were anxious to hear anything about the war.

Also, the children started school today. Everyone goes now except Jark. Shannen only goes for a half day, and Margaret walks to meet her at school. Jark is not too happy about the other children leaving for school.

Last week we moved our beds back to their normal rooms from the sleeping porch. It always makes me a little sad to see summer end, but I do get tired of the humidity. Soon it will be the holiday season, and I do enjoy that, even if you are not with me.

Monday, October 12, 1942

Dear Arthur, we listened to President Roosevelt again on the radio tonight. It was another fireside chat about the war. We are thirsty for any information about what might be happening with Fred. It is so frustrating. Sometimes the news is good and we think the war will be over soon and then it's discouraging news again.

Saturday, October 31, 1942

Dear Arthur, we had fun today. The children had masks and costumes, and we had a very merry time. It was funny and cute to see Jark's reaction to everything. He wasn't sure about the ugly costumes, but he knew it was the children. I asked if he wanted to wear a mask, and he said yes but then he took it off and just carried it. This time, Margaret took the kids out trick or treating, and I stayed home with Jark to hand out candy to the neighborhood children. Jark was very curious but also it made him nervous. He stayed back whenever I opened the door. When Margaret and the kids returned home, they dumped their candy on the dining room table to see what they got. Jark definitely likes candy and seeing the children half dressed in their costumes and playing with the candy will probably make him like Halloween.

We let the children stay up late tonight and had a special story night. I made up a story about children who went out trick or treating and turned into ghosts for one night.

Thursday, November 26, 1942

Dear Arthur, it was our second Thanksgiving without Fred. It's sad that we are getting used to him not being here. It will seem strange and wonderful when he returns. We are thankful for our health, and we are thankful for Jark.

We have ordered our presents for the children from Sears and Roebuck. Fred likes to get our letters and wants to know what each child is getting for Christmas.

Serendipitous Rescue

<u>Saturday, November 28, 1942</u>

Dear Arthur, today has been unbearably sad. Fred has been killed. We had just finished breakfast and Margaret and I were washing the dishes when Alice called out that someone was coming to the front door. Margaret went to see and then I heard her cry out. I dropped the dish I was drying and ran to the door. Margaret was collapsed on the floor sobbing hysterically. The children came running to help. I was still drying my hands with the dish towel. The Western Union messenger boy gave me the telegram and left. His own face was sad. I helped Margaret up and into the big chair. I opened the telegram and cried. All the children were crying and hugging Margaret. After a few moments she went up to her room and closed the door. I took care of the children and we talked about heaven. I don't know what happens when we die, but there is a flood of souls passing on in this horrible war.

There are no words to describe how miserably sad we have been today. Little Jark doesn't understand, but he is sad because everyone else is sad. All the children loved Fred. I am still trying to understand the shock of the news. The future seems more uncertain than ever.

We had a late lunch. I fixed a big batch of spaghetti. After a while, Margaret came downstairs and I gave her a hug and got her a small plate of food. She ate a little and then just sat in the big chair with Jon and Shannen.

No one has been in a happy mood. The children have been crying off and on all day. We tried to do story night but couldn't think of any good stories. Margaret asked me to play "Nearer My God to Thee" on the piano so I did. Then I played "Amazing Grace." After that, she asked me to play "Danny Boy." We were both crying and the children were so sweet. There isn't a one of us in this house now who hasn't been touched by tragedy.

Everyone was gloomy but stayed up late. After the children went to bed I sat with Margaret. We didn't say much but every now and then she just sobbed and talked about how she was going to give Fred the best party when he got back, and someday take a vacation. All I could do was hug her. I told her we are sisters now.

Sunday, November 29, 1942

Dear Arthur, we listened to church music all morning on the radio. Nothing seems to help much. Jon and Shannen are still trying to comprehend that their dad will never come home. I don't know what to say to Margaret. I feel so bad.

Tuesday, December 8, 1942

Dear Arthur, we received official notice in the mail that Fred has been killed. It hasn't made anyone feel any better. Margaret was hoping that somehow the telegram could have been a mistake. It's been hard trying to be normal. We do our best to get the kids ready for school and take care of everything but the sadness is everywhere.

Thursday, December 17, 1942

Dear Arthur, Margaret received a Gold Star service banner today. She can't decide if she wants to put it in the window or not. It's hard to believe that Fred is gone.

Saturday, December 19, 1942

Dear Arthur, we are slowly adjusting to our new way of life. We got more money from Fred, but it will probably be the last time. Margaret put the service banner in her bedroom window. She has saved a lot of money but now we have to be careful.

We got a very nice letter from a man named Bill Maguire who knew Fred in the war. He told us about one of the battles on the Guadalcanal island. Fred was driving a radio truck when he was hit with a bomb and was killed instantly. At least he didn't suffer. Now we know what happened. The letter also told about how the younger men looked up to Fred. They all shared pictures of home and found it interesting that Fred helped take care of orphans. He said Fred always carried his pictures with him. He said he was so sorry for us and hoped it helped to know that Fred was respected and well liked and that he loved his family.

Margaret put the letter on the fireplace mantel where we have the picture of him and all of us. She took off the necklace that Fred gave her and placed it on the letter.

Later in the afternoon, Margaret decided we needed a Christmas tree and took Jon, Shannen, Bobby and Shirley to get one. It was a nice medium one, about my height. I know she did it for the children, but I wish I could have driven the car. Maybe it was good for her to get out.

We had as merry a time as we could. We let the children decorate the tree, and Margaret made popcorn. I played Christmas songs on the piano and everyone sang, but it wasn't as cheerful as last year. Bobby and James are good at fixing the lights. Jark is fascinated with the lights and wants to touch them, but it burns his fingers.

After everyone had gone to bed, I stayed up with Margaret. We sat on the couch in the darkness for a while. She didn't say much. I thanked her for getting the tree. She thanked me for letting her read our story.

Friday, December 25, 1942

Dear Arthur, it was a Christmas of mixed emotions. It started out as a somber Christmas day. Only the youngest were cheerful. Then a very sweet thing happened. Bobby opened his first present that was a set of toy soldiers and quietly said, "Thank you Mr. Barclay." Then the other kids did the same thing. Each time someone opened a present they said, "Thank you Mr. Barclay." Jon and Shannen said, "Thank you Dad." It was very touching, and Margaret had tears.

After we were done opening presents, Mark said he wished he got a gun for Christmas so he could go kill Japanese people. We had a talk about war and how bad rulers make people fight even when they don't want to. We talked about sad little Japanese children whose fathers had also been killed. Their fathers didn't want to go to war either. I told them about you, and how you were from Germany, but you weren't bad like Hitler. I told how there were even Japanese men in America who went to fight against Japan.

All in all it was a sad Christmas.

Thursday, December 31, 1942

Dear Arthur, what a year this has been. Some joy and so much sorrow. We have gained Jark and lost Fred. At school, the kids know other children who have lost fathers or other family members. Some people say it's the end of the world. When we go into town people are sorry for us but there are others who are hurting too. It's going to be a different life for Margaret.

I have moved my things from the hall bathroom to Margaret's bathroom. It was her idea.

Tuesday, January 12, 1943

Dear Arthur, I had a nice birthday today. Margaret helped the kids make birthday cards for me. Once again it is bright and cheerful for my birthday. There is lots of snow outside, and it is bitter cold, but the sun is reflecting off the snow and shining through the windows and making the house bright.

The children have been calling Jark "JJ." They don't like the name "Jark." I don't mind either way. He goes to sleep easily now. We have a small bed in my room for him. I play my little music box, and he likes to listen while he goes to sleep. It's handy that he doesn't stay up late because Margaret is up a lot at night, and we just sit on the couch downstairs and talk with most of the lights out.

Monday, March 1, 1943

Dear Arthur, we celebrated JJ's birthday today. He has seen the other birthdays for the other kids, and I think he was ready for this. You wouldn't know that he was once a sad little boy.

On the news has been the sad story of the Sullivan brothers. All five were killed when their ship was sunk by the Japanese a few months ago. I can't imagine the sorrow of their mother and father.

I told Margaret she should open a bank savings account and put Fred's money in it. She thought that was a good idea and did it yesterday. The bank trouble we had from the crash has been fixed and the government now guarantees savings accounts.

Serendipitous Rescue

<u>*Sunday, May 2, 1943*</u>

Dear Arthur, there was another fireside chat this evening on the radio and President Roosevelt talked about coal. He wanted to make sure that all the coal miners keep working for the war effort. I guess there has been some trouble. It made me think of the coal mine and those happy times with you at the school.

We had a fun story night last night. I read "Alice's Adventures in Wonderland" and Alice thought it was all quite fun. The other kids enjoyed it too.

It has been six months since Fred was killed. Margaret is doing better but I know how hard it is. She will never recover but she will learn to cope, and I will help her. She has already helped me.

<u>*Thursday, November 25, 1943*</u>

Dear Arthur, we had a very nice Thanksgiving in spite of everything. It has been nearly a year now since Fred died. I'm afraid that Thanksgiving has become a time when we will remember the news from that awful day last year.

My sadness is easier for me to bear, but Margaret has a long way to go. I have been thankful for little JJ. I know it's wrong, but I think of him as my own child. He is with me much of the time but he also plays well with the other children. I believe he will be fine.

I am thankful for our health and that we have been spared serious illness at this house. Toward the end of summer there was another child taken with polio here in town. A little girl, but I understand she will live.

<u>*Sunday, March 5, 1944*</u>

Dear Arthur, we celebrated JJ's fourth birthday a few days ago, and now I think of you. It seems like it's been forever since you died and at the same time it seems like just yesterday. I do love these children and thanks to you we have this wonderful house. I wish you could see it all. It hurts me to think you died feeling that you failed me.

When the ladies from the farm came by this week, they told how they saw women working on the roads. It's amazing how many women are working in factories and in the steel mills. It's very practical considering so many men are away.

Wednesday, July 4, 1945

Dear Arthur, we had a lovely Fourth of July. Germany has surrendered, and Hitler is nowhere to be found. The war is over in Europe. Everyone is happy and believes it will soon end with Japan. We all walked into town yesterday to buy some fireworks and sparklers. People are happy and optimistic. Others, like us, are permanently scarred.

We have moved out to the sleeping porch again. I love our big house and all the things that remind me of you.

Little JJ will be starting school in the fall. You would just love him. He is a funny little boy and is curious about everything. He can count to twenty-five, knows the alphabet, and can read simple words. He listens when I'm helping the others with their numbers and reading. He sleeps in a room with Mark and Jon now.

Alice, Patricia, and Barbara have all graduated to the girl's home in Pittsburgh. Alice and Patricia are thirteen. Barbara is almost twelve but she wanted to be with her sister (Patricia). It breaks my heart when they leave but they write frequently. Shirley is almost eleven and will probably be here for a few more years. We now have Carol who is four, Linda who is six, and Janet who is also six.

Saturday, August 25, 1945

Dear Arthur, the Japanese have surrendered. The second big war is finally over. The world is very different. So many women are working everywhere. Euphoria is everywhere.

Margaret has been sad lately, thinking of the men who will be coming home soon. She had wonderful plans for Fred. We all wanted to have such a celebration.

Serendipitous Rescue

We have registered JJ for school. Sometimes I feel like he is the child we never had. I shouldn't feel that way because he will leave us one day. I don't know how I will ever handle that.

Margaret and I are determined to be friends forever, but I don't know what we'll do when we have to leave this house. We have fourteen more years. By then JJ will be nineteen. It's upsetting to think about having to leave and what might happen to little JJ. I must try not to worry about the future.

<u>Saturday, September 22, 1945</u>

Dear Arthur, you should have seen the commotion these past few days with Jimmy Stewart coming home from the war. He flew B-17 and B-24 airplanes and dropped bombs on Germany. He is a war hero. We are all happy for him and his family.

Margaret had me come to the bank with her and added me to the account for Fred's money. If anything happens to her or if there is an emergency I will be able to withdraw money if necessary. We have nearly $2800 saved, but we want to keep as much as we can for the future. Margaret says that someday they will probably shut down the orphanage and we will have to find something else to do. That money will come in handy then.

I finally received a letter from Darcy. They are still living in Dublin. They are fine but some houses not too far from them were bombed during the war. She is a grandmother now. I can only remember her as a young girl.

<u>Friday, April 5, 1946</u>

Dear Arthur, I have received such wonderful news today. Margaret and I are so excited. A letter from our old friends Scott and Susan came today. They will be coming for a visit. They are driving a car to California. Sadly, Susan has cancer, and they are not sure how long she has, maybe a year or more. They have always wanted to take a vacation, and now they are doing it. They want to pass through our little town and see their old house and see me too. I am sad for them but excited to be able to see them after all this time. Margaret, is excited as well. She knows them from reading my diary. They will be here in three weeks. I immediately wrote back and told them they must stay with us. Margaret wants it too. She drove to the post office to mail my letter to them. It will only be Scott and Susan and no children. Scott and Susan have nine grandchildren.

Little JJ loves kindergarten. I have been walking him to and from school. It's not too far from here. It's cute how he thinks he needs to study after school like the big kids. We go over numbers and reading together. We are doing simple adding, and he likes it and is actually learning. He can count to one hundred, and we are reading easy words like cat and dog. His teacher said he is the most advanced child in the class.

<u>*Friday, April 19, 1946*</u>

Dear Arthur, we had a nice birthday for Margaret.

We are starting to see more men in town return from the war. There are lots of men in uniform nearly everywhere. It's hard for Margaret to see all this, even though we are happy the war is over.

We are both looking forward to Scott and Susan visiting next week.

<u>*Sunday, April 28, 1946*</u>

My Dearest Arthur, what a wonderful time we have had these past few days. I have tears now, but it has been the most wonderful weekend. Margaret and I were on pins and needles all Friday until Scott and Susan arrived. They got here in the afternoon, and I can't tell you how wonderful it was to see them. They have changed so much, but it was easy to tell it was them. We all have wrinkles and gray hairs.

I kept watching out the window, and as soon as I saw them arrive and park their car in front of the house I ran out to meet them. We hugged and cried, and it was so wonderful. Margaret came out, and they were happy to meet her and she was happy to meet them. They already had driven by their old house. They have a nice car that is new.

We helped them bring in some suitcases and take them upstairs. Margaret fixed the main bedroom for them. We set Margaret temporarily in the room that Scott and Susan used to stay in. Scott and Susan said we shouldn't have done that, but it was really the most practical thing to do. Susan was interested in how the house looked and meeting the orphan children. Our big house no longer looks new.

They were thinking of taking me to the restaurant but I said we were already working on dinner and let's just eat here.

JJ and the children were interested in our visitors and Margaret explained that these were my friends from long ago. We had such a lovely dinner. We all had so much to talk about. Their family is doing well and has grown. The husbands of Stefani and Mary both went to Europe for the war but returned safely. Their boy John got called up, but the war ended before he left for the Pacific.

I can't begin to write down all the things we talked about. We naturally had to take care of the children and get them ready for bed, but Scott and Susan were used to kids and didn't mind. I think they enjoyed the whole environment. We had a jolly time.

We stayed up late. It seemed like old times, except you aren't here, and we're all older. Once again I wonder what you would look like now if you were here. Susan said it seemed perfectly natural to have children running all over this big house.

Saturday was just as fun. For breakfast, we had eggs and sausage and toast and orange juice. Margaret has been such a dear and used some of Fred's precious money for a little splurge for food. We can now buy orange juice frozen at the store but we don't get it often.

After breakfast we all took a walk with the children. Susan commented on how the trees are all bigger and everything looks older. There was so much to talk about. We came back and rested in the living room with the radio on. Susan gets tired easily, but we didn't talk about the cancer.

Susan told me that they gave that old refrigerator that we gave them to Stefani when she got married and it still works. Scott and Susan are doing well. I am happy for them. Scott is now head of a department.

Little Janet asked if Scott and Susan would be staying for story night. I had to explain what that was and they said they sure would. We didn't eat until almost 6. It has been wonderful having all of us sitting around our dining room table.

For story night, I played the piano again and then we had cookies and milk. I asked what stories we should have. The children wanted the ones I made up like the magic snowman, the fairies, the rock, the magic people on the island, and so on. We had such a wonderful time, and Scott and Susan were quite amused. Little JJ stayed by me the whole time. Once the children were in bed, we visited until late. There just is not enough time in the day.

Of course, we talked about you. It was hard not to be sad that you weren't with us. Scott said you were the nicest man he ever met.

This morning we had breakfast and then they left. They will stop in Pittsburgh and spend the night there before heading out to see the West. Waving goodbye brought back the memories of that sad day when they left in 1929. This time I know for sure that I will never see them again.

I thanked Margaret for everything she did this weekend and told her that Scott and Susan were my best friends from my past, but she was my dearest friend and sister.

Friday, May 3, 1946

Dear Arthur, we got a postcard from Scott and Susan. They were in Columbus, Ohio. They thanked us for a nice visit and said they wanted to send a few gifts for the children. Their daughter Stefani would be ordering something from Sears and Roebuck and have it delivered.

I have been selfish thinking about missing my friends. Margaret doesn't talk about her friends or family much. I haven't thought about her story. I only know there was some trouble with her family in Cleveland. Now that she doesn't have Fred I am the only friend she has beside the children. I will try to be a better friend for her.

Wednesday, May 15, 1946

Dear Arthur, what a surprise we got today. A big delivery truck stopped in front of our house, and the man started unloading boxes. There were four bicycles for boys and three bicycles for girls plus a tricycle and a new wagon. There was also a set of new mixing bowls, new dishes, new glasses, new bowls for breakfast, and new towels for the bathrooms. There is no way we can thank Scott and Susan enough. We can't even contact them. I can't imagine what it must have cost them. I wrote a letter to Stefani to thank them and to please let her mom and dad know.

When the children got home from school, there was excitement all afternoon. The bicycles needed to be put together, so Bobby and James took charge of that and we all tried to help. They got the bicycles for the younger children done first, and now the younger kids need to learn how to ride a bicycle. Carol was happy riding the tricycle.

We have received post cards from Indianapolis, St. Louis, Kansas City, Denver, Salt Lake City, Las Vegas, Los Angeles, and Hollywood. They are enjoying their trip and have seen the ocean.

<u>*Saturday, May 25, 1946*</u>

Dear Arthur, Scott and Susan are traveling home now. We have received post cards from Flagstaff and Albuquerque. They are taking the southern route back to Allentown so we won't have another chance to see them. This will be the last thing they do, and Susan will spend the rest of her time with her children and grandchildren.

Our children here have been overjoyed with the bicycles. Only Bobby and James know how to ride their bicycles. Margaret's Jon almost has learned. Linda, Mark, and JJ are getting close. It was such a nice thing that Scott and Susan did. School is almost out for the summer, and this will give the children plenty to do.

<u>*Wednesday, June 19, 1946*</u>

Dear Arthur, we took all the children to the movie theater today. The Mills Movie Theater lets the kids come for free on Wednesdays during the summer, if we come around noon. The movie today was a story about a dog named Lassie and I can't believe how much little JJ liked the movie. It was a very sad story until the end. I thought JJ would be too young, but all he talked about this afternoon was Lassie. All the kids liked the movie. I must confess I enjoyed it too.

Almost everyone can ride their bicycles now, including JJ and Janet. Little Carol loves the tricycle and the new wagon. School is out and everyone is having fun.

We have received post cards from Oklahoma City, Little Rock, Memphis, Nashville, and even Allentown. I wrote another letter to Susan and Scott. I told them how much the children are enjoying everything and how much we enjoyed having them here.

Thursday, July 4, 1946

Dear Arthur, we had a wonderful 4th of July. We all walked into town to see the fireworks show at the park.

We have taken the children to the movies a few times. I have the telephone number of the Mills theater office, and I call the day before to see what sort of movie is playing, and find out if the movie is a good one for children. Yesterday we watched a movie about a girl named Velvet who learned to ride a spirited horse. Two weeks ago we saw another movie about Lassie. This time, it was about a boy dog named Laddie that was the son of Lassie. These movies are so much nicer than the silent films we used to watch, and many of them are in color. Little JJ adores Lassie and wishes we had a dog. We've gone to the library to get the Lassie books. He has learned to read them by himself but he also likes me to read to him. I believe it's good for him.

Thursday, August 15, 1946

Dear Arthur, we had a very nice day today visiting the farm. The ladies came by this morning, and we drove both cars to the farm. It takes about an hour to get there and the children had so much fun. We were there for several hours and had lunch, too. The children learned about many of the animals. They got to feed chickens and helped feed the horses. They learned about milking cows, taking care of animals, and where the eggs come from. The older kids got to milk a cow. We even made butter. It has been a wonderful day. Little JJ was interested in everything.

Serendipitous Rescue

<u>*Saturday, September 21, 1946*</u>

Dear Arthur, we had a bit of a scare this past week. A middle-aged couple came from Pittsburgh because they were interested in adopting a young boy. They were particularly interested in JJ because of his age. I had been nearly sick from worrying about losing him. The people were here Thursday afternoon and came in a nice new car. They were dressed very well. They talked with us while we waited for school to be over. Then Margaret told me to stay and she would go and walk JJ home. I was surprised since I'm the one who walks him home after school but the way she looked at me I didn't argue. Margaret and JJ were late getting here, and I couldn't believe how messy and dirty JJ looked. Margaret told me to take JJ upstairs and get him cleaned up. He told me that he and Mrs. Barclay had a lot of fun on the way home. I got him cleaned and when I came back down the stairs the people were gone. Margaret told JJ to go out and play again and to have a good time. I asked what happened, and Margaret said that when she explained how much trouble JJ was they decided they weren't interested. Then she just smiled and went into the kitchen. I don't know what to think, but I love her dearly.

<u>*Tuesday, December 31, 1946*</u>

Dear Arthur, another year has ended. It has been one of my better years since you died. We've had a wonderful visit from Scott and Susan and the holiday season has been pleasant. Margaret has her moments, and even I sometimes do, but we are coping. The world is getting back to being good like before the crash. Winning the war has made everyone feel good and with the men coming home everyone is happy. It seems that everywhere ladies are expecting babies. There are jobs for everyone. I asked Margaret if she considered being a school teacher again. She said no, it wouldn't be enough money to pay for a house and food and everything else. Besides, she loves working with these children and me. I love working with her, and she is the best friend I've ever had.

Little JJ got his own Lassie book for Christmas. We managed to find a used one for a good price. He keeps it in his room and loves to look at the picture on the cover. He can read much better than I could at his age.

Friday, January 31, 1947

Dear Arthur, such a wonderful thing has happened. Right after the holidays the electric washing machine that we bought so long ago stopped working. It was completely worn out, and we had to wash by hand. Margaret decided we should use Fred's money to buy a new one, and I agreed. It's definitely something Fred would have wanted us to do. We took all the children in the car and drove to town to Stewart's Hardware and asked them to order us the cheapest one. Yesterday Mr. Stewart came over with a helper and their truck. They brought in a nice big fancy washing machine. At first we panicked and said there has been a mistake. He said there was no mistake. He said his church took up a collection and got enough money to buy a really good washing machine, and it wouldn't cost us anything. His helper hooked it up for us and took away the old broken one. Tomorrow we will all make a nice letter to him and his church.

Wednesday, June 18, 1947

Dear Arthur, I got the sad news today about Susan. Stefani said her mom passed away at the hospital in Allentown. All her children were able to be with her.

It has affected me more than I thought it would. They are good people and a wonderful family. Their house was always a home. Outside of Darcy and Mr. Stewart, she was my last connection to you. Thankfully I have Margaret and JJ and the children but my old life is gone.

17

A New World

Tuesday, June 15, 1948

Dear Arthur, Larry Johnson and his wife were by today to fix the problem with the water heater. He takes care of the orphanage in Pittsburgh and other buildings. He and JJ have been working on the old lawnmower, and they got it running. I don't know how that boy figures things out, but he does.

I enjoy getting letters from the girls who used to live here. They will always be my children.

Thursday, August 19, 1948

Dear Arthur, we had another nice visit to the farm. We have been there every August for the past few years. JJ got to milk the cow like he did last year. I wish you could see what a nice clever boy he is. It's hard to believe he has been here for six years. I wish he could stay forever. He now has three Lassie books.

Tuesday, February 8, 1949

Dear Arthur, little JJ is in the third grade. He does well in school but gets picked on. I suspect it is because he does better than most kids. He is smart and polite. The teachers all like him.

Several children have been sick with sore throats and fever. You would just love the way little JJ likes to help out. I don't recall him getting sick so far. Now that the war is over I worry that he will get adopted.

My biggest worry is to see him leave and be lost forever. I envy Margaret for having two children of her own.

Tuesday, August 16, 1949

Dear Arthur, we were married thirty years ago. Who could have imagined the life that was ahead for me? I am grateful for having had you in my life and for all that you have done for me.

Margaret and I fixed hamburgers for dinner and we had Coca Cola.

Saturday, June 17, 1950

Dear Arthur, we are worried. The management people said they don't need our orphanage anymore and can barely afford to keep it running. They said they can handle everything in Pittsburgh now. They want to close down by the end of the year and said we will lose the lease in a few years anyway. I don't like the idea that we will have to leave even sooner than we originally planned. At least I have Margaret as a friend. She and I have been so upset. I looked through all my old things in the attic and found the stocks we bought. We have some shares in the Coca-Cola Company and some others. I talked to the management people on the phone and told them they could have all the stocks if it would help keep our orphanage open. They said they will check it out. I worry what will happen to the children, and especially JJ if the children are transferred to Pittsburgh, and where we will go.

Tuesday, June 27, 1950

Dear Arthur, we had good news today. Our home is safe for now. Those stocks we bought so long ago are worth enough to keep the orphanage running until 1959. They even sent us $500 that we can add to Fred's money. There are no words to describe how happy Margaret and I are. It gives us more time to figure out what to do.

The bad news is that another war has started. This time in Korea. We had to look it up to see where Korea was. Hopefully, it will not be another big war. It makes us worry.

<u>*Sunday, December 31, 1950*</u>

Dear Arthur, I must say that I'm glad to be alive. As another year ends, I think about the past few years and how nice things have turned out. The children still enjoy the bicycles Scott and Susan gave us. JJ uses one of the bigger bicycles now. People donate things from time to time, and we have not had to use too much of Fred's money. Best of all is having the children. We occasionally hear from some of the girls who left and, of course, there is JJ. You would love him. I hope to live and see JJ grow up. I worry what will happen to him in the future and hope he will stay in contact with me after he leaves here. I'm sure he will.

<u>*Sunday, May 20, 1951*</u>

Dear Arthur, it has now been twenty years since the worst day of my life. You have been gone from me longer than our time together. My short time with you was worth all the years I could ever live. I'm grateful for my life now and that I am back in our wonderful home with Margaret, JJ, and the children. I saw your grave today and touched our tree.

<u>*Friday, June 1, 1951*</u>

Dear Arthur, school is out for summer soon, and the children are excited. JJ is particularly happy. He tries to avoid a kid who bullies everyone at school and is glad for the summer.

This evening the ladies from the farm came over, and JJ fixed their truck. We could tell it wasn't running right from the sound it made. While they were inside, JJ did something to the engine and then it was fine after that. He is really clever, and I must say he is smarter about some things than you or I.

<u>*Wednesday, June 6, 1951*</u>

Dear Arthur, we all walked into town to see a movie today, "Alice in Wonderland."

The big surprise was the little dog we found by the back porch when we got home. The children were delighted, but JJ was the most taken by it. He has named it "Laddie" and claimed it as his own. I'm not sure how this is going work out.

Saturday, June 9, 1951

Dear Arthur, it was difficult to have story night because of the dog. JJ doesn't like it when Laddie is outside and crying. He ended up spending the evening outside with Laddie. We have been walking around the neighborhood trying to find out who might have lost a dog. I fear JJ has bonded with this dog. I have no idea what we should do.

Monday, June 11, 1951

Dear Arthur, I'm certain JJ has been sneaking Laddie into his room. I have been beside myself with worry. Getting rid of the dog will crush him. All the children love to play with the dog during the day. After the children went to bed, I spoke with Margaret, and she has agreed that we should try to keep Laddie.

Tuesday, June 12, 1951

Dear Arthur, today has been horrible. My heart is broken, and I am worried sick. JJ and Laddie are gone. I can't stop crying, and Margaret is upset as well.

When we got up this morning, JJ wasn't in his room, and the dog wasn't in the garage. At first we thought he was out walking but when he didn't show up we walked around the neighborhood and the park. We finally called the sheriff. Margaret feels terrible and blames herself. I said it's not her fault but we are very worried.

Margaret went out with the older kids again this evening looking around the neighborhood. I stayed here in case the phone rang or JJ turned up, but no one called.

We both made dinner. Nothing like this has ever happened before.

It's very late now, but I can't sleep and neither can Margaret. We're hoping the phone will ring with news. All I can think of is little JJ out there in the dark. I've not been this sad and worried since you died. I pray he is safe.

Wednesday, June 13, 1951

Dear Arthur, we are so relieved. JJ is safe and sound. He still was not back this morning but then we got a phone call from the sheriff that they found JJ. They brought him home and told us about him saving the life of an old lady living on a farm. We were all crying and happy to see him. The sheriff said JJ is a hero. After the sheriff left, Margaret told JJ he could keep the dog. This will be a big change for us.

JJ took a nap while some of the others went to the picture show. Margaret took most of the kids. I feel like I have been through the wringer. There is so much to think about.

Thursday, June 14, 1951

Dear Arthur, it will be a lot to get used to with a dog in the house. The children think it's jolly, and all want to play with Laddie. Margaret says our job is to take care of children who have no home and maybe it makes sense to take care of a lost dog as well. The dog has been difficult for her but she is trying.

A lady from the newspaper came over to talk to JJ about how he helped the old lady on the farm. I have to admit it was an interesting story. JJ was happy to talk about his adventure.

After dinner, we got a telephone call from Mrs. Robinson. She is related to Beverly Garver, the lady that JJ rescued. She asked if they could bring Mrs. Garver over tomorrow. It will be interesting to meet these people, but it unnerves me for some reason.

Friday, June 15, 1951

Dear Arthur, this has been another strange day. We met the Robinsons when they brought Mrs. Garver. They came after dinner. Mr. Robinson brought a newspaper to show us the article about JJ saving Mrs. Garver. She is still not well but is doing better. It was an odd feeling having them here. Mrs. Garver likes JJ, and he seems to like her. For some reason it bothers me that he likes her so much. She is a widow and lost her boy in the war.

The strangest part of today was when Margaret suggested the idea of placing JJ with the Robinsons. I am still shocked by the idea, and I cannot sleep. The thought of having JJ leave here brings tears and worry, but Margaret has a good point, and she usually has good ideas. This whole situation is very troubling and upsetting to me. Things have been good for a long time and now this worry. It's bad enough that we will have to leave this place in a few years.

Saturday, June 16, 1951

Dear Arthur, we had a very nice story night. It was interesting having the dog with us in the house. JJ told us the story about his adventure again, and the children had so many questions. It's all made me realize that little JJ is growing up. He is now more interested in the dog than wanting to be with me. It seems to happen as the children grow up and their interests change. I just didn't expect it to happen so suddenly with JJ.

Monday, June 18, 1951

Dear Arthur, the Robinsons came over with Mrs. Garver and had dinner with us. JJ showed Mrs. Garver his room and seemed happy to see her. I feel like I am being replaced by a dog and a stranger. They seem like good people, though. They have been damaged by the war like us. Margaret has invited them for story night. She is pushing this relationship but it makes me uneasy.

Tuesday, June 19, 1951

Dear Arthur, I feel much better tonight. JJ has been such a dear today. He has helped me with the laundry and even the cleaning. It's almost as though he is reassuring me. I also had another talk with Margaret tonight. She is very logical about things, and if there is a chance that we can keep JJ here in town as he grows up, it will be worth the effort. It's just that so much has happened so quickly. I try to imagine how you would handle things.

Saturday, June 23, 1951

Dear Arthur, it was a very nice story night. The Robinsons and Mrs. Garver were here again, but Margaret shocked everyone by asking the

Robinsons to consider taking JJ to live with them. Everything is happening so fast. I hope she knows what she's doing. It's late, and I can't sleep.

Sunday, June 24, 1951

Dear Arthur, I couldn't sleep last night, and Margaret got up and we talked. The Robinsons are nice people. Mr. Robinson even fixed Carol's bicycle that Scott and Susan gave us. Living with the Robinsons would be good for JJ but it would be hard for me. I know what you would say if you were here.

Monday, June 25, 1951

Dear Arthur, I had a bad dream last night. I was outside, and Scott and Susan came by in their car. At first I was glad to see them. Then it wasn't them in the car anymore but was the Robinsons instead. JJ came out of the house and ran to the car and got in. Then they drove away. I was just standing all alone and then woke up. Margaret said maybe it means the Robinsons will be our new friends.

Thursday, June 28, 1951

Dear Arthur, Mr. Robinson called to say they are going to take JJ. They will be here for story night again. No matter how I try to think about things I can't help myself from being upset. It seems too fast and too soon. Margaret is right about how maybe there will never be another opportunity like this, and we need to take advantage of it. JJ seems happy but surprised and worried. He admires Mr. Robinson and is impressed that Mr. Robinson can fix things. Margaret and I talked with him after the other children went to bed. Margaret explained how we love him and we don't want him to leave but it will happen someday. He is a good boy and said he understands and will try to make things work. He hugged both of us and said he will always stay in touch no matter what happens. It gives me some comfort.

Serendipitous Rescue

<u>*Friday, June 29, 1951*</u>

Dear Arthur, I had another good talk with Margaret. She is right, and we must do our best to make this happen. Sometimes the right thing to do is painful in the moment but is the best thing in the end.

<u>*Saturday, June 30, 1951*</u>

Dear Arthur, this is the day I have dreaded for many years. JJ is gone. I know Margaret is right, but I am having a hard time. Seeing his room empty is almost as bad as seeing your empty chair after you died. Margaret has kept me company and reminds me that we're doing the right thing. My heart has been broken so many times. It is hard not to worry. I feel frustrated and helpless. I want to do something, but I don't know what.

<u>*Sunday, July 1, 1951*</u>

Dear Arthur, I knew the day would come eventually. Even normal families say goodbye to their children at some point. Margaret's boy Jon is seventeen and will be leaving us one of these days. I know it's our job to prepare these children to leave us, but it's not easy saying goodbye. The best we can hope for is that they remain close by.

I wasn't ready for this and I'm worried. The house seems empty. I'm not sleeping well. I wish life wasn't so hard. Why are all the good things in life taken from me?

<u>*Monday, July 2, 1951*</u>

Dear Arthur, Margaret is such a dear. She wants things to be nice for the 4th and suggested that we use some of our savings to get some fireworks. The children here are excited. We will have more fireworks than last year.

I have a hard time keeping my mind on things. I've had lots of tears and no appetite. I don't know how I'll get to sleep tonight. We can't tell how things are going with JJ, and I know Margaret is concerned. All I can do is pray that things work out. I mustn't be selfish.

Wednesday, July 4, 1951

Dear Arthur, we had a delightful 4th of July. Margaret and I are much more at ease about everything.

Mrs. Garver came over with JJ and the Robinsons and everyone seemed so cheerful. I don't know what happened, but Mr. and Mrs. Robinson seem happier than before and JJ was excited to tell us about working with Mr. Robinson. Mr. Robinson hurt his hand and JJ is helping him at his job. They almost seem like different people. I can tell that Margaret is pleased.

This was the best 4th of July since you died. We had sparklers and a nice display of fireworks. It was almost like old times. It felt like you were with me. JJ and Mr. Robinson took care of lighting the fireworks. Once more it caused me to realize he is growing up.

JJ said he would see us for story night. Margaret gave me a hug tonight and said we don't have to worry about JJ or the Robinsons.

Saturday, July 7, 1951

Dear Arthur, I feel much better about everything. We had a wonderful story night. JJ, Mrs. Garver, and the Robinsons were here. Everyone seemed happy. Margaret says JJ has already changed their life.

Right after dinner Mr. Robinson went outside with JJ and Mrs. Garver. He and JJ fixed little things on the bicycles and other toys. I can't believe how well JJ and Mr. Robinson are getting along. The other kids like Mr. Robinson. Mrs. Garver talks continuously about how well things are working out.

Saturday, July 14, 1951

Dear Arthur, we finished the Dr. Doolittle book last week, and Shannen said we should start reading "Swiss Family Robinson" since the Robinsons were here. Some of the children thought it was funny, and I asked Mr. and Mrs. Robinson if they minded. They seemed amused and liked the idea. Margaret said maybe we should have Mr. Robinson read the story. The children thought it was a wonderful idea, and Mr. Robinson agreed to read the story. It never ceases to amaze me how clever Margaret is.

Serendipitous Rescue

Saturday, August 18, 1951

Dear Arthur, We had an interesting story night. I don't feel nearly so worried about things. I learned more about the Robinsons tonight in a sad kind of way.

It has been warm, and after Mr. Robinson read a chapter from "The Swiss Family Robinson" book, the children wanted the magic snowman story. When I finished, Mrs. Robinson had tears. I found out that they had a little girl who died from scarlet fever a number of years ago. I'm nearly certain it was the little girl we heard about back then. I felt so bad for them. They have turned out to be such nice people. Margaret was so right about them.

When they were getting ready to leave, I told Mrs. Robinson I was sorry and didn't know about their little girl. She said it was fine, and it was a wonderful story and wished she had had a magic snowman.

They are making a nice home for JJ.

Tuesday, October 23, 1951

Dear Arthur, this has been such a good day, and you would be so proud of our little JJ.

We have been having trouble with the furnace lately. Sometimes the radiators wouldn't come on when they were supposed to. It was stuck again today, and Mr. Robinson brought JJ over right after school. They both worked on it and found the problem. We will see them Saturday for story night.

The other good news is that Patricia called me on the phone. She is twenty years old now and is a secretary and is engaged and can drive a car. She will be bringing her fiancé along with Alice and Barbara for story night. Alice is a nurse and Barbara is an operator at the telephone company. I am excited to see them, and so is Margaret. JJ will be here with the Robinsons and maybe Mrs. Garver too. It will be like a grand party. It's days like this that make me glad to be alive.

Wednesday, October 31, 1951

Dear Arthur, this has been the best Halloween since you died. We all had so much fun. The Robinson's brought JJ and their aunt along with Laddie. Tom went out with JJ and the children. We ladies stayed here to give out candy. I enjoyed visiting with Laura, Mrs. Garver, and Margaret. Margaret says we may very well have new friends and I believe she is right.

Thursday, November 22, 1951

Dear Arthur, on this Thanksgiving day there is much to be thankful for. I'm especially thankful that Margaret had the idea to have JJ go live with the Robinsons. There is no doubt that we will be able to see him often. Things are working out but Margaret and I are concerned about what we'll do in eight years when we have to leave. For now I will be thankful for what I have.

Tuesday, December 25, 1951

Dear Arthur, it was a bittersweet Christmas. Not having JJ here at Christmas time was sad for me. Jon is in JJ's room now. The reality of JJ being gone is final. I missed him so much this morning. The children opened their presents and it was very merry, but it was empty not having JJ here. At least he is with nice people and is here often.

Tom, Laura and JJ came by last night to wish us a Merry Christmas. JJ is happy. I'm glad he loves to see me. He gave me the nicest hug. Tom said JJ is learning quickly and knows almost everything about the business. I'm not surprised.

Saturday, December 29, 1951

Dear Arthur, what a year this has been. It is ending on a nice note. Tom finished reading the "The Swiss Family Robinson." It always makes me sad to think the family in that story would rather stay on the island then to go and see their son get married. I could never make a decision like that. I hope I live to see JJ get married and have children.

Serendipitous Rescue

<u>Wednesday, January 9, 1952</u>

Dear Arthur, the final step in JJ's adoption was completed today. It was a beautiful and comforting ceremony at the court house. We were all there. I thought I might be sad but when everything was done I felt peace. It's as though the last lose ends are done. Beverly Garver and I got to be part of the ceremony. The judge was very nice. Afterward we all went over to the restaurant. Tom paid for everyone, even the children. I had a hamburger and a Coca Cola.

Yesterday I got a letter from Darcy. She enjoys being a grandmother. I sometimes feel bad that we never had our own children. I'm grateful that you built this house. I feel that all the children who have lived here are our children.

<u>Saturday, January 12, 1952</u>

Dear Arthur, you certainly have not failed me. What a wonderful birthday I have had this afternoon. It's hard to imagine I am now 50 years old.

We had such a nice party here. It's like my birthday was celebrating JJ's adoption. Tom and Laura brought JJ and Beverly Garver. Even Patricia and Alice and Bobby came. Laura told us she is expecting a baby, but Margaret and I had already guessed. We are happy for them.

It's always cold on my birthday, but it was warm in our nice big home. With everyone here and all the children, it was a noisy affair. It has been even better than the parties we used to have here, at least for me.

Margaret gave me another new pen for my birthday, plus a new empty diary book to write in. Laura and Beverly brought a nice birthday cake they made.

It's quiet now, and everyone is asleep. It seems that no matter how nice the day has been I still miss you. I wish you could see the result of what you made.

<u>Saturday, July 26, 1952</u>

Dear Arthur, Tom and Laura came over this evening with JJ and his new little sister. It was fun to see them. They didn't stay long, but it was a wonderful visit. They have named the baby Lois. JJ and Tom have been so busy that we haven't seen them for several weeks. They met Mr. Mills, who owns the theater. They are doing air conditioning work at the movie theater and also in Pittsburgh. They have been very busy. It's nice to see how much JJ and Tom get along. Margaret has been especially pleased.

I have come to love them.

Monday, September 22, 1952

Dear Arthur, another sad event has occurred. Beverly Garver passed away. I really got to like her. They were just here for story night. She was a widow and lost her only boy in the war. She had a sad life like me but because of JJ, her last year was happy. It will be sad for them. They have gained baby Lois but lost their Aunt. Life can be cruel and wonderful at the same time. At least Beverly lived a long life.

Thursday, November 27, 1952

Dear Arthur, once again there is so much to be thankful for. Things have changed so much and have worked out better than Margaret or I could have possibly imagined. JJ and Tom are working with Mr. Mills. Laura is such a dear. They are sad not to have their aunt with them. I miss her too.

JJ and Tom got our car working again. It hasn't been working for a few days. It's hard to imagine all this. I don't think I have ever felt so secure since you died. I don't have to worry about losing JJ, and I often hear from the other children who used to live here. My only worry is having to leave this wonderful home in a few years.

Saturday, December 13, 1952

Dear Arthur, what a wonderful day this has been. I have not known so much happiness in all these years.

The Robinsons came over after lunch and we all went to get a Christmas tree. We had such a good time. They have a truck now for their business. Margaret drove our car and we had children in the car and the truck. The Christmas tree place was selling hot chocolate and

Tom bought some for everyone. Tom also paid for the Christmas tree for us and we got a big one. Setting up and decorating the tree brought such memories. We had dinner and story night too. Margaret and I love visiting with Laura and the baby. They will never know how happy they have made me.

Tuesday, December 24, 1952

Dear Arthur, I can't imagine having a nicer Christmas. It is very late now and everyone is asleep. I have my candle in the window and am exhausted but happy. Margaret and I have set out the gifts for the children for tomorrow, but Christmas has already started here.

This evening the Robinsons came over for dinner but the big surprise was the presents they brought in the truck. Tom and JJ brought in several bags of toys but that wasn't all. First we had music and singing while dinner was cooking. The children sang the songs we practiced and then JJ read "The Night Before Christmas" poem.

After dinner, the children opened the presents that the Robinsons brought. Then Tom and JJ brought in a huge present for me and Margaret. It was an air conditioner for the summer time. I don't know how this works, but they said it will keep us cool, like a magic snowman. Tom is now a partner with Mr. Mills, and they are doing very well. I hope their business keeps doing well, and we don't have another crash. It's worrisome thinking about the good times you and I had and how they ended.

Saturday, June 6, 1953

Dear Arthur, today has been another day to remember. All this past week people have been working on our big house. It almost felt like we were building again. The house has been painted and looks like new. A fence has been put up around the side and backyard.

Right after lunch we got to meet Mr. Mills. Then people from the newspaper came and so did people from the television station in Pittsburgh. It turned out to be quite an affair.

Tom and JJ had cut a hole in the living room wall and installed the air conditioner there. We all gathered around to see me turn on the air conditioner. It was amazing to have cold air coming out. It works much better than the electric fans. I wish you could see all these things.

Saturday, July 4, 1953

Dear Arthur, we had a nice celebration today, even better than before. The Robinsons brought Kevin Connor and his grandmother, and even Mr. Mills was here with the lady who helps run their business with her daughters. We had lots of food and fireworks and Tom and Mr. Mills paid for everything. There were so many people we ran out of room at the table. It was like the grand parties we used to have and was very festive. I wish you could have been here to meet everyone. They are all nice people.

It was the first time we got to meet Kevin Connor. He's a big fellow, and I can see why JJ used to stay away from him. I'm glad they are friends now. His grandmother seems like a nice person.

When it started to get dark, JJ and Kevin lit the fireworks and helped the children with sparklers. Tom supervised and everything went well. The children really had a good time.

When everyone left it was late but we still had a lot of food left over. We put the younger ones to bed and others wanted a snack. It has been a wonderful day. Tom and Laura have been good to us.

I miss you on these special occasions.

Saturday, September 12, 1953

Dear Arthur, it's been a sad day for Margaret and all of us. Her boy Jon has left on the train for Cleveland. She has family there who run a large store, and Jon will work there for now. He said he wished his dad could see him go. Margaret said to go and build a good life to honor his father.

We have both been sad to see him leave, but it's not that far away, and he already has plans to return for Christmas. Time moves on, and things change. Sometimes it seems that tears are the price we must pay for happiness.

We are getting a young boy this next week so that will keep us busy.

Serendipitous Rescue

<u>*Thursday, December 24, 1953*</u>

Dear Arthur, it has been a fun Christmas Eve. Not only were Tom, Laura and JJ here, but so was Mr. Mills, Kevin Connor, and his grandmother. Jon is here from Cleveland. We had a wonderful time. Tom and Laura brought presents again, and we had a little Christmas program.

The big surprise was Mr. Mills talking to us about an idea for them to buy our big house. If they can do it, we won't have to leave in a few years. It's only an idea now, but it's exciting to think that Mr. Mills will try.

Their business is still going well. It's different than building houses like we used to do, but JJ likes it. It seems that the air conditioning business will be good for a long time.

<u>*Sunday, November 14, 1954*</u>

Dear Arthur, Tom, Laura, and JJ were here for story night last night. I always love to have them here. JJ's baby sister Lois is so adorable. Tom says that things are moving along with Mr. Mills' plan to buy the house but it takes time. Mr. Mills is an important and successful person, and if he thinks there is a chance, it gives hope to Margaret and me.

My collection of pictures is growing. I have stayed in touch with most of my children who have left here and they sometimes send photographs. I love to get their letters and hear how they are doing. Many of them live far from here and some are having babies. It's interesting to see how life moves on.

<u>*Saturday, January 12, 1957*</u>

Dear Arthur, what a wonderful birthday this has been. Tom, Laura, JJ, Lois and Laddie came over for my birthday and story night. JJ has a girlfriend named Anna and she came with them. Anna seems very nice and I enjoyed meeting her. She plays the piano well. I had a good time visiting with her. I can tell JJ and Anna really like each other.

<u>*Sunday, March 3, 1957*</u>

Dear Arthur, it's hard to believe JJ is seventeen years old. Tom, Laura, JJ, Lois, Anna and Laddie came over for a visit. JJ told us his friend Kevin is now engaged to a girl named Patty.

It was a very nice evening. Anna and I played the piano together and had a lot of fun. I can tell by the way JJ and Anna look at each other that they are in love. I remember that day so long ago when you first told me that you loved me.

<u>*Saturday, March 30, 1957*</u>

Dear Arthur, JJ came for story night with Anna and brought his friend Kevin Connor too. Kevin brought Patty. I can't describe how wonderful it is to watch these kids grow up and know that they will always be in my life. They came by themselves because Kevin can drive, and he has his own company truck.

Shannen is married, and Jon has a daughter. Fortunately for Margaret, Shannen lives here in town and Jon visits often. It's like we both have grown children.

<u>*Saturday, October 19, 1957*</u>

Dear Arthur, JJ and Anna came over today with Tom and Laura. JJ and Anna are engaged and look so happy. I'm happy, too. I just love that girl. Anna and I played the piano together again and had a lot of fun. Laura is expecting another baby, and everyone is in a good mood.

<u>*Tuesday, December 24, 1957*</u>

Dear Arthur, it's been another wonderful day. This evening JJ and Anna were here along with Tom and Laura. Besides having a wonderful time with Anna, Tom told us to get ready to talk to the state people about the house. They are almost ready to finish their deal. Tom seemed very confident about things. Margaret and I are in an especially cheerful mood.

Serendipitous Rescue

<u>*Tuesday, January 28, 1958*</u>

Dear Arthur, JJ called this evening to announce that he has a new baby sister. They are naming her Catherine. I feel like they are all a part of my family. Anna is such a dear. I always look forward to having them over and playing the piano with Anna.

<u>*Friday, May 30, 1958*</u>

Dear Arthur, it's hard to believe that JJ has finished high school. Tom and Laura picked me up and I was able to see JJ get his diploma at the graduation ceremony. Mr. Mills and Kevin and his grandma and Anna and her parents were there. It was nice to meet the Kurzmanns. We had quite an evening. Margaret stayed here to watch the children. I know she wanted to be there. Afterward we all went to the little restaurant that you and I used to go to. It is different now. Mr. Mills paid for dinner for everyone. Tom said Laura worked there during the war.

Seeing JJ get his diploma made me wish I could have gotten one. I don't feel bad, though. I did get a wonderful education, and you taught me so much. You were a wonderful teacher.

<u>*Saturday, September 20, 1958*</u>

Dear Arthur, this has been another day I will never forget. To see JJ and Anna get married has been one of the highlights of my life. How I did miss you today. I thought of our day back in the mining camp, and how it began a wonderful life for me. Laura had me sit with her, so it was like we were both JJ's mother. Tom and Laura are such dear friends. Between Margaret and the Robinsons and Mr. Mills and Anna I have been blessed more than I could imagine.

The wedding was at the farm where Beverly Garver used to live. It was the place JJ ran away to. That was a horrible time for me but being here today at the wedding and to see how this all came together, I am glad that JJ found these people.

Margaret and the children were there too. They all had a good time. If it wasn't for Margaret this might not have happened and who knows where JJ might be. The children made a nice card for JJ and Anna and all wrote their names.

As we were waiting for things to get started, I almost got a little sad, wishing you were with me. Then Laddie came running looking for JJ. Everyone was amused but then JJ handed Laddie to me and I sat down with him on my lap. For some reason it gave me great comfort. It seemed like Laddie was interested in everything.

Today really felt like we were all a family. There were lots of pictures taken of all of us. The way the Robinsons introduce us to others, you would think we have known each other all our lives. Margaret got to meet the Kurzmanns. Anna is such a nice girl. I can't imagine anyone else I'd rather see JJ spend his life with. The whole day has been a wonderful experience.

I think of JJ and Anna starting their lives, and I remember when we started our life together in that little apartment in Carbondale. I wish you were here watching me as I write this.

Wednesday, December 31, 1958

Dear Arthur, this has been one of the nicest years I have ever had. JJ and Anna are married and he has a new sister. He has finished school and is doing well with work. Our big house has been secured, and we have no money worries. Tom and Mr. Mills have said we can stay here as long as we want. I am relieved to be able to stay in the castle you made for me.

We do miss JJ and Anna being here for story night. They now spend most Saturday nights in Pittsburgh with the Kurzmanns. I can understand how her parents must want to see them. Fortunately they are here often, and so are Tom and Laura. Just this last Saturday Tom and Laura came over with Lois and the baby for story night.

Between them and Margaret and the children who live here, my life is full.

Monday, January 12, 1959

Dear Arthur, what a nice birthday this has been.

JJ and Anna came by this evening and had a box of oranges they brought from Pittsburgh. I could tell from Margaret's smile she must have put them up to it. I had a hard time not getting emotional. Tom and Laura brought the kids and we had a wonderful birthday party. Anna played the birthday song for me and everyone sang. This has been one of the best birthdays I ever had.

Laddie always comes to me for a treat when they arrive and I always have something for him. I love the way he looks at me. Laddie has always liked me, probably because I fed him when he first showed up.

Monday, July 13, 1959

Dear Arthur, we've had such a lovely evening. JJ, Anna, Kevin, and Patty came by. Kevin loves to be here, and we love to see him. Kevin and Patty are expecting sometime in September.

We have managed to wear out the washing machine that Mr. Stewart and his church got us. JJ and Kevin brought a new one and installed it this evening. It is quite different from the first one we bought so long ago. This one is nicer and easier to use and even bigger. You would love to see how they take care of me and our castle.

Even though we can easily get oranges at the store here in town, JJ and Anna continue bringing oranges from Pittsburgh. Usually they come Sunday evening and Anna and I play the piano together. I love her dearly.

Saturday, May 20, 1961

Dear Arthur, it has been thirty years since you died. My life has been such a joy these past ten years. I wish you could see all the wonderful things that have happened. JJ's company is doing well, and they take care of us.

Margaret has been my dear friend all these years. I'm glad we are all cared for by such wonderful people. JJ and Anna are often here on Sunday afternoons, along with little Laddie. She plays the piano much better than I did at her age.

I received a nice letter from Barbara. She is living in California. She sent a lovely photograph of her and her husband and her two boys.

It's hard to imagine that there was so much trouble in the past. It makes me worry that something dreadful could happen.

<u>*Friday, January 12, 1962*</u>

Dear Arthur, I am sixty years old. I don't know if you would recognize me now.

I haven't been sad for a long time, but you are always on my mind.

Mr. Stewart died last year right after Christmas. I haven't seen him in a long time. Jimmy is older now but is still in movies.

The past keeps fading away, but my new life gets better and better. Tom, Laura, JJ and Anna are good to us. I have no complaints about my life.

<u>*Sunday, November 24, 1963*</u>

Dear Arthur, the past few days have been dreadful. Our president, John Kennedy, has been shot and killed. I couldn't help but remember when you taught our little school class about when Abraham Lincoln was assassinated. I can't believe such a thing has happened again. It has been the news on the radio and on the television. Everyone is shocked and saddened.

<u>*Tuesday, December 31, 1963*</u>

Dear Arthur, it has mostly been a good year for us. The country has been sad about President Kennedy but JJ and Anna have built a wonderful new home where Beverly Garver's house used to be. I'm happy for them. Their business continues to do well and it seems the future is bright.

<u>*Friday, September 17, 1965*</u>

Dear Arthur, what a wonderful day we had today. While most of the children were at school, JJ and Anna and Laura came over and had an early lunch with me and Margaret. Then they took me and Margaret with them to the movie theater to see "The Sound of Music." Laura stayed here to take care of the younger children. Margaret and I really liked the movie and I would say it was the best movie I ever watched. It was a wonderful story about children, and a rich man who married a poor woman. It was based on real people during the time when Hitler was taking over Europe. It had a happy ending and wonderful music.

Saturday, September 18, 1965

Dear Arthur, we had an especially fun story night this evening. Tom and Laura and the kids came with JJ and Anna. They brought a record with them which has all the songs from the movie we saw yesterday. We have been playing it all evening on the record player. Margaret and I have really enjoyed it. I'm practicing to play the songs from that movie.

Lately, after I give Laddie a treat, he jumps onto your big chair and rests. He's not bouncy anymore and neither am I. It seems he likes to watch me when I'm playing the piano. I wonder what he's thinking.

Saturday, June 15, 1966

Dear Arthur, what a fun evening we had. JJ and Anna came over for story night. He brought a new camera that can take a picture and in a minute you can see it. The picture comes out of the camera and slowly comes into view like magic. He took pictures of everyone and let each child have their own. We all had a lot of fun.

I wish I had the photographs of you and Scott and Susan that got lost in the flood. That time seems like a dream now.

18
Part 2 End

<u>Saturday, June 15, 1968</u>

Dear Arthur, JJ and Anna came over for the afternoon. Unfortunately they were headed to Pittsburgh and didn't stay long. They were so sweet and invited me to come and live with them. I must say that I am quite tempted. They want me to retire. I don't know what I will do if I have to leave this place. It's nice to know that they want to care for me. At least I have no worries about having a place to live. Even though I love them dearly, living with them would seem strange to me. I think they are trying to figure out how to help me live here. They are such dears. I know I'm being selfish, but I wish I could stay here until I die.

<u>Saturday, July 13, 1968</u>

Dear Arthur, This past week JJ and Kevin have been installing a motorized chair for me to go up and down the stairs. They finished it today and it is rather fun. It is wonderful how everyone takes care of me. I am feeling the effects of age and just don't move as fast as I used to. We made potato salad today and I had a hard time mixing everything. I don't remember it being so difficult before.

JJ and Anna have arranged for me to stay here as long as I want.

<u>Tuesday, December 31, 1968</u>

Dear Arthur, another year is gone, and so much is changing. At the beginning of the month, we got a new aide to replace me.

Serendipitous Rescue

Margaret had been interviewing several ladies and decided on a lovely girl named Lisa Carter. She has not married yet so who knows what will happen down the road. She started working here on December 2nd and sleeps in the bedroom at the end where Scott and Susan used to stay. She and Margaret have decided that when the weather warms we will get a dog to live here. The children do love animals, and they love to visit the farm. Miss Carter seems to have plenty of energy.

Our little town is quite a bit bigger than when we moved here. That's good for JJ and Tom's business. I don't worry quite so much anymore for them. They take very good care of us. We have a new washing machine, a clothes dryer, a dishwasher, even television. They even pay for our electricity and other expenses. Margaret and I live very comfortably in our castle.

Saturday, August 16, 1969

Dear Arthur, it has been fifty years since that wonderful day when we were married. The short time we were together changed my life in a wonderful and marvelous way. After you were gone, I had sadness, but my happiness these past years has made up for it. I wish we were both growing old together, and I wish you could see what a nice, loving family I have. Perhaps you do.

My life is very different now. I try to help out but Lisa and Margaret take care of most everything. We have two dogs here now. I feel like I am becoming an observer of life. I feel guilty for not helping more but everyone wants me to be comfortable. I look forward to visits from JJ and Anna and Laura and Tom and the children.

The news is often disturbing. The war in Vietnam is troublesome. Dwight Eisenhower has passed on. Even Judy Garland has died. I liked the Wizard of Oz movie.

Other news has been interesting. We watched the men land on the moon. It's hard to imagine all these things. The world seems so busy now.

Wednesday, September 23, 1970

Dear Arthur, such a sad day. JJ's dog Laddie has passed away. Laura called me on the telephone to give me the news. That little dog was the beginning of an extraordinary story that changed our lives. I sometimes wonder if you had something to do with it.

It is a time for reflecting and remembering. I've had plenty of time lately to think about our life, and the past we shared. I think about JoAnn Cummins, Mr. and Mrs. Ranta, Mr. Stewart, Scott and Susan, the ladies I worked with during the depression, Arabella, and dear Fred. I think about my mother, my father, my stepmother, Darcy and her family. And of course, I think of you, who rescued me and gave me so much.

I think of little JJ growing up and all the children I've known. JJ reminds me so much of you. He is now about the age you were before all the bad things happened to us. I often dream of our little apartment in Carbondale. I am blessed to have so many wonderful memories.

I don't do much around here anymore, but I'm happy. I don't have the energy I once had. Sometimes I gaze out the window toward our tree. The words you carved fifty years ago are now as high as my window and I can look straight out to see them. My eyes don't work so well but I can see those words as clearly as the day you made them. What a wonderful life I've had.

Saturday, October 10, 1970

Dear Arthur, I have dealt with what life gave me the best I could. I shall soon be with you. There was once a time when I wished for death. Later I was glad for life. Now I accept my fate.

You once said you would build me a castle and we would have lots of children. You once said that hopefully we would both die in this house. Things have not worked out like we wanted, but they have worked out. You should be happy to know that this house has been a wonderful home all these many years. I expect it will continue to be so for many years to come.

Story night exhausted me. I played the piano, and Miss Lisa told stories. She is very good with the children. In a way, it's nice to know that I'm no longer needed. JJ and Anna were not here, but I think of them every day. Because of you, they will have a good life. You have given me a good life and improved the lives of many others.

I feel that I am finishing my time. Aches and pains plague me constantly. I get cold easily and have a hard time warming up. I may finally be ill. It will soon be Halloween. Perhaps I will be a ghost.

It makes me happy that JJ and Tom have many of your good qualities. They are smart and kind. They work hard and care about me, this place, and the orphans. I'm glad for Laura. She has a wonderful family and a wonderful life. She deserves it. I'm happy that Anna and JJ found each other.

I have written my final letter to Darcy. We have both had good lives and we both have good families.

Saturday, October 17, 1970

This will be my last entry. I have finished the book about my life.

I wish for Margaret to have my things, except for my diaries, which I want for JJ and Anna. I want them to understand that sadness is a price we often pay for happiness, but we must not be afraid to pay it.

I have never seen the ocean or been on a train or an airplane or even been out of Pennsylvania. In many respects, though, I've had a better life than most. I've had the love of a wonderful man, and once rode in an automobile and held hands. I have experienced abundance and poverty. I have experienced great joy and great sorrow. I have experienced loneliness and enjoyed wonderful friendships. I've had the love of many children and can remember each and every one. I have seen the best of humanity. I'm sorry that Arthur could not be with me in all this. I look forward to seeing him again, and others that have gone before me.

No one could want a friend or sister dearer than Margaret. I thank her for everything, and for helping me to have a wonderful life.

I can't imagine a family more wonderful than what I have had with Tom, Laura, JJ and Anna, Mr. Mills, and the others.

I suppose life is like a train, with people getting on and others getting off at different stations. I feel like I'm getting off the train now. Soon I'll be standing at the station waving to my loved ones as they move on.

My only regret is not being able to see JJ and Anna have their family. I have confidence that Margaret will find the right situation. She has always been good at working out things. I want the best for them.

For these past many years I have been blessed with loving friends and family. There is nothing in all the world more precious than that.

Part 3

1971 - 2020

JJ and Anna

Fireflies in the night

1

The Storm

Martin was running late. He was on the phone with his twin brother, Mark. "You still there?" asked Mark, impatiently.

"I'm on my way right now," said Martin.

"Hurry up," said Mark, with a laugh. "Everyone's here."

Mark and Martin were celebrating their 40th birthday. Martin quickly locked the door to his small but prosperous pipeline business. The rest of the office was already at the party. The future was bright. Only two months ago their company had landed their largest ever contract with the county.

Martin smiled as he walked hurriedly to his brand new one-ton long-bed pickup truck and climbed into the cab. The truck was his pride and joy. He started the engine and stepped on the gas. Gravel flew behind as he sped out of the parking lot and onto the highway.

Martin drove fast, over the speed limit. He thought of his friends and family, and the big birthday party waiting for him. He pressed his right foot harder on the accelerator pedal. As he came to a curve, a concrete truck ahead was slowing down traffic. Martin turned slightly to the left, preparing to pass the truck.

* * * * *

Oleg and Lena Dzbinski were on their way home in their old Dodge. Lena had picked up Oleg from work. Oleg was driving. As they came around the curve, a pickup truck was heading straight for them. Before Oleg could react, the truck and its driver blotted out the rest of the world. Time slowed down. Metal crumpled. Glass shattered. Lena's head rushed toward the windshield. In the few seconds before she died, intense sadness and terror consumed her. As she faded into unconsciousness, there was only time for a single thought. *Please, God, my children.*

* * * * *

It was a Thursday evening in the spring of 1971. Eleven-year-old Eryk had been in charge of his younger sisters, seven-year-old Janina and four-year-old Anatola, while their mom went to pick up their dad from work. It had been a shopping day, and their mom had needed the car. Eryk was young, but he was a trustworthy babysitter.

Their parents were late. Eryk thought perhaps they had to get a few more things from the store. But they had never been this late before. Dinner was ready and just needed to be heated on the stove. Eryk was getting irritated that they had been left alone for such a long time.

When a policeman knocked on the door of their second-floor apartment, the sun was nearly set. Janina said, "My mom's not home right now," but Eryk got a sick feeling. The policeman asked if everyone was ok, and said he would be right back. Eryk peered out the window to see the policeman go to his car on the street below and talk on the radio.

When the officer returned, he had a smile and asked the children if they would like to come to the police station for some ice cream. That didn't make any sense at all. They hadn't had dinner yet. Something was wrong. Eryk wondered if his parents were in jail. The policeman only said they needed to come with him.

When they arrived at the police station, several people came to meet them, but it was upsetting not to see Mom and Dad. A lady took them into a room and closed the door. Her name was Dora, and she tried to explain what had happened. A head-on collision with a pickup truck. Their mom and dad were dead, along with the other driver. The girls could hardly understand. Eryk felt like he was falling into an abyss. This couldn't be true. He almost cried, but Janina was hugging him and crying. He needed to be strong.

The children spent the night in a strange place. The next day was Friday. They kept hoping their parents would show up. It seemed impossible that they weren't coming for them. Friday night should be pizza night. Nothing seemed real. Over the next few days, the horrible truth became undeniable. Life as Eryk knew it was over.

It was Eryk's job now to protect his sisters. That thought never left his mind. He guarded the girls carefully as they spent time in various places. Going to bed at night was the worst of all. Not having the security of their own beds and their mom and dad made it difficult to sleep. Eryk and Janina would talk with each other, and wonder about what was going to happen. Little Anatola was only four years old and could fall asleep quickly. Janina would eventually fall asleep, but Eryk hardly slept.

Kind people tried to help them. With no family in America and no friends who could take on three kids, it was up to the children's services to do what it could.

A lady named Mrs. Barclay showed up. It appeared to Eryk that the authorities knew her. After visiting with Eryk and his sisters, she was quite insistent that they should come with her.

Mrs. Barclay had a nice car and drove the children back to her house in another city. She had a room for them in her big house so they could all stay together. They were able to bring their clothes and toys, but it felt as though they were living in a bad dream. Other children lived in the big house.

Mrs. Barclay did what she could to make them feel comfortable. The other lady, Miss Lisa, was also helpful, but the knowledge that they were orphans only brought sadness. A few days later Eryk was sitting outside in the backyard with his sisters and met JJ, Anna, and their dog.

Lassie had jumped onto Anna's lap and tried to lick her face. Anna laughed cheerfully. "Here, do you want to hold our dog?"

Janina asked, "Is it your dog?"

"Well," said JJ. "She's going to be a family dog."

"What's her name?" asked Janina.

Anna smiled and said, "Her name is Lassie."

"That's a nice name," said Janina.

"Are we going to live with you?" asked Eryk.

"Yes," said Anna. "If you want."

"And Lassie too?" asked Anatola.

"Of course," said Anna with a smile.

"When?" said Janina.

"We'll have to work things out with Mrs. Barclay," said JJ. "But I'm sure it will be pretty soon."

Mrs. Barclay opened the back door and called out, "Who would like some cookies?"

The other kids who were playing outside ran toward the back door. JJ and Anna had been sitting on the grass with Eryk, Janina, and Anatola.

"I'd like some," said JJ, as he helped Anna up.

"Me too!" said Anna.

"Me too!" said Anatola.

Lassie barked and ran toward the back door. Kids and dogs went into the house and to the dining room table. JJ followed Mrs. Barclay to the living room.

"Well, what do you think?" asked Mrs. Barclay.

"I'm not going to argue with fate," said JJ.

"It's going to be very different from your experience," said Mrs. Barclay to JJ. "But I'm confident you can make it work. Their father, Oleg Dzbinksi, didn't make a lot of money. Lena stayed home to take care of the kids. From what I can tell they were good parents. They don't have any family here. I've got all their things – pictures, a few toys, clothing."

It was story night at Tutu House. JJ and Anna spent the evening with Mrs. Barclay, Miss Lisa, and the children. Mrs. Barclay had JJ tell the story of his life. It was a good way for Eryk, Janina, and Anatola to learn about their new guardians. The children spent one final night at Tutu House.

The next day JJ and Anna brought the kids home. Compared to the apartment they had lived in before, JJ and Anna's house seemed like a mansion. Even though there were plenty of bedrooms, the children spent their first few nights together.

Lassie was a huge help. She was genuinely happy to have the children there. JJ moved Lassie's bed so she could sleep near the children. No human could have been as therapeutic as Lassie was that night.

Anna stopped working at Mills and Robinson and stayed home with the children. There were still a few weeks of school left, but under the circumstances, they decided to wait until the following school year to put the kids back in school.

The next day the kids met Tom, Laura, Lois, Catherine, and their dog Maggie. Lois was home from college, and Catherine was thirteen, only two years older than Eryk.

The following day they met Kevin, Patty, and the twins. Timmy and Sue were twelve. JJ and Anna were pleased to find out that Patty was going to be Janina's teacher when school started after summer.

"Do you like school?" Patty asked.

"It's okay," answered Janina shyly. "Eryk helps me. He's good with numbers. I have to use my fingers."

Kevin held up both hands and said, "Me, too, but I can only count to seven." He said it seriously, but then he laughed, and everyone laughed with him. Eryk liked Kevin.

The following weekend Anna's parents came from Pittsburgh. For Eryk, Janina, and Anatola, this was a big family. The weekend after that, JJ and Anna had a barbecue and invited everyone, including Uncle Howard and Gloria.

Stability slowly returned to the children's lives. Mrs. Barclay had explained how important it was to create routines and consistency. Friday night was pizza night again, even though it wasn't the same. Every week there was a visit to or from Kevin and Tom. There were frequent trips to Tutu House. Even though they had stayed there only a short time, Mrs. Barclay represented something familiar from the recent past. Their new life was taking shape, but Eryk was annoyed when Anatola began to call Anna "mom."

"He's been in protective mode ever since the accident," explained Mrs. Barclay. "It's going to take some time for him to be able to accept you as his parents."

It bothered Eryk that the girls enjoyed shopping and doing things with Anna. JJ and Anna bought the kids anything they wanted. Anna read stories to the children almost every night. Eryk liked that well enough, but the girls sat close to Anna as they read together on the couch. Anna never hesitated to put her arms around them. To Eryk, it was a betrayal. It was still hard for Eryk to sleep at night. This wasn't his "real" house, this wasn't his "real" bed, and these weren't his "real" parents.

Nighttime was when Eryk thought about the unfairness of everything. Life had become a complicated paradox. On the one hand, being sad seemed like the right thing. On the other hand, he was glad to see his sisters being happy. Then there was Lassie. Lassie liked Eryk and Eryk liked Lassie. When Lassie sat on his lap, Eryk's wall became thin and frail.

Mrs. Barclay explained to JJ and Anna that barriers usually fall over time. "Sometimes you can find a crack," she had said, "to help break it down." JJ wished he could find a crack to work on. It wasn't the new bicycle, and it certainly wasn't new clothes. So far, Lassie was their only hope.

Janina was helpful. "He's good with numbers," she had said. "He likes number puzzles."

JJ and Anna bought several puzzle books, and Eryk seemed to enjoy them. The trouble was that he was still sad. They say "time heals all wounds," but it isn't so. Some wounds can only be soothed.

One afternoon, Janina and Anatola were coloring with crayons. On one page of the coloring book was a picture of a tree house. Anatola did the best she could, and then tore the picture out of the book and gave it to Eryk. "Here – it's for you," she said.

Anna noticed and was curious. "Is that for Eryk?" she asked.

Janina didn't look up from her work and nonchalantly said, "Yeah, he likes tree houses."

When JJ got home from work, Anna told him what she'd heard. That evening as they were eating dinner, JJ announced that he wanted to build a tree house. He said he had always wanted one and asked if there was anyone who was interested in helping. Janina promptly said that Eryk wanted one too. Eryk said he would help.

They chose the tree that was the furthest back, the one under which JJ and Anna had been married. JJ asked Eryk for suggestions on how they should start, where the platform should go, and so forth. During the last month of summer, it slowly took shape, as Eryk helped. JJ and Anna were happy to see Eryk being interested in something.

By the time school started, it had been nearly four months since the children had come to live with JJ and Anna. The girls were doing well, and Eryk was coping. Hardly a night went by when JJ and Anna didn't talk about how to help Eryk. They placed a picture of Lena and Oleg Dzbinski on the fireplace mantle, next to the picture of Nancy and Arthur. They felt bad for Eryk and hoped for a breakthrough. But fate, or God, or serendipity itself, decided to lend a helping hand.

A week after school started, on a Friday night, the great storm struck. It had been warm and humid all day. Dark clouds began forming in the afternoon. It started sprinkling on the way home from school and got windy. The wind became so strong, the kids pretended they were being blown away. By the time JJ got home, it had cooled down and was raining. Eryk and JJ went to pick up the pizza for dinner. It felt like they were driving through a hurricane. As they paid for the pizzas, the power went out. The wind made it hard to open the car door. The rain stung their faces. The pizza box almost flew out of

Eryk's arms. By the time they got home, it was raining hard. Darkness came early.

The wind blew harder than JJ could remember. With the power out, the near darkness made the howling wind all the more unnerving and scary. They got flashlights, and JJ was about to start up a generator, but Anna said, "Let's just do candles."

They ate pizza and ice cream by candlelight. Eryk was worried about the tree house and tried to shine a flashlight toward the back of the yard, but couldn't see anything through the rain. Every crack of thunder scared the girls. Sometimes the howling wind turned to a shriek. Small branches and other bits of debris occasionally hit the house, making scary sounds. Eryk pretended to be brave. Lassie was nervous and shivering.

"I don't know if I've ever seen a storm like this before," said Anna.

"I know," said JJ. "I sure hope Tutu House is ok."

At Tutu House Mrs. Barclay's only worry was Eryk. She had been caring for orphans for more than 33 years and had seen many storms and troubles. Not since 1951, when JJ had been placed with Tom and Laura, had she been so invested in a family situation. Now, a fragile set of children was living with JJ and Anna, and for one child, the outcome seemed uncertain. On one hand, she was confident that this was the right thing. And yet, she felt unsettled. She spent the evening apprehensive, sometimes looking aimlessly out a window, sometimes checking on the children in her care.

Anna read a scary story by candlelight. JJ decided this was an adventure and fixed up the living room for everyone to camp in and spend the night. The storm carried on until past midnight. Gradually the winds slowed but kept blowing all night long. Occasionally the rain came down hard. The girls giggled while they went to bed, camped on the living room floor. JJ was glad the children felt safe. The house was still illuminated by candlelight as the children drifted off to sleep.

The next morning, Saturday, was a shock. Eryk was the first one outside. The first thing he did was run to the tree house. It was destroyed. Pieces of wood were strewn about the backyard. Only part of the platform remained. Eryk stood by the tree and sobbed. It was the first time JJ or Anna had seen him cry. "What's the use?" he lamented.

"It's ok," said JJ. "We'll get it fixed."

While JJ and Eryk gathered up pieces of wood, Anna got on the phone. Her first call was to Kevin.

"Hi, Kevin. It's about Eryk. The tree house has been ruined by the storm. I'm afraid Eryk thinks it's a metaphor for his life. We could sure use your help."

"Say no more," said Kevin. "We'll be right over."

Anna called Tom and explained the situation. It didn't take long for Tom and Kevin to show up. Kevin brought a big truck. Naturally, it didn't take Kevin long to size up the situation and figure out what they needed. Before lunch was ready, they were back from the lumber store. Even Howard Mills showed up.

Kevin took charge of the project. JJ, Tom, Eryk, Sue, Catherine, and Timmy followed Kevin's instructions while Lassie and Maggie watched. Tom and Sue cut boards as Kevin called out the length needed. Catherine and Timmy handed the boards to JJ and Eryk, up on ladders. Kevin helped JJ and Eryk place them in the tree. There was no pausing to think. Kevin directed and kept everyone busy. Anna, Laura, and Patty cooked hamburgers on the barbecue for dinner. Gloria showed up. It was turning into a family event.

They worked until dark. JJ brought out lights. Kevin had convinced them to redo the platform floor, and now it was bigger than before. It was obvious this was going to be a great tree house. It was getting too dark to work. Kevin said, "I believe we can get this finished up by tomorrow night."

Laura served a late night snack of ice cream.

"That was fun!" said Janina.

It was a good day, thought Eryk. If only his parents could have been there. That night he dreamed he was building a tree house with his father.

The next day was Sunday. They started early in the morning and worked all day. Professional builders wouldn't have worked any faster, even with a blueprint. When Kevin saw something in his mind, he saw every detail. Eryk enjoyed working with Timmy and Sue. It was nice that they were nearly the same age as him. Eryk was surprised at how well Sue could work. She seemed more at home with a hammer and saw than Timmy. The three families ate breakfast, lunch, and dinner together.

By dinner time, the tree house was nearly done. It was bigger and fancier than before. It had walls, three windows, and a nice roof. The floor had an entryway in a corner with a ladder to the ground. Eryk was astonished at how fast things got done.

It was getting dark again. Eryk climbed into the tree house and sat there. He wished he could have done this with his own father. Anna called everyone to dinner, but Eryk sat in the tree house thinking about the day. He watched everyone go to the house and was glad to be living here. He just wished he could get rid of the ache in his heart. He wished the girls weren't calling Anna "mom."

It looked like it might rain again and tables were being set up inside the house for dinner. Laura was still outside barbecuing chicken and Tom went to help. Eryk sat in the tree house trying to make sense of everything. He heard someone coming up the ladder.

"Hi there," said Kevin. He climbed in and sat on the floor with Eryk. Kevin looked everything over and said, "Well, I think it feels pretty solid. No storm is going to take this down."

Eryk said "Yeah. Thanks for your help. This is a great tree house."

"You're welcome, Eryk. We're family. We help each other get through troubles. You're our family now."

"I guess so," said Eryk. He was getting a lump in his throat. "I just miss my mom and dad."

"We're all sorry about what happened," said Kevin.

They sat in silence for a moment.

"It just takes time," said Kevin. "You'll get to like it here."

"I do like it here," said Eryk. "But somehow it bothers me."

"Like how?" asked Kevin.

"I don't know," said Eryk. "It's like we can have anything we want here. We were poor compared to this, but we were happy."

"Yeah," said Kevin. "I know."

Eryk didn't say anything. A light breeze blew gently through the tree house windows. Off in the distance were clouds.

Eryk thought for a moment. Then he said, "My sisters like everything here, but it seems like they're forgetting our parents."

"They're just younger," said Kevin. "Loving JJ and Anna doesn't have to mean they don't love your parents."

They sat in silence again. Eryk shifted his weight.

"I don't know why all this had to happen," said Eryk. "You don't know what it's like. You're all rich."

"That's true," said Kevin. "I don't know what it's like. I hardly knew my own dad. He was mean and violent. He died in prison."

Eryk was shocked. "I didn't know that," he said.

"You're lucky," said Kevin. "You had good parents who loved you."

There was silence again. Then Eryk said it bothered him how Anatola called Anna "mom."

Kevin thought for a minute and said, "They can't be your mother and father, but they can be your mom and dad."

Eryk didn't say anything. A tear fell from his cheek. He didn't want another mom and dad.

"Your parents were good people, weren't they?" asked Kevin.

Eryk nodded his head slightly.

"These are good people," said Kevin. "If it weren't for them, I wouldn't have met my wife, and Timmy and Sue wouldn't be here. My own life was broken, and they fixed it. Tom is like a dad to me, and he is going to be like a grandpa to you. I know it's unfair what happened to you, but give these people a chance. Let them build a new life for you."

Eryk wiped another tear from his eye. There was more silence.

"If your father and mother could send you a message right now, what do you think they would tell you to do?" asked Kevin.

"I don't know," said Eryk. But he did know.

Kevin put his left arm around Eryk, so his left hand was plainly visible, and said, "They would probably tell you to be careful and not chop off any fingers."

Eryk couldn't help but let out a quiet laugh as he wiped his eyes again. Then he put his arm around Kevin.

"I'm going to be your new uncle, you know," said Kevin. "Well, sort of."

Inside the house, Anna asked where Eryk was. JJ said he was in the tree house with Kevin and started toward the back door. "I'll go get them," he said.

"No," said Anna. "Leave them be."

After a while Kevin and Eryk came back to the house, walking together. "Eryk wants to eat his dinner in the tree house," said Kevin.

"Can we come too?" asked Sue.

"Sure, I guess," said Eryk.

Timmy, Sue, Janina, and Catherine accompanied Eryk back to the tree house, each carrying paper plates and trying not to spill their food. JJ and Kevin brought them drinks. The children ate their dinner on the floor of the tree house, using light from the work lamps.

That night, Eryk had another dream about his parents. They were having a barbecue. JJ and Anna were there, too. Everyone got along.

Over the next few days, there were other repairs to make. The storm had broken a large branch at Kevin and Patty's house. A section of fence at Tom and Laura's had blown over in the wind. Everyone worked together on these projects after school. It was easy to see that they had all made his tree house more important than the other projects. Eryk was glad to be able to help.

A week later was "back to school" night. It was JJ and Anna's first time. It was extra fun because Patty was Janina's teacher. While they were standing around afterward, one of Eryk's new friends came over and said, "Hi Eryk. Is this your mom and dad?"

"Yes," he said.

* * * * *

Christmas and Thanksgiving might have been melancholy if it weren't for all the activity. As the holiday season approached, JJ and Anna explained about shopping for the kids who lived at Tutu House. Eryk, Janina, and Annatola had fun helping JJ and Anna pick out presents and clothes. They were all going to be "Santa's helpers." Tom and Laura had started the tradition twenty years earlier. Eryk and the girls were enthused about being part of this tradition. Buying Christmas presents for orphans gave the kids a whole new perspective. They say a good way to cope with your troubles is to help someone else. There would still be tears on Christmas, but the children were adapting to their new life.

Mrs. Barclay was immensely pleased with the outcome. But as spring gave way to summer, she was tired. Her last great accomplishment was fulfilling Miss Nancy's dying wish to get a family for JJ and Anna.

Living at Tutu House was not the same without Miss Nancy. When Shannen moved to Cleveland to work in the family business with her brother Jon, Mrs. Barclay decided it was time to move on.

An experienced couple, Mr. and Mrs. Halsey, were hired to replace Mrs. Barclay. They were both fifty-one and had grown children. They took over Mrs. Barclay's room.

Jon came from Cleveland to drive his mom to her new home. It was another sad day for JJ, Anna, Tom, Laura, Miss Lisa, and all the children who lived at Tutu House. Everyone stood in front of Tutu House and waved as Mrs. Barclay drove off with Jon.

*****

During the following year, Eryk, Janina, and Anatola were legally adopted. The only trouble Eryk was having was the idea of changing his last name. The girls clearly wanted to be a Robinson. Eryk had been a Dzbinski all his life, but he didn't want to be different from his sisters. As much as he accepted his new family situation, not being a Dzbinski seemed hard to bear. It might have been an easier decision if JJ and Anna had pressured him to be a Robinson, but they were leaving it up to him.

Tom, Laura, Lois, Catherine, Kevin, Patty, Timmy, Sue, and Mr. and Mrs. Kurzmann all came to the courthouse for the adoption procedure. When they got there, JJ was shocked to recognize Judge Hansen. He was twenty years older, but so was JJ.

"I thought you looked familiar," said JJ. "I'll bet you don't remember me."

"As a matter of fact," said Judge Hansen, "I do. When I saw your name on the docket, I thought I remembered you. I checked my files and there you were."

"Judging by this crowd," said Judge Hansen, "I'd say things worked out for you."

"Yes, they did, your Honor," said JJ.

Judge Hansen looked over the small crowd and said, "I can't begin to tell you all how happy it makes me to see how you are all doing."

Judge Hansen initially invited just the three kids into his office to ask some questions. As he talked with Eryk, he could see Eryk's dilemma.

"You know," said the judge, "We can do pretty much anything with your name at this time. Can I give you an idea to think about?"

"Sure," said Eryk.

"How about changing your middle name to Dzbinski and your last name to Robinson? You don't have to make up your mind right now. It's just an idea."

"I like it," said Eryk. And so on July 12, 1972, Eryk became Eryk Dzbinski Robinson. His friends called him "Eryk D." He loved it.

* * * * *

Mrs. Barclay began her new life as a doting grandmother. But as JJ and Anna's family grew stronger, Mrs. Barclay weakened. For the first time in decades, she was away from the home she loved. It was bad enough when Nancy Kappel died. Now she lived in Cleveland, retired, with her children and her family. Life was comfortable, and yet, empty.

As a young girl, Margaret Parker had happily worked in the family store in Cleveland. Parker's Department store had been founded before the turn of the century and had become the largest store in the city.

Margaret was the favorite child of Great Aunt Edna, the family matriarch. At a young age, Margaret was energetic and learned quickly. She was cute and witty. At family gatherings, Great Aunt Edna loved to have Margaret sit on her lap and recite poetry.

Margaret grew up smart, pretty, and opinionated. Aunt Edna boasted that Margaret would someday be the head of the family, and would eventually run the store. But Margaret had her own ideas about things, and wanted to make her own life.

After she graduated from a two-year college, she became an elementary school teacher. This was a disappointment to many in the family. Aunt Edna believed that once Margaret's youthful ambition was satisfied, she would return to the family business.

Then came Fred.

Fred Barclay worked in the toy department on the 4th floor. Chance meetings became friendship, and friendship became romance.

Aunt Edna did not like Fred. She considered him to be too "common" for the Parker family. And, he was a Quaker. Aunt Edna had her eye on the son of a prominent attorney.

Margaret, however, was not interested.

Fred was not as educated as Margaret, and he was not in the same class as the Parker family. But he was clever, worked hard, and had a sense of humor. He could repair almost any broken toy. He worshipped Margaret and treated her with respect. By Margaret's calculations, he would be a good father to her children.

Aunt Edna, along with Margaret's parents, repeatedly attempted to introduce Margaret to other eligible bachelors. Then she had Fred fired. The Great Depression was underway, and losing one's job was a catastrophe. Aunt Edna figured that would make Margaret reconsider, but she was mistaken.

Fred had a brother working in Pittsburgh. So, despite the ongoing depression, he and Margaret eloped and moved to Pittsburgh. The promise of a job didn't work, but Fred was able to do odd jobs, and Margaret volunteered at their church.

As the Great Depression worsened, the Quakers were able to secure a lease on a building in a nearby town for just the price of property tax payments, where they established an orphanage. Fred and Margaret readily accepted the offer to work there. When World War II broke out, Fred declined to be a conscientious objector and was drafted, never to return home. Margaret's life and dreams were shattered. Nancy Kappel became the most important person in her life, besides her children. The Parker family would forever live with the guilt of rejecting Fred, and by association, Margaret.

Margaret's parents divorced over the matter. Her mom never forgave her father for siding with Aunt Edna, and moved to Chicago. Her father worked hard, but became an alcoholic, and died early. Edna became reclusive, and gave control of the company to her nephew Harold. On her deathbed, she begged unseen spirits for forgiveness for letting vanity tear the family apart.

When Margaret's boy Jon turned 19, he was welcomed with open arms by the Parker family and began what was to become a successful career working at the family business. Margaret's mother tried to make amends, and moved back to Cleveland to be with Jon. Eventually, Shannen moved to Cleveland to be with her brother, and to work in the family business. By the time Margaret's mom died, old wounds were mostly healed.

Jon and Shannen were glad to have their mom with them in Cleveland. Margaret was back where she started, but it wasn't home anymore. She was no longer the captain of her ship. She was sailing amongst friends and family as a passenger, in unfamiliar waters.

As the months passed, Margaret's clouds of depression worsened. Nothing she could ever do would compare with the satisfaction of working at the orphanage, and helping JJ and Anna get their children. Every day she woke up disappointed, reminded that she was not living in Tutu House. Without Nancy or Fred, she felt that she had no home. At least she was with her children and grandchildren.

Jon and Shannen were discouraged that their mother was not thriving. Margaret was a good grandma and loved to babysit the grandkids. She loved her family. But when she went to bed at night, her thoughts drifted back to an earlier time. Every night she would read from the copy of Miss Nancy's diary that JJ had made for her. Her favorite part was the day she and Fred met Nancy Kapple.

A few days after her fourth Thanksgiving in Cleveland, Margaret's storm finally subsided. Shannen found her lifeless mother in bed, with Miss Nancy's diary opened to the time when they had been notified of Fred's death.

JJ, Anna, and their children came to the funeral, along with Tom and Laura, and Kevin and his family. It was truly the end of an era.

2

Growth

The corner of JJ and Anna's backyard where Aunt Beverly, Princess, and Laddie were buried became a memorial garden. It was Janina's idea. She was now eleven.

They made plaster "pancakes" upon which they could write names. These were placed in the memorial garden as small monuments for Miss Nancy, Arthur, Aunt Beverly, Baby Karen, Laddie, Princess, Little Maggie, Lena, and Oleg, and Mrs. Barclay.

Anna returned to Mills and Robinson, working part-time while the kids were in school.

The tree house was a frequent gathering place for friends and family. When Eryk's pals came over after school, they ate snacks up in the tree. Eryk liked it best when Kevin and Patty came to visit. Eryk and Janina got along well with Timmy and Sue.

Anatola was now in the third grade. Janina was in sixth grade, and Eryk was a sophomore in high school.

One Wednesday afternoon, Anna brought a box of papers and documents with her from the office. JJ wasn't home yet, so she asked Eryk to carry the box into the house.

"What's all this?" he asked, as he set the box down on the kitchen table.

"The books are out of balance," said Anna.

"What does that mean?" asked Eryk.

"Well," said Anna, "The totals for all the invoices and payments don't match what's been recorded in these ledgers. Someone made a mistake somewhere and I have to find it."

"Hmm," said Eryk, peering into the box and lifting out a journal. He set the journal down on the kitchen table and opened it.

"The rows total on the right, and the columns total at the bottom," explained Anna, as Eryk examined the last page of the ledger. "The totals of the rows have to match the totals of the columns on each page. Anyway, they don't match, and I have to find where the bad entry is."

"I see how this works," said Eryk. "Can I take a look?"

"Be my guest," said Anna. She handed Eryk a stack of papers wrapped with a rubber band. "Here are the invoice copies that the ledger entries came from."

"Oh great," joked Janina. "Another numbers game for Eryk!"

Eryk went to the most recent page and began scanning each column and row. He turned the pages back and forth, comparing the entries.

When JJ got home, he kissed Anna, hugged the kids, and asked what was for dinner.

"We're going out to a restaurant tonight," said Anna with a smile.

"Okay," said JJ. "What's the occasion?"

"It's Eryk," said Janina.

"He already found the problem," said Anna, with a smile. "The books are balanced. I don't have to work tonight."

"Wow!" said JJ. "Good job!"

"You should get a computer to keep track of this," said Eryk.

"Well," laughed JJ. "Maybe someday when we're bigger and can afford a million dollars."

Eryk was soon helping on a weekly basis. He loved how they kept track of their work, inventory, and other business matters. He began coming to the office after school. Others at the office joked that Eryk could spot a wrong number from across the room. Before he finished high school, he had a real job earning money as the company bookkeeper.

He also had a crush on Sue. He had admired her for a long time, ever since she helped rebuild the tree house. She was tough, but nice. She even worked with her dad sometimes on weekends. She knew a lot about air conditioning. Eryk asked her to the prom. She said yes.

* * * * *

Anna had been giving piano lessons to Anatola, who had a natural affinity for music. Anatola was soon taking weekly piano lessons from a professional teacher and practicing daily with Anna.

Lois graduated from college with a degree in architecture. She married and moved to New York, working for a firm that designed bridges.

Gloria's daughters went to medical school in Pittsburgh. Howard Mills sold all his theaters, except the local one in town, to pay for their education.

In 1976, Catherine graduated from high school. As it turned out, so did Kevin, who had been helping Patty twice a week in the afternoons. The kids in Patty's class liked Kevin and the way he explained things. There were always a few kids struggling with reading or arithmetic, and Kevin had a way to make learning fun. Sometimes he would hold up his left hand and say "Remember..." and the kids would respond, "You can't count on your fingers!"

At Catherine's graduation ceremony, the entire "family" was there. As the last diploma was handed out, former principal Dennis, who had become the state superintendent of education, came to the podium.

"I have one more special award," he announced with a big smile. "I would like to honor a former student who has made a great contribution to our community and to the school."

He paused for a moment, then said, "Would Kevin Connor please come up here?"

Kevin and the kids were all shocked. Patty and Tom smiled. Kevin stood up, looked around, and then walked up onto the stage and to the podium. He stood next to Dennis, wondering what was up.

Superintendent Dennis spoke into the microphone. "I am pleased to present this honorary diploma to Kevin ..."

Kids started cheering and clapping. Kevin's family stood up, followed by his friends. So many kids who knew Kevin stood up to clap and cheer that everyone else stood as well. Kevin's grandma was as proud as she could be. Superintendent Dennis shook Kevin's hand and handed him the diploma. Kevin had never been more surprised.

It was a festive evening with dinner at their favorite restaurant. As they were eating, Uncle Howard stood up. "I'd like to say a few words. First of all, I'd like to congratulate Kevin. We're all proud of him and how he's helped our company. We wouldn't be where we are without his help."

"Secondly, it's time for me to start taking it easy and let Tom, Kevin, and JJ run the company. I'll still be hanging around to keep an eye on things, but I'm turning control over to them. We're on the right track. I like that Sue is involved, and that Eryk here is minding the books."

"Thirdly, I think Gloria should be retiring while she can still enjoy her family. As you all know, I've been selling many properties that I've had for a long time. I've got a check here for a million dollars. It's for you, Gloria."

Uncle Howard gave the check to Gloria, who almost fainted. Her daughters and their husbands gathered around to see.

Howard continued. "If it weren't for Gloria, our company wouldn't exist."

* * * * *

The following year, Kevin's grandma passed away.

Timmy and Sue attended the Indiana University of Pennsylvania. Timmy majored in education while Sue majored in business. The following year, Eryk graduated from high school and joined them, majoring in business and accounting. Sue changed to a trade school and majored in construction and HVAC (heating, ventilating and air conditioning).

Eryk and Sue were happy to be spending time with each other. They enjoyed working together on weekends, when Eryk would balance the books for Mills and Robinson. Their romance was both surprising and pleasing to JJ, Anna, Kevin, and Patty.

Timmy and Janina's friendship seemed as normal as Eryk and Sue's. It was pleasant to see it also develop into romance.

* * * * *

Life was busy and getting busier. Eryk suggested to Tom and Howard (who still came to the office on occasion) the idea of franchising. Eryk was a sophomore in college but his idea made sense. Tom and JJ spent time selling the concept to small service companies in the smaller towns and even in Pittsburgh. By joining the Mills and Robinson company, smaller outfits could take advantage of the brand name and reduce their bookkeeping overhead. Kevin had been put in charge of training to make sure new franchisees and new employees understood the company standards. The plan worked well, and the company continued to grow.

Janina graduated from high school and majored in computer science at the Indiana University of Pennsylvania. She and Timmy started getting serious about marriage.

On top of everything else, Anna needed shoulder surgery. Years of using crutches had taken their toll. It was easy to take time off from work because there was now a small army of office employees. The surgery was scheduled during July, so the kids were out of school. Anna's parents came to help.

When Anna arrived home after spending two days in the hospital, Janina and Anatola were ready. JJ had planned to hire a full-time housekeeper, but the girls wouldn't hear of it. Janina and Anatola loved caring for Anna. They pampered her day and night.

"My goodness," said Anna with a laugh. "You treat me like I'm helpless!"

"But, Mom," said Anatola, "You are!"

* * * * *

1982 was a year to remember. First, there was the double wedding in May. It was a big wedding. Eryk was getting married to Kevin's daughter Sue, and Janina was getting married to Kevin's son Timmy.

There was only one place for a big wedding like that – the backyard of JJ and Anna's house where JJ and Anna had been married. Two brides and two grooms stood together with two sets of bridesmaids and groomsmen. They all stood under that same tree. Who could have imagined 30 years ago when Kevin and JJ became friends that they would eventually become in-laws to each other?

It would have been impossible not to be emotional. Off to the left was the memorial garden. JJ thought about how Laddie had been with him when he and Anna had been married. Eryk looked up at the tree house. It remained strong and sturdy. Children still played there.

As the ceremony was about to begin, Janina, in her wedding dress, walked over to the memorial garden and opened the gate. Then she returned to her place. No one said anything. It was as though she was inviting those who had gone before to join them in spirit. Anna held Lassie on her lap.

Next was the trip to France.

It was an adventure Tom had dreamed of all his life, to find the place where his cousin Jack had been buried.

As they sat on the jet plane and looked down at the endless ocean, it hardly seemed they were moving. There was plenty of time to reflect on the past. In Tom's coat pocket was an envelope containing a spoonful of dirt and ash from the memorial garden. That ground had once belonged to Aunt Beverly, Jack's mom. Their destination was the Epinal American Cemetery and Memorial in Dinozé, France.

When their plane landed in Paris, it was late afternoon. They rented a car and drove to a nice hotel where they had a reservation. They spent the next day touring the city and relaxing. Tom was nervous about the trip to Dinozé. The hotel management had provided a map and had outlined the route. Everyone at the hotel was helpful and respectful.

Tom and Laura left early the next morning. The cemetery was a little more than a four-hour drive east of Paris. After three hours, Tom stopped for gas and directions in a small town. A road closure had made following the map difficult. No one at the "petrol station" spoke English, but when Tom showed his destination on the map, an older man was eager to help. He made it clear Tom should wait for him as he went into the station. He returned with a young man. The young man said, "You follow me."

The older man smiled and shook Tom's hand.

"Merci," said Tom.

"No," said the old man as he pointed to Tom's destination on the map. "Thank you."

Tom got back into his rental car and waited.

The younger man walked over to a small motorcycle and kick-started it. He looked back to make sure Tom was ready and motioned with his hand. Then he began driving. Tom followed for a few miles until they came to the main highway. Tom waved a "thank you" to the young man who waved back and left.

"That was very nice of them," said Laura.

An hour more of driving brought them to Dinozé.

At the cemetery, they met an old Frenchman, Monsieur Lachance, who happened to be visiting that day. He visited frequently, and volunteered to help find Jack Garver's grave.

The cemetery was divided into two large sections. Monsieur Lachance walked with them to the eastern side and headed toward the north end.

"We are cousins, you know," said Monsieur Lachance, with a French accent, as they walked among the graves. There were thousands of crosses, marking neatly manicured gravesites.

"When you were young, we helped you with your independence. And then, when you grew up, you rescued us in our time of need." He looked at Tom and smiled.

He talked while they walked. "During the war, my family lived on a farm in the town of Aurillac. The German soldiers had taken most of our food. One by one they killed our animals for food. Times were very desperate. The way some soldiers looked at our family made us worry about the girls. Then one morning they were gone. That afternoon, the Americans came. I will remember that day as long as I live."

Monsieur Lachance looked about, turned here and there, and soon came to Jack's grave. "I will leave you now," said Monsieur Lachance. "I will always be grateful for your sacrifice."

A mild breeze blew as Laura stood and Tom bent down. He carefully opened the envelope from his pocket. "I know you're not here, Jack," said Tom. "But I've brought some earth from your home, and some of your mom's ashes. We've all done good. I guess you know we took good care of your mom. I guess you're all together now. I don't know what else to say. I just wanted to see this place. It's real nice here."

Tom sprinkled the contents of the envelope on Jack's grave. Then he stood up and took Laura's hand. They paused for a while before walking silently back to the visitor's center. They didn't see Monsieur Lachance again, but they would not forget him.

* * * * *

The following year was another busy one. Eryk had been urging Tom, JJ, and Kevin to move the company to Pittsburgh. Most of their business was now done in the big city. Mills and Robinson was growing up and needed a larger and more prominent office. They bought a building in a business park. It hadn't been difficult to find a new home for the company. So many steel mills and other factories had closed since 1950 that there were plenty of buildings available. Nearly half the population had left for other parts of the country. It was said that you could find a Steelers football fan just about anywhere in America.

JJ and Anna, Kevin and Patty, Eryk and Sue all began looking for new places to live in Pittsburgh. JJ and Anna remained in Indiana for one year until Anatola graduated from high school. Timmy and Janina stayed in Indiana and lived in JJ and Anna's house. Tom and Laura also remained in Indiana.

"It's time for me to let you guys take over anyway," said Tom.

Anna's parents, who already lived in Pittsburgh, were nearly 70 and happy at the prospect of having Anna and JJ close by.

Despite his young age, Eryk became the chief financial officer at Mills and Robinson. Sue Connor was now Sue Robinson and worked daily in the field: teaching, installing, and supervising. Her father, Kevin, worked mostly at headquarters with JJ. Eryk and Sue made a great team. Sue knew everything about the service business, and Eryk knew more about money and business operations than anyone. JJ and Kevin were free to meet with clients, manage, and play golf.

During the spring of 1984, the move was made. Mills and Robinson had new headquarters, and finally enough room for everyone.

Howard established the Mills Foundation to assist orphanages and help foster kids get established after they turned eighteen.

* * * * *

The company continued to grow in spite of Pennsylvania's slow economy.

Catherine graduated from veterinary school and began practicing in her hometown. Eventually, she took over after Dr. Rogers retired.

In 1985 Eryk and Sue had a girl named Megan. Timmy and Janina had a boy named Don.

JJ and Anna were thrilled to be grandparents. "I don't feel old enough to be a grandpa," said JJ.

"You're older than you think," laughed Kevin.

In 1987, Eryk and Sue had another girl named Gwyndalyn. It was fun that JJ and Kevin shared the same grandchildren.

That same year Anna's father, Mr. Kurzmann, died. Mrs. Kurzmann moved in with JJ and Anna. Then Lassie passed away. Eryk took it pretty hard, even though he had been living away from home for some time. He had always enjoyed seeing Lassie when he visited his mom and dad. Lassie had been there when he started his new life. Lassie had given him comfort during his worst time.

"The little animals that we love teach us to appreciate what we have," said JJ, remembering what Laura had told him when Laddie died.

Eryk was glad for his wife Sue, and his two little girls.

* * * * *

In 1988, at the age of twenty-two, Anatola got married to a man she met in college in Pittsburgh. Within a few months, it was apparent that there was a problem. She stopped her frequent visits. She didn't seem herself.

"Something's wrong," said Anna to JJ. They had invited Anatola and her new husband for dinner but ended up eating alone. Anatola had made an excuse for why they couldn't come.

"She's probably just busy," said JJ. "Remember how we were when we were first married?"

"Something's not right," said Anna. "I just feel it."

The way Anna said it made JJ uncomfortable.

After they finished their dinner, Anna called Anatola on the phone. There was no answer. "They've got caller ID now," said Anna. "She knows it's me."

"Maybe they're not home," said JJ hopefully.

Anna dialed the number again. She let the phone ring a number of times. Finally, she heard Anatola's voice on the other end.

"Honey, are you okay?" asked Anna

"I'm fine," said Anatola. It sounded like she had been crying.

"We're coming over," said Anna. "We'll be there in twenty minutes."

"No, really, it's ok," said Anatola.

"I'm on my way," said Anna. "I love you."

Anna hung up the phone. JJ was already getting ready. They drove to the apartment building where Anatola lived. They rode the elevator to the 5th floor. They knocked on her door. Anatola opened and let them in.

JJ and Anna were shocked to see bruises on the left side of Anatola's face and arm. Anatola cried and hugged her mom.

JJ asked, "Where is he?"

"He went out after you called," said Anatola.

"You're coming home with us," said Anna. "JJ, help her get packed."

Anatola wiped her tears as she helped her dad pack her clothes and things into plastic garbage bags and a cardboard box. JJ took a couple bags of clothes to the car while Anatola continued packing.

"Some of this stuff I don't want anymore," said Anatola.

"It's ok," said JJ. "Don't worry about anything."

They took Anatola back to their house. The company attorney recommended a divorce lawyer. Eryk was so mad he would have killed Anatola's husband if he had run into him.

Anatola's soon-to-be ex-husband refused to sign the divorce papers. Kevin and Patty were visiting JJ and Anna. "We'll get an annulment," said JJ.

"I know how to handle this," said Kevin as he took the papers. "I don't know what's wrong with some people."

The next day after work, Kevin was gone most of the evening. He got home late, but the papers were signed. Anatola's ex-husband left town the next day and was never seen or heard from again. No one discussed the matter after that. Anatola never re-married. She returned to Indiana and worked part-time in the town library and part-time at the Jimmy Stewart Museum.

In 1989, Mrs. Kurzmann died.

* * * * *

Howard Mills had been struggling with heart trouble and had been in and out of the hospital. Gloria's youngest daughter, Julie, now a doctor, was always there to make sure Howard was doing as well as possible.

One evening, Julie called to let them know the situation was serious. JJ and Anna came to see him at the hospital, along with Tom and Laura. Howard Mills knew he was dying. "I hope you guys won't forget me," he joked with a smile.

"Of course not," said JJ, now 49 years old.

"I want to tell you a story," said Howard.

Tom, Laura, and JJ sat in chairs next to the hospital bed. Anna was in her wheelchair. Julie stood behind them.

"Back in 1918," began Howard, "When I was thirteen years old, I had a friend that I met while riding my bicycle. That's the year you and Laura were born," he said as he looked at Tom and Laura. "The same year Miss Nancy began writing in her diary.

"Well anyway, we lived in a nice little middle-class house on the Northeast side of Pittsburgh. My dad worked at one of the steel mills and made decent money. That summer I made friends with a kid named Greg. Greg Larson.

"He lived in an orphanage about twelve blocks from my house. I used to ride my bike all around during the summer. That's how I met him. He and his younger brother Charles were heading to play in an abandoned junkyard further out to the east. They invited me to come along with them. I'd never been to that place before, and it sounded fun. We had a good time and became friends. Every day I'd ride my bike to the orphanage and knock on the door for Greg and his brother. Then we'd head out to the junkyard."

Howard paused again, thinking about the past.

"On the way, we would stop at Pop's Dependable Market. It was the old kind of store with vegetables and apples out front. They had a butcher shop right in the store with sawdust on the floor. I can still smell the aroma of that place. Anyway, it was summer, and we helped clean out the back and hose down the garbage area. We got each other all wet which was good because of the summer heat. The job didn't take us long. They gave each of us a Coke and apple, which we carried to the junkyard. Those were great times.

"The orphanage where they lived seemed funny to us at the time. We called it a haunted house because it was very old and creaked in so many places. The house wasn't level, and if you dropped a marble on the floor, it would always roll toward a wall."

Howard gave a quiet laugh as he thought about the old memory.

"It was the best summer of my life. Greg and Charles didn't have much. I'd bring my BB gun, and we'd shoot bottles or old car windows, or whatever. They loved shooting. We had a lot of fun. We even made slingshots out of old inner tubes. I had a pocket knife we used to cut inner tubes and sharpen sticks. Greg once said he wished he had a knife like that. I wish I'd just given it to him. We climbed trees and dug holes. We built imaginary fortresses. One time we made a giant slingshot by stretching an inner tube between two cars. It's a wonder none of us got killed.

"Right as school was starting my family moved because my dad got a different job. It was several miles away. In October, I rode my bike to the old neighborhood and to the orphanage to see Greg and Charles. It was a Saturday. When I got there, the place was empty. A sign on the front door explained that the building was condemned. I stood there for a long time, trying to comprehend the meaning of it. I looked all around the house, but there was no one there. I rode my bike home, devastated. My mom asked why I was home early and I just said that they moved. I pretended I didn't care, but that night I was angry and sad. I even cried. I promised God if only I could find Greg and Charles again I would help orphans.

"Later I told my mom what happened and asked her to help me try to find out where they moved. There were hardly any phones in those days. She wrote a letter to some agency, but we never heard anything. It was my first tragic experience in life. I never did find Greg or his brother. Then there was the awful influenza outbreak. It was just one bad thing after another. I was sick for a while but not bad. I recovered and made new friends. I grew up, graduated from high school, got a job at the steel mill, and got married.

"Like most everyone else, we started playing the stock market. But my dad was skeptical and nervous about all that. By 1927 he had sold his stocks and wanted me to do the same. My wife Helen wanted to keep buying. In the fall of 1928, I followed my father's advice and sold my stocks. We made a lot of money. For a while, I wasn't sure I'd made the right decision because the stock market kept going up. Then there was the crash.

"Overnight I became rich, only because so many others became poor. In those times you could buy anything cheap because of so many people selling everything they could. That's when I bought the movie theaters. Helen wanted them. Thank goodness I did. Then Helen got sick with polio. That's when Gloria was our housekeeper. She turned out to be more than a housekeeper. As Helen got weaker, Gloria took over the paperwork and bookkeeping.

"Boy, those were some times. Lots of people went to the movies during the Depression. I had plenty of money. I got along well with Gloria's family. Gloria took over all the bookkeeping stuff for my little company. She really had a knack for organizing things. I bought lots of property and Gloria managed that, too. Everything was so cheap. The Depression was bad for so many people, but it was good for me.

"Gloria's husband Louis always called her his 'Sunshine.' He'd sing that song about her being his sunshine. Their daughters were his 'Sunbeams.' Anyway, my instincts about Gloria and her family were right. Then there was the war. I promised Louis I would take care of his Sunshine for him."

Howard paused for a moment and looked at Julie, then continued.

"Well, as you know, I met JJ here in 1952. I immediately liked him. You remember that day you guys fixed my car?" asked Howard as he looked at JJ.

"Of course," said JJ.

"Anyway, Laura had mentioned that JJ had lived in the orphanage. It was like an electric shock went through my body. All those memories from 1918 came back to me. Getting you guys to do the air conditioning was more than just solving a problem for me. Then there was that 4th of July when we were at Tutu House for fireworks. When I heard that they would have to close down, my old promise was staring me right in the face. As every day passed, I knew I had to do something. I talked it over with Gloria and then Tom here, and you know the rest."

Everyone sat in silence for a moment. Then Howard said, "We did some good things together, didn't we, Tom."

"Yes we did," said Tom. Howard gave JJ's hand a squeeze.

Later that night, in a quiet, dimly lit hospital room, Howard Mills' heart gave out. A doctor named Julie Walker Michaels held his hand. Another era had ended, and another monument was added to JJ and Anna's memorial garden.

* * * * *

The world was changing faster than ever. The World Wide Web became popular, along with cell phones. Then came Amazon, Google, and the "dot com" boom. Eryk helped the company adapt. Janina designed a fancy web page. The company expanded into all areas of service and repair. Over the next 20 years, Mills and Robinson became one of the largest service and repair companies in the Nation. Eryk remained the chief financial officer while Sue Connor Robinson became the President and CEO of Mills and Robinson. JJ and Anna eventually returned to their home in the town of Indiana.

3

The Final Chapter

An old man stood in the Lowe's hardware store, looking at a stack of window air conditioners on sale. It was an early Saturday afternoon in the spring of 2020. As he examined the various models, a young man walked over to him.

"Good afternoon, sir. Can I help you with anything?"

"No," said the old man, with a smile. "I'm just admiring how efficient these are."

"Yes they are," said the young store clerk. "Are you interested in a particular model?"

"No," said the old man. "I'm fine. I was just thinking about the old units we used to install."

"Are you in the business?" asked the young man.

"Used to be," said the old man. "Retired now." Then he reached out to shake hands with the store clerk.

"JJ Robinson," said the old man, "Of the Mills and Robinson company."

"Oh wow," said the young man. "It's an honor to meet you, sir. I'm Peter Barclay. I know about you."

"Barclay?" asked JJ. "Any relation to a Mrs. Barclay who used to run the orphanage?"

"She was my great-grandmother," said Peter.

"Well what do you know about that," said JJ. "I was one of her orphans!"

"I know," said Peter. "I read about you."

At that moment, an old lady came around the corner in a fancy electric wheelchair.

"Anna! Anna!" cried JJ. "Come here!"

"My goodness, JJ. What in the world is it?" Anna asked as she came to a stop next to the two men. She had a tray of flowers in her lap.

"Anna! This is Peter Barclay! He's the great-grandson of dear Mrs. Barclay!"

"Oh my goodness," said Anna. "What a wonderful surprise!" She shook his hand. "Here, give me a hug."

Anna started asking questions: "Are you married? Do you have kids? Who's your mom and dad? Is your family still in Cleveland? How long have you been living here? My goodness, you need to come and have dinner with us."

"I've always wanted to meet you," said Peter. "My great grandma had a copy of a diary that her friend kept. It was given to my grandfather, and he let me read it. My wife and I have been fascinated by the story of my grandfather growing up."

"I made that copy for your great grandma," said JJ with a laugh. "Almost 50 years ago. Your grandfather must be Jon Barclay."

"That's right," said Peter. "He died last year."

"I'm sorry to hear it," said JJ. "We kind of lost track of each other."

"What time do you get off work?" asked Anna.

"Today's my early day," said Peter. "I'll be off in an hour."

"Go and get your wife and come over for dinner," said JJ. Then he looked at Anna. "What are we doing for dinner?"

"Um..."

"How about pizza!" said JJ. "You like pizza don't you? Anna – get me something to write with."

JJ gave Peter his address and phone number. Then Peter took them to an empty register and checked them out.

A little after 5 pm, the doorbell rang. JJ and Anna's dog Buddy barked at the front door. JJ opened the door and welcomed Peter Barclay with his wife and five-year-old son.

"This is my wife, Elaine," said Peter, "And my son Freddie."

"We're sure pleased to meet you," said JJ as he gave Elaine a hug.

"We're happy to have you here," said Anna, as she came over in her wheelchair.

"It's a pleasure to meet you," said Elaine. "You have no idea! We're excited to talk to you about Peter's great-grandmother."

Little Freddie walked over to Anna as Buddy sat down beside her. He looked at Anna's wheelchair and asked, "What's that?"

"Freddie!" said Elaine.

"It's ok," said Anna cheerfully. "I had polio when I was four years old, and my legs never got all the way better."

"What's polio?" asked Freddy.

Anna didn't say anything for a few seconds. That thought made her smile. Then she said, "It's something that no one has to worry about anymore."

As they ate dinner, Peter told how the Parker family had sold their store a long time ago. The building was eventually demolished. An Amazon distribution center stood there now. He talked about how he had loved the stories his grandfather told about living in Tutu house as a child, and how he had read the copy of Miss Nancy's diary.

JJ talked about his life growing up with Peter's grandfather. He talked about Miss Nancy and Mrs. Barclay. He explained how their current home was the place he ran away to, except it was an old house and barn back then. JJ and Anna took Peter and his wife out back to the memorial garden. Peter and Elaine looked at the small monuments to Mrs. Barclay, Miss Nancy, Arthur, and the others. Anna had already planted the flowers they bought at the store.

"That's really nice," said Peter.

As they walked back to the house, JJ asked, "Have you been to Tutu House yet?"

"We drove by a few weeks ago," said Elaine.

"Would you like a tour?" asked JJ.

"Oh brother, would I," said Peter.

"It's barely past six," said JJ. "We can be there in a minute."

JJ, Anna, Peter, Elaine, and Freddie climbed into JJ and Anna's van. It only took a couple minutes to get to Tutu House. They walked up the ramp to the front porch. JJ knocked on the front door and then opened it and walked in.

"Hello there!" he called out as he and his guests made their way into the house. Several children and some older people were finishing dinner. A young lady and a man came over to see them.

"My goodness," she said. "What a surprise! What brings you here?"

"Hi Gwyn," said JJ. "We've brought a visitor to see the place. This is Peter Barclay and his wife Elaine and his son Freddy. He's the great-grandson of Mrs. Barclay."

"Oh wow," said Gwyn.

"This is Gwyndalyn and her husband Daniel," said JJ. She's one of my granddaughters and runs the place with Megan, one of my other granddaughters."

At that moment, Megan came in to greet the visitors. "So you're a great-grandson of Margaret Barclay," she said. "Do come in. We're just finishing supper."

"Sorry to intrude," said Elaine.

"No problem," said Gwyn. Then she asked JJ, "Have you guys had dinner?"

"We just ate," answered Anna.

"Why don't you show our guests around while we clean up?" said Gwyn. "Then we'll have some cherry pie and ice cream."

"Sounds good," said JJ.

A six-year-old boy came over to see Freddie.

"Tyler," said Gwyn, "Why don't you take Freddie into the play area and share some toys?"

"Ok," said Tyler as he took Freddie's hand.

"We don't just take care of kids anymore," explained JJ. "We also have older folks living here. It's kind of a combination old folks home and foster home."

"What a great idea," said Elaine.

"It's worked out quite well," said Gwyn's husband, Daniel, as they headed for the stairway. "The older folks like having the younger kids around, and the kids often enjoy stories from the older ones."

JJ took Peter and Elaine upstairs. Anna rode the chairlift.

"This was your great-grandmother's room," said JJ. "Gwyn and Daniel live here now."

"And over here," said Anna, "Is where Miss Nancy lived. I still imagine her fussing around and taking care of everyone."

"I'll show you where my room was," said JJ as he took them upstairs to the attic rooms. "We've got the attic all heated and cooled now."

After walking around the house, and meeting the children and older residents, JJ took them outside. Peter and Elaine immediately walked over to the tree nearest the house and looked up.

"Is this the tree?" asked Peter.

"Yes it is," said JJ. "Arthur's words are one hundred years old. You can barely see 'em."

"What a romantic story," said Elaine, as she held Peter's hand.

Megan opened the back door and called out, "Dessert's ready."

"Wow, this is great," said Peter, as they made their way back inside.

At the same time, a fifty-three-year-old lady came in the front door.

"Aunty An!" cried little Becky as she ran to the front door. JJ also went to greet her.

"Hi, sweetheart," said JJ as he hugged his daughter.

"Peter, this is my youngest daughter, Anatola."

"Pleased to meet you," said Anatola.

"This is Peter Barclay and his wife, Elaine," said JJ. "He's the great-grandson of Mrs. Barclay."

"Oh my word!" said Anatola. "I was such a little girl when I saw her last. I barely remember."

"Your great grandma really was a great person," said JJ to Peter. "My family exists because of her. Anatola comes here to play the piano for story night. It's a tradition we've kept for a long time."

"I'm getting arthritis," said Anna. "Anatola is our musician now."

"We're just sitting down for dessert," said JJ to Anatola.

"Is this homemade pie?" asked Elaine.

"Yes," said Megan. "I hope you like it."

"It's wonderful," said Elaine.

"I assume you're staying for story night," said Gwyn.

Peter looked at Elaine. She nodded. "Sure," said Peter.

As everyone started gathering in the main living room, Peter asked, "Is this Arthur's chair?"

"Yes," said JJ. "And this is Miss Nancy's piano."

Seeing the chair and the piano always brought wonderful memories to JJ. Having Mrs. Barclay's great-grandson here amplified the feelings.

"The chair looks brand new," said Elaine.

"Geneve re-upholstered it last year," said Megan.

"That's one of my other grandkids," said JJ.

"She did a great job," said Elaine. "What a talented family."

Peter asked, "So whatever became of your friend Kevin?"

"My grandpa died six years ago," said Gwen.

Peter looked confused. JJ explained, "They're his grandkids, too. His kids married my two oldest."

"Wow," said Peter.

By now, everyone was sitting comfortably, either on a couch, a chair, or a blanket on the floor. TVs, computers, games, and movie players were turned off, along with cell phones and tablets. The two youngest sat in the laps of older guests. Only one boy sat alone upstairs, playing a computer game. It wouldn't be long, though, before he would adapt.

"We're reading 'Charlotte's Web,'" said Gwyn, who opened the book to the middle. Gwen and Megan took turns reading.

After several chapters were read, Anatola played the piano. The children liked the music, but the real fans were the older folks. For half an hour, as the kids got ready for bed, Anatola played songs requested by young and old. It was nearly nine o clock by the time JJ and Anna got ready to leave with Peter and his family.

"We're going to put on 'Forrest Gump' for the late-nighters," said Gwen.

JJ explained that a few older residents had trouble getting to sleep at night and stayed up late. Megan accompanied JJ and his guests to the front door.

"It was nice to meet you," said Elaine.

"You're welcome any time," said Megan.

On the ride back to JJ and Anna's house, Peter thanked them. "That sure was nice," he said.

"You can go there anytime you like," said JJ. "Especially for story night, if Freddie likes it. As far as I'm concerned, you're family."

That night, as JJ and Anna sat in bed, Anna said, "I think about Mrs. Barclay and Miss Nancy and the good times we had."

"I know," said JJ. "I wish we could live forever."

After a moment, Anna said, "We're going to have to tell the children about my cancer."

"Yeah," said JJ. He gave a sigh. "Anatola will be here tomorrow. We'll talk to her first. You seemed to do pretty good today."

"It was a nice day, wasn't it?" said Anna. "We've had a good life."

"We certainly have," said JJ. "The world is so different from our time."

"Yes," said Anna, holding JJ's hand.

"I worry about our grandkids growing up in this day and age," said JJ. "Everything is so different."

"It's not difficult for them," said Anna. "It's what they're used to. Our own world was very different from the one our parents grew up in."

"Yeah, I guess so," said JJ.

"I think we all just remember the world of our childhood," said Anna. "Imagine how different our world seemed to Miss Nancy."

"I know," said JJ. He kissed his wife and turned out the light next to the bed.

The next day, Anatola came by in the late afternoon. For many years she had been checking on her mom and dad nearly every day. From the time she was little, she and Anna had a special bond.

"Hi, what are you guys up to?" asked Anatola as she came into the living room and sat down on a couch by JJ and Anna. The giant TV screen was on. An old black-and-white science fiction movie was paused. "Oh for Pete's sake," said Anatola with a laugh. "Are you watching that movie again?"

"Well, we like it," said Anna with a smile. "It was our first date."

"How was your day?" asked JJ.

"It was fine," said Anatola. "How about you? Did Peter Barclay enjoy his visit yesterday?"

"He sure did," said JJ. "I expect we'll be seeing them often."

"That's fine with me," said Anatola. "They seem nice."

JJ turned off the TV.

"That's ok," said Anatola. "You don't have to stop your movie. I'm just going to steal a plate of food if you don't mind."

"Go right ahead," said Anna. "We do want to talk to you about something."

Anatola returned with some potato salad and a piece of leftover pizza.

"That looks appetizing," joked JJ.

"I know, huh?" said Anatola with a smile. "So what's up?"

"Well," said JJ. "It's about Mom."

Anatola got a serious, worried look on her face. She put down her food. "What?"

"Well, sweetheart, I have cancer," said Anna. "Lung cancer."

"Lung cancer?" asked Anatola. "How can you have lung cancer?"

"I don't know sweetheart. Sometimes you just can."

"So what's the treatment?" asked Anatola.

"I'm afraid we didn't catch it in time," said Anna. "It's been spreading. There's nothing we can do at this point."

Anatola got up and then sat down next to Anna. They held each other's hands. Anatola had tears in her eyes. "How long?" she asked.

"I'm not sure exactly," said Anna softly. "Not more than a few months."

"Oh Mom!" sobbed Anatola. "It's not fair."

"Honey, I'm eighty-one. It's ok. We're all getting older."

That evening and for the next few days, cell phones rang, text messages were sent and received, children and grandkids gathered, and plans were discussed. Anatola moved back into the house to help take care of Anna. Eryk and Sue left Mills and Robinson in the hands of capable employees while they spent time with the family. JJ and Anna signed the deed to their home over to Anatola.

The worst problem Anna faced was her lifelong fear of suffocating. In the old days, polio had claimed many lives that way. Now, cancer was threatening to make it hard to breathe. Anna had talked with JJ about it before. Now they talked again. "I can't die that way," she said.

"I know," said JJ.

They had made a choice together. In one way, it was difficult. Yet, in another way, it was easy. For Anna, there was no other option. Eryk, Sue, Janina, Timmy, and Anatola were called to a family meeting.

"The reason I want to talk with you," said JJ, "Is that your mom and I have made a very serious decision."

JJ looked at Anna, and then continued. "Your mom doesn't want to wait until she is barely alive, gasping for air. She could live for another few months or more but..."

"Can't you do chemo or radiation or something?" asked Eryk.

"Yes," said JJ, "But the cancer has already been spreading. At best, it would give her an extra few weeks. She would suffer more than it would help."

"So what are you thinking?" asked Eryk.

"We've given this a lot of thought," said JJ. "Rather than spending time in a hospital, we're going to do hospice. Mom will be given all the medicine necessary to relieve pain and suffering."

Janina got up and sat down next to JJ, and took Anna's hand. Anatola took the other hand.

"It would be different if I were younger," said Anna, as she looked at each of her kids. "I don't want you to think I'm not brave. I just don't want to spend my remaining time in a hospital."

"Your mom has been brave and courageous all her life," said JJ. "We've talked to several different doctors in Pittsburgh. Even a specialist in Texas about the new treatments."

"I wondered why you took a trip," said Eryk.

"We didn't want to say anything until we were sure," said JJ. "We were hoping for a miracle."

"But you see," said Anna, still holding hands with Janina and Annatola. "I already had my miracle. The day I met you, the day I met your dad, the day your children were born. I've already had so many miracles."

Eryk wiped tears as he hugged his mom. "We're so lucky to have you," he said.

A week later, at 2:45 in the morning, Anatola awoke to the sound of her mom coughing and crying. She rushed to her parent's bedroom. JJ was doing his best to help Anna, who was sitting on the edge of the bed. Anatola patted her mom on the back and held her hand. Anna was starting to catch her breath. Anatola could plainly see the panic in her mom's face. After a few minutes, Anna said, "I'm ok now. Thanks."

The next day, Anatola tearfully discussed the situation with her brother Eryk and her sister Janina. "We've got to let mom go," she said. "If we don't, she's just going to suffer."

"I know," said Eryk.

Losing another mom was going to be hard, but he was a man now, with his own children. Eryk loved his mom enough to let her go.

After another episode in the afternoon, Anna decided that tomorrow would be the day.

That evening, JJ and Anna sat in bed together for the last time. They talked about their lives and their children. They talked about their childhood and about growing up.

Anna had difficulty breathing, but said, "I remember the day I looked out my window to see you and Laddie by my fence. From the first moment I saw you I wanted to be with you. I could just tell by looking at you."

"The first time I saw you," said JJ, "you made me nervous. I guess I was in love and didn't know it."

"I love you so much," said Anna.

After a moment she said, "I don't think I can sleep tonight."

"We don't have to sleep," said JJ.

They got up, went into the living room, and sat on the couch, in the dark. JJ opened the curtains so they could see out to the backyard. A few fireflies were bobbing here and there in the grey shadows of the night. "It's easier for me if I sit up," said Anna.

Anatola woke up and came into the room and sat next to her mom. JJ liked watching the fireflies in the dark.

"Thank you for helping me with this," she said to JJ. Then she looked at Anatola and squeezed her hand. "Thanks for being such a wonderful daughter."

Anatola couldn't say anything because of the lump in her throat. She just held her mom's hand.

"I would do anything for you," said JJ as he put his arms around Anna. They sat in silence for a minute.

Then Anna said, "In the grand scheme of things, we're all so insignificant really. Like a little firefly in the night."

Then she said, "I was thinking about Miss Nancy. Hardly anyone remembers Arthur or Nancy anymore except us, and soon we'll be gone. To Arthur, Miss Nancy was the most important person in the world. That's the beauty, isn't it? The least significant person in the whole world is the most important person to someone."

JJ thought for a moment. "Arthur and Nancy forever."

"Yes," said Anna. "The house they built, the people they cared for, it still lives on. Their love changed the world in its own way, and that will last forever, just like our love."

"Just think," said JJ. "If Arthur had been like his brothers, our story wouldn't exist. He took control of his life and created a world for Nancy and the rest of us."

"Yes he did," said Anna.

"I wish I could have known him," said JJ.

Anna held JJ's hand and kissed him on the cheek. "You are my Arthur."

JJ, Anna, and Anatola sat for a while until Anna fell asleep with her head on JJ's shoulder. Anatola decided to leave them alone and went back to bed in her room. She lay in her bed and wept as softly as she could.

Eventually, JJ dozed off.

As the sun began to illuminate the backyard, Anatola returned to the living room. Anna was starting to stir. JJ woke up.

Neither JJ or Anna were hungry for breakfast. By 9 am Eryk, Sue, Janina, and Timmy arrived. Anna and JJ went into their bedroom. They sat on the edge of the bed together. "I don't want to leave you," she said. "I'm just having so much trouble breathing. I'm scared."

"It's all right," said JJ, as he hugged her. "I want you to do what's best for you."

They embraced for a few minutes. Anna coughed, then looked at JJ with a tear in her eye.

"It's ok," said JJ, as he hugged her.

Anna drank from two small bottles. JJ helped her back into her wheelchair and they rejoined the children in the living room. JJ looked at Eryk who then came over to the wheelchair. The others followed.

JJ slowly pushed Anna out the back door. Eryk, Janina, and Anatola walked with them. Timmy and Sue followed. They gently pushed Anna across the patio and across the yard. They pushed her toward the back of the yard by the tree house. They stopped under the tree and helped Anna down onto the grass. Anna looked up at the tree. "This is good. Right where we were married."

JJ sat on the grass and held Anna in his arms. He had no words. Janina and Anatola held Anna's hands, while Eryk put his hand on his mom's arm.

"I love you all so much," said Anna. "You're the best family a woman could ever want."

As Anatola sobbed, Eryk hugged his mom and said, "Thank you for being my mother."

Anna looked back at Eryk. "Thank you for being such a wonderful son."

After a moment, she said, "It's so beautiful here. I couldn't ask for a better life."

After a few more minutes, Anna closed her eyes and said, "I'm starting to get sleepy."

JJ held her in his arms and kissed her forehead. He stroked her hair as he cradled her head. Anna closed her eyes and smiled. Her children gently squeezed her hands as she fell asleep. Anna's breathing gradually became slower and slower, until finally, it stopped. The children hugged their mom, and then each other. They helped lift Anna back into her wheelchair and bring her back to the house.

Eryk took charge and called 911. There was a big funeral. "At least she didn't have to suffer," said Janina. All agreed.

"Mom and dad really loved each other," said Anatola.

"They still do," said Eryk.

✳ ✳ ✳ ✳ ✳

Eryk and Sue returned to Pittsburgh to run the company. As best they could, the family returned to normal. Anatola and Janina made a small monument for the memorial garden.

Anna was cremated. Her ashes were saved in an urn. JJ and Anna planned to have their ashes mixed together, and be buried in the memorial garden, near Princess and Laddie.

JJ was never the same. The void in his life was immense. Every normal activity was no longer normal. He was glad for the company of his family. He was glad Anatola was living at home. He enjoyed the Fourth of July party. He enjoyed story night at Tutu House. He enjoyed seeing Peter Barclay and his family. He admired the way Gwyn and Megan took care of Tutu House. He would often say to them, "Arthur and Nancy would be proud of you."

At home, Anatola played the piano for her dad every evening. "You're just like your mom," he would say.

In the fall, a small celebration was planned to commemorate the hundred year anniversary of the 1920 completion of Tutu House. The party was scheduled for the Friday after Thanksgiving. Mills and Robinson would be closed, although some employees were on call for emergencies.

Anatola drove JJ to pick up Kevin's wife, Patty. They arrived at Tutu House by late morning, before the rest of the family. Patty was in good health and still enjoyed helping at family events. By noon, the rest of the family began arriving. Peter and Elaine Barclay came too.

It was a wonderful party. For the residents of Tutu House, it was like having a second Thanksgiving. Megan and Gwen had cooked an extra large Thanksgiving dinner in order to have plenty of leftovers. Additional tables had been set up to accommodate the crowd. By 1 pm, dinner was ready.

JJ stood to make a toast. Everyone but a few children stopped to listen. "As you all know, this wonderful house was completed one hundred years ago. Our family exists because of this place. I make a toast to Arthur, Nancy, and Mr. Ranta, for building such a strong and sturdy house."

As JJ sat down, glasses clinked at all the tables around the house. It was just the kind of party that Miss Nancy and Arthur would have loved.

I wish Arthur and Nancy could see our grand party, JJ thought to himself. *I wish you were here, Anna.*

JJ was pleased by how the Robinson family took care of the company and the house. His children and grandchildren would continue for many years to come. They had already begun shopping for Christmas gifts for the residents, young and old.

After eating, adults sat around to visit, and children played. Some had video games, some texted friends, and some played outside with the animals. The outside air was chilly. Snow would soon be sticking to the ground. The sound of a TV came from the other room as one of the adults turned down the volume. It was the kind of setting JJ loved. He kept expecting to see Anna.

JJ wondered if the attic heating was working properly. He decided to check it out. He climbed the stairs to the second floor, but as he started up the stairs to the attic, he was out of breath. He rested for a moment and then decided to go back down and visit. He used the chairlift that he and Kevin had installed fifty years earlier.

He walked back into the main living room and sat down next to Patty to watch the great grandkids. Some of the older residents were also in the same area, visiting. "I guess us old folks need to stick together," JJ joked to Patty.

"How are you holding up?" asked Patty.

"I'm doing fine," said JJ. "I just miss her."

"I know," said Patty. "I still miss Kevin."

JJ just nodded. He missed his old friend, too.

It was one of the best days JJ could remember. Only Anna's absence had made it imperfect. The afternoon slowly faded into early evening. It was starting to get dark early now. He hated saying goodbye to family members as they gradually left.

By seven o'clock the environment at Tutu House had settled back to normal. JJ sat down in the big chair next to the piano. It always made him feel happy to sit there. The sounds of people moving around and cleaning up were pleasant. Anatola sat down at the piano. "How are you feeling, Dad? Would you like some music?"

"Sure," said JJ, as he closed his eyes. As Anatola played the piano, he felt peaceful. He thought about his kids growing up, his friendship with Kevin, meeting Howard Mills, and growing up here in Tutu House. He thought about working as a boy with Tom. He thought about Anna. His heart filled with happiness. He dozed off and began to dream.

In his dream, he was a young boy, living at Tutu House. It was late Fall. He was standing outside on the front porch. The wind was blowing, and he was cold. He wandered toward the street. He could hear the piano playing "Danny Boy" inside the house. He felt melancholy. He wanted to go back into the warmth of the house but felt compelled to keep walking.

JJ bent down to pick up something from the street. It was his toy dog, "Barky," lost before he came to the orphanage as a baby. It's what he had been trying to say when they thought he was saying "Jark." JJ smiled to think about it.

Far down the road, he could see a dog. It looked like Laddie. JJ started walking, but it ran away. JJ ran toward the dog but lost track of it. He stopped and found himself in an unfamiliar neighborhood. The wind had ceased, and the air was calm. He glanced back toward Tutu House but couldn't see it anymore. He was older now, a grown man. He found himself standing in front of a house he didn't recognize, uncertain what to do next.

The door opened, and Anna walked out. She was smiling and cheerful. "There you are!" she said as she took his hand. "Come on in. It's the best Thanksgiving ever."

Anna led JJ into the house. He saw Tom and Laura, Kevin, Laddie, Uncle Howard, Gloria and her husband Louis, the Kurzmanns, and Aunt Beverly with her husband and her son Jack. Everyone was happy to see him. Anna pulled JJ further inside. There was Mrs. Barclay with Fred. Finally, he came to Miss Nancy, who said, "Hello, JJ, I don't believe you've met my husband, Arthur."

Danny Boy:

Oh Danny boy, the pipes, the pipes are calling
From glen to glen, and down the mountain side
The summer's gone, and all the flowers are dying
'Tis you, 'tis you must go and I must bide.

But come ye back when summer's in the meadow
Or when the valley's hushed and white with snow
'Tis I'll be here in sunshine or in shadow
Oh Danny boy, oh Danny boy, I love you so.

And if you come, when all the flowers are dying
And I am dead, as dead I well may be
You'll come and find the place where I am lying
And kneel and say an "Ave" there for me.

And I shall hear, tho' soft you tread above me
And all my dreams will warm and sweeter be
If you'll not fail to tell me that you love me
I'll simply sleep in peace until you come to me.

Truth and fiction

The backdrop of actual historical events portrayed here, along with historical figures of the era, is meant to be true and accurate. The characters in these stories themselves are fictional.

Some specific exampes:

Indiana, Pennsylvania really is the Christmas tree capital of America. The actor, Jimmy Stewart, really did grow up there, and the Stewart family really did run a hardware store. Alex Stewart, Jimmy Stewart's father, died in 1961. Jimmy Stewart died in 1997.

The Mills Movie Theater is fictional, as is the Mills and Robinson company, and Tutu House.

Anthracite coal in America is primarily found in Northeastern Pennsylvania. Carbondale is a small town near Scranton.

The influenza pandemic of 1918–1919 was one of the deadliest natural disasters in world history. About 500 million people were infected and between 50 million and 100 million people died.

Diseases like tuberculosis, polio, smallpox, and scarlet fever plagued humans before vaccines were developed. The development of the polio vaccine was one of medicine's greatest achievements.

Trolleys were a big part of the history of Scranton, PA. Scranton was once known as the "Electric City" and was one of the first to adopt electric lights.

The Great St. Patrick's Day Flood of 1936 in Pittsburgh destroyed 100,000 buildings. Steel mills near the river were flooded and 60,000 steel mill workers were put out of work. To this day, some downtown buildings have markers showing how high the floodwaters reached.

The radio was just beginning to develope when WWI broke out. Radios were strictly prohibited for the duration of the war. After the war, demand for radios was high. In 1920, radio station KDKA in Pittsburgh broadcast the first ever live results for the election of Warren G. Harding. On August 5, 1921, KDKA broadcast the first baseball game, between the Pittsburgh Pirates and the Philadelphia Phillies.

During WWII, the five Sullivan Brothers were all killed. They served together on the USS Juneau which was sunk during one of the battles of the Guadalcanal Campaign. After that, the War Department adopted the "Sole Survivor" policy.

The "Red Tails" were African American WWII fighter pilots who flew planes with the tail often painted red. They were the "Tuskegee Airmen." Their job, as fighter pilots, was to protect B-17s and other bombers on bombing runs. They were also known as "Red Tail Angels." Despite severe segregation on the ground, their success in shooting enemy aircraft and protecting American bombers gave comfort to bomber pilots when they spotted the red-tail aircraft.

"Always remember, be nice to people."

-   Jimmy Stewart

ABOUT THE AUTHOR

Lowell Dunn is married to the former Karen Rush, and is the father / stepfather to six children and fourteen grandchildren, as well as a number of dogs, cats, birds, and other animals.

After a successful career in software development and a lifetime of informal storytelling to younger siblings, around camp fires, and to children and grandchildren, *Serendipitous Rescue* is Lowell's first effort as an author. It is meant to be a tribute to his mother, Lois Olsen Dunn. The stories cover an era when she would have been growing up and then raising a family of her own.